# HYPNOTIC STATE

## DELTON ANTONY PINK

## ABOUT THE AUTHOR

Delton Pink is a London - based writer born in the 50s on the beautiful island of Jamaica. Since arriving in the UK as a six-year-old, he has enjoyed a varied career holding posts in many different sectors, but none as important as raising two very independent and wonderful children.

The same children who, after running out of traditional stories for their nightly bedtime routine, inspired his passion for creating original stories to satisfy his young audience.

Eventually turning his talents to writing for adults, Hypnotic State is his debut novel.

An accomplished musician, who has played at venues such as the legendary Ronnie Scott's Jazz Club in London. Delton's flair for storytelling continues with unique projects on the horizon spanning music, drama and film.

deltonpink.com

# Hypnotic State

Delton A Pink

Published by Not By The Book 2020
Copyright © 2020 Delton Antony Pink
First Edition

A CIP catalogue record for this book is available from the British Library.

ISBN-13: 978-0-9926283-7-6

To my friends and family who read the first 28 pages and insisted that I complete the journey.

# CHAPTER 1

Even with half a brain, you would expect the government that had been in power for seventeen years to have more ideas about tackling rising crime, which is being fuelled steadily by their own stealth austerity measures. It's Monday 19 April 2027 and setting aside the historical significance of the date, there's a whole generation of voters that have never experienced the policies of any other political party. That given, it's no wonder the government appears nonchalant when faced with the evidence of a slowdown in world trade. With the government appearing to sideline any debate on the prospects of another recession, everyone else is under no illusion that for the government to have any chance of an unprecedented sixth term, they must fight the next election on the current issue of law and order. With opposition parties preoccupied with trying to second-guess dates for the next general election, the government steals a march to share early information on its manifesto. Their proposal to reduce the taxpayer's burden hides a much wider plan to denationalise courts and prisons for England and Wales, and the complete sell-off of all assets.

. . .

Following the last election, the government settled for the blind bid auction as their preferred sell-off criteria. Warned about its higher risk, it was still two years before they discovered that someone had hacked the cloud data. While the breach was being investigated, they had no choice but to delay announcing that a Chinese company called 'Lotto-Guard' had won the bid. Under a commissioned security review, it found that several highly classified memos leaked precise details of the government's full sell-off plans. One memo showed the extent and effect it would have on unemployment for thousands of civil servants. After finding and plugging the security hole, the government's IT contractors, 'The Hackers Employment Agency', gave the all-clear. Even the contractors, at one point, were under suspicion. But with no evidence to the contrary, they could only request a change of personnel. Whoever's involved with the leaks is keeping one step ahead of detection.

The government viewed the leaks as an unfortunate distraction from their bidding process and, in the confusion, missed their own deadline to halt the sale of prison land. They kept ownership of prison buildings purely by luck, since they were actually being sold under a separate contract. With the government seeking to minimise all risk of a backbench revolt, they arranged a televised broadcast to announce a ministerial reshuffle and deny many of the leak's claims. Appointing a new Minister of State for Prisons and Probation and the third in as many months. The Cabinet welcomed the appointment as a positive that they could sell to the public. The new minister's proven negotiation skills are enough to bring the Lotto-Guard deal back on track and over the line.

Given the green light, Lotto-Guard unveiled their laser base system. Code-named Pinpoint, its function is to support the government's policy of zero tolerance. Projected from the outset, the new system will see more people imprisoned for minor crimes. When presented as a visible crime deterrent to the public, the government adopted the plans as their own statement of intent. Lotto-Guard's glossy presentation showed crime levels peaking at twelve months, followed by significant falls as the public became more informed and aware of the new system.

Provisionally set for Thursday 10 June, the upcoming general election will test how well the public receives the government's outsourcing policy, while a much-welcomed drop in crime rates will measure the success of Lotto-Guard's new justice system.

Three months ago, vehicle crime was at an all-time low, with the police credited for much of this success. However, information recently received about a new car audio system is changing everything. The manufacturer's claim about their chip technology, which ranges from basic digital cameras to weapons classifications, is making them the number one target for criminals and subversives alike. With redesigned aerials making fitted cars more identifiable, news of the entire stock being lost in a fire at a Hong Kong factory has added thousands to the value of all existing chips. With good intelligence secured from a paid informant, the police have set up a surveillance trap on one of London's busiest roads in an attempt to reverse this crime wave.

The dark blue unassuming van used for surveillance contains the latest high-tech listening devices and is capable of picking up everything within a 300-metre radius. Parked among the cars in this affluent neighbourhood, its presence does not go unnoticed, as its tinted windows are a throwback that attracts curious stares from a handful of vehicle enthusiasts.

It's a humid and warm evening and the sky is covered in a low blanket of grey clouds. It's weather that's perhaps unusual for so early in the year – for Britain at least. Energy-efficient LED streetlights add to the overall air of security, given that evenings since the clocks went forward are getting lighter.

The van contains several occupants. A communications engineer, hired from the Hackers' agency, is there to take charge of the computer installation. He's a tall, thin and wiry figure, with rust-coloured dishevelled hair concealing much of his face and talent. These agencies are perfectly respectable these days, working for many businesses that practise the revised strategy "If you can't beat them, hire them."

The commanding officer in charge is Ryan Chase: as tough as they come, ex-army, and from his demeanour an old mercenary for certain. He's known for one of two expressions, anger or contempt, and his marked face carries his life's experiences for all to see. He never switches off, takes his work seriously and takes it home. There are also two armed police officers, distinctive in their black and chrome uniforms. Two recent recruits, categorised as plain specials – 'plain' being the operative word – make up the rest of the crew.

The van's position is six vehicles behind the target car. To maintain complete silence, all non-essential equipment, including the air conditioning, is off, even though outside temperatures are already reading two degrees higher than the forecast. Inside, the men's body heat is adding to the already clammy environment. It's a waiting game – but one for which they're already briefed and prepared.

A watch alarm sounds, inviting a fixed stare from the commander, reminding the wearer that it should have been on silent.

'What time do you have there?' the commander asks, in a relaxed tone.

'A minute after half past, sir,' the watch's owner stutters, looking at his wrist to confirm. He exhales a swift sigh, relieved at not being taken to task as the only one who didn't have his watch on silent.

'Four-Two, Four-Two, report please,' the commander growls. Operative Four-Two is in the Indian restaurant opposite the target vehicle. His seat by the window gives him the widest view of the area and vehicle.

His whispered voice comes over the radio, muffled by the sound of him eating.

'Four-Two reporting, all clear. No, wait a second... Two males fitting the descriptions are heading past the van now.'

'Your extra popadoms, sir,' a background voice interrupts over the radio.

'Four-Two, stand by, we have them.'

The infrared camera mounted on the roof rotates in the tense silence. With the two figures picked up, its autofocus takes over to enhance the night view. The suspects are walking at a casual pace as they pass the van heading in the direction of the target vehicle. To a nonpartisan observer their actions could not be less suspicious, but the informant's vague description of clothing is enough for them to warrant closer attention. Those watching, though, won't act without positive orders.

'Right, this could be it; stay alert, don't lose them. One-Seven, do you have a confirmed eye on the targets yet?'

One-Seven's position is only metres from the target vehicle. Waiting in the reception area of a health club, he answers as the two suspects enter his view.

'One-Seven reporting, eyeball is affirmative, sir.'

The area outside the health club is well lit by the reception lights and the neon sign advertising the name of the kebab shop next door. The two suspects stop, setting their sports bags on the pavement. It's clear they're smoking while enjoying a light-hearted discussion.

'There goes my New Year's resolution,' says Ox, a twenty-two-year-old, melanin-rich six-foot young man of Afro-Caribbean descent. He's clean shaven, with close-cut curly hair. His athletic frame is a good fit for his designer tracksuit.

'Yeah, I agree. If we want to make progress, we need to get more serious about our fitness and martial arts.'

'Then we need to stop smoking altogether.'

'Okay, then let's give them up, starting right now.' Chan agrees; he's Ox's Chinese friend of the same age, who, at five foot five, and in the correct light, could pass for a young Jet Lee. Ox nods his agreement and takes a last look at his cigarette before one final puff, which causes a slight cough, forcing him to cover his mouth.

Synchronised, they drop their cigarettes, extinguishing them with the soles of their trainers.

'My teeth aren't looking yellow, are they?' Chan asks, flashing his full set at Ox.

'Don't let it worry you. You're yellow all over,' Ox jokes, as always accompanied with his cheeky smile. Chan bends down to the wing mirror on the target vehicle to check for himself, unaware of what has been triggered.

'All units go, go, go!' Commander Chase shouts, putting the operation into motion.

Four-Two explodes into life and leaps from his restaurant table, almost colliding with the waiter. One-Seven also begins his exit from the health club. Everyone on the radios can hear the waiter in the restaurant bellowing, 'Stop, stop! You've not paid for your meal yet!'

Chan and Ox turn towards the noise and see a figure running towards them from the restaurant.

One-Seven, stationed in the health club, stands up to makes his way outside. Too eager to exit and forgetting which way the glass door opens, he slams into it.

Both Ox and Chan get distracted by the sudden thud and twist their heads to witness the comical situation. They smile and shake their heads as One-Seven grabs the door handle and finally yanks it open. They've no reason to sense danger and are unaware that Four-Two has reached the target vehicle. He catches Ox off-guard, shoving him towards the health club's doors. Ox stumbles as he sees the glass door looming and looks for a safe place to place his hands as an ankle buckles and his knees hit the ground.

One-Seven, now outside, selects Chan as his target and moves to grab his loose tracksuit. Ox, on the ground, foils One-Seven by tripping him. The momentum catapults him into Four-Two, who stumbles heavily and loses his balance, smashing an arm through the target vehicle's window.

'Tell them you'll pay up!' shouts Chan.

'Pay what?' answers Ox. 'It must be you they're after?'

'No! I don't know anyone who's not Chinese. Except for you.'

Four-Two extracts himself from the smashed car window and turns towards the friends.

'That's it, I've seen enough!' Commander Chase fumes at the debacle unfolding on the camera monitors in the van.

'Go! Get out there and put an end to this fiasco,' he says to his armed officers. The door to the van swings open, striking the side panel with a violent thud. The pair step from the van, the streetlights reflecting from the shiny metal clips on their body armour. One takes a deep breath and glances at his partner before moving off purposefully.

Chan moves closer to Ox; standing back to back, they raise their hands and prepare for further attacks. One-Seven, with the help of Four-Two, cuts off their escape, while the armed policemen raise their guns, aiming them straight at the friends.

'You know the drill!' warns one.

'Now!' the other shouts, backing him up.

Ox and Chan don't know what's occurred, nor why or how to defuse it. They're sure, though, that there's no escape, as a brief scan confirms the overpowering force around them. So, raising their arms, they take the only option left. With no explanation, the two men are slammed onto the car's bonnet while the armed officers stand guard.

'Hey, what's all this about?' shouts Ox.

'Keep it shut!' a policeman orders.

Commander Chase has made his way over from the van.

'Link them,' he says, taking off his cap to reveal his bald head.

They allow both the men to lower their arms to aid attaching electronic bracelets, placing one on each wrist. The devices exhibit the current date and a unique serial code. They allow their hands to drop into more natural positions. The commander replaces his cap and adjusts it, using the shiny surface of an armed officer's lapel as his mirror. He looks in the other direction and signals towards the van. The links snap together, taking on the look and feel of conventional handcuffs. Commander Chase detaches a large handheld from a pocket on his left sleeve. Silently, he enters several codes, activating the units, and without looking up, he speaks in a clear tone.

'You're both under arrest for attempted vehicle theft.'

'What are you talking about? I see no evidence of that,' Chan argues.

He's introduced to the seriousness of their situation when one policeman jabs him in his stomach with the butt of his gun.

'Don't talk unless you're told to,' the other armed policeman informs Chan, with a stare equal to his blow.

'As I was trying to say before you rudely interrupted,' Commander Chase continues, 'you're accused of attempted theft... and this broken car window here' – he points towards the car – 'is all the evidence we need.'

Chan and Ox stare angrily as the commander continues reading from his handheld.

'You are both now linked to the central crime computer. Your crime number is 1792. If you can't read or you forget it, it's there visible on the bracelets. This means a curfew for you between six pm and six am until your court appearance. Should you break your curfews, GPS sensors linked to the Pinpoint lasers will target you. Do you understand what I'm saying?' He looks up to gauge their responses, seeing their faces for the first time.

'Now, sign these penalty notices. Then you're free to leave. Once you've paid at court, they will remove the bracelets. So, questions?'

'That means you can talk now,' one policeman informs them.

'Yeah, you're sure? Because the law says we don't have to sign anything and you can't force us either,' says Ox.

'Come here,' the commander says, grabbing hold of Ox by his shoulder and dragging him to one side.

'What's your name, boy?'

'My name is Ox, and I'm not your boy,'

'Well,' he starts then whispers up close, 'not being able to knock the shit out of your kind anymore doesn't mean we don't have other ways of controlling you. Especially ones like you, who think their smart. I hope that's not too much for a small ethnic brain to remember.'

He pushes Ox back together with Chan.

'Since you refuse to sign, you're required by law,' – he emphasises the last word – 'to attend a court hearing at ten am, in three days, where you'll either get formally sentenced or be given bail. Now, you've got roughly about one hour to get the fuck off my streets' – the sergeant checks his watch to confirm – 'before those links become active again. Now piss off.' He seems happy to add.

With the links deactivated from the van, their hands are finally free again. Chan and Ox retrieve their bags, then leave. Two figures blend into the shadows away from the light: the real thieves, perhaps, taking their leave. The target car's alarm finally goes off in a blaze of horns and flashing lights.

Commander Chase looks back at the car and sees no one anywhere near.

'Foreign rubbish,' he mutters to himself while climbing back into the van.

# CHAPTER 2

Sir Edward Long MP is the recent appointment to the post of prisons minister and the main link between the government and Lotto-Guard. Sir Edward, as he prefers to be addressed, is, despite his name, a man of average height. However, his blue eyes and semi-permanent smile conceal the assassin-type nerves he brings to negotiations. Unless he's holding all the aces, he rarely gambles, and takes pride in dressing to be noticed, never forgetting to match his waistcoats to the patterned handkerchief sitting in his breast pocket.

Loyal party supporters are calling for greater scrutiny of Lotto-Guard's Pinpoint system. Complaints have been on the increase following several unfortunate deaths not related to crime. They warned that a deterrent that's killing innocent people is not a vote winner, and in an election year, these types of choices could mean the difference between being re-elected and finding yourself in opposition or, worse, out of a job altogether.

The time is nearing 4 pm on Tuesday afternoon and Sir Edward is sitting at his desk, working on last-minute notes. His impending weekly session with the press, interested parties and pressure groups is fast approaching. The intercom on his desk buzzes.

'Yes, Amy, what is it?' he answers.

'Sir Edward, your wife is on line two, sir.'

'Okay, please put her through.' He picks up his telephone.

'Hello, dear.'

'Hi, honey, you haven't forgotten what day this is, have you?'

'No, no, I haven't forgotten.'

'So, should I expect you home on time then?'

'Well, you should, but my appointments are running behind schedule, so I may have to meet you at the theatre.'

'That's okay. Just know that you'll be eating dinner after the show, though.'

'Don't worry, I'll grab a sandwich or something before I leave.'

'I'll see you later on, then. Love you.'

'Love you too.'

Ending the call, he collects all the notes for his meeting and deposits them into a dark leather-bound folder.

Sir Edward Long's rise to the elite of government has been rapid. His ascent was aided by the expulsions of three ministers deemed corrupt and the subsequent public outcry for direct action. He's held this new post for two months since his promotion from transport. Sir Edward is eager to oversee new, sweeping reforms to the prison service. The party's claims of being the party of law and order is again under the microscope and he very much hopes that his solutions will also be part of his legacy.

With the folder secure in his briefcase, Sir Edward leaves his office to attend his weekly meeting.

The extra time taken to answer his wife's call means Sir Edward is the last to arrive.

'Good afternoon, everyone and sorry for the delay. If you

would all like to take your seats, we can begin. Let me also apologise before we start for the briefness of today's session. A prior engagement means I'll only be answering a handful of questions before leaving today. However, my colleague will be more than happy to continue in my absence.'

The reporters have all found their places and sit in readiness. The minister opens his case and removes his folder. He opens it, turns two pages, then raises his head and nods.

'Minister, overcrowding in our prisons is at a crisis point. How does the government propose to tackle this issue?'

'The government is working with the bid winners, Lotto-Guard, to secure a reduction in prisoner numbers. They will achieve this through the use of new technology, by understanding the social problems at the root of crime, and targeted training.'

'Can you elaborate any more on this, Minister?' The reporter extends his arm to get his microphone closer.

'Yes, studies have shown that we need to identify and break the cycle of social crime. They have recognised this cycle as being at the core of today's crime figures. Surveys have also determined that when you remove the family breadwinner, it often leads, in a majority of cases, to other family members turning to lawlessness to support the family. The introduction last August of the Pinpoint system has seen a significant reduction in street crimes. Regrettably, during this same period, fatalities have also occurred. As a result, in trying to get it right, I've temporarily suspended the programme pending further safety checks.'


The minister lifts the jug on the table and pours himself a glass of water before he continues.

'I can take one further question, Yes, you, Laura,' he says.

'Minister, how can this government justify spending millions, yet again, on trying to deal with problems which are a clear hangover from the last decade? Are we not allowing services such as national health and transport to suffer?'

'I think the question of funding is best directed at the Chancellor. But, to answer your question, the government sees law and order as the single most important issue of public concern today. Let me reassure you that this government is looking to the private sector to play their part. We are talking about new commitments and funding for pre-existing projects.'

Before anyone raises a new question, the minister adds.

'The government will publish, later today, further details about our partnership with Lotto-Guard's funded automated court system. It's installed, configured and ready for use as of tomorrow. This measure alone should see a fall in the number of backlogged and pending cases and mark an increase in the speed at which we're able to dispense justice and deal with new offenders.'

'Minister!' George, the reporter known for his scoops, shouts.

'I'm sorry, George, as I conveyed earlier, this is a short session for me today. I will answer no further questions, thank you.'

'Sir Edward! What can you tell us about Lotto-Guard's safety record and their human rights policy in South America?' George asks his question anyway to Sir Edward's back as he departs the room.


'George, you went after him like a bloody greyhound snapping at a rabbit's tail. What have you got on this Lotto-Guard lot anyway? Unless you're working on an exclusive and can't share?' Mike, from the rival paper, whispers to his colleague.

'Not much, other than it's a registered Hong Kong company that on paper has established an impressive reputation along with amassing huge fortunes.'

'And that's all?'

'It's all I have. The company is cloaked in so much secrecy, publicity-shy – it's a wonder any information on their operations comes out at all. Even their associates display similar traits, you know, quietly occupying key positions of power here and there.

With their influence and contacts, doors never stay locked for long. And I guarantee, once opened, huge sums of money or bribery must be keeping them so.'

'Then maybe some of my contacts can help? Any other info?'

'Well, all I've dug up so far is they started operating lotteries in Asia before expanding into South America. Then when they sought new revenue streams, the security industry presented itself as the challenge. With crime on the increase worldwide, governments and organisations were soon keen to embrace their private service. After that, using heavy advertising and key partnerships, they perfected it.'

'Well, if I dig up anything, I'll be sure to let you know.'

'Failing that, we'll just hijack him again at the next press briefing.'

'Yeah, see you next week, George.'

'See you, Mike.'

Back in his department, Sir Edward requests a cup of tea from his secretary before entering his office. Once seated at his desk, he picks up the telephone and dials.

'Ah, Doctor Minn, it looks like we have a deal. One moment, please.'

He covers the mouthpiece as his secretary enters with his tea. With the tray resting on the corner of his dark oak desk, she mouths, 'Shall I pour, sir?'

'No, please just leave it there. Thank you, Amy, that will be all.'

He continues once Amy has departed and closed the door.

'Hello again, it's really just a courtesy call, letting you know the government will make public the contract details with Lotto-Guard later today. I'm sure we'll be able to talk further once they've been confirmed.'

Replacing the receiver, Sir Edward takes a minute to pour a

cup of Earl Grey tea for himself. He takes out a notebook from an inside pocket in his jacket and, after a cursory glance, replaces it. He gathers additional papers, placing them into his briefcase. He allows himself a single mouthful of his favourite drink before taking off for the day and his date at the theatre with his wife.

As Sir Edward arrives at the theatre five minutes after the show's official start time, his wife, Lady Elizabeth, is one of only a handful still in the foyer.

'What kept you, dear? Don't you know these are the hottest tickets in town,' she says, greeting him with a kiss.

'I'm sorry, love, the traffic…' is all he's allowed before she cuts his explanation short.

'Never mind explaining now, let's go inside… quick.' She takes him by the arm, shuffling through the swing doors in her long evening frock that sweeps the parquet floor.

Cutting it fine, they take their seats literally seconds before the lights dim and the chatting settles. Following a drum roll, the show is ready to start. A lone spotlight falls on the unopened velvet curtains. Then the compere's confident voice announces the first act.

'Ladies and gentlemen, he's appeared on countless television shows. He's known the world over for his unique style. The Readers Theatre is proud to present hypnotist extraordinaire Mr Ian Gilby!'

The audience cheers in anticipation of an entertaining evening. Ian Gilby enters stage left, microphone in hand, to sustained applause.

The clapping tapers off as soon as he raises his hand to speak.

'Good evening, everyone,' he begins, with a rush of energy.

'My name is Ian Gilby. I'm a hypnotist. My deaf former father-in-law thought I'd said I was a hippy.'

The crowd enjoys his opening joke and launches into even

more generous applause. He continues talking as he wanders from one side of the stage to the other, ensuring that he's seen from every seat in the theatre.

'Now, tonight, I'm looking for five volunteers – five people up here on stage with me. So, who will be first? How about you, sir? Yes, you; come on, folks, encourage him. Make your way down to the front and up the stairs at the side of the stage, please. Who will be next? How about you, sir, the gentleman wearing the striped shirt? Don't be shy about wearing your pyjamas in public, it's fine to come on down, sir.' The audience laughs as the man makes his way towards the front. Ian continues. 'Where are all the ladies tonight?' He looks straight at the front row and points. 'I don't mean you with the handbag, sir.'

A curvy woman in a red top and white jeans stands up. The audience cheers and wolf whistles as she flicks her long dark hair behind her ears before making her way towards the aisle at the end of her row.

'Come on, everyone, give her lots of encouragement. Two more, I need two more… I'll even take a couple. Sorry – Mum, Dad – you're excluded, they might think it's fixed.' He draws another round of laughter from the now warmed-up audience. A brave couple leave their seats and, hand in hand, head towards the stage.

'Ladies and gentlemen, please give our lovely volunteers an enormous round of applause.' Ian stops and clutches the microphone under his arm to join in applauding the volunteers before resuming.

He moves amongst them, asking if they have ever met him before and if they believe it would be possible for him to hypnotise them. Then he turns to the audience again.

'I'll need about ten minutes to prepare them. In the meantime, please give it up for Miss Lisa Thompson singing her latest single "Only a Night Away".'

The applause signals the temporary exit of Ian Gilby with his five volunteers in tow. The huge velvet curtains neatly fold upwards like clouds being lifted by the wind to reveal Lisa Thompson and her dancers as the music swells to accompany her advance to the front of the stage.

At around the ten-minute mark, Ian Gilby returns to the stage with his five volunteers. The stage has been transformed and made ready, with chairs laid out in a semicircle. Ian invites all the volunteers to sit.

He then walks behind each of them and, placing a hand on each of their shoulders, repeats the word 'sleep'. Each volunteer's head slumps as if they're sleeping. He walks back to the front of the stage to address the audience.

'Right, what we will do next, ladies and gentlemen, is to have a little fun. I will suggest random scenarios to these volunteers. The first will be to this lovely lady, telling her she's a chicken. When she's asked questions, she won't be able to resist clucking before giving her answers.' He moves back to the woman who is sitting in the middle of the group.

'Listen to my voice and my voice only. When I tell you to wake up, you will open your eyes and be alert. While awake, every time you're asked a question, you will feel the urge to cluck like a chicken before answering. Wake up.'

The woman raises her head and appears awake and alert.

'Stand up, please. Can you tell us your name?' Ian asks.

'My name is – cluck – Mary,' she replies, sending the audience into hysterics.

'Do you feel hypnotised, Mary?' Ian asks.

'Cluck – no,' Mary says, bringing further laughter from the crowd. She looks bewildered. Ian asks Mary to sit down again, touching her on her shoulder while saying the word 'sleep'. Mary appears to slump back into a hypnotic state.

Ian moves to the front of the stage to talk to the audience again.

'What we will do with the next gentleman is to get him to imagine that a ring of fire surrounds him and he's unable to cross it.'

Ian moves back and stands behind the man with the striped shirt. He places his hand on his shoulder.

'Listen to my voice. When I tell you to wake up, you will wake to feel there is a ring of fire surrounding you. There is no way you can cross it and you can't tell anyone, because you believe you're the only one who can see it. Wake up.'

The man wakes up and looks around at the audience, trying to pick out his wife.

'What's your name, sir?'

'Andy, Ian,' says the man.

'Andy Ian. What an unusual name, Andy Ian.' The audience laughs.

'No, just Andy,' he says with a smile.

'Anyway, please stand up for me, Andy,' Ian asks. Andy gets to his feet almost at once and he's led to the front of the stage.

'Andy, now tell me, do you feel hypnotised?'

'No, I don't, Ian,' he says, still smiling.

'Okay then, thank you for taking part, you may go back to your seat now. Andy, ladies and gentlemen!' Ian claps and the audience joins him to applaud Andy back to his seat.

Andy looks around at the floor. A few of the audience laugh while others are willing him to step outside the imaginary circle of fire. After about two minutes, all bar a few are enjoying the laughter at the man's expense. Ian places him back under hypnosis and the show continues.

# CHAPTER 3

Having walked a little after the show before taking a cab, Sir Edward and Lady Elizabeth are finally home and preparing to retire for the night. With the door to the en suite ajar, Edward stands by the sink while Elizabeth sits in the bed, propped up and centred by two smooth luxurious silk pillows. Finding the remote, she puts the television on for some late news. Over the familiar music that signals the start of the nightly round-up, she asks Edward a quick question.

'Did you enjoy your anniversary treat? I found the one… er… what's his name? The man?' She has to raise her voice as the music coming from the television concludes with a crescendo. 'I think his name was Andy, he was so funny, don't you agree?' she recalls, and takes a moment to smile to herself. 'Fancy not being able to move outside that imaginary circle? Are you listening in there?'

'Of course, dear, and next year it will be my turn to choose the anniversary treat. You've set that bar high for our first anniversary.' He squares up to his image in the mirror, allowing the electric toothbrush to reverberate vigorously over his teeth. Then, in a flash, he gets a thought which halts his nightly routine, a 'eureka' moment that so overwhelms him he removes the toothbrush without first turning it off and gets a speckling of toothpaste across the mirror and his face.

'Could that work?' he says a little too loud, but not enough, he assumes, for Elizabeth to hear.

'Were you talking to me, dear? Could what work?' Elizabeth calls out. 'If so, I didn't altogether catch whatever you said,' she adds.

'Oh, nothing,' he replies. Sir Edward is not in the habit of sharing everything with his second wife, and that was a major factor in the break-up and eventual divorce from Kim, his first. Before their marriage, Elizabeth worked as Sir Edward's research assistant for three years. Over the long periods spent together away from home, their relationship finally caught up with the rumours.

He stares again into the mirror, positive he may have stumbled upon a solution to the problem of overcrowded prisons. It could work and help the government achieve its cost-cutting targets. Sir Edward is not a man to miss an opportunity for adulation or the lining of his increasingly deep pockets either.

A quick dab with his face towel, before he uses it to clean the mirror, then he can see his knowing smile again. Sir Edward pulls the cord that turns off the light before going back into the bedroom. For a moment, news emerging from the television sidelines all his thoughts.

*'We are receiving details from France tonight regarding a seized Eurostar train in Calais. French authorities say a large group of migrants are trying to reach the United Kingdom. In the last few minutes, the Home Office has said the border forces will consider cutting power to the tunnel as a way of halting the train's progress. In other news today, Microsoft, the world's former largest software business, announced they are to enter voluntary liquidation. This news comes following a spate of unexplained fires in its factories around the world. Earlier today, a Microsoft spokesman confirmed that global stocks of*

*their final i9 Pentium chip, code-named 'Omega-X2', have been wiped out. And now, let's take a look at tomorrow's weather.'*

Sir Edward glances away from the television to focus on his wife. Sitting on the bed next to her, he kisses her first on the neck then her lips as she turns the television off and slides under the sheets.

'I'm just going to double-check that I've locked the front door. Won't be long.'

Following his nightly routine, Edward descends the stairs to the hallway. Turning right, it's only a few steps to the front door, where he applies the brass chain. He turns the lights off but turns them on again when the house telephone suddenly rings.

'Hello?' he answers.

'Help me, Edward. You've got to help me.'

'James, is that you?'

'It was an accident. I didn't mean to.'

'Calm down, James. You're not making any sense.'

'Don't know what came over me. I lost it and strangled her.'

'You've done what?'

'She was demanding too much, Edward. She threatened to involve you and the family.'

'I've always said your brains were either in a bottle or your trousers.'

'But I was thinking of you, Edward. I didn't want her to ruin your position...'

'Don't drag me into this, James! You've messed up time and time again, haven't you? Now murder, that's big time!'

'What do I need to do? Please, Edward, tell me!'

'I don't know, I've got no ideas. Besides, I'm going to need longer than a single phone call to figure this one out. Where are you now?'

'I'm in my office, but I can't leave.'

'Why, what do you mean you can't leave?'

'I'm too scared! Edward, the police have fitted me with one of those new link things. I made it to my office, but if I leave now, I might never make it home.'

'Then I guess that's one choice you don't have to make. I don't understand though, why didn't you go straight home?'

'Because it happened in the flat and I had to move the body to stop it being linked back to you.'

'Tell me you didn't use the car?'

'I had to use it.'

'You should never have used that car. That was Father's pride and joy; he loved that car. Now you must get rid of it.'

'I came here because it was close and I needed something to steady my nerves.'

'Really?' Edward is frustrated that he can't raise his voice with Elizabeth just upstairs. 'After everything that's happened, your first thought was more drink? You're my brother, James, but sometimes I question how we can be so different. Anyway, nothing can happen tonight. You'd better get some rest, and I'll speak to you in the morning. Oh, one last thing – what's the number on the bracelet?'

'Hang on a second while I look. It's one-eight-seven-five.'

Sir Edward jots the number on the notepad next to the telephone. He separates the sheet from the pad and puts it in the inner pocket of his coat, which is hanging next to the front door.

'Okay, I need to go. Don't forget what I said. Get shot of the car. Oh, and make sure you have something to eat. I don't want your diabetes to kill you either. Goodnight.'

Hanging up, he heads back upstairs. A sick thought comes into his head. What if James were to die of diabetes? Would it be a bad thing? It would rid the family of his issues.

Edward enters the bedroom, and Elizabeth is quick to pick up on the change in his demeanour.

'Who was that calling at this hour?' she enquires as he sits on the edge of the bed with his back to her removing his socks.

'Ah, nobody. Those bitcoin firms have no shame calling this late.'

'Maybe we should think about changing our number?' she says, turning off her bedside lamp.

'Maybe,' he says, turning off his and swinging his legs into bed.

Elizabeth feels so isolated in the dark, even with her husband lying inches away. Her thoughts about the past make her feel insecure. She sympathises with what his first wife, Kim, must have felt while they carried on behind her back. Her mind is awash with jealous thoughts. Why, for instance, was he unable to come home before their theatre visit? In her mind, those familiar elements of Edward and his ex-wife's relationship are causing her own doubts. She abandons any thoughts of intimacy as they both drift off to sleep in silence.

In the morning, when Elizabeth opens her eyes, it's clear that Edward had been up and away early. A focus on his empty pillow only serves to bring back last night's thoughts. The more she dwells on it, the more she feels vulnerable. She's given her husband everything. Paid close attention to every detailed complaint about his ex-wife and what she did and didn't do. As claimed by Edward, his ex-wife Kim spent all her time on her mobile, absorbed in simple, repetitive games. Then, at the end of an evening, she was often too fatigued to pay any attention to their relationship. Elizabeth is sure she has steered clear of those pitfalls, so what else could be distracting him? Why is he so uninterested? Putting her thoughts aside for a moment, she gets out of bed and goes into the shower.

'Oh, that's cold!' she screeches, before the water reaches her desired temperature.

The shower's jets massage her slender body, while the mint-scented shower gel does its best to calm her. Relaxed enough to think, a thought enters her mind. When she leaves the shower, she picks up the telephone and dials 1471.

'Telephone number 0201 457 1692 called yesterday at eleven thirty-five pm. If you would like to dial this number, please press hash.'

Elizabeth is slow in replacing the receiver. The number is not unfamiliar. She recognises it straight off as being the office number of her brother-in-law, James. She is all too aware of James's playboy lifestyle, having experienced one of his drunken episodes in the past.

She is always conscious to guard against any connections the press could use to damage her husband. Elizabeth feels no better knowing for sure that her husband has lied. She has good reasons to think beyond whatever seems innocent on the surface. Even a tenuous link is likely to have other connotations. Far from allaying her fears, the realisation widens her thinking. Finding out why her husband lied will be her next task.

Her mobile rings, but the caller has withheld their number. She answers it and, being cautious, allows the caller to speak first.

'Lizzy?' Her suspicion turns to delight – there's only one person who still calls her that.

'Dad! Is that you?'

'Yes, my little flower, it's me.'

'I didn't recognise the number. You call from a different one each time.'

'Just another drawback to being in prison. And before you ask again, the answer still remains no to any visits. Too many people would see the advantage in knowing you're my daughter.'

'But I'm married to the prisons minister now. I'm sure I'll be able to help you.'

'Lizzy, I can probably do more to help you from here than you can manage from being outside prison. I hope this doesn't sound like your father isn't appreciative of your suggestions, but I fear you would open yourself up to unavoidable dangers.'

'Then why call me if it's dangerous?'

'Just to hear your voice. You have no idea how that keeps me going for weeks, Sorry, but I have to go. Don't forget, any problems, you let me know in the usual way – right? I'll call again soon, I promise. Bye.'

The phone falls mute, giving Elizabeth no chance to say goodbye.

∼

In his office, Sir Edward removes a ticket from his pocket for yesterday's evening show. He places it on his desk and picks up his telephone, dialling a number from memory.

'Sir Edward Long here,' he declares. 'I need information, and you can trawl as deep as you like on this one. In fact, I want everything and anything.' He picks the ticket up, flipping it front to back and back again between his fingers.

'What's the name?' the voice asks.

'It's Gilby, Ian Gilby.' Sir Edward rests the ticket back on his desk. He listens to the sound of heavy keyboard typing over the phone while he waits.

'There's quite a substantial amount of material here.'

'How refreshing. I need you to extract anything special and package it for me. Then bike it over. You know the sort of incriminating things I need; same as the last three, which helped to clear my path to this post.'

'Do you want him picked up as well? I can arrange it.'

'No, under no circumstances. I just want you to send two hard copies, then bleach the files.'

'All expenses plus extras?'

'Without question. I'm looking forward to receiving it.'

After replacing the telephone, he picks it up again. He dials the number for the management agency printed on the reverse of the ticket, and a female voice answers.

'Mayday Management, good morning. How can I help you?'

'Oh hello, good morning. I'm trying to contact a Mr Ian Gilby.'

'Are you a promoter?'

'No, I'm not a promoter. I'm with the government.'

'Is it about his late tax return?'

'No, it's nothing of that nature, and he's not in any trouble. Could you have him call me please, today if possible, on 0207 194 5222? It is important.'

'May I take your name then, please?'

'Yes, my name is Mr Edward Long.'

'I'll see he gets the message, sir.'

'Thank you ever so much. Goodbye.'

He replaces the receiver, picking it up again for a third time. Up to this point, Sir Edward has spent the morning on the telephone. None of his calls, yet, are official government business. He waits for his next call to connect.

'Hello, Minister.'

'Good morning, Doctor Minn.'

'You're a little premature if you want your money; they have announced nothing yet.'

'I'm not calling about the money. I need a huge favour.'

'Favours are costly things, Mr Long, I'm sure you'll appreciate that.'

'I don't care what this one costs; you can keep the two hundred thousand. And I'll consider the job as paid.'

'You have my full attention, Mr Long. What is this favour?'

'My foolish brother has got himself into serious trouble and now he's part of your Link programme. I need to know if you can bleach his record.'

'If by bleach you mean destroy, then the short answer, Mr Long, is no. In fact, one of your government's key requirements for this system was the inability to remove or amend any data once entered.'

'What I'm trying to impress on you, Doctor Minn, is that if he's convicted, then my family's name also gets dragged through the courts. This is not a scandal that I, the government or Lotto-Guard can handle right now.'

'I fail to see how Lotto-Guard has any links to this. It's a matter for you and your family.'

'Believe me, Doctor Minn, my political family includes you, me and the government. There is a lot riding on this. It's an election year, and if one trips, we all fall.'

There's a long silence before Dr Minn responds.

'Even if we are family, as you say, it doesn't change facts. There's no way we can delete any data. However, the possibility to swap, say, one case for another, might still exist.'

'Do it,' Sir Edward orders, without even a second to think it through.

'I must warn you, swapping crime numbers will only ensure that someone else gets tagged with it. How's your conscience today, Mr Long?'

'My conscience is fine. Whatever it takes, get the job done.'

'And the lottery numbers, Mr Long, do you have them?'

'The numbers are one, eight, seven and five. Have you got that?'

'I have.'

'Good. Then goodbye, Doctor Minn.' Sir Edward returns the handset to its base.

He takes a full deep breath and wonders if a stiff drink would be out of order to take the edge off what he's done. He dries his clammy palms on the thigh of his trousers; a glance at the clock on the wall suggests what beverage would be more appropriate for the time of day.

After a minute, when the shaking stops, he's able to focus again. His secretary enters with the morning post and his cup of Earl Grey.

'This arrived by courier, marked private, for your attention, sir,' she says, handing Sir Edward a large brown envelope.

'Thank you, Amy.'

Once alone, Sir Edward opens the envelope and digests its contents. A calming feeling of being in control returns again. He compares it with the power he'd witnessed being wielded by the hypnotist at the show last night.

# CHAPTER 4

I t's an early start for everyone at the new courthouse, especially though for those arrested or detained over the last seventy-two hours. However, it's understood that a faulty television broadcast link seems to be why invited dignitaries and members of the public are facing the problem of a twenty-minute delay. A team of technicians have been working all morning trying to ensure the historical event gets recorded and televised live around the rest of the world. For this momentous occasion, a specially constructed stage and grandstand sits to the left of the court's main steps. The raised stage extends out from the multi-tiered seating to display its sleek glass podium. All the important dignitaries are seated in the front row.

Lord Taylor, the Lord Chief Justice of England and Wales, receives a ready media signal and stands up from his seat. He steps forward into the sunshine, casting a shadow that trails him all the way to the special podium.

'Lady Mayor, ladies and gentlemen, honoured members of the world's press and invited guests. Today marks an important and historical moment in the legal justice calendar of the United Kingdom. The government, together with Lotto-Guard, is proud to present the world's first Automated Robotic Court System, which I will henceforth refer to as ARCS. Please welcome the CEO of Lotto-Guard, Doctor Do Hi Minn, to share a few words on this amazing project before cutting the ribbon.'

The crowd's applause is generous. When Dr Minn reaches the podium, and draws a deeper breath to speak, the clapping dies away.

'Good morning to all. The ARCS program has existed since 2007 and is modelled on the great chess computer "Deep Blue". We present to you today our vision of justice in partnership with artificial intelligence. Our computer database already has two billion cases programmed to date and capable of processing well over of one hundred thousand cases per second when reaching decisions. We hope that this installation will herald a new era for justice, a first for Britain and a fairer and quicker way of dispensing justice for all. Thank you.'

Dr Minn's brief keynote ends with rapturous applause. Even defendants scheduled for this new experience applaud the passion of the address. The Lord Chief Justice returns to the fore.

'Now, it only remains for me to ask Doctor Minn to cut the ribbon and declare this court officially open – Doctor Minn.'

Lord Taylor hands Dr Minn a pair of scissors that's adorned with a decorative bow and stands back while he cuts the red ribbon, which falls obediently to the ground in two halves.

The world's media are thirsty for their first glimpse inside the courtroom. Photographers rush for vantage points, trying to bag that exclusive and historic money shot. Officials opening the sliding doors shield their eyes from the bank of flashing lights that's more intense than a violent thunderstorm. With the doors wide open, the press and public file in to take every available seat in the main gallery.

Inside, the courtroom is bland, simple and unassuming, with décor that wouldn't be out of place in a sterile hospital, with its radical departure from traditional Victorian oak-panelled walls. A two-metre QLED flat-screen covers the far wall; according to the official handout, this is the only interface between ARCS and the defendants. It's pre-loaded with prosecution and defence evidence and indexed to a unique crime number. Court-appointed solicitors are on hand for defendants who attend court unrepresented. A conveyor belt bordered by a grooved handrail replaces the conventional dock.

The atmosphere builds, with the anticipation comparable to gleeful fans awaiting the appearance of their rock star. It's time; everyone waits for the first case, to witness history and a glimpse at the future.

A computer-generated voice fills the courtroom, informing every one of the two-minute countdown to proceedings. It reminds patrons that all mobiles must be off and warns against any type of recording.

Footsteps puncture the chatter, which fades when the first defendant enters. His heavy steps seem out of sync with his gait as he appears to take forever to reach the conveyor. Officials flank and then encourage him to hasten his pace onto the conveyor belt before calming him. There's a sharp clunk as the links lock into place that startles him.

Within seconds, the case number appears on the huge screen. The synthesised voice again fills the courtroom, commanding a stilled silence.

'Case 1462, how do you plead?'

'Not guilty,' the defendant stammers, scanning the courtroom, uncertain if he needed to include 'Your Honour'.

'Case 1462, the prosecution has withdrawn its case after receiving fresh evidence. Case dismissed. You're free to go.'

The links immediately spring open, freeing both hands. A free man, he steps from the conveyor belt, rubbing his wrists, his face showing the joy of his relief. As he exits, the media surround him like vultures, picking over every aspect of his experience with a deluge of questions.

'What's it like to be the first person freed from this new system?' asks one reporter.

'Any idea, sir, what the new evidence is?'

'Would you like to give the press a quote, please?'

'Anything?'

'No comment.' A family member steps in to block and fend off reporters and their questions. 'We just want to put this unfortunate episode behind us.'

They leave the courthouse still pursued by a few reporters. It's fair to presume from their silence that there's every chance their story is already sold.

The next case, hoping for similar justice, is James Long, the prisons minister's older brother. He holds his head low on the walk towards the conveyor belt. He's feeling thankful to the new system already, for not identifying defendants by name. James steps onto the conveyor belt and tries without success to place his trembling hands onto the rails. One official steps forward to help guide them. The system takes over again, locking them in place to read the information. Holding his head low, James's eyes work the courtroom, hoping for any signs of his brother.

'Case 1875.' The voice focuses James's attention. 'How do you plead?' A profound silence occurs, prompting the repeated question. 'Case 1875, this is your first repeat. How do you plead?'

'Ah, guilty, Your Honour,' James answers hesitantly.

'Case 1875, the court accepts your guilty plea for attempted theft. This being your first recorded offence, you're duly fined three hundred pounds, payable today, before you leave the court.'

Still trembling, James moves immediately to conceal his face the moment his hands are released.

Sir Edward, watching from the sideline, hears the verdict and slips away without talking to his brother.

Officials escort James to the fixed penalty machine, where he pays the fine and has the links removed.

Free again, James's immediate and only plan is to vacate the courtroom in the shortest time. He forces his way through the waves of reporters still congesting the court and really can't believe he's free.

Chan and Ox meet up outside the court building.

They start up the steps towards the main entrance together. They halt when they see two of the police officers who arrested them exiting the court. The officers negotiate the revolving doors, taking care not to catch their bandaged limbs.

Entering, Chan and Ox are processed through security, having the links scanned to verify attendance. They find two empty seats near the courtroom and wait. After ten minutes a well-attired man approaches, after being redirected by a court officer.

'Good morning, are we…' – he studies his electronic notepad – 'Mr Chan Yip and Mr Oxford Earlington?' he asks.

'And who are you?' asks Ox.

'I'm the court solicitor, appointed to represent you or just to offer advice. Now, I've reviewed your files, and as these are your first offences, there's a good chance that, if you both plead guilty, you'll be in and out of court, ten minutes tops.'

'Guilty! Guilty of what?' says Ox.

'And if we don't?' Chan suggests, less confrontational.

'Then I suspect it might become more arduous, because as I understand it, the mitigations module has not yet been linked to the new computerised system.'

'So, we're just lab rats yeah, that is right, isn't it?' says Ox, standing. He wanders a few paces then returns.

'Not in such simple terms, Mr Earlington. A guilty plea as it stands is by far your best chance of wiping your slates clean.'

'Plead guilty even when we've done nothing wrong – would you do that?' argues Ox.

'Look, I can only recommend it. That ultimate decision rest with you both.'

'We need time to think,' Chan suggests.

'Well, get it wrong and time is the one thing you'll have plenty of, so good luck with that,' says the solicitor, who then turns and leaves them to their own thoughts. Another fifteen minutes pass before they're called into court. They've agreed between them to take the free solicitor's advice and plead guilty.

They're conscious of all the eyes watching from the time they enter the courtroom. As directed, both men stand on the conveyor belt, placing their hands on the rails. Once again, the links snap into place with a familiar clunk. The crime number flashes onto the screen for the court to view.

'Case 1792, how do you plead?' says the now familiar synthesised voice.

'Guilty,' says Chan.

'Guilty,' adds Ox.

'Case 1792, you have both entered the plea of guilty for the murder of Miss Jade Meredith.'

'Murder! What murder? Hey! What are you talking about? Where does the murder come from?' Ox shouts.

'We're supposed to have done something relating to cars!' bellows Chan.

Panic sets in as the pair struggle and kick at the rail, powerless to free themselves. The court computer volume gets louder to compensate for the raised noise level.

'In view of your guilty pleas, we've set your sentences at fifteen years, reduced from twenty. Due to the severity of this crime, it's further recommended that you both serve a minimum of twelve years.'

The conveyor belt sparks into motion with two extra guards added between the conveyor belt and the court audience. Ox and Chan, still protesting, are removed from view. At the end of the conveyor belt they pass through a door that opens and closes behind them automatically, where they're met by waiting prison officials.

After experiencing the highlight of the day so far, the courtroom becomes disruptive and loud. The synthesised voice asks for calm but the debate continues, with opposing opinions being shouted across the court. Again, the voice repeats its request for order, getting louder. There's not a real judge on hand to control proceedings but the court is equipped for most scenarios. Without further warning it activates its 110-decibel siren. This causes some to rush from the courtroom while others cover their ears. The siren lasts a mere ten seconds, but it has the desired effect of silencing the court. The new system has created drama and fear on its first day in service. It summons the next case.

Far away from the public pandemonium, Chan and Ox had not been expecting prison when they arrived in court this morning. They're both in deep shock over something they know they haven't done, and it took only a few minutes to go from them being accused of being car thieves to receiving fifteen years for murder.

Sir Edward sits in his office, his chair reclined, the cup of tea on his desk untouched and now cold. In silence, he reflects on the consequences of the action he has taken to preserve his family name. He knows his faults, even understands how, of late, self-preservation and greed may have clouded parts, if not all, of his recent judgements. His telephone rings, and for a moment it goes unnoticed, until its incessant tone catches his attention.

'Yes, Amy?' He asks.

'Sir Edward, I have a Mr Gilby holding on line two for you, sir.'

'Mr Gilby?' He repeats.

'Yes, sir, he claims to be returning your call.'

'Oh! Yes, I remember, I'll take the call.' He covers the mouthpiece and clears his throat.

'Mr Gilby, good afternoon, and thank you for getting back to me so promptly.'

'Mr Long, is it? I understand from my office you're not an agent, promoter, nor a fan, so I'm a little short on why you would think we have things of interest to discuss.'

'Well, Mr Gilby, you seem to have special talents for a few

things, but only one which I'm keen to explore. Any arrangements could be of benefit to both our interests.'

'I'll make this clear for you then; benefits or not, I'm not interested. I don't do sideshows and I'm not about to start.'

'That's not what the file in front of me shows,' says Sir Edward.

'File, what file?'

'I'm sure you're aware of the individual events but not that we have combined them in a file. In fact, none of your so-called real fans, or the press, knows of its existence, for now, anyway.'

'What events are you talking about?' snaps Ian, his tone sharpening.

'Let's just say, Mr Gilby, that these pictures, well... they tell an interesting and comprehensive story, even to someone who can't read.'

'I see. Then you'd best meet me in the Stuffed Pheasant. It's a little pub only two doors from the theatre – in say an hour and a half?'

'Yes, I agree we should meet, and I'm able to make that appointment.'

'And Mr Long, please don't forget to bring the file with you.'

'I'm looking forward to our meeting, good—' The conversation ends suddenly. Ian hung up without even a cursory goodbye, which Sir Edward views as just poor manners.

# CHAPTER 5

Walls filled with theatre memorabilia identify why it's a favourite hangout for actors, whether working or not. The Stuffed Pheasant has everything for those who still hanker for the bygone era when silent or black-and-white movies ruled. The cheap and chirpy atmosphere creates a setting ideal for thespians but offers nothing special for ordinary punters apart from the favourable drink prices. Sir Edward arrives early, allowing him to secure a seat in a corner facing the entrance. Knowing what Ian looks like gives him the edge, but by the time Ian arrives, the place has filled; standing customers obscure his view, voiding any advantage.

Sir Edward's three-piece suit distinguishes him from any other person in the pub – apart from the eccentric bartender who, in addition to his handlebar moustache, wears a pocket watch with his waistcoat.

A man wearing a dark full-length leather coat, light purple scarf and tinted glasses with silver rims appears in front of his table.

'Mr Long, I presume?' he enquires, tilting his head forward to peer over the rim of his glasses.

'Mr Gilby? Please have a seat.'

Ian unbuttons his coat, pinches his trousers at the knees and slides into the seat opposite. Sir Edward doesn't remember him being so pale but quickly appreciates how make-up must play a huge part in his theatrical illusion. He notices Ian's recent neat haircut, which infers that he cares about his appearance.

'Do you know? I saw your show for the first time, on Tuesday night.' Sir Edward says, with a smile, and hopes he comes across friendlier than in their earlier conversation.

Ian leans forward, placing both elbows on the table, and rests his thumbs under his chin. He spends a moment studying Sir Edward's face before removing his glasses. Without them and close up, Ian's eyes give little insight into his character or soul. They're captivating, mysterious and a good conversational topic, as one eye is green while the other is blue. Ian rests his glasses on the table, then leans back.

'So, you've seen my show? Fact-finding purposes? Or you enjoyed it?' he says through slightly clenched teeth.

'Actually, I enjoyed it, really. It was an anniversary treat from my wife.'

'Then, if you're a fan of my work, why go digging into my past?'

Before Sir Edward can answer, a young waitress interrupts.

'Can I get you both something?' she asks in a cheery voice.

'Nothing for me, thanks,' answers Ian, keen to get on with the meeting.

'Oh, another tea, please,' Sir Edward says, offering his empty cup to the waitress.

'Sir,' she says, accepting the cup before heading back behind the counter.

'Well?' Ian continues, pressing for an answer.

'Let's call it insurance,' Sir Edward replies.

'Insurance for or against what?'

'Well, if you are half as good as I've seen live, then it's my insurance to keep you from stepping out of line.'

'So, once we set aside your few nice words, what are we left with? Blackmail, perhaps?'

The waitress returns with Sir Edward's fresh cup of tea, breaking the conversation for the second time. Ian sits back in his chair, waiting until he's free to continue. After a sip of tea, Sir Edward appears ready to reveal more. Ian resumes his original position, elbows back on the table.

'Far from it,' Sir Edward assures Ian. 'Tell me, Mr Gilby, how much do you gross per annum? Thirty thousand? Forty maybe, in a good year? Could you perhaps feel comfortable earning, let's say, four times that amount?'

Ian sits back again, picks up and puts on his glasses. Sir Edward sits back too; he has no way of gauging Ian's response with his eyes covered. Seconds pass, and the two men sit staring at each other in silence, until Ian speaks.

'Sure, Mr Long, who wouldn't, if there were no strings attached?'

'Call me Edward. Look, if you're prepared to work with us, then I could arrange for whatever you earn to be treated… as tax free.'

'It might help to know who you mean when you say "us".'

'I'm with the government, Mr Gilby.'

'Well, since we've reached this far, you might as well call me Ian.'

Sir Edward nods his acknowledgement.

'If that's a genuine offer, then it's tempting. But I still don't know what the hell you want from me.'

'The government has been under increasing pressure to come up with a solution to tackle our overcrowded prisons.' Sir Edward pauses, taking a sip of his tea which allows Ian to interject.

'Build more prisons, is your answer.'

'No, they're keen for a more long-term solution, one that will not waste public resources or risk putting the public in danger. Now, watching your show the other night, I came away with a distinct impression that it's possible to control an individual in such a way as to prevent him or her from engaging in any unlawful acts.'

'I guess there must be an English translation for all that,' Ian says under his breath, looking away.

'I beg your pardon?' Sir Edward says.

'Let me get this right,' Ian says, removing his glasses. Are you saying you are considering hypnosis as a tool for controlling criminals?'

'In a nutshell, Ian, yes, if it's possible. Is it?'

Ian thinks before answering.

'Well, can it work?' Sir Edward presses for an answer.

'First you need to understand that not everyone can be... hypnotised, that is.'

Ian's statement equates to a traffic light at amber for Sir Edward, who moves to get it to green and shore up his fragile idea.

'Well, any reduction, even one per cent, in the prison population would be significant, in the greater scheme of things.'

'If you're honest, you know you're not solving the problem. You're just creating a "hypnotic state",' suggests Ian.

'I understand why you may not share my vision. But I can foresee a time when the need to build more prisons doesn't exist. They could manage sentences in the community, and perhaps without reoffending.'

'You seem to have it all worked out. But I'm more on the side of caution. My only question is, why me?'

'You're reputed to be one of the best hypnotists in this country, if not the world. If you join me, I think it would load the odds of success in our favour. What do you think? Are you in?'

Ian goes into one of his silent moments again. He's driven, like most, by the thought of earning vast amounts of money. That's the only principle bending him towards the government's view – if it's the government's and not Edward's.

He nods, then looks up at the ceiling before making eye contact with Edward again.

'Okay,' he says.

'Okay? Is that a yes, you'll do it?'

'Listen, you have me at a disadvantage, so I guess it's really no surprise to you that I'm saying yes.'

'Welcome on board,' Sir Edward says, affording himself a smile and extending his hand over the table. Ian mirrors him and the two men shake on their deal.

'There are just a few technical details to get through. As of now, it classifies you as a civil servant. What we've discussed here is not for public ears. You'll be working for me directly… and only me. Questions?'

'Yes, I'll have that drink now, while you tell me what will happen to the information you're holding on me.'

Sir Edward attracts the waitress's attention, beckoning her to the table.

'For now, your file stays with me.' Sir Edward extracts and slides a folded single sheet of A4 paper in front of Ian, who lifts one edge to confirm the existence of the information. Ian makes a second fold in the paper before placing it into his coat pocket.

'You beat me to it. I was about to ask to see proof,' Ian comments.

'I've taken the trouble of having the originals erased from all databases. In essence I'm the only one with all copies. But in say, two months, I hope to be handing it over to you. By then, I hope you will have gained my trust and I yours and the point where I would feel there's no need to retain it anymore.'

'What can I get you both?' says the waitress, arriving at the table.

'Nothing more for me, thanks,' says Sir Edward.

'A whisky with ice for me, please,' says Ian.

The waitress scampers off towards the bar again.

'Now, where were we?' says Ian. 'You mentioned some technical details.'

'Tomorrow you will receive a package containing your full

security clearance. I've used the picture from your Oyster file for speed.'

'I thought personal information was data protected?'

Sir Edward leans closer.

'You haven't heard this from me, but that's just fiction, put out to keep the public happy.'

'And my clearance level?' asks Ian.

'You will have complete access to check records and interview any prisoners you think suitable for the first trials.' Sir Edward pauses. 'I know it's only been a moment, but it's so important I'm saying it again. You are to report—'

'Yeah, I got it, only to you,' Ian interrupts.

'Now that's out of the way, I have a question for you.'

'Surprised you'd have anything further to ask me, given what you've already dug up.'

'I'm curious about your eyes. It's not something you would find in notes, not from my sources anyway. Were you born like that... the different colours?'

'No, and apart from the conversations it spurs, it's given me no advantage in life.'

'Look, you don't have to say if you don't want to, it's nothing I could use anyway.'

'It's not a secret, more a tragedy if you really analysed it. You see, my stepfather was an abuser and drug dealer. But he wasn't always like that. I can remember my earliest memory of him when I was about three. He might even have been around longer but I couldn't say with any accuracy that I can recall. I know my mother wasn't the struggling, teenaged single parent anymore who could barely feed me, let alone herself. And she never questioned where the money that bought the food and toys came from. We weren't hungry, and we had a roof over our heads, so why would she? Soon she became pregnant by him; I got a half-brother, and she got a family. About four years later I noticed a change in him, the way we were living, everything. Then, when one of his deals went tits up, whoever he was dealing with threatened to harm one of us. He had no way of replacing the stuff he'd either lost or used, so I think he made a batch himself.'

'Here we are,' the waitress says, placing the whisky in front of Ian. 'Ready for another tea, sir,' she says with a carefree smile. 'Anything else at all, gentlemen?'

'No, that's all for now, thank you,' says Sir Edward. She turns and leaves.

'Sorry, please continue.'

'You know, he used to play this game with us. He would hide sweets around the house and if we found them, they were ours to eat. So, one day I found this bag of what I thought were sweets, hidden in a shoe box under his bed and obviously shared them with my brother. At that age, you crave any connection. I knew that he wasn't my real father but I wanted him to be. I took any form of contact as a way of bonding, hoping he would stay and look after our mother. Well, my brother was sick instantly; he brought everything up. But I ...wanted to be his real son and took more. After that, my only memory of it was waking up in a hospital with a light being shone into my eyes. I heard the doctor say she couldn't be sure if they could save my eyes. Then, after five weeks, I was well enough to go home. He came for me and we took the bus... I thought it was a treat at the time, in fact it was all we could afford and cheap. I started noticing that everyone we passed would stare at me. I mean everyone, and I wasn't sure if it was just a spot on my face, but it soon made me self-conscious. When we got home, I found a mirror and stared, as everyone else had, at my eyes. But you're only seeing a coloured contact lens that hides the real damage.'

'Where was your mother during this?' Sir Edward takes another sip of his tea which by now must be cold. Ian pauses, then downs his whisky in one shot before he continues.

'Physically she was there, but her eyes showed that she was not, if you know what I mean.'

'I'm afraid I don't,' Sir Edward says. He has encountered no social deprivation in his life.

'My stepfather... well, anything he did affected the whole family. He turned my mother into an addict but committed the ultimate sin when he took her life.'

'I'm sorry, how did it happen?'

'It was a day when she was not too spaced out. I remembered it, purely because it was my birthday and she had bought a small cake. She confronted him about a rumour she'd heard at the shops that he'd fathered a baby, a girl, I think. The argument got loud very quickly, so loud that they didn't even notice when I took my brother and hid in the wardrobe. I covered his eyes, but I witnessed enough of an intense argument, something an eight-year-old shouldn't have to. Something fell or was maybe thrown and hit the wardrobe door, and it shut. He had no idea that she was carrying another child for him. He just never enjoyed being questioned by anybody. The paramedic who attended couldn't save her and even he felt sick. He said something like "he'd never seen anything so sad".'

'What became of your father?'

'Just sat down on the floor by her body, placed his hands on his head and waited. Her lifestyle masked how far on she was in the pregnancy and for that he received two life sentences.'

'That must have been a bad experience for you and your brother, and the drugs culture is just another area my government is battling to find solutions for.'

'Well, unless you're prepared to tackle things at the source, then you have no way of solving that problem either.'

'I think it can only become a bigger problem if we don't try.' He takes another sip of tea.

'I can't disagree with that,' Ian says. He finishes the rest of his whisky by tipping his head back and emptying the glass.

'I'm sorry, I have to be somewhere. You must excuse me.' Ian puts his glasses on and stands up. Stepping into the aisle, he buttons his coat.

'Yes, I need to be getting back myself. Don't worry about the bill,' Sir Edward tells him.

'Oh, I'm not. Goodbye,' Ian says.

'Goodbye,' responds Sir Edward. 'I'll be in touch,' he adds.

'I'm sure you will,' Ian replies, moving away.

Sir Edward remains and settles the bill, then, as inconspicuously as he arrived, he leaves the Stuffed Pheasant.

# CHAPTER 6

Downing Prison is a little over five years old and already considered the flagship of the UK's penal system. The contemporary, single-storey complex is built on a reclaimed landfill site bordering the Hertfordshire countryside. Designed from the ground up, it was an architect's dream to be handed a blank canvas on which to express forward-thinking ideas. The design set out to avoid old failings; the result, an ever-evolving upgrade on its Victorian predecessors.

Bricks and mortar alone have changed little of the attitudes, least of all the thinking of convicts or staff. Perhaps what have changed over time are the powers that prison officers once wielded that are now reduced to mere tokens. Its corridors are a glowing example to other prisons and the first place offered by the government for press and photo calls. Like most prisons, though, it has its fair share of troubled and troublemaking prisoners. While most inmates at Downing are Category C or less, they're still deemed dangerous enough to warrant being locked away from the public. A small category identified as IPPs have little to no chance of ever seeing freedom again.

Paul Gilby is a twenty-four-year-old small-time burglar. Arrested on yet another break-in, he's six weeks into a five-year sentence. His apprenticeship in the art of taking without permission began at the delicate age of five. Inducted into crime by a family member at such a young age, it's no wonder he knows little else.

In his cell, Paul lies relaxed on his bed, passing time by perusing an old copy of *Hello!* magazine. He's resting, having just come back from a two-day stop in the infirmary following a chest infection.

His former cellmate, there for the first four weeks of this sentence, has left following new evidence presented by his solicitor. His replacement arrived yesterday before Paul returned and occupies the other bed in the cell.

Paul's new cellmate hasn't said a word since arriving. For the time being he's even avoiding full eye contact, choosing to keep pretty much to himself. Even without words, Paul feels something isn't right about this slight figure with stalactite teeth and a dodgy ponytail, and he hasn't decided yet if he's trustworthy. Two of Paul's personal items have mysteriously disappeared, but he has no evidence to suspect his new cellmate. Paul hopes it's not him, especially when there's no idea how long they could be sharing.

Paul lowers his feet to the ground and sits upright on the edge of his bed. He places the magazine on the bed beside him before standing. It's almost time for lunch. His cellmate, also knowing the drill, does the same, placing the book he appeared to be reading on the table between the beds. Paul glances over at the book's cover – maybe he can get an idea of his cellmate's character by what he reads.

He stares, horrified, at one of his missing items: his daughter's photograph, being used as a common bookmark.

Paul is angry at this blatant disrespect for someone else's property. That photo is the only thing he has left of his daughter, after his girlfriend, fed up with his prison career, walked out taking their daughter with her.

'Where did you get that?' asks Paul, pointing but calm.

'What?' A shrug of the shoulders accompanies the cold reply.

'That photo, there, in your book, where did you get it?'

'I found it.'

Paul steps over to within a few inches of his cellmate's face.

'You'll find nothing in this cell unless you go digging for it, and that includes trouble. Now, if I find you anywhere near my stuff again, I'll break your skinny little arms. I hope I'm making myself clear.'

Paul pushes his cellmate aside, ignoring his contemptuous look, to retrieve his daughter's photo from the pages of the book. Placing it in his pocket, he moves back to his side of the cell.

'Look, I'm sorry! I found it on the floor, honest. As long as we're cooped up in here, we need to get along, right? I'm Vincent.' He extends his hand.

Keys in the cell door interrupt their encounter.

'Come on, get busy, if you want your food hot,' says the guard, opening the door wide. Paul stares at Vincent but declines the handshake, choosing to just exit the cell.

Mates or not, Paul looks back after leaving his cell to notice Vincent is yet to move. He doesn't seek confrontation, and he's determined to make this his last stretch, vowing never to end up in prison again. This promise he has made to himself he's broken several times in the past. However, for it to work he knows that trying to keep out of trouble is his first step.


After collecting his food, Paul takes steps to avoid sharing the same table as Vincent for lunch. He finds an empty seat next to Ox on the end of a long table. Chan sits opposite as they settle to the daily business of first identifying, then eating, what someone has classified as lunch.

'You guys new here?' Paul asks, glancing at Ox and Chan in turn.

'No, we've been here a couple of days now, and you? We haven't seen you before either.' Chan notes.

'No, I was in the medical wing for a couple of days with a chest infection, so I guess that's how we might have missed each other. Anyway, my name is Paul, by the way,' he says, extending his hand.

'Chan,' – meeting Paul's hand across the table – 'and he's Ox,' he adds, looking in his direction.

Paul moves his focus to Ox, extending his hand, but is completely ignored.

'Okay,' he says, retracting his hand before he begins eating.


Vincent sits at the table behind and appears every so often to whisper something to the others at his table. Alert to the positions of the meal supervisors, Vincent picks a few peas from his plate and, disguising his throw, strikes Paul on his left shoulder. Paul looks over his shoulder and the group seated with Vincent notice him.

Things seem to quieten after the throwing incident. Soon the loud piercing noise of a bell sounds the end of lunch and a return to the cells. The long walk back always appears harder on a full stomach.

Paul strolls just in front of Chan and Ox as they are all corralled back towards the cells. Suddenly a nudge parts Chan and Ox; a huge hand comes between them to rest on Paul's shoulder, halting his forward motion. The assailant spins Paul, gripping him by the throat and thrusting him against a wall. Everyone continues filing past, keen to distance themselves from any trouble. Even to witness such an act is to invite unwanted danger to your own existence under the unwritten rules amongst inmates in the prison.

Chan and Ox aren't afraid, but they are unschooled virgins when it comes to getting drawn into prison conflicts. And now they have a close-up view of the assailant, a man known as Dozer.

A whale of a man, Dozer is a unique individual within the prison. The guards hate him even more than other prisoners. His size alone ensures that he can only use one of the staff toilets, which he enjoys leaving in a foul state. Paul is showing signs of distress as the colour drains from his face. Dozer presses even tighter under Paul's chin, while Vincent looks on over his shoulder with his mocking smile. Paul, using both hands, tries harder to loosen the grip and get a little air as Dozer speaks.

'We heard you're sharing your cell with a thief, and we don't like thieves in here,' he says, looking around at his two lookouts. 'But do you know what's hated in here even more than thieves?' He loosens his hold, enough to allow Paul to shake his head. 'People who interfere with children.'

Paul can't understand why he's a target. He fears things are getting out of hand.

'I've got no idea what you're talking about,' Paul says, struggling to protest while Vincent goads Dozer.

'Check his pockets, if you don't believe me,'.

Dozer beckons one of his lookouts to hold Paul, before searching each of Paul's pockets, finding a small picture size photo of a baby in a top shirt pocket.

'No idea, hey?' Dozer says as he ploughs a stiff punch straight to Paul's stomach.

Paul is being propped up and is unable to collapse. He hangs like a shirt on a clothesline, gasping for air.

As soon as he can breathe again, he coughs out his plea: 'It's a picture of my daughter!'

'Now, why don't I believe you?' Dozer smiles.

'If the guy says it's his daughter, why wouldn't you?' interrupts Ox.

Dozer turns to face the voice that dared to interrupt him, ignoring Paul for the moment. He forms a fist which he changes into a gun, placing his finger dead centre to Ox's forehead.

'I hope you're not a gambling man, because in here there isn't much to gamble with except your life.'

'I guess this should be your first gambling lesson then,' Ox replies, as he grabs Dozer's fingers, twisting them away from his body, before planting a side-kick just under his ribcage.

From the faint sound that follows, and Dozer's immediate clutching of his shoulder, there's no doubt that his shoulder is at least dislocated, at worst broken. Dozer drops silently to the ground, as does Paul, released by the others who were restraining him.

Ox picks up the photo from the ground and, helped by Chan, steadies Paul before escorting him back to his cell. As the tail end of the line of prisoners files past, it clears to show Dozer on the floor and in some pain, with his two accomplices standing over him. The guard escorting the end of the line draws his baton.

'What's wrong with him? And which of you did it?' he shouts.

'He tripped on the soap,' says one.

'What?' says the guard.

'He tripped… on the back of someone's sole – not soap. You know what I mean, the heel.'

'He's dyslexic, sir,' says the second prisoner.

'Is he hurt?'

'It's his arm; it may be dislocated.'

'You have my authority to get him to medical, now!'

'Yes, sir.'

'Just one of you. You, back to your cell.' He points out whom he has selected and the direction he's expected to take.

The sight of the prison bully being taken towards the medical centre is a sure precursor for everyone to expect more trouble and soon.

Paul recovers a little with each stride, rubbing his stomach and stretching his neck as they move towards the cells. Once he feels able, he asks a question.

'What did you do to him?'

'It doesn't matter, forget it,' Ox answers.

'Yeah, but—'

'If the man says forget it, just let it go,' says Chan.

'I owe you, mate, big time,' says Paul.

'You don't know me, so you don't owe me.' Ox spells it out and hopes Paul get the message.

They arrive at Paul's cell door.

'I don't know you guys, it's true. But remember that story about the lion and the mouse? Sometimes even someone small can help.'

'I don't understand, or wish to know, what the hell you're on about,' says Ox.

With that, Paul enters his cell, leaving Chan and Ox to continue on to theirs.

After waiting long enough for them to leave, Vincent follows Paul into the cell. He moves straight onto his bed, picking up his book. He pretends there's nothing else that interests him.

After five minutes, the cell door is locked. Paul is now sure he's sharing a cell with a thief and a liar, and will need to guard against information of any sort being passed to others in the prison.

# CHAPTER 7

Ian Gilby sits comfortably in the soft leather back seat of his official chauffeur-driven car that picked him up. It's the start of a new week and he's en route to his first prison visit and he uses his time efficiently, going over papers he's received from Sir Edward. Offered several locations to conduct his trials, Ian chose Downing Prison and was surprised how Sir Edward acceded readily to his request.

Stopping short of the gates to the prison visitors' entrance, the driver lowers his window and waits for the advancing security officer. Then, after the driver presents his official documents, the officer leans in to talk with him.

'Sorry, sir, going to be a slight delay, so for the moment please switch off the vehicle's engine while you wait.'

'Can you tell me what's going on?' the driver enquires.

'Engineers are putting the finishing touches to the new security entry system. Should be fully operational by your next visit. If you'll excuse me, I'll be back after checking your documents.'

After a short delay and the returned papers, they're moving again through the first layer of security. The vehicle is then manually scanned before it enters the belly of the prison, where Ian is escorted from there on foot.

Through many security gates, weapon detectors and bag search areas, Ian gains a real perspective on prison procedures. He's conscious of his own dread of such places but excited too about the prospect of being reunited with someone he hasn't seen for some years. At visitor reception, someone waits to greet Ian officially and escorts him to the governor's office.

Having being assigned the highest level of clearance, Ian is not subject to any of the normal checks. The experience so far makes him consider how an innocent person could feel anxious at a time like this.

They reach the governor's secretary's office in a little over seven minutes from the gate. Not seeing the secretary, Officer Newport moves to knock on the governor's door only to have it snatched open, with Cynthia emerging a little red-faced.

'The governor is expecting you, please go right in,' she says, holding the door open before re-knotting the tie on her white blouse.

They find the governor sitting behind his polished oak desk. Ian's first impression is he's a serious man, maybe even ex-army. Then it occurs to him that it could be the nature of the job rather than the person himself.

'Come in, Mr Gilby,' the governor says, rising from his chair to shake Ian's hand across his desk. 'I'm Governor Riley. Please, take a seat.' The governor scans through a printed document which he lays face up on his desk.

'You come with some heavyweight authority behind you. It also says here' – he checks again – 'that you are to have full cooperation and access to all prisoner files. Well, Senior Officer Newport here will be at your service throughout your visit. He will, amongst other things, be in charge of your safety. Put your trust in him and your experience here can only be a pleasant one.'

The governor draws breath. 'Now, Mr Gilby, do you have any questions?'

'Er, no, nothing for the time being, Governor, thank you,' Ian answers.

'Okay, then if you would be so kind as to wait for only a few minutes in my secretary's office, Officer Newport will be out to take you through our safety briefings, issue your vest which I'll stress must be worn at all times while in the company of any prisoners.'

They stand shaking hands again. The governor walks Ian to his office door, closing it once Ian has left. Walking back to his desk the governor turns to instruct officer Newport.

'Keep an eye on him. I want nothing going on inside this prison I'm not aware of, have you got that?' He says taking his seat.

'Sir,' Newport responds with a confirming nod as he opens the door and exits the governor's office.


The governor is a suspicious man by nature, and while there is no evidence for it, he feels that the government, in their need to cut costs, are carrying out these stealth visits hoping to unearth something they can use to support their interference, or even perhaps his ultimate removal.

After the fitting of Ian's hi-tech vest for protecting vital organs, Officer Newport takes Ian to the room where he will conduct all his interviews. It's a sparse room: two tables stand by the back wall, facing the door. The desk to the left contains a computer monitor and keyboard, while the one on the right has just a telephone. Presented with the prisoner records as requested, Ian sits at the desk on the right to begin his selection.

'Should you require any additional information,' says Officer

Newport, 'then this computer here will give you access to the prison records. I should say, though, you only have basic access.' Officer Newport tips him a knowing smirk.

'Password protected, I'm sure?' says Ian.

'But of course, and your password is "prisonbreak". All one word and lower case.'

'What?' Ian says, smiling.

'Yeah, I know, I chose it.' Newport smiles at what he believes is a slick play on words and the initial rapport between them.

Twenty minutes has elapsed before Ian is anywhere near ready to start the real work of seeing prisoners. Officer Newport sits at the computer desk, pretending he has no interest in what's taking place in the room. Each time Ian raises his head, he catches Newport straining to glimpse the names he has so far written in his open notebook.

'Ah, let's see now,' Ian says, loud enough for Newport's ears. 'Interesting,' he adds.

'What is?' asks Officer Newport.

'Oh, sorry. When I say interesting, I mean to the trained eye.'

Officer Newport stands up, moving towards Ian's desk. 'Perhaps you might permit me to look. I'm trained not to miss any details,' he spouts confidently.

'Well, you see this photo here,' says Ian, pointing to a passport-size photo in a file.

Newport positions himself to the left of Ian's shoulder to get a better view. 'I can't see anything unusual about it,' he says frowning.

'Perhaps a closer look at his face,' Ian urges, as he circles his finger around the photo. 'Can't you see it, the aura?'

Ian's fingernail contains a thin layer of a chrome mirror-like substance that reflects the ceiling lights with dazzling effect.

'No, I can't see a thing,' insists Newport.

'Concentrate.'

His finger's circling motion, coupled with the light bouncing from the chromed nail, leaves its own trail that mimics a delayed photographic exposure. The colour also appears to change, becoming a softer shade of pulsating orange.

'Can you see it now?' Ian asks again.

'Yes, yes I can.' Newport's answer is delivered in a monotone.

'Listen to my voice and only my voice: sleep.'

Officer Newport's head slumps, allowing Ian to begin.

'You will observe everything I do until you hear a trigger word. Your trigger word is "tea". When you hear this word, it will immediately erase all information gathered in any preceding hour from your memory. Do you understand?'

In the same trance-like drone, Newport answers, 'Yes.'

'Wake up on my count of three,' Ian says in a bright tone. 'One, two, three!'

'Just a second. Yes, there's a glow around the face,' Newport says.

'This is thirsty work,' Ian says, changing the subject.

'Give me a minute and I'll arrange for refreshments. What would you like?' Newport enquires.

'A cup of tea would be just fine, thank you.'

The expression on Newport's face changes to puzzled.

'Now, what were we talking about?' The question confirms Ian's procedure has worked.

'You tell me,' says Ian.

'That's funny, I can't seem to remember. I best get that tea organised. Do you take sugar, Mr Gilby?'

'Yes, two please. Also, I would like to see this gentleman first.' He shares his choice with Officer Newport.

Officer Newport, still aware of Governor Riley's instructions, sets about trying to gain Ian's confidence.

'Paul Gilby. I suppose you chose him because you share a similar surname?' He jokes.

'Well, I suppose starting with someone who sounds like he could be related helps make my choice easier,' replies Ian with a fake smile. 'What can you share with me about this prisoner anyway?'

'There's not much to tell. He's a quiet one; I don't think you'll have any trouble with him. Others in here, though, might have a pop at you just for fun.'

Officer Newport uses the telephone in the room both to request refreshments and to call for someone to bring the prisoner to the visitor block.

Paul arrives just ahead of Ian's tea. The initial surprise visible on Paul's face goes undetected by Officer Newport as he enters the room. Nor does Paul let slip that he and Ian are in fact related, as joked about by Officer Newport earlier. Asked to take the seat opposite, Paul plays the perfect and passive inmate.

'Mr Newport?' says Ian.

'Yes.'

'I wish to interview this man in private.'

'Well, Mr Gilby, the prison rules handbook – namely section nine, subsection two, paragraph eleven – clearly states that no prisoner should be alone with a member of the public, unless it's their legal representative.'

'You yourself were only saying a few moments ago that there's nothing to fear from this prisoner. I don't understand what's changed.'

'Yes, I confirm those were my words, but rules are rules, Mr Gilby, and breaking them is how people like him end up here in the first place.'

'Officer Newport, I think you'll find that my letter of engagement covers this specific area and, with my time here limited today, I would appreciate you clearing this with the governor as soon as, so that I may continue.'

After contacting the governor, Newport concedes to Ian's request, which is backed up by authority.

'Well, it seems you're right and your remit does override prison rules. I'll just be outside should you require anything else.'

Alone, Paul feels able to be open with his half-brother and wastes no time in resurrecting past gripes.

'Ironic, isn't it?' he says.

'What is?' asks Ian. 'What's my brother – or, should I say, half-brother – got against me now?'

'Well, on balance, and given your taste for risk taking, you were the more likely of us to end up in a place like this.'

'It just goes to show you can't always judge a book solely by its cover.'

'The same way you can't say it's a good book unless you've read it from cover to cover,' Paul counters.

'Look, Paul, I'm not here to rake over what happened to us as kids. You were too young to understand why I left after Mum died.'

'Then why are you here and how did you find me anyway? Because when you left that showed me you didn't care.'

Ian tries not to raise his voice.

'Didn't care? If I didn't care, Paul, then why did I spend years searching only to find that you had changed your name by deed poll? This is just a job. But I've looked into it and there's real potential to get you out.'

'That would take a miracle, since I still have over four and a half years of my sentence left, maybe less for good behaviour.'

'The authority to get you out of here sooner depends on my recommendations that would be sent in an official letter. I can get your name on that. But...' He pauses for a few seconds. 'I have to have your complete trust, and more important, you must follow my instructions to the letter.'

'If it means getting out of here, living a normal life and perhaps even seeing my daughter again, then it's an easy decision. I'd piss on the Pope's head if that's what it took.'

'Trust me, you won't need to go that far,' Ian says, smiling.

'Then just tell me whose head I need to piss on, cos I'm on board, brother.'

'Take this,' Ian says, producing a small clear plastic pouch from his pocket.

'What is it? There's nothing in there.'

'I told you to trust me, Paul, which will also mean no questions, none.'

Ian stands up and goes over to the door, watched by Paul. He looks out the small window set into the top half of the door. It's obscured by the broad shoulder of the guard who escorted Paul from the main block. He returns to his seat.

'Okay, now listen. Inside the bag, you'll find a pair of contact lenses.'

Paul runs his finger over the transparent plastic pouch, detecting them.

'On Wednesday, I'll be back to start conducting the hypnotic tests. Based on them, they're expecting me to recommend individuals for the trial release. Be prepared so that whenever you're called you're wearing them. They will protect you from the process. You must also act out any instructions I give you for the benefit of any observers, but we're only talking amateur dramatics, and minor parts at that.'

'How convinced are you this could work?' asks Paul.

'Well, if everyone does their bit, there's a ninety-nine per cent possibility you can walk free from this prison within weeks, with a one per cent chance of being randomly interviewed before release.'

'Can you answer a personal question, please?'

'Depends on what it is.'

'In all these years, did you ever wonder about Dad?' Paul asks, which makes the expression change on Ian's face, showing it's the last question he wanted asked.

'Why would I? He's your father, not mine, and the only one responsible for Mum's death.'

'That's what you've always said but you don't know the full story.'

'Don't try and tell me that, Paul. Remember, I was there.'

'Well he was too, but tells it differently.'

'I bet he does. Sounds like you've been in touch with him and he's brainwashed you around to his sick way of thinking'

'Yeah, I'm in contact, but it was more like he filled in the blanks about all the questions that were left unanswered because you were not there for me to ask.'

'Let's drop this, Paul. I'm here to help, not fight you. If you want to help yourself don't talk to me about him. I've got plenty of other things to waste my energy on.'

'Okay, I see.'

Ian's initial visit to Downing Prison is over. Despite having only met one prisoner, and a relation at that, Ian has collected valuable information to aid his task going forward. Paul has gained too, returning to his prison routine with a positive prospect of early freedom.

Later, while Paul makes his way towards the dining hall, he's still carrying a smug smile from his brother's visit. As each wing merges into a single line, it's his good fortune to find himself once again in the company of Chan and Ox.

'You're looking pleased,' says Chan. 'Good news?'

'Well, let's say I've found my ticket out of here,' Paul whispers, unable to resist smiling.

His mood soon changes as they turn a corner and encounter Dozer. His six-foot-four frame doesn't give the impression of someone who's ever missed a meal. He's flanked either side by his two associates. Dozer's twenty-two-inch neck turns and he looks behind him, a sling supporting his arm. They have confirmed his injury as a break, which will at some point need an operation to insert pins. Dozer looks at Paul and nods, which is as much as saying his injury is Paul's fault.

'Your pretty paedophile defenders aren't with you twenty-four seven,' he says.

'You need to take care of that mouth of yours or it will be more than your arm next time,' Ox says, answering for Paul. Dozer shifts focus to Ox, stepping in closer to face him. His towering figure blocks all the light.

'When it's your time, oh, I'll enjoy messing you up proper,' he tells Ox.

The line shuffles along, which forces Dozer to do the same.

'You don't want to mess with him,' Paul informs Ox.

'He doesn't scare me.'

'Well he scares me and almost everybody in here. If the rumours are true, then you should be scared too.'

'What rumours?' asks Chan.

They hold back slightly, obliging others to file past, and Chan also lowers his voice to reveal information only a few prisoners would know.

'Over the last three months, we've had two unexplained deaths in here. Victims just stopped breathing. No marks, nothing. I overheard one of his guys boasting about how they held someone down while Dozer sat on his chest until he stopped breathing. The deaths were all recorded as some sort of virus. Even the post-mortems found no clues, so trust me, he's dangerous.'

'How does that clumsy oaf run a place like this?' says Ox.

'He doesn't; the set-up here is all Fat Fingers'.'

'Fat Fingers? Who's he?' asks Chan.

'They say he runs things from his cell, and as his name suggests, he's got fingers in everything going on in here, some say right up to the governor's office.'

'Wow, sounds like this place is full of people we wouldn't want to know outside of prison,' Chan concludes.

The line continues moving as they enter the food hall.

# CHAPTER 8

Whether you're a prisoner or guard, there's a routine every day at Downing Prison. Sometimes a simple event can transform the whole energy of the prison from an edgy but calm place to a tense, reactive and volatile one. At 7 am sharp, it all starts with a loud klaxon announcing the new day, signalling another round of challenges and conflicts, unless you're lucky enough that it happens to be the day of your release.

Every inmate has to make his own plan on how to survive a prison sentence. If you're lucky and get it right then you stand a good chance of waking up to the same sound the following morning. Sometimes your personal journey is fated, depending on which groups you associate with.

Like all prisons, there's a hidden, unspoken subculture where the key to survival is how, like water, you can quickly find your level. Downing has an important role to play in the modern approach to rehabilitation: a vision designed to give free education to even those deemed too dangerous for society. There's also free advice from just about every inmate, ready to persuade a captive audience about their foolproof methods for not getting caught next time. For those experiencing incarceration for the first time, the shock may kick-start them into not wanting to experience it for a second time. For others, though, it will be the start of a long relationship with prison, one that for some will last their lifetime.

The line for breakfast snakes towards the canteen. Somewhere near the back, Dozer and his cronies are forcing their way up the line towards the head of the queue. Paul, nearer the front, stands tiptoed trying to locate the whereabouts of his current nemesis. Noting Ox and Chan only metres behind, Paul invokes the first rule of prison survival: avoid being caught isolated. He weaves back through the queue as Dozer advances the other way. From his height, Dozer also catches sight of Paul and knows the first rule also. But he's hungry and has no intention of interfering with Paul. Not in public anyway or while Ox and Chan are that close.

'Hi, guys,' Paul says as he reaches them.

'You do know breakfast is the other way?' Chan points out.

'Yeah, I know. I wanted to talk to you guys about something.'

Dozer draws level. He stops for a second and stares before moving off again.

'Phew! Close,' Paul says with a nervous laugh.

'If it's him you want to talk about, not interested,' Ox says.

'No, it's something more important. But I can't say here.'

'There's nothing more important for us than getting out of here,' Ox says, stepping across Paul to continue moving.

'Apart from finding out who set us up and why?' Chan adds. Ox looks back, acknowledging the missed point.

'I might be able to help with one of those,' Paul whispers.

'And why should we believe you?' says Ox, walking backwards.

'Because I...' Paul stops himself as he notices others taking an interest in their little tête-à-tête.

'Because I owe you guys my life and this might be my one and only way to pay you back,' he whispers.

'We've already said, you... owe... us... nothing,' Chan says, also going ahead of Paul.

'Why don't you wait until you hear what it is, then make that decision?' Paul's question attracts interest from inmates who know the value of information, either to use themselves or to sell.

Chan and Ox only stare at each other, allowing Paul to continue talking.

'There would be nothing to lose, and besides, it might help pass the time quicker.'

The queue approaches the canteen doorway. Ox picks up three trays, handing them out. The line narrows to single file as they pile their plates with the allowed quantity of sausages, beans and toast. A simple breakfast, designed to give the nutrients needed to maximise their energy, especially those who will work in the harsh environment of the prison workshops.

Securing seats, they start breakfast against the clock. Everyone gets the same ten minutes to eat, clear plates and return trays to the collection points. All canteen entrances have sensitive metal-detecting devices with built-in Tasers. This makes the concealment of any metal object dangerous. Anyone who violates the rules gets twenty seconds to own up before being stunned. On its initial trial, that time was ten seconds but they found out this was unrealistic when an old man with a pacemaker couldn't persuade them in time. He got confused by all the flashing lights and buzzers and couldn't think quickly enough. So, after that fatality, they increased the reaction time to twenty seconds and now even the new prisoners are made aware of this in their welcome pack information sheets and that seems to be working.

Conversations during the morning period are invariably difficult owing to time constraints; dinner time allows the opportunity to at least start one. With military rigour, two thousand men eat three meals every day. Once through this culinary experience, those who have been unlucky in securing daily work can enjoy half an hour in the yard, to digest food and take vital exercise to combat the long spells of being locked up.

Less athletic inmates seek employment in or around the canteen, with extra inches around the waist guaranteed. The library is popular amongst those thinking themselves intellectually superior to others; although in prison what you did outside may not count the same because everyone's been tagged as a stupid convict for getting caught. To brag about who you were outside is of limited interest to the majority. What has influence is the nature of your crime, with the information used to establish where you fall in the pecking order. Too low, and you're considered a target for those offering protection at a price, anything from a little kick about with your head to losing a limb or even your life. Depending on what you've got yourself into, there are no blueprints or survival kits to pull out and use in an emergency. Each individual has to work things out themselves, and the quicker they do, the easier their time inside will be.

Others separate along racial lines, a feeling of safety in numbers for some. It's also strange how further division sees religion playing its part. Black inmates too, of which there are many, split into two unique camps: those who listen to a particular musical style and those from specific postcode's, that identify exactly where you're from.

As the prisoners exit from the shadow of the building after breakfast, the sun blankets their skins with vitamin D. The yard has apparatus to build and test strength and agility. Some prisoners ignore the benches provided, using the equipment as a place to sit, making it obvious that not all groups are permitted the use of them.

Chan, Ox and Paul venture towards an unoccupied bench, only to find Dozer's men barring their path by sitting down first.

'There's another one,' claims Paul. They change direction towards the other bench.

'You know why they're doing it, don't you? Because of him,' says Ox. 'We agreed to keep ourselves quiet and avoid trouble in here.'

'Haven't you noticed?' says Chan. 'Everywhere you look in here you'll find the ingredients for trouble.'

'That's why I'll get you guys out,' says Paul.

'If you really have a plan for escaping from here, it had better be good,' says Ox. 'This is real, it's not *Prison Break*.'

'I know, and I won't be making promises I can't keep.' Paul sounds assured, but he still needs to ask them a key question.

'So, you're trying to tell us you can get us out?' asks Ox. 'Yet you seem powerless to get yourself out. Funny that, isn't it?'

'Not really, I have an answer to that.'

'Which is?'

'I need your promises first.'

'I was wondering when you'd get around to the sweetened part of whatever you're trying to sell,' says Ox.

'Let's see, would it involve protecting you?' says Chan.

'It does, but that's the only way I'll be able to ensure it happens.'

'Nice as you're trying to make it sound, you're either a dreamer or a time waster, or maybe both.' Ox stands up and starts towards a free bench press.

'You can see where he's coming from. One moment we're free, the next we're accused and branded murderers,' Chan says.

'You've killed someone?'

'I'm not sure why everyone just ignores the word "branded". We didn't do it.'

'I believe you,' Paul says.

'And what about you? Another injustice, no doubt?'

'No, they caught me red-handed.' Paul sighs. 'You know, I used to have this one recurring dream, a nightmare where I would wake up from it at the same point. I was dead and outside the pearly gates, although the gates looked like an ordinary door. That was odd, given my lifestyle as a burglar. I presumed that being dressed in white, with everything white around me, meant that's what it was. When I say white, the clothes didn't look new, just bleached white. There was a sign on the door: *'Back in eight and three-quarter hours'* it read. Well, it was just a wall, and when I looked up, it seemed to rise to infinity, and the gate, well it was only a door. Did I say that already?'

'Yes, you did,' says Chan.

'I must have been thinking about it, and then one day it happened. I'm a burglar, right, a damn good one, but I suppose there is only one measure of that, and maybe being here says I'm not that good. So, I thought the next time I'm in the dream again, I'll use my skills.'

'What was behind the door?' Chan asks.

'Nothing.'

'Hold up! What do you mean nothing?'

'Well, I picked the lock, the door was open. I eased it a little, with no idea what to expect. Through a gap, I could see it was pitch-black in there. I had progressed so far, and if I was dead I couldn't die again, right, so curiosity took me the rest of the way. The second I stepped through that door, this blinding light hit me! I couldn't see a thing. It was so bright it woke me up. I was sweating, and my pillow was soaked.'

'You must have discovered what was behind the door the next time?' Chan asked.

'No! On my very next break-in, they caught me. I never experienced that damn dream again either.' Paul lets out a sigh.

'Must have been one of those premonition-type dreams,' says Chan. 'You know, warning you about something. Maybe as long as you remained outside the door you were unlikely to be caught.'

'You might be right. I was never good at puzzles anyway.'

'You have a good imagination while you're asleep though.'

'Look, that was a dream. What I'm talking about is real. My brother is working with the government now, on ways of releasing prisoners into the community.'

'There's nothing new in that,' says Chan.

'Yeah, but get this: without tags or having to report to the police every couple of days.'

'So how will they monitor them?'

'That's where my brother comes in. He's one of the top hypnotists in England, maybe even the world.'

'Hypnosis?'

'Yeah, but obviously, it only works on those who can be hypnotised. And the best part is, he's told me how I can get out of here without being in a trance, like the others. So, what I've been trying to say is, I can get you guys out too.'

'You're certain about this?' asks Chan.

'I told you, I owe you. Do you want me to arrange it?'

'But you don't know for sure that your brother will go along with it, do you?'

'Don't worry. If I don't get you out, you can let Dozer crush the living life out of me.'

'Well, if you can pull this off, we're certainly in,' Chan says. Paul looks over at Ox.

'Don't worry about him; he'll be all right with anything that gets us out, even if it's just for a day.'

'Well, I'm going to need your full names,' Paul says.

'And that's all?'

'Yeah, for now. My brother is back here Wednesday.'

A bell rings, ending recreation time. The happily employed are escorted to work while everybody else is shipped back to their cells.

# CHAPTER 9

Today Sir Edward has arrived at his office an hour earlier than usual. Ongoing issues are causing him to lose sleep, and not wishing to waste this time, he hopes to clear the backlog of work already being generated by the new system. A note scribbled in his own version of shorthand near one corner of his ink blotter translates to 'Call Ian', and it's deliberately obscured just in case anybody should attempt to read any reminders he's written to himself.

There's also an important call to Dr Minn pending, he remembers, but, as always, Sir Edward puts family first and dials that number from memory.

'Hi, how are you?' he asks informally, showing he knows the person well.

'Will I be seeing you today, Edward, like you promised?'

'No, not today. In fact, it might not be possible for a while. I'm tied down with work.'

'But you promised me last week that you would this week—'

Sir Edward cuts in, wary of long arguments that always start "But you promised me".

'Yes, I realise what I promised. But I'm having to work extra hard here, clearing up other people's mess. Nothing is straightforward and I'm restricted by time.'

'You know I still miss you, don't you? And I was too reckless in the past, taking my mind off things that mattered to both of us, and still do, even now. But looking at things from the other side, I get it and don't blame you or her anymore.'

He listens, and for a short moment her voice commands his full attention. His eyes are closed, and a flickering light for another telephone line goes unnoticed until they're open again.

'Look, don't worry. She should be the last person to complain. It may take a little more time to win her over to the idea that we can all get along, but we can, just give it time. Kim, listen I must go now, I'll try to call you again tomorrow. You take care.'

He switches to the other line. 'Yes?'

'Sir Edward, there's a gentleman here from the Home Office.'

'Okay, Amy, please send him in.'

There's a short knock at the door, and Sir Edward calls for his visitor to enter. It opens quickly and the visitor strides in, moving straight to the front of Sir Edward's desk.

'Good morning, Sir Edward.'

'Good morning. It's Trevor, isn't it?'

'It is, sir, you have an excellent memory.'

'Thank you. What brings you to my office, and this early, Trevor?'

'May I?' he says, looking to the two empty chairs facing the desk.

'Please. I didn't offer, hoping it might just be a quick question.'

'I'm afraid not, sir,' Trevor says, planting himself down. 'We're getting reports of a fresh wave of migrant activity near the Eurotunnel complex, sir.'

'I hope the bloody French are on top of this,' he says, tutting. 'And what's been our response?'

'Well, the Home Secretary repeated yesterday that they're prepared to do whatever's needed, including cutting the power in the tunnel.'

'Yes, I heard his similar statement on the incident last week, which doesn't seem to have had any impact.'

'So, as long as the trains remain in the French half of the tunnel, we regard it diplomatically as being a French problem.'

'Frankly, that approach is highly simplistic and too damn dangerous. We can't be seen to be sitting on our hands and not reacting to these sorts of issues. Remember the public backlash to the Syrian migrant scandal?'

'Vaguely, Minister,' Trevor replies. His mobile rings. 'Would you mind, sir?'

'Please, go ahead.' Sir Edward leans back in his chair, thinking.

'Yes?' Trevor says into his phone. 'Right. Okay, okay. And definitely secured now? Yes, I understand. Keep me updated the minute you hear anything else,' he says, ending the call.

Sir Edward couldn't her the caller's voice but has a good idea what it's about.

'So, what is the latest?' says Sir Edward, bringing his chair back to its upright position.

'Well, it seems the confusion at Calais may have been a deliberate distraction.'

'What do you mean when you say a distraction?'

'It appears security cameras picked up several figures exiting the tunnel at Dover last night.'

'Is that the politician's several, meaning we don't have a damn clue how many?'

'Some did slip through our net, sir. But they arrested five and have already transferred them to our high-security police station in North London for questioning.'

'Five! Only five?'

'Yes sir.'

'That's all we need.' Sir Edward sounds disappointed.

'Well, we're counting on at least one of them revealing whatever is being planned. There's clear footage from reporters stationed near the tunnel of what we now suspect were decoys. A frequency distortion on equipment from the micro-scooters used to travel through the tunnel alerted them. However, they only began filming once they realised what was happening. So far, the intelligence gathered is rather sketchy – they seem well organised and we're having to play catch-up.'

'Okay, the minute anything happens you're to inform me, got that?'

'Yes, Sir Edward.' Trevor stands and heads for the door.

'Oh, and Trevor?'

He spins. 'Yes, Sir Edward.'

'Thank you.'

Trevor leaves the office, closing the door behind him.

Sir Edward pulls out his diary again, the black one. He flips through and selects a page. He opens the diary wide and flattens it on the desk to keep it open, then picks up the telephone to dial.

'Ian, it's Edward.'

'Edward who?'

'Edward. We met last week at the pub.'

'You mean Sir Edward Long?'

'Yes, Sir Edward Long. It's not a problem, is it?'

'On our first meeting, you opted not to give me your full title, didn't you? Well, that got me thinking that you must have a few secrets of your own.'

'My motives were nothing more than to appear casual and friendly, that's all.'

'Well, I've been thinking a lot about this arrangement.'

'And?'

'And, I'm worried about the effect on my career when my name gets associated with this scheme.'

'I don't think it could be any worse than what's associated with your name now.'

'So, is this what working with you is really like?'

'I'm sorry, that was rather a cheap shot. If you do as we discussed then I guarantee your involvement will not show up in any inquiries.'

'Anyway, just so you know, I've taken a few precautions of my own.'

'Dare I ask you to elaborate, Mr Gilby?'

'I guess I'm adding to my insurance too.'

'Let's hope, Ian, that you haven't done anything stupid. Failure to operate to my strict guidelines could have a catastrophic outcome, and I don't mean for me.'

The line is silent for a few seconds.

'It's a little recording of our first meeting at the pub, that's all. I was sure you were coming to blackmail me. That was before I found out who you are, and that you probably have more to lose than me.'

'Well, understand me when I say you're better off not having anything that someone can trace. My advice is to destroy it and stick to what's agreed. Is that simple enough?'

Ian's silence confirms compliance.

'Now, how did you get on at Downing?' Sir Edward changes the subject, making Ian refocus and return to the topic.

'The governor there is a suspicious man. The sort that could create trouble down the line.'

'You've learned that from a single visit?'

'You've seen my show. I take pride in being able to find someone's strength or weakness within seconds of meeting them. That's what I'm trained for and that's what I do best.'

'Well, you need to remember that your authority overrides anything the governor may fire at you. I may ask you to do one small but important thing that would underwrite what I'm working to achieve.'

'And that is?'

'Well, since you've already noticed how suspicious the governor is, I should impress on you that there's a need to convince him more than anyone. I was wondering if you could... say... hypnotise him?'

'Anything is possible. But I say again – going down this route you're plotting will take us towards being a hypnotic state.'

'One last thing, Ian. Perhaps when you're at Downing next, please try to see other prisoners, not just your brother.'

'How did you find out about him?' Ian's disquiet is clear. 'Did you bug me?' he asks.

'You want the simple answer, yes. In my defence though, it was purely for your safety.'

'And you're expecting me to trust that you'll honour our deal, when you're obviously still harvesting information behind my back. That's bullshit! And you know it.' Ian reacts with real venom in his voice.

Sir Edward moves to hold on to the little gains he has made.

'I had to give assurances you could be discreet, that's all.'

Ian remains reticent.

'Come now, Ian, you didn't believe I would be alone in this undertaking? What I can ensure is that this chapter of distrust is over. Please, this is my personal guarantee to you. There will be no further intrusion into any aspect of your life.'

Ian stays mute.

'Mr Gilby, are you still there?'

'Only just, but the sooner this is over, the better I'll feel.'

'I understand, and I have noted it.'

'Good.'

'I have another call coming through. Would you mind me putting you on hold for just a minute?'

'Go ahead.'

Sir Edward, puts Ian on hold, then dials another number from his black book.

'It's me. Stay on the line, but please remain totally silent.'

'I understand.'

Sir Edward presses a button linking all three lines.

'Mr Gilby, I'm back with you. Now, how soon will you be in a position to confirm whether or not the process is a workable option?'

'It depends on how many.' Ian answers.

'Initially, no more than say a dozen so we can conduct trials.'

'Then it's viable already, which I suspected from our first meeting. Just need the mechanics of a few minor details and we're there.'

'Excellent news. I can expect a positive briefing in the next few days then?'

'Yeah, things should be more or less set by then.'

'Good. We'll talk then. Thank you and goodbye, Mr Gilby.'

'Goodbye.'

There's a slight click as one receiver leaves the three-way loop.

'Well?' Sir Edward asks.

'Impressive, if it all works. And an even more lucrative future for both of us if it works well,' Dr Minn responds.

'I thought it would impress.'

'Sir Edward, I repeat, only if it works, and have you spotted any potential flaws in the idea so far?'

'One, at best two. But they are more, shall we say, problems of human nature, and I already know how I'll deal with them. I will let you know in a few days, and then after a trial, to ensure that the scheme delivers what we expect.'

'Will you please keep in mind the excellent testing facilities of my factory, should the scheme need testing under more exacting conditions?'

'Funny that you brought it up, Doctor Minn. I had planned to raise that same possibility in our next conversation, so I'm glad you recognise the desire for my proposal to be watertight. Once we've delivered, we're not certain of getting the genie back in its bottle. So, I think you're up to speed and we will talk again soon.'

'Sir Edward, if I may take a minute more of your time, please? I would welcome your knowledge on a personal and delicate matter.'

Having no idea what Dr Minn intends asking, Sir Edward is sure that no matter what it is, he's fully paid up on all favours.

'Go ahead, I'm listening,' Sir Edward says.

'I have a daughter, Mai Li. You are not in a position to know this, but she was most important in resolving your family problem. Back in 2005, when she was born, they only allowed Chinese couples one child. Since birth, taking care of her has been my duty. She is my entire family, Sir Edward, and I need to secure a British passport for her now her studies have finished, so she can remain here with me in England. Can you help?'

'Let me be honest, it's not as easy as it used to be pre-Brexit. Perhaps these days the best thing would be for her to find sponsored employment, and they can apply on her behalf. I would have thought, though, Doctor, that with all your millions, buying a passport would be no problem. But you didn't hear this from me.'

'It's considered unlucky for the Chinese to buy advantage. My daughter would feel cursed for life if she found out that was the case.'

'Well, I appreciate how you came through for my family, so let me suggest how we might kill two birds with one stone.'

'I don't want my daughter involved in any killings, Sir Edward.'

'No killings, just a figure of speech. I do have something in mind, though, that might just fit both our needs. Please have your daughter call me today and I'll arrange for her to be picked up early tomorrow morning.'

'Let me thank you on behalf of my daughter, and goodbye for now, Sir Edward.'

'Goodbye, Doctor Minn.' Sir Edward hangs up and sits back. His idea for pairing Dr Minn's daughter and Ian Gilby is his stroke of genius. In one move, he'll link the desire of Dr Minn to get his daughter a British passport with his own agenda to have actual eyes and ears monitoring Ian's activities.

# CHAPTER 10

W ith the automated court system now operational, the Pinpoint system is pressed back in service, to take control during what the government believes are the most vulnerable hours, between six in the evening and seven in the morning. The reduction in recorded cases suggests a slowing in street crime. The popular view amongst the governing party, and the one they preach at every opportunity, is that the present crime level more than justifies using Pinpoint, even though at the moment it only covers the extended congestion charge area. But the number of fatal accidents attributed to Pinpoint still shows a creeping upwards trend. Early studies have confirmed how close the fatalities are running to the agreed acceptable levels. If the next report doesn't show a marked improvement, then the natural and prudent course would be to ditch the scheme. The government doesn't want such unwelcome information made public in an election year, even when unofficial reports indicate that knife crime has been directly impacted.

Central London police headquarters: Squad room.

. . .

It's close to 5:30 pm and the shift supervisor gets up to deliver his briefing for the evening roll call.

'Listen up, everyone. That includes all you seated near the back. Now, as you can all see, we have a television crew with us this evening. They are making a documentary and, solely for the benefit of the lads, none of you will require more make-up.'

A raucous cheer goes up; the female officers don't react to the jibes of their male colleagues.

'Come on, everyone, settle down. All joking aside, this is a serious topic, and we should all be aiming to present the best side of policing. So, even if you're frustrated, let's keep those swear words to a minimum, folks, okay? Remember, the camera never lies and microphones pick up everything, ladies and gentlemen.' He looks down at his clipboard. 'Right, Chase, they will travel in your vehicle this evening. Please make certain they're kitted with vests; we don't need accidents. That's all, and remember you're not super heroes, so be careful out there.'

Chase stands up and wanders over to the film crew.

'Okay, I'm Sergeant Ryan Chase and this is my colleague, PC Sharon McCloud.'

'I'm Karen Brown. You may have seen me on television?'

'No, I don't watch television.'

'Okay, well,' Karen says, a little embarrassed. 'This is Shane, our cameraman, and Carlos, the sound engineer.'

The handshakes and 'pleased to meet you' palaver is over in seconds. The sergeant looks down at his wristwatch; he taps its face before looking back up at PC McCloud.

'I'll need this repaired again, it's still losing time.' He looks past the crew at the exit where the last attendees have just left. 'All right, please listen. We will head straight down to stores and from there it should only be around ten minutes before we're out of here. I'm not predicting any problems this evening, but please bear in mind we are a functioning unit and will respond professionally if called on. So, please follow me.'

The sergeant leads the film crew from the squad room, turning immediately left towards the reception. Using his security pass, he opens the unit doors leading to the reception and front desk.

Passing through, Chase notices two olive-skinned men seated opposite the desk looking nervous. A third smartly dressed man stands at the counter, engaged in an intense exchange with the desk sergeant. Steering the crew past the mayhem, a curious Chase asks the film crew to wait with PC McCloud by the stairwell while he checks something with the desk sergeant.

'Sergeant, may I have a brief word, please?' he interrupts.

'Can't you see I'm busy, Chase? Or should I be calling you Detective Inspector Chase?' He commits the last part of his statement to a whisper.

'Okay, keep it down, it's not official yet,' Chase replies.

'You're one lucky bastard, Chase. But, to be fair, you're hard-working too, I'll grant you that.'

'This won't take long. I'm interested in why someone has pulled them?'

'Why do you always seem more interested in the foreigners?' the desk sergeant says, still whispering.

'All right, forget I asked. I'm busy too.' Chase turns to leave.

'Okay, you see those two,' the desk sergeant says pointing. 'We picked them up last night wandering about inside Victoria Tower Gardens, Westminster, near the fence by the Houses of Parliament. No identification, and their interpreter here just keeps repeating "political asylum" but can't provide me with so much as a name. So, unless you speak their language, then your twenty seconds are up.'

Sergeant Chase rejoins the television crew, leading them down two flights of stairs, past the canteen, towards the rear of the building. He enters a security code to enter the stores area then selects three vests, handing them to the sound engineer, cameraman and reporter.

'I wonder if I could have a smaller size, please?' asks Karen, the reporter.

'Why?'

'Well, if you have had any experience of women, you would have noticed that I'm a size twelve.'

'Well, on this occasion my experience overrides your fashion sense.' Chase tightens the straps on either side of her vest. 'There,' he says when he's finished.

'Do we need these vests because we're likely to encounter the Pinpoint system in operation?' asks Carlos in his Spanish accent.

'These vests wouldn't shield you from Pinpoint. They're designed to combat knives, and with a lot of luck – and I mean a lot – maybe a bullet.'

PC McCloud knows about the sergeant's 'black-and-white' attitude to everything, so tries to soften the message.

'We're not expecting any trouble. Let me help you with that… it's on back to front.' She corrects the sound engineer's vest after turning it the right way around.

'Gracias.'

'Don't mention it. Okay, all ready? Let's roll, as they say.'

From the stores, it's a short distance to the station's back entrance. A gentle push on the door bars and they're outside the building. The police van is twenty-five metres away, parked against the boundary wall. PC McCloud opens the doors by remote before they approach it. She gets into the driver's seat and adjusts the rear-view mirror before starting the engine. Sergeant Chase opens the side door, allowing the crew to occupy the second and third tiers.

They spend another five minutes setting the camera and sound levels, and then they leave through the automatic rear exit, away into a chilly evening. With the early kick-off of England's European Championship qualifier, the timing should ensure the documentary goes smoothly. Karen uses the time to build a background story which will help present the facts later. She asks a question.

'Sergeant Chase, I'm aware that the bracelets form a crucial part of the Pinpoint system, but what's to stop an individual removing them? And how would the police detect if someone had removed it?'

Chase looks back over his shoulder before facing forward again.

'First, it uniquely identifies each bracelet as a pair. Just like your mobile phone, its position is tracked at all times. Now, unlike its predecessor – I'm speaking here about the traditional ankle bracelets – should someone gain an advantage in removing one of them, the remaining bracelet will deliver a serious shock. If, sadly, your health is suspect, then that in itself could be fatal.'

'Is that how they happened, the casualties we've all read about?' Karen asks, presenting her microphone over the seat towards the sergeant.

'No, they've all been from the main Pinpoint system and—' Something distracts Chase and he pivots and peers out his window.

'Stop!' he orders. PC McCloud brings the van to a halt. 'Back up to the alley between the shops, please.' He stares in the nearside wing mirror as the van reverses, the gears whining to produce a distinct tone.

Opening his passenger door, Chase steps out onto the pavement. There are ten minutes to curfew, and a small puppy sits just outside the shadow of the dimly lit alley. The dog has a length of blue sailing rope serving as its lead. Chase drifts towards the puppy, bends and scoops it up into his arms.

'Hey, little fella. What are you doing here alone?'

'He's mine,' says a voice from the darkness. A young man steps out from the shadows onto the well-lit pavement holding the other end of the rope.

This catches the documentary crew off-guard but they are quick to spot and recognise a great story. They leave the van to form a small media scrum behind Chase.

Sharon also leaves the van to stand with the film crew.

'Darrell, you know they've banned you from central London; what are you doing here? It's less than five minutes to curfew.'

The cameraman films a close-up of the bracelet visible on the young man's wrist, its LED light pulsating.

'Does he know him?' Karen whispers to Sharon.

'Darrell is a familiar acquaintance from the council estate behind his house,' she answers.

'I'm fed up of being pushed around,' Darrell says, reclaiming his puppy from Chase's arms.

'Look, I'm trying to do you a favour here, Darrell, so don't be silly.' Chase checks his watch again. 'You have a few minutes. I suggest you go straight down to the underground station around the corner and get off home now. And consider yourself lucky that the scheme extension doesn't come into effect in our area for another two weeks.'

Darrell places the pup on the pavement and ambles off. The pup keeps resisting and glancing back. It stops again to sniff at anything interesting but Darrell tugs the rope each time to encourage it to keep walking. They watch until he's about thirty metres away before filing back into the van. Sharon starts the engine while Chase gets in last after closing the side passenger door.

Suddenly, two red beams flash with lightning intensity, converging at the exact spot where Darrell is walking. He slumps to the pavement like a discarded garment. The rope tightens around the pup's neck, its yelps amplified by the empty street. It tugs, desperate to breathe and free itself.

Sharon gets straight on the radio.

'Mobile unit twenty-three, requesting an ambulance at quadrant five WC 1, officers in attendance.'

'Roger that, unit twenty-three,' confirms the voice over the radio.

Chase leaps from the van and races towards Darrell. Sharon drives the van closer as the passenger door slaps shut.

'Are you getting this? Is the camera still recording?' says Karen, excited by the action.

The van moves forward, screeching to a stop by the kerb where Chase is kneeling beside Darrell's body. He shakes his head, placing one hand over a gaping wound in the side of Darrell's abdomen. His action does nothing to hinder the flow of blood, and it diverts through his fingers, pooling on the pavement. Darrell tries to raise himself.

'Keep still, Darrell,' Chase urges. He drags the rope free with his other hand.

'I should have listened to you, shouldn't I? You're the only one that's ever looked out for me.' Darrell coughs then winces at the pain.

'Let's have that conversation another time. Save your energy, try not to talk.' Chase looks up at Sharon. 'Find me something to cover this.'

'Like what?'

'I don't have time to bloody think for you! Anything!'

'Will this help?' says Karen, stepping closer. She reaches into her handbag, pulling out a sanitary towel She rips off the plastic wrapping and hands the towel to him.

Without thinking, Chase takes his hand from the wound and swaps it for the pad. He grips it tightly, applying more pressure. He looks up at the reporter.

'Thanks,' he says.

'If I don't make it…' Darrell swallows. 'Promise me you'll look after my dog? His name is Clive.' Darrell forces the words through his pain. 'This pavement is so cold.'

'He's going into shock,' Chase says.

The rise and fall of Darrell's chest is becoming less obvious and his head lists to the right. Chase checks Darrell's neck for a pulse but can't detect one.

'Where is that damn ambulance?' he says, raising his voice.

'I'm on it.' Sharon, desperate to be of use, moves back to the van to radio again.

'Forget it,' says Chase. 'He's gone.' The faint sound of a siren breaks through the sound of his breathing.

'That's so sad,' says Karen. 'He looks ever so young.'

'There are many Darrells out there,' says Chase. 'What future are we building for them?'

Sharon gets an ETA response on the radio.

'Two minutes, copy.'

'Mobile unit twenty-three Scratch that last request. Better off sending a hearse.' She tosses the radio onto the van's dashboard.

The cameraman stops filming and the sound engineer lowers his microphone.

A paramedic team soon arrives but it can only confirm the worst; there's nothing more they can do.

The police's part in the victim's life will end once they've filed their report back at the station. Chase picks up the puppy and they return to the van. He strokes it while it sits relaxed in his lap. Under the cover of the flashing blue ambulance lights they leave, heading back towards the station.

'Sergeant, listen, we've decided not to use any of the footage,' Karen says from the rear seat.

'That's your decision. It could serve as a deterrent. Or the excuse for a small minority to create further trouble.'

'Are you going to take care of his dog like he asked?'

'No, if someone doesn't take it, then it gets put down. Unless you want it,' he says, his tone serious.

'Well, I don't know if I have the room…'

'I'll take him,' says the cameraman, Shane.

'Really?'

'Yeah, sure. My nephew's birthday is coming up in a few days and it would really piss off his parents.'

'Thanks,' says Chase, 'but that solution falls short of what Darrell would have wanted me to do. I'll just hang onto him for a few days and see what else turns up.'

'I didn't mean it would come to any harm,' Shane is quick to add.

'No worries. It was just me trying to find a quick solution.' The puppy makes a small sound as Chase strokes it.

'I think he likes you, Sarge,' says Sharon, turning to look at them.

'Just keep your eyes on the road. The last thing we need is another damn accident tonight.'

'Yes, Sarge.'

# CHAPTER 11

The sound of the brass knocker falling against the recently varnished front door echoes through the quiet evening air. It triggers barking from the neighbour's dogs in response as if someone is at their door. The detached four-bedroom house is distinct in design from any other in this well-to-do tree-lined avenue and while the caller waits for someone to answer, there's just enough time to straighten his tie and prepare one of two responses. Which one will he use? It will depend on who answers the door.

'Who is it, please?' a middle-aged female voice calls out, putting on the outside porch lights. She engages the security chain before peering round the narrow gap left between the frame and the door.

'Good evening, Christine,' Sir Edward says.

'Oh, it's you. What do you want? And it's Mrs Barton to you.'

'I'm sorry, Mrs Barton. I was wondering if Kim was still awake.'

'You have a nerve coming here. Don't you know this house doesn't vote for you anymore?'

'Well…'

'Who's at the door, Mother?' Kim shouts from within the house.

'No one of any importance, dear.'

'Mrs Barton, please. This visit is at Kim's request, although you can blame me for the late timing.'

'You're to blame for much more than that.' She starts to reply before the door closes suddenly then opens wide after Mrs Barton appears to have been eased from it and the chain removed.

'Edward, you should have warned me you were on your way.' Kim appears, surprised but happy, quickly adjusting her hair in the hallway mirror.

'Yes, I should have. I've been a little preoccupied of late, so… spur of the moment and all that.'

'Ah, where are my manners? Come in,' Kim steps to one side.

'Are you sure that your mother will be okay with that?'

'It's Mrs Barton to you,' she insists from behind her daughter.

'Mother, don't you think it's late? Aren't you going to bed?'

'Don't let him spin you more lies and worm his way back into your affections.'

'Okay, give me a second.' Kim takes her coat, which hangs in the hall, and picks up her house keys from the glass console table. 'Mother, I'm going out for a while.' She pulls the front door shut and walks down the steps. Sir Edward follows close behind.

Being the gentleman, he helps with her coat before they start a slow walk down the road, keeping about half a metre's distance between them but sharing frequent glances. If you weren't aware that their eleven-year marriage had ended, you could forgive any observer for thinking they were still a couple.

'I can't stay long,' Sir Edward says.

'You never used to bother giving me excuses for why you weren't home on time. What's changed?'

'Me, I've changed. I'm trying to make this one work.'

'Are you suggesting you never wanted our marriage that lasted eleven years, to work?'

'That's not what I meant and you know it. No, I'm just trying hard not to make the same mistakes as before, that's all.'

'By "mistakes", you mean getting caught?'

'Kim, you know you weren't exactly innocent in our break-up. And I only agreed to see you on the understanding that we're clear about the past. I was never sure if it was me or the lifestyle you loved more.'

'Yes, I take full responsibility for my part. I was immature and took what we had for granted. But I've changed too, and I wanted you to hear it from me in person.'

'Kim, please don't.' Edward stops walking while Kim continues a few extra steps before turning to face him.

'What do you mean "don't", Edward?'

'Look, every time we meet our conversations always end the same way, with you pleading for us to get back together. Think what turbulence that would cause, especially in this election year.'

'Forget about electioneering for a moment, Edward.' Kim looks up at him, staring into his eyes. 'We've done a lot more than just have conversations recently.'

'And I said that I was very sorry for that moment of weakness, which was months ago anyway.'

'I wasn't sorry, and do you know why? Because for that one moment, I felt like I did the first time we kissed.'

'Is this why you wanted to see me, just to say that?'

'No, it's not the only thing.'

'Then please get to the point, Kim. I'm already late getting home.'

'This really is a new you, isn't it? Hurrying home to the new wife.' Kim looks towards the ground.

'Whatever it is, you know you've always been able to talk with me about anything.' Edward moves to reassure her, placing both hands on her shoulders and looking at her. She sighs.

'In around seven months' time, you will increase your constituency and family by one. There!' She looks up for a reaction.

'Are you saying you're pregnant?' His voice rises ever so slightly with shock.

'Shush! Not so loud. But yes, I am.' Kim smiles, waiting for congratulation or just acceptance.

'You can't keep it,' Edward tells her, gripping her shoulders tighter.

'Why not?' She jerks herself free from his grip.

'Because you were the one who didn't want children. Is this to spite me because I'm with someone else now?'

'No. It's because I'm still in love with you, that's why.'

'Love? Don't label it as love. Christ! Entrapment sounds a far better word, Kim. What do you expect to gain out of this?'

'You. I want you back, Edward.' Kim's straight in with her reply, no hint or hesitation.

'You'd best go inside. It's getting cold, and look, it's started raining. I must go anyway.'

Edward avoids further eye contact. He walks silently towards the house with her. The pavement is speckled with rain and the dry spots are disappearing fast. Standing by the gate, he waits, hands in his pockets, for her to climb the few steps to her front door. The speckles morph into heavier droplets as the rain builds towards a full shower. Kim inserts her key then looks around, hoping to find Edward behind her, but he remains by the gate.

'Goodnight, Kim,' he says, turning towards his official car parked across the road.

'Goodnight,' she murmurs. She raises a hand to wave, but he has gone.

The rain has turned heavy. The wind is driving it against the car windows. His ex-wife's revelation has moved to the top of Sir Edward's pile of worries. 'Why now?' he asks himself, desperate for any answers. With the traffic moving slowly, there's more time to get his head around it. Sir Edward feels angry at being told eight weeks into the pregnancy. He likens it to hearing a starter's pistol in an 800-metre race, but only after other competitors have already completed their first lap. He fears for the success or otherwise of his only option, to persuade Kim to abort the pregnancy. It would save his career and perhaps his marriage.

But it's late and not worth the stress of thinking about it. The car glides to a stop by his gate. Sam, his chauffeur, walks around the car to open the passenger door. He opens a very large umbrella extending it over the door to shield the minister from the rain.

'It's okay, Sam, it's not too heavy now. I'll see you in the morning. Goodnight.'

Sir Edward steals away from the car in a quick shuffle towards his house. Unusually, the main bedroom lights are still on, a sign that his wife is also still awake. Opening his front door, Sir Edward wipes his wet feet on the coarse rug. He drops his keys into the oriental bowl that sits on the console table and his briefcase on the floor beside it. Edward removes his coat and drapes it over the banister. He's expecting a reaction for being so late and looks up the stairs in anticipation. Taking a deep breath, he begins his ascent.

'Ah, you're finally home,' Elizabeth says as he enters the bedroom. She moves a bookmark to the current page of the book, *Finding Arun,* that she's reading, before closing it and putting it on the bedside table to her left.

'The weather has turned bad tonight, don't you think?' he says, moving towards his side of the bed. He sits with his back to her.

'It's not the weather, dear. Your office said that you left hours ago.' She stares, but he doesn't turn to face her.

'Hours ago, that's probably right.' He removes a sock.

'Then where were you? I've been waiting. I have something important to tell you.'

'If it's to do with your mother it can wait until the morning, can't it?' He removes the other sock.

'It's not. And mother is fine by the way, thanks for asking.'

'Oh, I'm sorry, Elizabeth, I didn't mean it that way. Today was her hospital appointment, wasn't it? I remember you saying something now.' He tries to get back over a crossed line and not be on the wrong side of yet another mother-in-law.

'It was, yes, and she's fine. She'll probably outlive both of us.'

'I know you didn't wait up just to tell me that.'

'You're right, I didn't.'

Edward finally turns to face Elizabeth but she says nothing.

'Are you sick?' He leans over the bed and looks into her face.

'No, not sick. I thought maybe it was my biometric implant causing me to feel nausea, especially mornings.'

'Then what is it then?' He's tired and just wants to know.

'Pregnant! I'm pregnant Edward.'

'Pregnant?' He repeats turning away and sitting up, clearly startled, the lines on his forehead and eyes showing the extra brain activity.

'Yes, pregnant. The hospital appointment was really for me about the implant and mother only came with me for support. That's when they told me.'

She tries to glimpse the right side of his face, which is nearest to her, pass his broad shoulder.

'Aren't you going to say something?'

'Like what?' he says without thinking.

'Well, like how happy you are would be a start.'

'Let me, er, just get past the shock phase first. Give me a second. I need the bathroom. I've been holding it in and I don't want the excitement to show as me wetting myself.'

Edward goes into the en suite, closing the door. Placing both hands on the sink, he looks up to confront the image staring back at him in the mirror.

'What have you done? What have you bloody done that's different in the last couple of months?' He spends several minutes thinking over scenarios in his head, trying to work out what he needs to do next.

'Are you all right in there, dear?' Elizabeth calls out.

'Yes, I'm fine. Out in a second.' He flushes the toilet and takes his time brushing his teeth. Then he opens the door, pulling the cord to turn off the light.

He goes to her side of the bed and sits on the edge, leans in and gently kisses her lips.

'I'm thrilled. I'll admit the shock felt like being hit by two buses.' It's Edward's cryptic way of saying that after waiting a long time, two pregnancies have arrived together.

'And this can be another thing that Kim never did for you,' she whispers.

Edward stands immediately and walks to his side of the bed.

'What's wrong?' she says.

'Did you have to bring Kim into it?' He climbs into bed. 'I thought we agreed not to mention her at all?'

'Yes, but—'

'No buts, Elizabeth, she nearly ruined my career.' He looks away, hiding the guilt in his eyes.

'I'm sorry, dear. It must be the hormones. I promise I'll try harder not to mention her again, promise.'

She turns her bedside lamp off and slides over to his side of the bed. Resting her arm across his chest, she cups his face with her soft fingers and drifts contentedly off to sleep.

# CHAPTER 12

I n the dew of the early morning countryside, Downing Prison sits centre frame in a serene picture. Against the backdrop of the lightening sky, daybreak brings fresh hope and perhaps freedom for at least a selected few.

Ox is already awake, and has been for some time. He's having unsettled nights of late, ever since learning about Paul's child. He also has a child, and a girl too, she'll be nearing her second birthday soon, which is why he feels so guilty after promising he'd always be there. When the alarm sounds, he ignores it for a moment more of deep thought. His anxiety is perhaps his own fault, for telling his former girlfriend never to bring their daughter to the prison. In his opinion, allowing it would only fuel the views of those still preaching that people of colour are more genetically predisposed to criminal activities. He'd had her whole life mapped out, from the first moment he held their little miracle in his arms. There were tears; both parents overwhelmed that they had created life, beating the odds given by doctors. It took Ox two whole days to stop crying, promising himself that he would provide all things he deemed missing from his own life.

Every night, while asleep, he somehow distances his mind from the traumas of real life, only to be reminded by the same flaky dull grey walls each morning when his eyes finally open. The reason he and Chan are in prison still evades him. Once he's awake, his thought process consumes every spare minute. He has raked over every aspect of that evening, but no matter how he recalls the details, there has to have been a gross injustice. Did the colour of his skin make it easier for officials to stop seeking the truth? In a biased system, it might take years to become eligible for parole. He remembers the immigration experiences that his grandfather used to talk about when he was a boy. It's as if being black hasn't moved on since then. There's always been the same promise of equality but never a clear unrestricted path to it.

'Are you getting up for breakfast?' Chan pokes Ox's shoulder. They've been friends since primary school. The adopted 'Chinese' boy with two white parents and his then underweight black friend who stuck together. They were often the last two selected during playground elimination processes, as well as being picked on for choosing to adhere to parental advice to always try to better yourselves and not to waste free education, no matter your start in life.

'I'm up.' Ox swings his legs to the floor and stands. He stretches and groans while rotating his head and touching each shoulder lightly, one after the other. He pulls each arm at the elbow, stretching out his shoulder sockets, then performs a double rotation of his arms to finish.

'Well, you'd better get ready quick or we'll miss the good stuff.'

'I've had better food in my dreams,' he says, rubbing his stomach.

'For what it's worth, it keeps you alive,' says Chan.

'Come on man, you can't call this living?' Ox slips on a T-shirt.

'I know, I'm just stating the obvious.'

'Well, the less you mention it, the better I'll cope.'

'We will get out of here one day, so live up to your name – Ox – be strong.'

'Actually, Ox stands for Oxford, the seat of learning, not strength.'

'Then let's just tackle the bad food first, then who knows?' Chan concludes.

Outside their cell, they're confronted by an officer.

'Mr Yip and Mr Earlington,' he says, reading their names from a clipboard held exaggeratedly at eye level two feet from his face. 'Find your way over to the workshop in block F as soon as you've finished breakfast.' Then stares at them.

'Everyone says it can take up to eighteen months to get your name on the workshop list, so how come?' Ox enquires.

'Just following orders, lads, and yours are to get along to the canteen now or you'll turn up starving.'

The pair move off towards the canteen, still puzzled. They glance back a few times to see the officer still smirking.

As usual since his incident, Paul waits for them near the canteen entrance. As they approach, he smiles, causing Vincent to acknowledge their presence and move away sharply.

'Morning, guys, all good?' Paul says, holding up both thumbs.

'What's good about it?' says Ox. 'Same shit, different day.' He carries on straight into the canteen.

'What did I say wrong this time?' Paul asks, shrugging and throwing his arms out.

'Nothing, it's not you,' says Chan. 'He has other things on his mind. Don't let it worry you.' He places a hand on Paul's shoulder and pats it.

Paul's cellmate, Vincent, joins the table with Dozer, who despite his disability can still shovel large quantities of food into his face. He looks at Vincent and mumbles between chews.

'Why is he so happy?' says Dozer, nodding in Paul's direction.

'I don't know,' answers Vincent. 'He's been like it ever since some meeting he had on Monday.'

'With who?'

'No idea. Could have been anybody, maybe his solicitor?' He takes another mouthful as Dozer clears food stuck in his teeth.

'You don't know? Then what am I paying you for?'

'You don't pay me,' answers Vincent.

'You're on my discount scheme, which means I don't take cigarettes from you.'

'But I don't even smoke.'

'Is there somebody in here stopping you from smoking?' Dozer gets serious.

'No, but—'

'Then that's your problem. My charges for your protection are more than reasonable – you not having any local currency, now that is dangerous.'

'I don't smoke because I have asthma,' Vincent pleads.

'Your problem not mine; don't argue.'

'Okay, look, I'll try my hardest to find out who it was.' Giving in to Dozer's logic makes Vincent realise that maybe he's sided with the wrong set. There's little to no chance after his last stunt of forming even a fake friendship with Paul.

'You'd better. Nothing goes down in here without Fat Fingers' approval. You got it?'

'Yeah.' Vincent stands up with his tray, moving away from the table, giving others the impression they're no longer friends.

'Kevin Atkinson!' a warden shouts. 'Stand up.' Dozer is slow in getting to his feet. Everyone looks, checking to see what sort of trouble he's in. The warden walks over to him so as to discuss medical matters personally.

'Kevin, I have a date to sort out that arm of yours.'

'When?' asks Dozer.

'Friday the seventh, nine am.'

'Good. Wait! It's not this week, that's next week?'

'That's right, Kevin. Look, I shouldn't have to mention it but we do have to get specialist equipment in to cope with your challenges.'

'What challenges?'

'Just forget that, the earliest date we have for delivery is next Wednesday so from next Thursday evening at seven until after the op, you must have nothing to eat. You're allowed tea and water, nothing solid. Do you understand, Kevin?'

'Yeah, I heard you but I'm going to put in a complaint to the Governor.'

'You've also requested to be asleep for the operation, is that correct?' the warden asks, completely ignoring Kevin's rant.

'Yeah,' Dozer replies, his answer being noted.

'Right then, someone will come and fetch you early next Friday. Any other questions?' the officer asks.

'How soon after can I eat?'

'I think you'll make lunch next Friday, Kevin, no problem.'

'Sounds wicked, thanks.'

'No thanks needed. Our job is to get you back to your normal self as quick as possible.' The warden leaves Dozer to sit down and continue expanding his waistline.

On Chan and Ox's table, Paul whispers, glancing around before completing each sentence.

'Today, guys, I'll be getting you the good news I promised.'

'News about what?' says Ox. Paul looks at Chan.

'You didn't tell him about the additional information I gave you?'

'There was nothing concrete in what you said to tell, per se,' says Chan.

'You didn't mention it because you don't believe me?'

'Look, he's already finding it hard in here, missing his family, his little girl.'

'I'm right here, you know,' says Ox. 'And it's not your business to be discussing my business with him or anybody else.'

'Look, I was only trying to inform him you have other things on your mind, that's all,' says Chan.

'Okay, I get it. You need something tangible.' Paul looks around once again. 'My brother will be here tomorrow, Thursday, and you'll have all the proof you need.'

The canteen is clearing fast. The trio clear away their trays before leaving the canteen together.

'Where are you guys heading?' Paul asks.

'Prison workshop, where else?' says Chan. 'If you take out the kitchen and the library, that's the only other place to earn money, keep sane and beat boredom in here.'

'Your first time going to the workshop, isn't it?' Paul continues before they can answer. 'So, let me clue you up on a few things. Besides metal scanners, they'll weigh you going in and out.'

'Why?'

'You've got to appreciate that there is always someone in here up to no good; it's in their nature. So, if they can lose a few kilos while in there, they can then smuggle out materials that turn into weapons.'

'I would never have thought of that,' says Ox.

'Innocent people wouldn't. But if it's possible, someone in here will know how. Anyway, you better get going – late twice and you can kiss that privilege goodbye.'

They ignore Paul's warning and set their own pace to the workshop.

'You've only just made it,' says the officer at the entrance to the workshop.

'Sorry, it's our first day.'

'First day! That's no excuse; you're both on report.'

'How is that fair?' argues Ox.

'Do you want to try for the double on your first day, lad, and lose this opportunity to be out your cell, before you've even started?'

'No, sorry,' says Chan. 'We needed the washroom after breakfast. There was a queue and that's why we're late, sorry.'

'I'll tell you what, as it is your first day, I'll give you both a break. But you'll owe me, right?'

'For?' Ox says, before being nudged in his side by Chan.

'For which, we would be grateful, to you, for allowing us to start afresh.'

'You two will be my eyes and ears. Let me know anything suspicious or odd that you come across.'

'Anything?' Ox asks. The officer leans down from his six-foot-four frame to whisper.

'Anything. You tell me and I'll be the judge of how important or not it is.' Back at full height, he moves to one side, inviting them to step forward.

'You first.' He points to Ox with his pen.

Ox steps up onto a metal plate. It's about a metre square and bordered on two sides by thick metal columns. The officer notes down the digital reading from the display. An alarm sounds.

'Don't move. You have twenty seconds to identify any metal object we don't know about,' says the officer.

'Nothing,' says Ox. 'I have nothing... just this.' He points to the tiny gold stud in his left ear. The officer silences the alarm before using a handheld detector to verify Ox has nothing else on him. Ox steps off the plate and is made to remove the offending item. It's placed in a clear plastic bag and sealed.

'You can pick it up when you leave, but we prohibit the wearing of any metal while entering or leaving this workshop. Have you got that?'

Ox nods. Chan has witnessed the process and needs little prompting when checked in the same manner.

'This isn't any worse than airport security,' Chan says, attempting to lighten the atmosphere.

'He's lucky; the integrated Tasers could have fried him. Keep in mind you only get twenty seconds.' The officer beckons another inmate standing close to approach. 'He will be showing you around and telling you all the things not to do. He will also be assessing your suitability to work in this workshop so make sure you pay full attention. That way you'll remain safe in here, and I mean the prison, not just this workshop.'

'Hi,' says the inmate. 'I'm Kam, but you can call me Bob.' He leads Ox and Chan away from the workshop entry point.

'I suppose he told you you've got to be his eyes and ears?' Bob says.

'Yeah, how did you guess?' Chan asks.

'That's his little party trick. He tells everyone, and I mean everyone, sometimes forgetting he's told them several times already.'

They turn into an enclosed area and after twenty metres Bob halts.

'Okay, we stop here.' He reaches up over some pipes and extracts a mobile phone. Chan and Ox take a step back, looking around. They're in an unfamiliar environment and have a sudden and deep feeling that maybe they're being set up again.

'Wait! What kind of trouble are you trying to get us into here?' Ox challenges.

'We're not stupid you know,' adds Chan.

'Don't worry, it's safe here.' Bob, unfazed, dials a number on the mobile. 'He only wants to talk to you.' He holds the mobile out to them. 'Either of you, it doesn't matter which one.'

'Who knows we're even here?' whispers Chan.

'My boss. He arranged all of this to bring you here,' explains Bob.

Frustrated, Ox snatches the mobile from Bob's hand.

'Who is this?' he asks, irate.

'From that aggressive tone, you must be the one they call the Ox?'

'I said who is this?' Ox is getting even more irritated, more so at not being able to raise his voice.

'For this communication, Mr Ox, just call me Fat Fingers.'

'And what is it you want from us?'

'I like that about you, straight to the point. So, let me also get straight to the point. How would both of you like a job in here? You guys know how to handle yourselves. I've seen your references, and unlike Dozer... even though he claims to be grammar school educated, well, he's got more issues than he has uses, and one of them is not using his brain.'

'Look, we shouldn't even be in prison. There's nothing of interest here for us and nothing we're interested in. That's it.'

'But you're both of interest, seeing as none of my sources can tell me what you are up to in my prison.'

'Let me assure you we're not up to anything. We're not into anything except keeping to ourselves.'

'Oh! I see. Like Gerald Fitzpatrick and Patrick Fitzgerald?'

'No, no, no, I meant that we're keeping ourselves to ourselves, that's all.'

'Okay then, let me see if I got this right. You're just two faggots that don't wish to share. I get it.'

'No, you don't get it. Getting out of here and finding out who framed us are our only priorities.'

'Well, as long as you don't cross the lines in here, this conversation never took place. Put Kam back on.'

'He wants to speak with you,' Ox says, passing the mobile back.

'Yes, boss?' says Bob.

'Don't believe a word of shit from those two. You keep digging for me and we'll see what turns up.'

Bob replaces the mobile in its hiding place and leads them back to the workshop entrance. As they approach, the officer questions them.

'You can't have finished the full assessment so quick?'

'I'm afraid they're not ready yet to accept the conditions for working here. Maybe after they've been here a while, they can try again,' Bob suggests.

'Disappointed you two haven't taken this opportunity that others can wait months for.' He sighs. 'Okay, in that case, nothing more to keep you here this morning. So, get yourselves back over to the main block and if you hurry there's still five minutes of the breakfast recreational exercise time left. Don't forget this.' Ox is handed the clear plastic bag containing his tiny stud earing.

# CHAPTER 13

Elsewhere, in a leafy part of North London, a black limousine glides along a residential thoroughfare. It navigates each sleeping policeman and stops outside a private three-storey block of flats. The steady exhaust vapours confirm the engine is still running and that it's only a brief stop. After two minutes, the imposing figure of Ian Gilby appears in his dark overcoat and walks towards the limousine. Opening the nearside passenger door, he's confused and hesitates about getting in.

'Oh, I'm sorry. I assumed this was my car.'

'If you are Mr Gilby, then it's the right car,' a sweet voice answers.

'And you are?' he asks, sliding into the seat next to a well-dressed young Asian woman.

'My name is Mai Li and I'm supposed to be working with you.' She hands Ian two envelopes bearing official government seals. He pulls the door shut, attaches his seatbelt, and the car drives away. Raising one envelope to eye level he examines the seal, then looks across at the other passenger.

'May I?'

'Why are you asking me? It's your name printed on it.'

Ian opens the envelope bearing his name and glances over the contents. When he's finished, he puts both envelopes into his pocket and settles in for the journey to Downing Prison. After five silent minutes of counting lamp posts, Ian realises there is no chance that Mai Li might crack and speak first.

'Where are you from?' he asks, breaking the silence.

'From Hong Kong. Usually I answer "from my mother", but I've not done so for three years.' She half smiles. 'I would have thought it was easy to guess. Most people get at least the region right the first time.'

'I'm of the opinion that if I want to know something, it's just as easy to ask as it is to guess. So, then, which government agency are you working for?'

'None. Until three weeks ago I was an undergraduate.'

'What happened?' Ian asks.

'I graduated. What else did you think would happen?'

'A degree, okay, in what, if you don't mind me asking?'

'Computer science and human resources.'

'You'd be much too clever, then, to warm up for me.'

'Don't be getting any funny ideas,' she replies. 'My understanding is, I'm here for work experience, not fun.'

'Okay, I think I'll quit there while I'm ahead,' Ian says.

The rest of the journey takes place in silence. The driver listens to a news radio station with the volume higher than usual. Mai Li looks over at Ian occasionally but doesn't say a word.

The prison structure, even at some distance, draws eye focus away from the landscape and becomes even more prominent as the limousine nears the main gate. Everything bad that the prison represents is on the other side of the huge perimeter wall. The car stops short of the three retractable bollards protecting the gates. Each bollard is topped with lights capable of showing either red or green. On approach, the red lights are continuous, displaying a stop sign. The driver lowers his window and stares out into the eye-level security camera. A 3-D biometric green light scans the contours of his face. The lights on the bollards blink red, turning to green as they're lowered into the ground. Once flushed, the huge doors open inwards allowing the car to move forward and into the belly of the prison. A second set of bollards halts progress until the outer doors are closed and the first set raised. The vehicle is then photographed from all angles by high-definition cameras. They sweep under and around the car, looking for evidence of any illegal attachments. This last stage of entry is quick and brings them to the heart of the prison.

They're soon met by prison officials and escorted to the governor's office.

'Ah, Mr Gilby, so nice to welcome you back again so soon,' the governor says, reaching out his hand.

'Governor,' says Ian, accepting and shaking it. 'I'm not sure I share the same sentiments, not about you I hasten to add, I mean the place.'

'Well, at least you're free to leave at any point. But for staff, and the prisoners, we all serve a sentence of some sort, you know?'

'When you put it like that, Governor, I can only concede to your view.' Ian stands to one side to reveal the small, demure figure of Mai Li. She moves forward into the light. 'This is Ms Minn. She will be assisting me.'

The governor looks over Mai Li from top to toe.

'We have had no paperwork warning us of any additional personnel,' he says.

'Oh, sorry, I believe this is for you,' Ian says, handing the second envelope to Governor Riley, who turns away to read the enclosed document.

'Everything in order, Governor?' Ian asks.

'Yes, yes, it's all here,' Governor Riley says, spinning back to face them. 'You remember Officer Newport, don't you?'

Ian turns to face Officer Newport, standing to one side.

'Yes,' Ian says, nodding.

'Now, I didn't quite get what you were telling me last time about your business with these prisoners?' the Governor adds.

'I'm sorry, Governor, I can't seem to recall any conversations about prisoners, and I'm bound, as you are, by the Official Secrets Act.'

'I must be mixing you up with someone else then, forgive me. Officer Newport will escort you as before. Maybe, if I'm still here, I'll catch up with you before you leave.'

'This way, please,' Officer Newport says, holding the door open.

'Governor, I wonder if I may have a private word with you now, in case we aren't able to meet later?'

'Mr Newport, can you and Ms Minn wait outside please?' Riley orders.

'Now, what can I do for you, Mr Gilby?' the governor says once Newport and Mai Li have left the office.

'Governor, you're probably aware of why I'm here?'

'Well, I have my sources at the ministry,' he says, bluffing.

'Then I need not spell it out.'

'But I'd still like to hear it from you, on or off the record, so to speak.'

'Well, I didn't want to say anything in front of Officer Newport, but there are big changes coming to Downing, sir. If you know what I mean?'

'Say no more, Mr Gilby. I knew it would only be a matter of time before they recognised the thirty years of service I've put in.' He taps the side of his nose.

'Please call me Ian.' He pauses for a moment. 'That badge you're wearing, Governor, may I see it?' Ian points to the governor's blazer. Governor Riley obliges by removing the metal badge, handing it to him.

'Are you from a military family, Ian?' enquires the governor.

'I remember my uncle having one like it. What does this bit represent?' He points to some fine markings on the badge.

Governor Riley leans forward across his desk.

'Let me see. If I'm honest, I don't think I've ever looked at it in any detail.'

Ian's engaging conversation with the governor is for the sole purpose of using his skills to hypnotise him. He implants the trigger word 'vitamins' to use for easy hypnosis later.

'There you are, Governor. And thanks for the guidance.' Ian hands back the badge after bringing him out of the trance. The governor is a little unsure what advice he may have given but follows Ian to the door.

As Ian leaves, the governor stealthily signals to Officer Newport, who understands that his mission is still to keep a close eye on Mr Gilby.

After the mandatory vest fittings, Ian and Mai Li are led back to the interview room, where Ian sets up again with his writing pad and a list of prisoners. Mai Li sits quietly at the other desk, awaiting instructions. Officer Newport seems to have found something of interest on his mobile.

Ian's brief is the approval of at least twelve inmates for the trials. He's mindful that on this visit he must interview more prisoners. Despite the confidence he has in his abilities, he's also conscious of his actions and the effects they could have on society. Ian switches on the desktop computer then turns to Officer Newport.

'Is the password as before, Mr Newport?'

'Yes, it is. Do you recall it?'

'I do, thanks. Right, I think we're about ready now. If you would kindly fetch Mr Paul Gilby and then we can get started.'

'That's the same prisoner you saw last time,' notes Newport.

'Yes, you're correct. But I need to clarify a few things from last time. Once that's done I can interview the others on my list.'

'Well, depending on his whereabouts, it could take up to ten minutes to locate him.'

'In fact, that's perfect. I'll put together a list so you can round them all up and save time going back and forth. What do you think?'

'Well, if they're going to be here waiting, they'll all need to be supervised.'

'And that's where you're needed most. Perhaps you can get someone else to escort them back once I'm done with them?'

'Maybe I should wait until you've completed your list?'

'No, I have a few details I must discuss with my assistant first.'

'What details?' asks Mai Li. Newport looks at her but Ian ignores her comment.

'So, by the time we're ready for the second interview, I should have your list.'

'Fine, I'll fetch him right away then.'

'Thank you, Officer Newport.' Newport turns and leaves the interview room, leaving Ian alone with Mai Li.

'I would appreciate when you're not clear what's going on that your default mode is to say nothing,' says Ian. 'And if you have a question, keep it to yourself until we are alone. Is that clear?'

'Okay, we are alone now, so you can start by telling me what we're actually doing here?'

Ian takes out a photo and pushes it in front of Mai Li.

'What do you see?' he says, moving it closer to her. Mai Li looks down at the photo then back up at Ian.

'What am I supposed to be looking for? And who is this person anyway?'

'You're looking for the person's aura.'

'How can you see that in a photo?' she asks.

'I'm glad you asked. Let me show you something.' Ian rests his finger on the photo. 'Look here and focus,' he says, circling his finger around the face in the photo. The chrome mirror on his fingernail catches Mai Li's eye. The ceiling lights bounce off it with each rotation.

'Do you see it yet?'

'Wait, I see it now,' says Mai Li, sounding almost excited.

'Good, now listen to my voice and only my voice – sleep.' Mai Li's head lists, allowing Ian to begin. 'You will observe and remember everything I do until you hear your trigger word. Your trigger word is – coffee. When you hear this word, all information held to that point will be erased from your memory. Do you understand?'

'I understand,' Mai Li murmurs.

''You'll wake up on my count to three. One… two… three. You got it right, well done.'

'I did!' Mai Li sounds surprised.

'Yeah, I think we are more or less ready now.'

'So exactly what is my role?'

'When they, the prisoners, arrive, the first thing I will need you to do is to verify that their faces match the photos in our files.'

'That's why you were testing me with the photo, wasn't it?'

'That's correct.' He tries to keep the rapport going.

'So, what are you, like an optician?'

'You could say that. I'm more of a specialist in my field. I will also ask you to follow my example, as you saw in the governor's office earlier. That is not to discuss anything you see or learn here with anyone. That includes casual comments. As professionals, we must behave similarly to doctors; we soak up the information and keep it to ourselves. That way we'll build confidence and trust in what we're doing. When they leave here, they will talk. What we need to ensure is that they don't give the wrong impression to those we've not seen yet.'

'I get it.' She nods vigorously.

'Good, I think that about covers everything.'

A knock at the door signals Officer Newport's return.

'Come in,' Ian calls. Newport pokes his head around the door.

'If you're ready, Mr Gilby is outside,' he announces.

'Yes, you can show him in, please.'

'Come on, in you come,' Newport orders Paul, stepping aside to allow him to enter under his arm.

'Please take a seat. It's Paul, isn't it?' Ian says with a straight face. Mai Li checks his profile picture as instructed.

'Excuse me, Mr Gilby,' Mai Li interrupts.

'Yes, what is it?'

'I need to visit the ladies before we get started.'

'Officer Newport?' Ian redirects the question.

'Oh. If you'd like to follow me, miss.' He opens the door for Mai Li. 'We won't be long,' he says.

'Take your time,' says Ian. 'I've met Mr Gilby before. I'm not expecting any problems.'

With that, Ian and his half-brother Paul are alone once again.

# CHAPTER 14

As the door to the interview room closes, Paul wastes no time in getting to his point.

'I need a favour, and yes, I know you don't owe me squat, that's why I'm begging you,' he says, with his hands pressed together as in prayer.

'A favour? Isn't the risk I'm taking enough?'

'It is, but I need two more of those magic eye lens thingy things.'

'Why? Don't tell me you've lost them already, Paul?'

'No, I'm wearing them, like you asked.'

'Then trust me, that's all you need.'

'Look, Ian, they're not for me. I owe people in here, big time.'

'What happened to keeping this private between us? What do you think I'm running, a bloody support group?'

'No, but listen, please. It's that or I leave here in a coffin before your scheme can work.'

Ian stands and moves from the desk to think. He combs through his hair with his fingers, sighs heavily before sitting down again. Looking Paul point blank in his face, he jabs a finger at him.

'No more,' he says.

'No more! That's like you condemning me to death yourself.'

'Shut up, let me finish. No more after this, and that makes us even. You got that?'

'Absolutely, and thanks, you're saving my life, you really are.'

'What's their names?'

'Oxford Earlington and Chan Yip,' Paul whispers.

Ian looks through the list and makes a mark against both names.

'Tell them to answer "no" to my question about their eyes. That way I'll know they're wearing the lenses. Understand?'

Ian extracts two more sets of lenses from a hidden pocket and hands them to Paul.

'You had extra pairs ready?'

'Had a feeling you'd be asking for something. Just wasn't sure what.'

'So, I didn't need to beg. You bastard.'

The door nudges open, which signals Officer Newport and Mai Li's return and brings an end to the brothers' conversation.

'Ah, you're back, good. I've been able to finish my task with this gentleman, so luckily, I'm still on schedule. Now, give me a minute and I'll have that list I promised you.' Ian uses a blank piece of paper and prints the names of several inmates, including those given by Paul. He hands the paper to Officer Newport, who gives the list a superficial glance.

'And if you could keep to that order, that would be most helpful too,' Ian is quick to add, as Officer Newport reviews the list in more detail, smiling as he does so.

'This list tells me it's obvious you don't understand who these men are and why they're in here,' Newport gloats.

'True, Mr Newport, I don't. My task doesn't require me to take that into account. Besides, I must remain impartial, so I would prefer you said nothing, either personally or professionally. It helps me to keep my work honest.'

'Right you are then. I'll round them up. Okay, let's go, Gilby. On your feet, lad,' Newport barks his orders at Paul, whose chair makes a screeching noise as he pushes it back across the polished floor.

Officer Newport marches Paul out the door while Mai Li takes her seat and looks over at Paul's notes, which are still visible on the table.

'You know how to operate a computer, don't you? Why am I asking, you must do if you have a degree in computing.'

'Yeah, I can find my way around one,' answers Mai Li.

'Well, see what information they keep on this lot.' He points to the underlined names on his copy of the list.

Officer Newport escorts Paul Gilby back to the main section of the prison. He walks several paces behind, making Paul uneasy and worried about Newport's renowned random searches. These exercises, a trick he learnt during his army days, keep all prisoners anxious when he's around.

The gate looms closer with each step and the prospect of a search diminishes. Within metres of the recreational area, Newport signals for the steel gate to be unlocked, only leaving once he's satisfied that Paul is back under the control of the system. Officer Newport goes to the main control centre to make the announcement for the names on his list.

Once he's out of the guard's watchful gaze, Paul finds Chan and Ox. With the exaggerated caution worthy of any B-movie spy, he hands Chan the spare lenses through a simple handshake, then sets about delivering a crash course on how to fit them.

'Get this right and within weeks you can expect to walk out of here,' Paul tells them.

'Just like that?' Ox says, suddenly interested, after giving the impression he wasn't even listening.

'Yeah, just like that,' Paul says, nodding. 'Now, you better see if you can put them in… like now, this minute.'

Before Ox can try, a loud siren warns inmates to stop and listen for a general announcement.

'The following prisoners are required to make their way immediately to the visitor gate: Earlington, Oxford; Miller, Steven; Orbison, Mark; and Yip, Chan.'

Chan tilts his head back and inserts each lens with relative ease.

'Come on, Ox,' Paul urges. 'Do it now and quick, before you get there.'

'I'm not sure I can.'

'What do you mean not sure if you can? Don't be a wuss.'

'You want to watch your mouth, Paul. You don't have a clue what you're talking about.'

'So, you act all tough then let a little thing like this defeat you?'

Paul steps to the side so he can view the gate. Officer Newport is returning and two of the prisoners whose names he called are already there waiting.

'Look, it's up to you. I've done what I said I'd do. If you fail, we might all get punished. Oh, one last thing. When my brother asks questions about your eyes, you need to answer "no" – have you got that? "No" means the lenses are in.'

'Come on, let's go,' Chan says to Ox. They walk away from Paul towards the visitor gate. 'You've never mentioned a problem with your eyes before.'

'Only proves one thing; that you don't know everything about me,'

'As your best friend, I would like to think I do,' replies Chan. 'So, tell me?' He looks at Ox, who looks back in much the same way.

'When I was sixteen, I used to do a lot of that graffiti tagging stuff. But as it became more and more popular, finding fresh walls became an issue. Anyway, in my eagerness, I painted over the then main tagging king, and I was so proud of myself I signed my work. That made it easy for him to identify me. He lured me to the bridge by the canal one night, and while two of his gang held me, he deliberately sprayed paint into my eyes.'

'That must have been around the time you went missing from school for six weeks but never said why.'

'That's right.'

The conversation has to end as they're only metres from the gate and the ever-listening ears of the guards. The gate is unlocked, allowing the four inmates to file through.

'Okay, prepare to be away for most of the morning,' says Newport. 'Some will be away longer than others. You will not, I repeat not, talk during this process unless either I or the person you are seeing today speaks to you first. Have I made myself clear, gentlemen?'

There is a collective murmured 'Yes, sir.'

'Right, any questions, now is the time to speak.'

Ox is swift to raise his hand.

'Yes?' says Newport.

'I was on my way to the toilets when they announced my name.'

'And?'

'And I still need to go.'

'And?'

'Oh, I'm sorry. I still need to go, sir.'

'Now, that wasn't hard, was it?' Officer Newport walks over to Ox. 'Respect works both ways, lad.' He turns to the others. 'Now, anyone else for the ladies' toilets?' he says, looking around. 'No? Then off you go, Earlington. You have two minutes. Now move.'

Ox hastens towards the set of doors marked 'Toilets' in bold white letters. Inside, he quickly checks the few cubicles to make sure he's alone before moving to a sink and placing the plastic plug into the sink hole. The trauma of his childhood experience floods back overwhelming him, as he looks into a mirror with a large crack extending across the bottom left corner. With his confidence slowly evaporating he looks down at the sweat buildup in his palms, and rubs them together before drying them on the thigh part of his trousers.

There isn't much time and Ox is struggling to convince himself of what he needs to do. He looks in the mirror again and removes the clear package from his pocket and rushes to open it. With the lenses in his left palm, he searches for them with a trembling index finger from his right, gathering the first lens onto the tip of the finger. Then, with his little finger, he pulls down the lower lid of his right eye, blurring the vision as his finger gets closer to the eye. He holds his breath and composes himself to insert the first lens.

He blinks and checks the difference in the mirror before picking up the second lens.

'Hurry up in there,' Newport shouts from outside, causing Ox to blink and let the lens slip and fall into the sink.

'Three minutes for number twos, sir,' Ox shouts, fumbling in the sink for the dropped lens.

It's a good thing he had the sense before starting, to put the plug in, otherwise his search would have been futile. Hands still trembling, he feels frantically around the sink for the second lens. Thinking he's found it, he's unsure until it's gripped between his fingers. Composing himself again, Ox lifts the lens to try again.

After a third attempt, he succeeds and checks his eyes again in the mirror. Satisfied he flushes the nearest toilet, rinses his hands hurriedly under the tap allowing water to splash everywhere before he exits. Shocked to encounter Officer Newport about to enter, Ox squeezes past, keeping his head low.

'Another minute lad, and I would have been in to fetch you.'

'Sorry, sir.' He hurries away from the toilet door.

'Wait!' Newport commands. 'What's happened to your eye?'

'My eye, sir?'

'It looks sore. What have you done to it?' Ox checks by feeling his face underneath his right eye.

'There's a mark under your left eye,' Newport informs him.

'Is there, sir?' He switches his attention to the other side. 'Well, I don't know what you're seeing, sir. I can't feel anything.'

'You also need to work on your aim lad.' Newport says, referring to the wet patch on the front of Ox's trousers. 'Anyway, let's not waste any more time. We've already kept people waiting long enough.'

Outside, Newport gathers the other prisoners, marching them to the visitor centre.

## CHAPTER 15

'**M**r Earlington, you're up first, let's go.' Officer Newport knocks on the door and pushes it open enough to poke his head in. 'They're all here,' he says, entering with Ox.

'I was wondering what had happened,' says Ian, standing up behind the desk. 'Thank you, Officer Newport. Please take a seat,' he directs Ox as Newport backs out of the room.

'Right, let's get started. Mr Oxford Earlington, right?'

'That's correct, sir.'

Ian looks towards Mai Li, poised to note his response. Ox also looks over at her, and she blushes before glancing away, then sneaks another peek once she's sure he's not looking.

'First, how would you describe your general health?' Ian asks.

'I'd say good, because it is,' replies Ox.

'And your eyes, are they clear at the moment?'

'No.'

'Okay. I'll be carrying out a psychometric test requiring nothing more than your complete honesty. But, to guarantee this, it will be necessary for me to hypnotise you. Now, do you understand and are you willing to give your consent?'

'I'd be lying if I said yes I understood, but whatever it takes,' says Ox.

'That's okay, then let's make a start. I want you to look at this.' Ian places a picture containing hundreds of coloured dots in front of Ox. 'And concentrate on my voice, understand?'

'Okay,' says Ox.

Mai Li angles her head so she can get a better view of the picture herself. Ox sees the printed text forming in the picture. When he understands it, he's relieved he didn't read it out loud. Mai Li sees only the dots, forming no particular pattern or shape.

'Now, concentrate as the dots move. They're all blending into a single colour and becoming brighter and sharper as they do. You sense that your eyes can no longer stare at the intense light. They're closing, and the brightness is decreasing. They're now closed, and the light has stopped and you're asleep.'

The dotted text only seen with the lens warned Ox to close his eyes when told to do so. He's not in a trance but keeps still and silent, awaiting the next instruction.

'Mr Earlington, do you know where you are?'

Ox responds, saying 'Downing Prison' in a monotone voice.

'That's right, and you're now in the final week of your sentence and feeling light because your prison journey is ending. You are full of remorse and can never engage in anything illegal that would lead you back to prison. The word "payback" is your prompt. When you hear that word, a voice will control you directly with instructions. If you understand, move your head.' Ox nods. 'When I say, "rise", you will wake up refreshed and happy that your sentence is almost over. Rise.'

Ox opens his eyes and looks around the room, using the opportunity to check out Mai Li, who stares suspiciously out of the corner of her eyes. Ian gets up and moves over to the door, opening it.

'Officer,' Ian summons Newport.

'Yes, Mr Gilby?'

'Mr Earlington is ready for you now.'

'Earlington, don't just sit there. It's not the barber's chair, lad.

Your time is up. Outside please.'

'Sorry,' Ox answers, getting to his feet and moving quickly to leave the room. He remembers to add 'sir', lowering his head as he passes Newport in the doorway.

Mai Li stretches to get a better and last glimpse of Ox before he leaves.

'Miller, in you come,' Newport barks.

'What's all this about, anyway?' Steven Miller asks, looking pensive after waiting for some time outside.

'You won't find out from out here, so in you go,' Newport orders again.

'Please come in, Mr Miller, and take a seat.' Ian closes the door behind him and returns to his seat.

'Right. First off, there is nothing for you to worry about.' Ian waits for Miller's reaction but none is forthcoming. 'Okay. I'll be carrying out a psychometric test requiring nothing more than your complete honesty.'

'No.'

'No?'

'No, I'm not having you mess around in my head.'

'I can assure you—'

'You can assure anything you want. My answer is still no. I know my human rights… and what's she writing?' He's agitated by something not obvious to Ian or Mai Li. Ian immediately rules him out as a viable candidate for the release programme. Standing up, he goes to the door, his every step being observed by Miller. He opens the door, stepping outside for a private word with Newport.

'I think I need to reject this person. There appears to be something troubling him,' he says, starting a whispered conversation.

'I did try warning you. Knowing what a prisoner is in for goes a long way to understanding some mental issues we face here. Trust me, by not knowing, you've got no chance of understanding why they behave the way they do.'

'I still have to remain unbiased in my approach, Mr Newport. So, let's just carry on to the next one, if you please.'

'Well, the offer is there. I mean, if I knew even a little, anything, about what you were doing, I could filter out the nutters. That way you wouldn't be wasting your time. What do you think?'

'We're good for the moment, thanks. But I'll keep your offer in mind.'

They both re-enter the room.

'Time to go Miller, on your feet,' Newport orders with a raised voice. Miller swivels in the chair before standing and marching to the door. Newport checks his list.

'Orbison!'

'Sir.' Mark Orbison gets up and comes to the doorway, passing an agitated Miller as he leaves.

'Thank you, Officer. Come in Mr Orbison, please take a seat.' Ian closes the door again then takes his seat after Orbison has sat down. By far the oldest of the inmates being interviewed today, his unusual stare and facial tattoos that cover eighty per cent of his face, will make it tough for Ian, to read his reactions. Orbison folds his arms and looks across at Mai Li, paying her perhaps a little too much attention.

'Mr Mark Orbison, yes?' Ian brings Orbison's focus back to him.

'Yes, that's correct, sir.'

'First, let me repeat what I've told the others. It's important for you to be honest with me.'

'Who the fuck are you? And why was that last guy so scared? If you're looking for a confession, then you'll have to beat it out of me.' He stares straight at Ian, almost like he can see through him.

'First, can I ask you to respect that there is a lady in the room and moderate your language, please.' Orbison looks over at Mai Li, then straight back at Ian.

'Mr Orbison, I'm here carrying out tests, with no guarantees, but which could lead to your early release. My assessments, however, are carried out under the condition of hypnosis. I would very much like to have your approval to use it.'

'Hell, the fuck yes, if it means getting out of this shithole. Oops, sorry.' Orbison checks his language.

'First, some questions about your general health – how would you describe it?'

'Feeling pretty pumped right now after what you've told me.'

'And your eyes, are they clear at the moment?'

'My eyes! Man, they're crystal,' Orbison says, shaking his head and spreading his arms.

'I need you to study this.' Ian places the same picture, containing hundreds of coloured dots, on the table in front of Orbison. 'And concentrate only on my voice – do you understand?'

'Yeah,' Orbison nods.

'Now, look closely as the dots move. They are blending together into a single colour and getting brighter and brighter as they do. You'll feel your eyes can no longer look at the bright light and they're closing. The brightness is diminishing, your eyes are now closed, you're feeling deeply relaxed, and now you're asleep.'

Ian waits a few seconds before proceeding. He's not sure, but thinks he may have seen one of Orbison's eyes open and close briefly.

'Now, you're in the final week of your sentence, you're feeling light because your stay here will soon be ending. You feel remorseful about what you did and you can never do anything illegal again that would send you back to prison.'

'It's a joke, right?' Orbison says, opening one eye. It throws Ian and Mai Li off when he doesn't appear to be hypnotised.

'Mr Orbison, let me assure you, I don't see my work as a joke.'

'Then I guess you're in the wrong fucking profession.' Orbison is staring at him again.

'Mr Orbison, I'm thinking your inclusion on this programme may have been a little premature. So, in view of this, I'm ending this assessment until I can gather further information.' Ian gets up and moves to the door.

'What information?'

'Sorry, I'm not in a position to discuss that with you now,' Ian says, opening the door. 'Officer Newport, Mr Orbison is ready.'

'Whatever you're doing in there isn't taking you long,' Newport cynically observes.

'Mr Newport, can we hold the next one, please? I need five minutes.'

'Right you are,' Newport says. 'Let's go, Mr Orbison. Your normal routine awaits.'

Ian observes how Orbison exits the room without saying a word. Is it fear or respect that Officer Newport commands? Closing the door, he returns to his seat. He's already analysing possible reasons for his complete failure to hypnotise Mr Orbison.

'Do you need two eyes?' Mai Li unexpectedly asks.

'I have two, thanks.'

'No, not you. Do you need your subjects to have two eyes to make whatever it is you're trying to do work? I mean hypnotising them. Because this is nothing like any psychometric test I've come across.'

'And what would you know about it?'

'I know from Mr Orbison's medical records that he only has one eye. The other one is false, made of glass.'

'We don't have access to any medical records.'

'From what I've seen so far, I don't think you have clearance for any of this. So, I read his records on their system.'

'You better come out of there before they find out.'

'They won't. I've cloaked my entry.'

'I wouldn't know what that means. Just get out of it right now, please.'

'Okay, I'm out,' she says, pushing a few buttons, and the screen returns to normal. Ian can feel pressure building as his task gets harder. He acknowledges to himself that a glass eye could, in fact, stop someone from being hypnotised. Too little knowledge has its dangers – such as not knowing enough about Mai Li or her background. Ian thinks for a moment that he may have been too hasty in not allowing Mai Li to get the extra information. At the end of the day, he still has the power to erase her knowledge of it anyway. There is still one prisoner to assess before he can call it a day. A day that can't be considered successful with the characters encountered so far.

After six minutes, Ian goes to the door and asks Newport to send in the last person.

'Good morning, please take a seat,' Ian says, greeting Chan, who is busy exchanging glances with Mai Li. Ian takes his seat again to begin his final interview for the day.

'First, Mr Yip, I'd like to ask you about your general health. Would you describe it as good, fair or poor?'

'Good morning,' Chan starts, looking again at Mai Li. 'I'm in good health, Doctor.' He notices that Mai Li is taking as much interest in him as he is in her.

'I'm not a doctor, Mr Yip. Anyway, your eyes; are they clear at the moment?'

'My eyes? Oh, these eyes? Er, no.' He smiles at Mai Li then turns back to Ian.

Mai Li takes the opportunity, while Ian concentrates on Chan, to look up the prisoner's record. She's convinced from Chan's nervous answers that he must be a drug user – or, worse, even a dealer – however cute she thinks he is. Her discovery that he has been convicted of murder makes her physically shake, and she tries to limit any further eye contact.

'I want you to look at this.' Ian places the same picture containing hundreds of coloured dots on the table in front of Chan. 'I want you to concentrate only on my voice – do you understand?'

'Yes, I do.'

'Now, look closely as the dots move. They are blending together into a single colour and getting brighter and brighter. Your eyes can no longer look at the bright light and are closing.

Your eyes are now closed, and the light is going away, and you are able to relax and sleep.'

Ian's sure Chan has followed the instructions and is aware of what's happening as his eyes are closed.

'Now, you're in the final week of your sentence. You're feeling light because this journey is ending. You feel remorseful and will be unable to do anything illegal that would send you back to prison. The word "payback" is your trigger. When you hear it, the voice speaking will control you. If you understand, please move your head.' Chan nods a few times, almost too vigorously. 'When I say "rise", you will wake to feel refreshed and happy that your sentence is almost over. Rise.'

Chan opens his eyes, rubbing them to legitimise the deception.

'Well, Mr Yip, that concludes our assessment today.' Ian gathers all his papers, squaring them on the desk before placing them into his briefcase. He stands and makes his way to open the door, inviting Officer Newport back in.

'All finished?' Newport asks.

'Yes, thanks, done and dusted for today.'

'You're probably in need of some refreshments?'

'Oh yes, thank you. Tea or coffee, anything will do.' With the trigger words activated for both Newport and Mai Li, their memories of everything that's happened today is erased.

The prisoners are escorted back to the main prison block by the other officer, leaving Newport to take Ian and Mai Li to the governor's office before their departure.

'I'm still intrigued, Mr Gilby, to find out your exact business in my prison,' Governor Riley says, still fishing.

'No doubt in due course, Governor, everything will be public. My report will cover the excellent help afforded to us. I look forward to seeing you again next week.'

'Of course,' says the governor. 'Next week,' he repeats.

# CHAPTER 16

Paul sits on a bench in the main prison yard, watching the gate for Chan and Ox to return. He's impatient to find out the outcome and if they are finally ready to trust him. There's no particular reason they shouldn't but he needs to hear them say it.

It's almost lunch, an opportune time for having conversations under the cover of the canteen's noise. 'Here they come,' someone announces, alerting Paul that he's not the only one interested in their movements. It would have been better if no one else had noticed, but the earlier tannoy announcement means everyone knows when something is happening.

The gate to the prison yard opens and they reintroduce the four men back to their normal routines. Ox and Chan are making their way towards the canteen block and Paul starts off to meet them. He catches up just before they enter the dining area.

'So, was it as I described, gentlemen?' Paul asks on the quiet.

'When is it all happening?' Chan responds.

'He said it shouldn't take more than a few weeks once his tests are concluded, then maybe random interviews.'

'I thought you said once we've seen your brother that's all we needed to do?'

'I said that's the only complicated thing. Look, let me repeat what he said: only a one per cent chance of interviews happening. It will be easy from here, trust me. They can't block it unless they find reasonable cause. That means, don't freak out, lose your marbles or murder someone. Sorry, ignore that, it was just an example.'

'Changing the subject, did you see her, in the interview room?' Chan whispers to Ox.

'I did.'

'And what do you think?'

'What do you mean, what do I think?'

'Her and me?'

'What do I think? That it's conceivable you're starving and it's affecting your thinking. You have no chance now she's seen you in here.'

'It's been known to happen.' Chan is still absorbed by the possibility.

'Yes, anything could. But here's the reality, Chan: you don't know what information she's had the opportunity of seeing. So, work it out for yourself – is that a healthy chance?'

Chan takes a second to ponder.

'I'll admit it's not the perfect place to meet someone, but zero hope equals zero chance.'

'Did you even talk to her?'

'Are you joking, and spoil that moment? Her eyes did all the talking, and I heard every word. I felt that instant connection with her, and I bet she felt it too.'

'I'll assume that there's nothing amiss with your hearing. I'm hungry.' Ox picks up his tray and merges with the line.

Mark Orbison needs a toilet break before lining up for lunch. Pushing the restroom door open, he's immediately overwhelmed by the smell of stale urine. The toilets are supposedly cleaned regularly, but the odours accosting his nasal passages seem to live there. Mark could hold his breath for a brief hand wash, but this time it's more than a penny that he needs to spend. All the cubicle doors show traces of being damaged and repaired numerous times. His destination is clear; it's the only cubicle with a bolt attached by more than a single screw.

Mark confirms he's alone and enters the cubicle. He drops his trousers and takes a seat, bracing one foot hard against the cubical door. It's a position that leaves him more secure but less comfortable than he would like.

Suddenly, the door rattles noisily and with such ferocity that the vibration shudders through Mark's limbs.

'What do you want?' Mark shouts. 'Can't you see this one is occupied?'

Being caught anywhere in the prison with your trousers down, even in the lavatories, can spell disaster. He didn't hear anybody come in, which suggests a measure of pre-planning.

'Mark, we simply want a chat.'

'Information!' another voice adds, letting Mark know there are at least two people on the other side of the door.

'I'm a little busy, can't it wait?' Mark's legs quiver as the two men lean heavily against the door, increasing the pressure.

'Mark, give us the information we want and earn your comfortable crap.'

'What is it you want? Or think I might know?'

'Don't play smart. Tell us what went on in the visitor centre this morning and we're gone.'

'Information, Mark!' the other voice adds again.

'Look, it was just this random guy I'd never met before. He could have been a doctor, talking about when I get released… and some hypnosis shit.' Mark pauses but hears no response. 'The fact is, I'm not even due for parole for at least another eight years. That's all, I swear.'

It's silent now, except for the buzzing of a fly. Mark puts his foot to the ground and hastily concludes his business. He can't identify the individuals but knows for certain that the information will somehow find its way to Fat Fingers.

Mark opens the cubicle door, poking his head out first. He checks either side to verify he's alone. At the sink nearest the door, Mark washes his hands before he exits the toilet and heads back to the canteen.

~

Governor Riley and Officer Newport are in the governor's office after their superior three-course lunch in the staff canteen. The governor sits in his recliner while Newport hovers about his desk.

'So, what do we know so far about our friend Mr Gilby?' the governor asks.

'Well, he's had two sessions now with one prisoner, Paul Gilby.

'Have you followed it up to see if they are related?'

'I had the same suspicion too, sir, but strangely enough Paul Gilby changed his name from Salerno by deed poll. Maybe he's just doing a survey on the running of the prison.'

'I run this prison, Mr Newport, like a steady ship. Besides, pals at the ministry would tip me off if there's so much as a murmur about this place. No, I don't think it's the running of this place we need to worry about.'

'What do you mean, Governor?'

'Just some little details that the government is trying to contain.'

'Well, since you've alluded to something, Governor, are you going to fill in the blanks?'

'Let's just say, the soil under this prison building, Mr Newport, is no longer British territory.'

'Surely that can't be right, governor?'

'As I understand, it was accidentally sold off under some mad privatisation scheme.'

'Sold to who, though?'

'To a company called Lotto-Guard, who I believe are Chinese. But I'll emphasise again, this is not public knowledge,' he hastens to stress.

'So, these interviews, could they be related to that?' asks Newport.

'No, got to be something else, something we've overlooked or haven't even thought of. Then again, we might be trying to find problems where none exist.'

'Well, Mr Gilby's interview list so far turns out to be pretty random.'

The governor sees a folded piece of paper on his desk, secured by his paperweight. He opens it up and skims the contents.

'If we can't establish any ties between these inmates,' he declares, laying the note face down, 'we may have to accept that he's here for some other reason. Work more on the list, Mr Newport. Shake their files and see what falls out.'

'Right you are, Governor,' Newport says as he leaves the office.

The governor picks up the intercom connecting him to his secretary.

'Cynthia, this note left on my desk, what time did you leave it?'

'I don't recall leaving any notes, Governor. I've not been in there since the nine o'clock meeting this morning.'

'Okay, thank you.' He hangs up the telephone and reads the note again before scrunching it up and disposing of it in his bin.

His telephone rings.

'Yes, Cynthia,' he replies.

'The chief of counterintelligence is holding, Governor. He says he needs to talk with you most urgently.'

'Did he say what it's about?'

'No, sir, but he insists it's urgent.'

There's a hint of annoyance in Cynthia's voice. She knows the governor is duty-bound to accept the call.

'Okay, put him through.' The governor concedes.

'He's on line six now, sir.'

'Hey, Martin. What's so important you can't let my lunch digest first?' He greets Sir Martin Dupont like the familiar colleague he is.

'How are you, Rick?' Martin says,

'One cannot complain, what's up?'

'We've got an evolving situation that will require the secure resources of Downing.'

'Martin, it's me you're talking to. I'm sure you can give me more information than that.'

'Not on this one, Rick. It's only because we go way back I'm letting you in on this beforehand.'

'Plus, you know you can depend on me.'

'There is that too, but it's absolute hush on this one until we've cracked it, understood?'

'Yes, yes, I understand.'

'Okay. Well, last week we captured several asylum seekers. Economic migrants, call them what you will. The thing is, Rick, documents we discovered hidden are written in a language that we're still working to decipher. We don't know the entire scope yet, just a strong suspicion we may be dealing with some sort of terrorist threat. We're banking on the few who avoided capture not knowing the level of intelligence we've collected so far. I needn't tell you we have to isolate them. We may need to use techniques from our time in Iraq to extract information on what these people are planning.'

'I'm guessing off the radar?'

'Yes, we need them cracked and we need it done fast. We're more than sure they're collectively part of a bigger picture. We're also sure we're holding a huge chunk. But a chunk of what? That's what we don't yet know.'

'When do you propose bringing Downing into play?'

'If you're ready, Rick, I'd like to do so tonight. Sometime between, say, nine thirty and ten.'

'Do you recall our old army motto?'

'Born to live or born to die, but always born ready,' they chant in unison, then laugh.

'Martin, as ever we've got our country to protect. Anyway, leave it with me.'

'Thanks, Rick. They'll be with you later, as arranged. Bye.'

'Goodbye.'

The call finishes, and the governor asks Officer Newport to return to his office.

'We are expecting some highly classified guests this evening and must have this prison in full lockdown before nine. All prisoners need to be in their cells, tucked up and secured until tomorrow morning.'

'What reason can we use this time? We can't use another attempted prison break; we did that last week.'

The governor thinks for a moment.

'Say it's to allow outside contractors full access for preventative measures to contain a small outbreak of MRSA. Yes, that sounds good and should also cover any awkward questions.'

Newport nods in agreement as the governor's personal mobile unexpectedly rings in his pocket.

'That can't be them already,' he quips, while transferring the phone from pocket to hand.

'Hello, Governor Riley,' says the unfamiliar voice. 'Or would you prefer me to call you Patrick?'

'Who is this?' He pulls the mobile from his ear to see if it displays the caller ID on its tiny screen.

'It's me… your fat Jesus. I guess you're not yet familiar with my telephone voice, but give it time, it will grow on you.'

The colour drains from the governor's face like water sloshing from a bathtub. He pulls the mobile from his ear again to address Officer Newport.

'You have enough to get on with… you'd better make a start.'

'Are you all right, Governor? You look like you've seen – or heard – a ghost?'

'Yes, I'm fine, a small family matter. You get moving.'

The governor stalls until Newport leaves before launching his anger at the caller.

'How did you get this private number?'

'It wasn't easy, but while you continue to ignore my request to meet, I think I'm more than justified, given our links.'

'We have no agreement for you to contact me like this. Every three months there's a scheduled chat, that's what's in place. You must know not sticking to it sets up a trail that others can easily follow and use to link us?'

'Why should I wait three months just to tell you my records show you are being less than honest about our deal? We both know you're avoiding me.'

'It's clear you don't understand how a huge prison such as this is run. It's not avoidance.'

'Actually, between me and you, Governor, I could claim to be the better qualified, given the time I've spent in prisons over the years.'

'Look, I've got to put matters of national security before your games. And how did you get that note into my office?'

'Games, hey? I bet you don't even know what the interviews in the visitor centre are all about.'

'If you have information you wish to share, it would be well received and rewarded.'

'Of course, you would welcome it. Funny how the man running this prison knows the least about what goes on in here.'

'With three life sentences, you know just as much as I do. You won't ever leave here. So, you might as well tell me. You can't do anything with that information.'

'Governor, in here, information equals power. I'm enjoying our little power chat, but I've got another call coming through. Next time, we can talk about your wife's new BMW. She must be used to the controls by now, but only you and I know how you could afford it on your salary.'

'I know what you're trying to do, but trust me, I'm out of the loop on this one. You know there can't be any visible ties to you.'

'I have to go, Governor. But remember, no one can predict the future.'

The line goes silent, and the governor releases his mobile onto his desk in anger.

'Damn!'

He picks up his desk phone and orders Newport back to his office yet again.

'Close the door,' the governor says once he's arrived. 'We have a dilemma. There's a mobile phone in my prison. I want it found, today. There could be several, but this one alone threatens my way – I mean our way – of life, so find it and get it to me. I'm suggesting you focus most of your efforts on that "fat Jesus".'

'Fat Jesus, sir?' Newport asks.

'Mr Salerno? AKA Fat Fingers?'

'Do you still want me to investigate the names on the list?'

'No, put that to one side for the moment. Find the phone and anything that looks like a ledger, and we find a lot of answers.'

'Right you are, Governor.'

'Also, take these.' The governor hands Newport a small listening device and a walkie-talkie from the base drawer of his desk. 'Find somewhere secure to hide that. We can recover it later and see what we get. There's only two of these handsets and one channel.'

'I'll get on it right away, sir,' Officer Newport replies.

'When I think about it, it might be best to do it during the lockdown.' The governor amends the timing of his instructions.

# CHAPTER 17

By 8:15 pm the planned lockdown for Downing Prison is already in place. The favoured means of protest takes the form of prolonged orchestral discord, with mugs being clanged on any surface capable of making noise. Many long-term criminals have seen all this before and simply don't buy the preventative measures story and are convinced it's a front for some other activity.

Newport has ensured that all prisoners are in their cells ahead of the crucial 9 pm deadline. Just like on previous occasions, only time will reveal what's taking place. His other task for the evening is to organise a search of Fat Fingers' cell. Newport has hand-picked six of his best officers and positioned them outside the cell.

'Now remember, each of you face the same risk from the moment we enter the cell until we have Mr Salerno secured,' Newport whispers, establishing eye contact with each man and watching for their nods. 'We move in, we secure, we extract. Then we carry out a detailed search of the cell. What are we searching for? Any communication device. If you're uncertain, ask. Got that? It's important that we don't utter a single word or give any clues about what we're looking for. Right, everybody should be clear on what we're doing.'

Newport raises his left hand, then gives a nod, signalling the start of the procedure. The two officers with riot shields move to the front while they unlock the cell door. Using noise as their disorientating tool, four officers force their way into the cell. The noise ends as the lead officer stops the action.

'Mr Newport, you need to see this, sir,' he says.

Officer Newport moves to the head of the team and into the room. He's presented with a scene not unlike a child's room, with everything on the floor, including Mr Salerno, who sits, untroubled, with his back towards the door and his hands propped on his head.

'Looks like someone has beaten you boys to the fun,' he informs them.

'Shut up! No talking,' one officer orders, thrusting his shield between Fat Fingers' shoulder blades. His hands go down to the floor before he returns them to his head.

'So, Mr Salerno, I guess you believe you've outsmarted us?' says Newport. 'But we'll still be going ahead with the search of your cell anyway. Bag him!'

They yank a handcuffed Fat Fingers to his feet in two unsteady movements. Flanked by four officers, he's moved out of the cell, leaving the last two with Newport.

'Okay, gentlemen, do your job,' Newport orders. He talks into the walkie-talkie as he exits the cell.

'Governor, are you there? Come in, Governor, are you receiving?'

'Hello, Mr Newport…' An unexpected voice answers.

'Cynthia? Is that you? I thought you'd left for home an hour a go?'

'No, sir, the governor had me… doing overtime. He's here.'

'Mr Newport, anything? Over.'

'Not yet, sir. We're just starting the search now, but it looks like he had prior information about our little exercise. He's getting good intelligence from somewhere.'

'Keep on top of it, we need to sort this.'

'Without question, Governor, over and out.'

Officer Newport has specific orders direct from the governor. Their working relationship is a long-standing one, based on years of trust. Newport re-enters the room and moves a few things from the floor to a small table. He engages his officers to distract them.

'Anything yet?'

'No, sir.'

'Have you tried the obvious places, like those books and his shoes?'

'Not yet, sir,' one officer replies, his focus diverted to the books on the shelf.

The untidy scene in the cell is a perfect cover for Newport to introduce a listening device into the hollow leg of the metal bed.

'Sir, found something. A phone card in this book.' The officer turns and shows it, satisfied at his find.

'That's prison issue, son, continue searching. There's a reward in it if you discover something important.'

The officers appear animated at the prospect of being rewarded, especially since they're being ordered to clean up a mess they have, for once, not made.

Newport leaves the cell, heading for the isolation unit where Salerno was taken. For once, he had been a model prisoner and not resisted. Newport isn't fooled, though. No matter how placid Mr Salerno appears, he's dangerous.

When Newport arrives, Salerno sits calmly, hands and feet cuffed to his chair.

'Okay, Mr Salerno, you can make things much easier for yourself by telling me how your cell ended up in that condition.'

'Do you believe in the little people, Mr Newport? You must do, you're Irish.'

'That doesn't answer my question.'

'Sir, may I have a quick word?' an officer interjects. Newport follows him from the room, out of earshot.

'What is it?' says Newport.

'He may be under the influence of drugs, sir.'

'How sure are you?'

'Not a hundred per cent, but I worked in narcotics for three years before this, and he's showing signs consistent with stimulants.'

'Well done. It's good to have bright people on the team; you'll go far.'

'Thank you, sir.'

'That may explain why he's so passive, although his record up to now shows no drug use. Been suspected of dealing several times but we've never found evidence. Okay, get a kit, test him and try to identify the substance. Whatever it is, we need to find its source.'

The officer leaves and Newport gets back onto the radio.

'Governor?'

'Yes, Mr Newport, anything?'

'Nothing more than an interesting observation for the moment, Governor.'

'What observation?'

'One of my officers with drug experience thinks our Mr Salerno may have taken something. I'm having him tested as we speak.'

'You need to keep an eye on that officer and keep him well away from our operation.'

'Understood, sir.'

'Besides, Salerno has shown no interest in drugs in the past. I can't see him starting at his age. There must be another explanation.'

'I'll keep looking, sir.'

'Right you are, Mr Newport. Over and out.'

Newport returns to the ransacked cell where the men are a decent way through the clear-up.

'Progress?' Newport asks, looking around the cell.

'We're getting there, but so far all we've discovered is this.'

The officer hands over a small electronic device.

'Well done, but this one doesn't count, gentlemen. It's one I planted myself beforehand.'

'Are you testing us, sir?'

'I am. It's a requisite part of my duty to ensure I have complete faith in all my staff. Carry on.'

They're joined by the officer who alerted Newport to Salerno's possible drug use. Newport follows him back out of the cell again, allowing the other two officers to carry on.

'Well?'

'Unfortunately, I arrived after they had already given him sleeping tablets. My test wasn't necessary, though, because that was the first test the doctors carried out, and theirs came out negative. They allowed me to observe him for ten minutes while they prepared the results of other tests.'

'Well done for thinking outside the box. There's always opportunities in the prison service for sharp thinkers like you.'

'Thank you, sir. The tests suggested it's more likely food poisoning. Apparently, it's an acute reaction to garlic.'

'Garlic?'

'Yes, sir.'

'I thought that stuff kept you healthy?'

'Same thing my mother always said, sir.'

'Nevertheless, still excellent work.' He turns his attention to the two officers clearing up the cell.

'Can I guess at around another thirty minutes before we can reunite Mr Salerno with his cell?'

'Yes, sir,' answers the nearest officer.

'We all have homes to go to, so make that fifteen.'

'Yes, sir.' An internal text message arrives on the officer's phone and he checks it. 'What is it?' asks Newport.

'It's medical, sir. They're keeping Mr Salerno until tomorrow morning. They think it will take until then for whatever he's taken to work its way out of his system.'

'Okay. That being the case, you and the others can meet me down in prisoner reception for nine fifteen. That goes for you two also. Finish up in here and get yourselves over there.'

'Yes, sir.' Newport heads back to the governor's office. The protest from the prisoners is dying down, with only a handful still trying to sustain it, but the cacophony is dwindling.

'So?' says the governor as Newport enters his office.

'We found nothing, Governor, and I don't think there are any communication devices in that cell.'

'There's got to be. He's just too damn clever. That's what you get from being inside for so long – knowledge of how to beat the system. And a damn pity he hasn't used drugs either.'

'What do you mean, sir?'

'For my right-hand man, you're off point tonight. Who supplies all the drugs for this prison?'

'That's you, Governor.'

'Exactly! If he were using, it would have given me the advantage over him. As it stands, he's the only one in here that I have nothing on. How he covers his steps in this prison is still beyond me.'

'I still think somebody at a high level is helping him, Governor.'

'You may well be right, and we must be—' He stops to answer the telephone that interrupts them. 'Okay, right,' he says, replacing the receiver. 'I was going to say, extra cautious.'

'Without question, Governor, without question.'

'Right, it seems our special prisoners are only a few minutes away. So, we'd best make a start over there now.'

Newport opens the door and follows the governor out.

They arrive at prisoner reception to the sound of the van's reversing beeps. Officer Newport assumes authority, deploying his men either side of the van. Shutting the engine off, the driver exits his cab and together with the escorting police officer, moves to the rear of the vehicle, unlocking the doors.

'You may need a wheelchair,' suggests the police officer. 'One bastard has been sick in there, and I want him out first.'

Newport responds, speaking into his radio.

'This is Officer Newport at prisoner reception. We need medical assistance and a wheelchair right away, please.'

The police officer enters the narrow aisle of the vehicle to unlock the sick person's cubicle. Pointing the way out with one hand, he masks his nose with the other, twisting his head away from the smell. A dark hunched figure appears from the shadows, his beard matted with sick. Unsteady on his feet, he stumbles to the stone surface from the two metal steps of the vehicle, unable to break his fall. It's only then that the onlookers realise his hands are handcuffed behind his back.

'Is this what passes for modern police policy when moving prisoners?' asks a furious governor.

'Someone thought it best, seeing as they've refused any attempt at communicating,' says the driver. 'Our orders were to take no chances.'

The medical team, wearing face masks, step forward to support the man.

'Remove his cuffs,' the governor orders. 'This man is clearly in need of medical help. And get the others to solitary, quickly.'

They take the sick prisoner in one direction, aided by the medics and two guards, and escort the others to solitary.

Once the sick prisoner is secured in medical, a doctor gets on with cleaning him up while checking for any signs of injuries.

'Put these on and we'll get you seen to shortly,' says the doctor, handing him a pile of clean clothes.

There's no response. The prisoner sits staring, his eyes every so often rolling back into his head and moving rapidly and involuntarily, which is normally the sign of a type of seizure.

He holds his belly and his face shows real discomfort. The

doctor encourages him to discard the soiled clothes and puts the rancid attire into the incinerator bin. After cleaning his hands, the prisoner is offered a gown, which he has to be helped into.

Moving the prisoner to a prepared bed, the doctor holds back the sheets and signals for him to get in.

'Any chance of more water? My throat is dry,' Salerno asks from the adjacent bed.

'Two minutes, Mr Salerno,' replies the doctor, turning to acknowledge him before shifting back to his new patient. 'You rest. In the morning, we'll work out just what's making you so ill.' He's not sure anything said is getting through so turns to Mr Salerno, making sure that his glass is full and he has enough chilled water for the night.

It's late, almost eleven, and the medical unit is shutting down for the night.

The ward itself has no cameras but all exits are monitored from a control room. After a few minutes, the main lights dim and the pale glow from lights outside the ward filters through the translucent glass set in the wooden doors. It's quiet and dark enough to sleep.

'Hello, friend.'

'So! You can speak, and English?' Fat Fingers answers.

'Yes, that is most correct.'

'Then, what's wrong with you anyway?'

'Nothing.'

'Nothing! They're not convinced. You're not brought in here for no reason, so you must be sick.'

'It's a small trick I learned as a child, when I didn't wish to eat my food.'

'I take it your mother wasn't a good cook?'

'Mother never cooked at all. We had a kitchen full of staff.'

'So, you just messed up for the fun of it. What's the real reason? Since you haven't even tasted the food here yet.'

'To meet with you.'

'Me! I don't know who you've been chatting to, but they've given you poor information, my friend.' Fat Fingers rolls onto his side, exposing his back to the new arrival.

'My information is of the purest quality, Mr Fingers.'

Salerno rolls back and strains to see something of the man's face or outline in the semi-darkness. He sits up slightly in the bed.

'Who are you? And why go to these lengths to meet me?'

'My name for the moment has no significance to our conversation. I'm just the one chosen to meet with you, but there are many of us, each willing to sacrifice their life with something that will make the world and England take notice and save the plight of my people.'

'So, not a wild guess then – that you believe I'm able to help?'

'The word is, even locked up, you can still locate things.'

'Somehow I don't think I'd be gaining anything I don't have already by dealing with you.' Salerno turns away again.

'Does a quarter of a million, sterling, get me your attention?'

Fat Fingers turns to face him again.

'If you're offering a quarter of a million, then you must be making ten times as much.'

'Please don't consume your thoughts with what you think we are making. Our cause is about life not money.'

'I applaud your cause, but mine would be nothing less than half a million.'

'If that would put us in agreement, then I'm authorised to make that deal. I assumed negotiating with you would have been much harder.'

'Doubling your original offer is enough for me. Many people have called me evil, but no one has ever said greedy.'

Even in the dark, Fat Fingers shows little reaction. It's still good business, especially if it has little to no impact on his own activities.

'We can arrange payment details later. For now, your word, Mr Fingers, is enough.'

'Then, fill me in on what it is you need my help with.' Fat Fingers places his hands behind his head, sliding lower under the bed sheets.

'We are here to locate and acquire the chip.'

'Chips? Is that with the traditional fish?' Fat Fingers' grin goes unseen in the dark.

'Believe it or not, from studying here many years ago, I get your English humour. Being serious for one moment though, this chip you will know better as the 'Pentium Omega-X2'.'

'I stand by my earlier comment; you're working on out-of-date information. They don't exist anymore.'

'Again, my sources are right on the money. How else would I have found you here?'

There are footsteps in the hallway outside. The men's conversation falls silent until they have faded.

After a moment, Fat Fingers speaks, a little louder than a whisper.

'Look, the factory in Malaysia making those chips burned to the ground. Don't your sources follow the news?'

'That is true, but that incident was an unfortunate error. Explosives set to take out the security caused the blaze.'

'Well, with such first-hand knowledge, why come here?'

'Because we found some half-burnt invoices, showing a few of the chips had already shipped to Hong Kong and the United Kingdom.'

'Then I can earn that money in seconds before I go to sleep and advise you to search in Hong Kong.'

'Information about the Hong Kong buyer suggests he and the chip are here, in the south-east of England.'

'And you want my help to find them?'

'It's something I heard is easy for a man of your resources.'

'And why would you believe I'd help you?'

'Can you remember the riot about three years ago, when

someone made an attempt on your life, wounding you with a broken broom handle?

'I still have the scar as a permanent reminder but that attacker never lived to boast about it.'

'And do you remember who stemmed the blood long enough for you to get help, possibly saving your life?'

'I remember little from that night. After six days in hospital and a hundred and two pints of blood, I know someone had to have shown me great kindness, but I never got the chance to thank or repay them. Now why the interest?'

'Let's just say that he was a relative and you can still repay him.'

'And what do you need this chip for?'

'The chip will give us access to and control over the Pinpoint laser system.'

'So, a weaponised Pinpoint. Then what?'

'Then we seek the attention of the government and invite them to negotiate.'

'And if they don't?'

'Then we would be forced into unleashing a terror that London has not seen since the war.'

'And you trust me not to say anything?'

'In many parts of the world, half a million buys me your tongue, pickled, but we already know what sort of a man we are dealing with.'

'There's still one question that needs an answer.'

'Ask away.'

'What were the odds of you turning up here in the night and being brought into this unit to meet me?'

'Who knows? But I'm sure you'll appreciate, Mr Fingers, that money is one of the few things that can actually change odds.'

'You joke, but it's serious if someone around me is getting too close – that's how someone was able to stab me last time.'

The ensuing silence leaves both men reflecting on who may have benefited more from their first and possibly only meeting.

## CHAPTER 18

On the ground floor wing of Dr Minn's very large family home, Mai Li enters the pre-chamber to her father's special room. Although not off limits, it's her first time in this room in the house and she's feeling nervy. It's just gone 5 am, but she knows it's where her father spends at least half an hour each morning before he starts his business day. Sitting, she can't help but notice the calming fragrance from the scented candles and the many images of Tian Tan Buddha adorning the walls. Dr Minn parts the sliding double doors, emerging from his sanctuary and immediately catching sight of his daughter. He's surprised yet pleased to see her up so early and so close to where he draws his spiritual strength.

'You seem troubled, Mai Li. Maybe you should embrace our culture further.'

'It does nothing for me, Father. You forget I've been raised Christian.'

'Let's hope that being a Christian will not bar you from taking a little breakfast with your father.'

'I'm not sure I'm even hungry.'

'Well, I am. So how about just keeping your father company

then? We can discuss what you've learned from your work experience.'

'I don't wish to talk about other people's lives when I know so little about my own – or yours. You never talk about my mother, yet you've promised me you would since I was seven.'

Mai Li's outburst makes her father uneasy. He's used to hard-nosed business types; he has little experience of dealing with his emotional daughter, except throwing money at any issues that arise She sits down on a chair and averts her welling eyes from him.

'Are you uncomfortable with your lifestyle, Mai Li?' he asks, trying to divert her from the subject.

'You could have all the wealth in the world, Father, and still feel empty when there's something missing.'

'Why do you think something is missing when I can give you anything in this world? And all this is for you.'

'That's it, money again. It's always your answer to everything, isn't it?'

'So, would you rather I sold what you are destined to inherit?'

'You made it, Father, it's yours to do with as you wish,' she says, getting up to leave.

'Wait, sit down, please.'

He sits down beside her, taking her hand in his.

'I know being an only child must be hard for you, Mai Li, but it's even harder being a single parent. If I've kept my past from you, that's only my strange way of protecting you.'

'You can protect me, Father, by explaining what it is you are protecting me from. I bet you didn't have these problems when you were a child.'

'When I was a child? I grew up as bitter a young man as you could find. My father was a merchant sailor whom I saw once a month if I was lucky and the schedule of his ship happened to take him home to Dalian. We lived in a little town on the southern tip of the Liaodong Peninsula, where I was born. We were poor back then in every sense of the word. My parents barely kept their heads above water, even with them both working. When I was around twelve years old, I used to help my father loading his ship, but there were no extra rewards for that. It was only for the experience of spending as much time as possible with him before he set sail again. I missed him so much after each visit I decided I would leave with him the next time he came home. I told no one of this plan, not even my father.

'It was almost two months before he returned the next time, and I had counted each day. On that day he was due to leave again, I helped him load the ship as usual. Half an hour before the ship was due to depart, I hugged him so tight. The tears in his eyes told me I was making the right decision. When I left the quay, it must have seemed strange to my father; before, I had always waited until the ship sailed before leaving for home. In my mind, nothing had changed. I would follow my father. Being familiar to most of the crew made it easy to stroll back on board unchallenged. Once the coast was clear, I concealed myself in a lifeboat and stayed there until the ship sailed. I had no idea where the next stop would be, and I soon remembered the benefit of a good meal. I hadn't thought out the finer details of my adventure.

'Anyway, after a day and a very cold night sitting in the lifeboat's hull, I heard whistling. The tune I knew well. It was one of my father's favourites. I lifted the heavy tarpaulin and there he was, tidying ropes not ten feet from me. Making him aware of my presence was easy, but, while his face glowed to see me, he was furious at my stupidity. He was angry at the danger I'd placed myself and him in, not to mention what my mother would have been going through. He could see from my condition I needed food. But when they caught him stealing a second time, they bound him and threw him overboard.'

The emotion of having to relive the story brings tears to his eyes, and Mai Li also wells up. Composing himself, he continues with his story.

'He didn't tell them the reason he needed extra food. That saved my life, but they found me during a routine clean and sold me to a factory soon after arriving in Hong Kong. It was a few years before I felt confident enough to escape. Others had, but they were all caught and brought back. I considered myself lucky, and once I'd saved enough money doing whatever work I found, I returned home to Dalian. I was too late, arriving home two days after my mother had died. She had no money, so I couldn't imagine the life she must have had without us. I swore then that one day I would avenge the cruel treatment of my father. I would make money in any way possible and as soon as I was able I would buy that boat and make every crew member and their family redundant and suffer as I did.'

'And did you?' Mai Li asks, hoping to hear how her father avenged her grandfather's death.

'I bought it, yes. But two wrongs don't make a right, and it still makes me money to this day.'

'Thank you, Father,' she says, wiping her eyes. 'I can see now how painful this is for you.'

'I'm even hungrier for my breakfast now,' he says, standing up. 'Are you sure you won't join me?'

'Maybe I can manage a piece of toast,' she says, smiling.

Leaving the room, they start together down the corridor, turning left at the hallway walking towards the kitchen.

'You must try to enjoy life, Mai Li. It's the one thing that's guaranteed to be shorter than you expect.'

'I don't think that far ahead though, Father.'

'Then you should. You must be aware I'm not getting any younger. Who will I leave all this to?' He turns in a circle, pointing out the spoils of his success.

Mai Li doesn't answer, and the rest of the journey to the kitchen is made in pin-drop silence.

As they enter the kitchen, they see Chi, Dr Minn's bodyguard and driver, sitting at a separate table in the corner.

'He makes me uneasy,' Mai Li whispers to her father at the kitchen entrance.

'Who? Chi?'

'Yes. And are you aware that all the other staff call him "the Full Midget". He's always watching me. I've seen him.'

'He's effective but harmless. It's better than having a guard dog, and having to clean up all the hairs afterwards.'

Chi smiles and Mai Li quickly links arms with her father to move past him and get to a large table, where she sits adjacent to her father at one corner with her back to Chi.

The chef comes to the table as they sit and bows before speaking.

'Are you ready for breakfast, sir?'

'Yes, two poached eggs on brown, please.'

'And for miss?' the chef asks.

'Toast, please.' She looks over at Chi, who is looking in her direction.

'See, Father, he's looking at me again.'

'Forget about him. Tell me what you learned from the prison visit and your boss.'

'I learned it's not a particularly nice place.'

'They do not mean these places to be holiday venues, you know.'

'Why are you so interested in him, anyway?'

'I'm more interested in your boss's methods.'

'He's not my boss,' she snaps. 'It doesn't even feel like a real job.'

'If you want to remain here, you must respect him as your boss.'

'I don't disrespect him. I know nothing about him.'

'Good. Now, I'm still waiting to hear something of interest.'

'There's nothing interesting to tell, Father. He asks everyone the same questions. So apart from him not being able to predict or control their answers, there is nothing.'

'So, you really haven't learned anything?'

'I was taking notes. Anyone could have done that, even a stupid tape machine.'

'It's a waste of your talent, true, but it will be worth it. Please have faith.'

'Why can't I do more of those computer amendments?'

'That was a one-off. That computer glitch is patched now and the data restored from the backup.'

Their breakfast arrives and the conversation stops. The chef sets the food out on the table before them.

'Will there be anything else, sir, miss?'

Mai Li shakes her head.

'That will be all, thanks,' Dr Minn says.

Mai Li puts down the toast she's eating and addresses her father without looking at him.

'You know everything you told me upstairs about your life and Grandpa's?'

'Do you have a question about it?'

'No, and I appreciate what little you've told me.'

'So why do I fear there's a "but" coming?'

'Because you've never told me about my mother. Don't you think I'm mature enough to handle whatever it is you are shielding me from?'

He stops eating, wipes crumbs from his lips and places the napkin beside his plate. Pausing as if to construct his response, he raises his head slowly and turns to his daughter.

'My daughter, why do you choose the one subject guaranteed to bring tears to my eyes and hurt my heart?'

'Because it's the one thing missing from my life and it causes me to cry too.'

'Thinking about that part of my life is painful.'

'But I need something, Father. Something of my mother to hold on to, just for me. I get these strange feelings every so often, as if she's alive. But you've always said she isn't, so it's hard to explain.'

'How often do you feel like this?'

'Most days, when my thoughts aren't occupied by something

else. I even felt it while in the prison when I should have been distracted. That's why I need to know all I can about her, and maybe that will stop me going mad.' She looks down then buries her head in her hands. He places a hand on her back attempting to comfort her.

'I too wish she were still with us. And soon, when I feel strong enough, we'll talk about her.'

'Is that a real promise this time, Father?' she asks, lowering her hands looking over at him.

'It's a promise that I will make real.'

Mai Li leans across and embraces her father.

'Thank you. Thank you so much,' she says, her eyes now softened and teary. 'I don't even know things like how you both met.'

'You really want to know? Is that what interest's young people these days?'

'It's only interesting because it's you, Father. And when you can finally trust me with the information, it will become part of my history too.'

'It's not a matter of trust, Mai Li. This leaves me open, vulnerable even. All the things I swore would never affect my life again. By telling you, it will undoubtedly affect yours too. So, believe it or not, I'm always thinking about you in all my life choices.'

'But I'm strong enough, Father.'

'When you were a little girl, I'd practice telling you this. Knowing that you were too young to understand or ask questions. It kept me focused on why I needed to protect you.'

Dr Minn pauses for a moment.

'I had gone on a pre-wedding celebration with five friends.'

'You can say the word "stag do" you know, Father.'

'If you keep interrupting, I can do this another time.'

'No, no, I'm sorry. I'm listening.'

'Anyway, we ended up in a nightclub, a place alien to my culture, my everything. I was trying to fit in by pretending I could cope. The drinking, the loud music, a different experience they were calling fun. Anyway, your mother must have been standing somewhere behind me, because my first encounter was her silky soft voice. I turned around and there she was. I had nothing to say because my mouth was dry and felt as twisted as my stomach. After a few moments of staring at each other, a random man approached, trying to engage with her in conversation. All the time she kept looking at me. Her eyes were telling me she needed rescuing, so I stepped closer and said, "There you are, darling". The man got the message and blended back into the crowd. She thanked me and offered to buy me a drink, but I declined, as my father always said it's a man's job to provide for a woman. Our relationship was on one day and off the next, and it made no sense, I couldn't see why. She was also away a lot. It was sometimes up to two weeks before I'd see her again.'

'Where was she?' Mai Li asks, trying to keep the tap of information running.

'I don't know. I thought it was work, or perhaps something to do with the government.'

'And you didn't think to ask her directly? That's unlike you, Father.'

'No, I didn't ask her. Somehow I felt that at that stage of knowing her it might have driven her away.' He takes a bite from a piece of toast and looks at his daughter, sitting focused on his every word. A moment of realisation washes over him, and he considers that maybe, just maybe, he should have done this a long time ago, as he'd promised.

He heaves a huge sigh, looks into his daughter's eyes, and continues. 'Things changed,' he starts, then looks down at the table. 'Things changed.' He appears to not know what his next words should be.

Mai Li tries to put him back on track. 'Things changed?'

'Yes, things did, especially when she told me she was pregnant. I suppose my first thoughts were that it was not my child. That was because of all the time we spent apart, and I still didn't know where she went or who she was with. The prospect of having a child soon overwhelmed those thoughts, though. I tried to get things into perspective and told her how I would look after her and our baby, but it wasn't enough. She disappeared once again and this time she didn't come back after two weeks.' He takes another sip of tea. 'After a few weeks, I gave up searching. In China, you won't be found if you don't want to be.'

'So how come I'm here with you if you couldn't find her?'

'Chance, luck? Maybe a combination of both, I suspect. Who knows? I'm just glad it happened. It was a call I got out the blue one day from a friend who had attended the stag do. He told me he had seen her at a private maternity hospital, where his wife was giving birth. I didn't know what to think, but I've always chosen the path that offered greater enlightenment. When I got there, to tell the truth, I didn't know why I'd bothered at all. It wasn't like she wanted to see me. She knew where I was throughout her pregnancy and yet it was someone else who told me. It wasn't visiting time, but you soon learn the value of money when you can pay a nurse to get you in.'

'She must have been excited to see you, though?' asks Mai Li.

'Her reaction was more like shock. She looked pale. Her face and arms were bruised. Her beauty... her beauty was, for that moment, gone.'

Mai Li's hands cover her mouth. She shakes her head but continues to listen.

'I feared even touching her. I could see the pain in her eyes. She told me I couldn't stay but offered no reason why I should leave. There were two cribs in the room; in one was a tiny baby wrapped in a cotton blanket, eyes closed, sucking the air. I stood there and watched for a few moments and the baby shuddered as if she was being disturbed in a dream.'

'Was that me?'

'Yes, it was you.'

'So, what happened?'

'Your mother said, "If you want your child, you better take her and leave now". I asked about her, but she insisted that I needn't worry about her and should concentrate on giving you a better life. I pleaded with her that whatever it was we could get through it, there was still a future. But she insisted that I leave with you and forget her. She helped put a few things into a plastic bag, put you in my arms and almost pushed us out the door. When I got home, I rang the colleague to thank him, but what he said shocked me.'

'What did he say, Father?'

'He congratulated me on the birth of my twins. That's why there were two cribs in the room. And before you ask, yes, I went back straight away, but she had gone. Girls in China in those days had little to no value. When I think back, I was lucky that I got there in time to save you.'

'So, I'm a twin and my brother is out there somewhere?'

'I couldn't say and I have no way of confirming it. Raising you became the only focus of my life.'

'And you couldn't have raised it with the authorities to try to find them?'

'You're listening yet you're not hearing, Mai Li. China's one-child policy meant trouble or even death for anyone involved in breaking the law. They would have taken you away and who knows where you would have ended up. Thankfully the police were corrupt, so I moved as soon as I could to Hong Kong.'

'You have nothing, not even a photo?'

'The plastic bag contained this.' Dr Minn unbuttons the top two buttons of his shirt and extracts a gold pendant. It measures about two inches in diameter and has a unique design of a dragon on one side and a lotus flower on the other.

'That looks familiar,' says Mai Li.

'And it should. It's your birth scar, which is an exact imprint of this lotus flower.' Dr Minn turns the pendant round to show her.

'And what does the other side look like? Do you mind if I see it?' Mai Li holds the pendant in her hand and flips it over.

'It's all I've ever had of your mother apart from you,' says Dr Minn.

# CHAPTER 19

It's the morning after lockdown at Downing Prison, bringing a delicate but serene calm following the rowdy protests that only petered out sometime after eleven last night. In the main, most inmates realised early on that no measure of protest would do anything other than disrupt their night's sleep. Earlier, during his rounds, the doctor informed Mr Salerno he was all clear and well enough to expect an early return to the familiar environment of his cell.

The sick prisoner who arrived last night has just woken and sits up in bed. Fat Fingers, well aware they'll come for him before the prison gets busy, starts a conversation.

'Something I should have asked last night,' he declares.

'What troubles you?' the man asks.

'The plans you have for the chip, should I worry about innocent people getting hurt?'

'No less than the propaganda your country feeds to the world.'

'I'm not sure that's an answer.'

'According to the United Nations, one child dies every two minutes from the causes of war in my country, yet the people of this country are blind to this suffering, caused by the arms they supply to the Saudis. The real question, Mr Fingers, is does my answer invalidate our deal?'

'No, I stand by my word, but it's worth you knowing it's my conscience asking that question.'

'Mr Fingers, I—' He starts then halts mid-sentence as the doors to the ward burst open and a group of prison officers enter, with Officer Newport at the helm and the doctor trailing behind.

'Right,' exclaims Newport in a loud authoritative voice, 'listen up. You know me, and the instructions I'll give will be given once and once only. To question them or stall is a direct threat to my authority and will be dealt with as such. If you follow my instructions, we will all make breakfast in a better mood.'

'Excuse me, Mr Newport, a private word, if you please,' the doctor requests.

'Yes, what is it?' Newport turns to face the doctor, annoyed at being stopped in mid-flow.

'The chap who arrived last night.'

'What about him?'

'Well, he needs to stay here for at least another twenty-four hours.'

'But I can't see anything wrong with him, doctor,' Newport says, looking over at the man sitting up in bed.

'That's why I'm the doctor here and you are not. Look, if we release him without identifying whatever illness he arrived with, we run the risk of infecting the whole prison. Now, will you take responsibility for that?' Newport looks disappointed.

'Fine,' concedes Newport. 'Okay, Mr Salerno, looks like it's just you today, so let's show this foreigner the standards we expect at Downing. Let's have you standing facing your bed with both hands behind your back.'

The officers move to apply handcuffs to Fat Fingers before flanking him.

'Prisoner on the move,' Newport says into his radio, before turning to lead the way out of the ward.

~

In the army, the labels 'interrogations' or 'interviews' used to be applied to the process needed to extract information. Done right, you would be hard-pressed to notice one approach as being better than the other. During his military service, Officer Newport had used and was skilled at both, unlike the modern approach, where prisoners' rights are often at the forefront of the interrogators' mind even before they take any action.

Downing's windowless interview room boasts plain rendered walls, a table, two metal chairs bolted to the floor and the all-important cluster of lights suspended from the concrete ceiling. The whole interview is overseen and captured from an adjacent room.

Governor Riley sits observing Officer Newport and his team from the control room. The first of the men picked up from the Channel Tunnel enters the room to be interviewed. He looks tired, or maybe he's just bewildered.

He's unshackled and seated facing Newport. The chaperoning officers take up positions either side of the exit while Newport and the prisoner stare at each other, until the prisoner breaks eye contact to take in his surroundings.

Newport stands and takes a few steps around the table. He half sits on the table with one foot still on the ground.

'Okay! What would you like us to call you?' He looks down at the prisoner, who stares back in silence. 'Where have you come from? And what is your purpose for entering this country?' Newport moves around the prisoner and sits on his other side. The prisoner's eyes track his movement in silence.

'English! You understand? *A kupton? Ant tafahum?*' Newport tries his limited Albanian and Arabic. The prisoner remains mute in response to all questions.

Newport looks at his wristwatch then covertly signals to the control room, holding up four fingers.

'Stop recording,' the governor orders the operator.

Newport removes his cap and extracts a hypodermic needle from its lining in full view of the prisoner. Placing it on the table, he sets his cap to one side, then removes his jacket, hanging it on the back of his chair. With his back to the prisoner, he rolls up his sleeves and nods to the two officers, which signals their move forward, one either side of the prisoner. The prisoner glances between the officers standing over him.

Newport picks up the needle, tapping it to force any air out. He expels a small amount of fluid from the needle as he nods again to the officers, who grab an arm each. The prisoner resists and fights back, pushing an officer off him and freeing one hand. The prisoner grunts, groans and grits his teeth in a show of defiance.

The officer still holding one arm forces it behind the prisoner's back, while the other grabs his head in a chokehold. Still struggling, the prisoner only offers animal-like groans. The officer with the chokehold forces the prisoner's torso down onto the table, then, using a strong forearm, he pins the prisoner's head. The prisoner grimaces and gasps for air, but he's held tight.

'This is so unnecessary, but it's still not too late. Keep him still,' Newport orders, raising the needle.

The sight of it kicks off a fresh round of struggles but the officers have full control, pinning the prisoner to the table. Newport lowers and tilts his head, mirroring the prisoner to offer him a final chance to talk.

'Fucking mother of mercy!' He curses, as he straightens up quickly, turning away and makes the sign of the cross. 'Let him go he can't tell us anything.'

'How do you know, sir?' the officer freeing the prisoner's head asks.

'Because, even if we beat him to within an inch of his life, this man has no tongue.' He answers, putting the needle back into its cover then into his hat. Smoothing his hair back into place after the shock with his fingers, Newport shares his immediate thoughts.

'Someone has gone to a lot of trouble, to guarantee his silence.'

'Sir, have a look at this here,' says the officer still securing the prisoner's arm.

'What is it?' Newport moves closer.

'There, on his wrist, see it?' The officer struggles to keep the hand still.

'No, let him go, we'll have a better chance of seeing it.'

The officer loosens his grip, allowing the prisoner to sit up again in the chair. He rubs at his wrists, tender from the ordeal.

Newport takes his seat again and reaches for the prisoner's hand. He resists at first but Newport coaxes him into allowing him to see. Tattooed on the palm-side wrist of the left hand are four numbers.

'I want photos taken of these numbers before you take him back. Then pick another one, at random, for the next interview; have you got that?'

'Sir.'

'Okay, get going. Wait! One more thing.'

'Sir.'

'I want them monitored twenty-four seven. Whether they're sleeping, eating or taking a dump, we need to know their every movement. Got that?'

'Yes, sir.' The two officers handcuff the prisoner, then escort him away. Newport walks the short distance to the adjacent control room where Governor Riley swivels his chair round to face him.

'What's your thinking on this so far? Your hunches are often on point,' the governor asks.

'Maybe once I've seen a few of the others, I'll have a better idea. But as for gut instinct, I've got nothing so far.'

After twenty minutes the monitors show the two officers

returning to the interview room with the second of the Channel Tunnel prisoners.

'I'd better get back in there,' Newport announces, leaving the control room. The monitors show Newport as he re-enters the interview room.

'Okay, let's try a different tack,' Newport says, sitting down, placing his hands on the table. 'Don't remove the handcuffs, it should make things easier. We'll start by seeing what's in his mouth.' He sits back in his chair as one officer moves to restrain the prisoner, holding him from behind around the neck. The second officer pinches the prisoner's nose. After less than thirty seconds his mouth opens as he struggles to breathe. Newport leans forward to look. Just like the previous prisoner, this one's tongue is also missing.

'Let him go. We just need to check his wrists.' With the prisoner still handcuffed, it's easy for the officers to manoeuvre him into a position where his left wrist is visible. Once again, there are tattooed numbers, a clear sign that some kind of link exists, at least between the two men seen so far. Newport stands and walks towards the door. The prisoner watches him all the way.

'I want all their hands photographed. I also want all the others checked to confirm if they're also missing tongues. Once that's all done, bring me the results,' he instructs before returning to the control room, where he takes a seat this time.

'Excellent job, Mr Newport,' the governor says. 'You would have thought it would be the first thing the police should have picked up on.'

'They're all about human rights these days, Governor, and that Geneva shit. I bet that's the only reason they sent them to us.'

'It looks like you've stumbled onto something. However, the security services are still looking for answers... like yesterday.'

'But you know yourself, Governor... there's information and there's quality information.'

'Well, do your best, as always. I've got a few calls to make back in my office, so the minute you have anything…'

'Sir.' Newport acknowledges the governor's departure.

Later, around mid-morning, Newport receives the requested data. Even with the photos spread out on his table, he's finding it hard to see connections between the pattern of numbers. Not knowing anything at all about the men bearing the numbers is not helping. Further information passed on by the governor confirms that they didn't apprehend all the migrants, which implies the data itself might also be incomplete. Newport's naturally inquisitive mind has drawn a blank this time. He feels a little nauseated, a feeling he gets only when his gut clashes with his logic. From the prisoners' hairstyles to their shoes, nothing is overtly obvious.

They must communicate somehow, he thinks. What about if they're being controlled? Maybe implants under their skin? He mentally takes his foot off the brake, allowing his mind to go full throttle, burning brain rubber. He picks up the telephone while that thought is still fresh, dialling a three-digit internal number.

'Doctor, it's Officer Newport.'

'What can I do for you, Mr Newport?'

'A question, Doctor. I was wondering if we have the facilities here at Downing to scan bodies for implants, say something as small as a microchip?'

'That's easy, Mr Newport, no. We're a prison not a vet's; anyway, budgets don't stretch to such extravagance,' the doctor says, laughing which Newport detects over the phone.

'It was only a thought. Thank you anyway.'

'I do have some good news for you, though.'

'Good news, Doctor?'

'Yes, all tests on the prisoner brought in overnight are now complete, and you're free to have him back as soon as you're ready.'

'And the risk of infection?'

'Gone, completely clear.'

'And you found nothing unusual about him?'

'Absolutely nothing. You seem to be questioning my expertise yet again, Mr Newport.'

'No, not at all, Doctor. Just trying to confirm that he has a tongue.'

'A tongue? Of course he has a tongue. Why wouldn't he?'

'That's even better news. I'll dispatch an escort for him right away. Thank you, Doctor.'

It's been half an hour since Newport spoke with the doctor. In the interview room, he awaits the prisoner and stands when he's brought in. He's already changing his tactics yet again for this interview, going for a less physical approach.

'Take a seat,' he says, careful not to sound condescending.

The prisoner looks at the chair before steering himself into it. Newport is assured of at least one fact: he understands English.

'Please place both hands on the table,' Newport instructs the prisoner. He complies and Newport orders that the cuffs are removed.

'Now, what is your name?' he continues.

'My name is Izsa Madas,' he replies, confirming he is not a tongue-less mute either. Officer Newport notes his answer.

'Where are you originally from, Mr Madas, and what purpose did you have for trying to enter the United Kingdom undetected? We know it's not for a holiday.' Newport turns Madas's hands over, checking them for tattooed numbers. The prisoner puts up no resistance and there's no evidence either of a tattoo, just a scar where he was anticipating finding it. Preoccupied in search of tattoos, Officer Newport fails to notice how the prisoner's hands are devoid of fingerprints.

'I want political asylum,' Madas answers. His voice is calm and his breathing natural.

'Well, before we can even talk about political asylum, we need to know your country of origin, then what it is you need protecting from.' Newport continues checking Madas's arms, rolling his shirt sleeves back further.

'If I tell you and get sent back, they will take my life.'

'If you don't, then we have the right to lock you up for the rest of that life.'

'Locked up or death – which would you choose, Mr Policeman?'

'I'd be happy to choose, once I know the facts.' Newport looks him straight in the face and finds his stare returned.

'How did you get this scar?' Newport asks, rotating the prisoner's hand, ensuring that it's visible.

'It was an attempt to take my own life,' Madas answers.

'And why was that?'

'I'm homosexual,' Madas reveals.

Newport gives up looking for tattoos, releasing Madas's arms. He sits back in his chair. He's forming an early opinion that Mr Madas may not have links to the others, but he still has niggling thoughts about everything.

'Mr Madas, how do you know the others picked up with you?'

'I don't,' he answers too quickly.

# CHAPTER 20

'Mr Newport! I've just this minute got off the phone with counterintelligence, where are we with our foreign problem?' The governor speaks, a little deflated, into the phone.

'With their physical impairment, things are proving trickier than we thought, Governor.'

'Well, they're now suggesting that the mutes are most likely monks.

'Monks, sir?'

'Yes, according to some professor of antiquities, documents found in their possession have been identified as ancient religious texts.'

'But what about their tongues and the tattooed numbers?'

'They understand it to be a vow of silence literally taken to its extreme to protect the secrets of the texts. It's thought the tattoos are just prison numbers.'

'And the one that can talk?'

'They're not sure about him but carry on for now.'

'There doesn't seem much point in light of what you've told me, Governor. However, I do have one last theory that may or may not turn up something. Anyway, before you go, Governor, we have another problem you need to know about.'

'Have you not been following my unwritten rule, Mr Newport?'

'The one that states that anything that distracts you from running the prison, I'm to deal with?'

'Good, glad you haven't forgotten.'

This is a sure-fire way the governor assures that others take the blame if things go wrong.

'Regardless of your rule, Governor, with respect I thought you'd be better off knowing why receipts are down this month on your pension scheme before you raise that question.'

The governor's pension scheme has little to do with his or prisoner's welfare and more to do with the future-proofing of his financial position. For years, through a network distributed by Fat Fingers, the governor has been the main source supplying cheap drugs to inmates.

'Okay, it's obvious you are itching to tell me something, so what is it?'

'The suppliers have mislaid one of the fire extinguishers. It would appear that our regular service engineer had a temporary helper. He may be the one responsible for leaving the unit in the wrong location.'

'The wrong location?'

'Well, the right location, but wrong for the scheme purpose, if you're following me?'

'Then you need to find it, along with who may have had any contact with it, then make the problem go away. Do you follow me, Mr Newport?'

'Indeed, Governor.'

Newport leaves his office for the interview room. He's determined to tackle one of his two most pressing problems. When he arrives, he acknowledges the two officers standing just inside the door. The prisoner already seated seems relaxed, only turning his head at the sound of the door closing.

Newport moves straight to the table, setting his papers down in a pile. The prisoner glances at the papers for a second before refocusing on Newport. Without words or eye contact, Newport removes his jacket, placing it on the back of his chair opposite the prisoner. He sets off, circling the table, while rolling up each shirt sleeve to a point below his elbows. The prisoner keeps his head still, only moving his eyes to follow Newport. After around two minutes Newport stops behind the prisoner, out of his view. Leaning over towards the prisoner's ear, Newport whispers, 'Mr Foreigner – I hope you don't mind me calling you that since I'm not sure I know your real name?'

The prisoner swallows hard, then speaks.

'It's Izsa, Izsa Madas. I told you this already, yesterday.'

Newport steps from behind to take his seat.

'Okay, Izsa. How are we spelling that? Never mind!' Newport says, interrupting him before he can answer. 'Instead, perhaps you could help me with another little question?'

'I'll do what I can,' Izsa says, half smiling.

'Take away that beard, and I imagine you probably have similar features to the others.'

'You mock my appearance.' Izsa acknowledges Newport's comment.

'It's just a general observation, that's all. So, the men arrested with you?'

'I don't know these people.'

He answers the question rather too quickly, like before, and Newport leans back in his chair, shaking his head.

'Call me suspicious, but I would bet your life that's a lie, Mr Izsa. Tell me about when you first met the others.'

'I don't know what you suggest, what you are accusing me of or what you wish me to say, Mr Policeman. You ask a question, I answer it, you ask the same again, what could I answer but the same again?'

Izsa, seems more agitated at the line of questioning Mr Newport has adopted.

'Look…' Newport leans forward again. 'The thing is, you've violated several laws just by entering this country. So, since we only welcome law-abiding people into this country, then we need to know why you broke our laws as your first step.'

'I want to claim asylum.'

'On what grounds?' Newport sits back, arms folded. 'You will need help, my help, to apply, but until I'm given satisfactory answers, I can't help you.'

'I claim because England is known the world over for upholding human rights.'

A knock at the door breaks the momentum of the interrogation. The door opens wide enough for a hand to pass a brown folder to one of the officers inside. The officer transfers the folder to Newport, who opens the folder for a brief look at its content before closing it and placing the folder on the pile of other papers.

Asking the officers to vacate the room, Newport holds up four fingers, his signal for those in the control room to halt any recording. He lowers his hand and directs his full focus to the prisoner.

'Okay, here's a little geography lesson for you. You want asylum in England, is that correct?'

Izsa nods. 'Yes, that's what I asked.'

'Well, right now we're not in England,' Newport says.

A wry smile appears on Izsa's face.

'I think it is you more than me in need of this geography lesson, my friend.'

'No, I assure you, we're not.' Newport is stone-faced and serious in his delivery.

'Then where do you claim we are?'

'China, and I don't claim.'

'I think you are joking at my expense. They say the British have the good sense of humour.'

'Mr Madas, no country jokes about matters of national security.'

168

'No, I still think you are having the game with me.'

'Okay, then let us make the game interesting. Please tell me where Guantanamo Bay is?'

Izsa affords himself a confident and broader smile.

'Cuba.'

'Wrong! That facility sits on US soil, which means they get to do whatever they damn well like. And I'm sure you've heard how they treat their guests?'

'So, this is America?'

'Wrong again.'

'Then where are we?'

'I've told you. Welcome to China, Mr Madas, where we'll guarantee your human rights. Oh no, wait! That's England, as you've rightly pointed out. Here we can guarantee you won't have any.'

Izsa's passive character changes. He seems to get the point, finally.

Newport signals for the recording to resume, standing up and pacing in a circle again.

'So, let me share with you what we know so far,' Newport bluffs. 'We know the others are possibly carrying codes. For who or what, we don't understand yet. It must be very important though, to go to such extremes as having their tongues removed. My gut feeling is that you're the link that binds it all together. Now, if we were to, say, eliminate you, then the whole plan stops. Am I right?' He concludes by sitting and facing Izsa again.

'I don't know if you are right or wrong because, I told you already many times now, I don't know those people. It is not unheard of for people who steal to have their hands removed or liars their tongues.'

'Then I'll let you into another of my little secrets. Ever since my Army days I've preferred the challenge of prisoners choosing the harder option, that's what gets me out of bed most days. So, you've told me your name; how about you tell me which country you're from?'

'I'm not prepared to say any more without a legal witness present.'

Newport picks up the brown folder again. Opening it, he slides out the single sheet of papers which he tilts away from Izsa's gaze to study. In his next action, he replaces the sheet and rests the folder back on the table.

'Yemen! Al Jawf Region, to be exact.'

'Where did you get this information?' asks Izsa.

'You told us.'

'I would have remembered making such a statement.' Izsa insists.

'Well indirectly. Let's just say DNA technology has given us an advantage. DNA, in your case, from blood taken to identify your mystery illness. Collected, mind you, to stop the spread of any virus throughout our prison – just a lucky move on our part hey. So, refusing to speak is only delaying us. We'll get there. But you could make things easier for yourself and your friends.'

'How many times must I repeat? I don't know them. And I don't understand why you keep insisting that's not the case?'

'You were all picked up together.'

'Nothing more than pure coincidence. Please, trust me.'

'Fine, have it your way for now.'

A knock at the door halts the interview and Newport goes over to see who it is.

'Yes, what is it?'

'The prisoner's legal representative has turned up and is demanding immediate access to see his client, sir.'

'Okay, give me two minutes then you can have him.'

Closing the door again, Newport returns to his seat.

'It seems like there's someone here to see you.'

'Who?'

'You'll find out soon enough, I just need to know what you would like me to put on this asylum application.' Newport opens another folder and waits.

'I may not need it, if they have come to secure my release.'

'Even if that were the case, paperwork would take days, if not weeks... so?'

'You put homosexual.'

'Okay. But just so you know, it's not something you want to be advertising in this prison. I'm sure we will talk again very soon.'

Officer Newport finishes writing his notes then gathers the folders before leaving the room. He informs the two officers outside to escort Mr Madas to his appointment.

As he reaches his office, the officer tasked with finding the missing fire extinguisher approaches.

'Sir, we've located the missing appliance. We found it near area seventeen, close to the staff canteen. But it's damaged and we can't see any sign it's been used. In fact, it's so clean, it doesn't look like they ever filled it.'

'It must be a demo one that got mixed up,' Newport says, thinking fast.

'That makes sense.'

'We'll leave it to the experts, hey? Just get it back to stores and I can handle it from there. Well done.'

He closes the door to his office and calls the governor.

'Governor, we've found the missing extinguisher, but someone has compromised it either accidentally or they know all about our operation.'

'Any suggestions?'

'Yeah, we suspend things. In the meantime, I'll check the security cameras. I'll also have a chat with our source to find out what's gone wrong.'

'Get it done, and quickly. Under no circumstances can we have a repeat of this mess, do you understand?'

'Completely, as always, sir.'

Newport wastes no time calling their supplier.

'You almost put us in the shit; don't you have control of your operatives?'

'I must apologise,' says a soft-spoken female voice. 'We were a man short, so the agency sent a replacement. If we didn't complete the servicing as per contract, there was every chance we could have lost the contract altogether. Think of the bigger risk that would have posed.'

'Are you sure that replacement was legit?'

'We have no reason to suspect him. In fact, he did a fantastic job, everything by the book, straight out of the training manual.'

'Then you'd better be careful. Any leaks and you're on your own.'

'I've never known it not to be the case,' she replies.

'Well, for the moment, let's suspend the next two deliveries. That should throw up a blank trail for anybody following.'

'What do I do with the stuff already in the pipeline?'

'Help me out here, for Christ's sake, and do some thinking for the level of benefits you've enjoyed up to now.'

'Okay, ah, leave it to me.'

'That's exactly what I will be doing. Don't mess this up. People higher up the chain are still not pleased about the previous break in their pension funding.'

Later, Newport's check of the security system boosts his theory that someone knows, as none of the cameras picked up or recorded any part of the incident.

# CHAPTER 21

The next morning at Downing Prison's staff entrance, the queue is moving but slow. Officer Newport stands just after the security desk waiting for his briefcase to pass its scanning test. His usual morning banter with the operator hasn't occurred as he's focused on finding out why a car occupies his personal parking slot.

'There's a car in my space.'

'If it's the dark blue one, then it's an unmarked police car.'

'What happened here during the night?'

'Unfortunately, there's been another death.'

'Do you know, who?'

'No, but I'm hearing it happened around the time of their evening meal. You'd have gone home by then.'

'Thanks.'

Newport picks up his briefcase and starts towards the security office, where he finds the night manager still there.

'Morning, Charles.'

'Mr Newport.'

'I hear we lost another one last night?'

'Yeah, another one of those scenarios where their heart just stopped. I'm slowly coming around to the notion that there's a virus in this damn place. But, the only thing stopping me is that the other two post-mortems don't bear out my theory. They've found no trace of any known virus.'

'Who was the unlucky sod that pegged it then?'

'One of the foreign intake from the other night.'

'Which one?'

'The only one that could talk it seems. Maybe it was natural causes – wasn't he sick when he arrived?'

'Damn, that's all I need, back to square one. Where exactly was he found? And have we interviewed whoever found him yet?'

'No witnesses. Our priority was to contain the other inmates so we could do a proper recovery of the body. He was in the toilets next to the canteen.'

'No witnesses? I want you to find out if anyone was watching him from the time he left his cell. And get that information to me ASAP.'

'Sure, but I'm about to clock off shortly, so I'll get one of the day mob to chase it up for you. They're expecting the post-mortem results this morning anyway and they might turn up something.'

'One last thing, Charles. How did the other foreigners react to his death?'

'From what was observed, pretty much business as usual.'

'We're missing something. The elephant in the room is getting bigger and we can't even see its damn trunk. Tell me at least we're still monitoring everything they do?'

'Yes, of course we are.'

'Good, then I want whatever you've collected so far brought to my office as soon as. And Charles, go home and get your rest.'

Newport leaves security for his office with nothing more than a steadfast determination to solve the problem of the tattooed sequence and what it meant.

After five minutes in his office, there's a firm knock at his door.

'Come in,' he orders.

'Sir.'

He looks up at the warden who has entered. 'Ah, it's you from the other night, isn't it? Our so-called drugs expert. How come that was the first time I'd seen you in this prison?

'Because it was my first time on shift and it did seem to be busy with a lot going on.'

'I suppose there was, so what can I do for you?'

The warden is about to speak when Newport's mobile, which is on his desk, rings.

'One second please,' says Newport. He glances at the phone, noting the caller ID before muting it. 'Right, go ahead.'

'I've got the surveillance information you requested about those prisoners downloaded to this USB, sir,' the warden says, presenting the device.

'How come they got you to do this?' says Newport, receiving the device.

'When you're new in any job, they take advantage and load you up with all the things no one else wants.'

'And how does that make you feel? Because when I first started over twenty years ago it was the same, a way of testing a warden's resolve to stick at a job in the prison service.'

'Oh, I can cope, sir. I'm used to my own company. I realise that sounds weird, but it's not really. And I'm not – weird, that is. I'm just a thinker, that's all.'

'If that's the case, if you've watched it, did you notice anything unique about these prisoners, to save me looking through every frame?'

'I did, not sure how relevant, being a bit more comical than anything.'

'What?'

'Well, at each meal they shuffle and reposition themselves into the same order. Not certain if it's a pecking order related to age, as they all look around a similar age. It may even be just their custom. Either way, it's consistent and they do it every time.'

Newport smiles. 'Like I said before, we need men like you who can think beyond the boundaries.'

'Thank you, sir.'

'One last thing. Can you identify and arrange them into that order?'

'Yeah, I'm sure I can.'

'Okay, here's what I want you to do. It might be a long shot, but my thinking is, when they were being tattooed they did exactly the same thing. I'm also hoping whoever controls them hadn't noticed it. So round them up. Wait! It might be better to allow them to line up for breakfast naturally. As soon as they are in order, I want you to move in and record that sequence of numbers and get it straight back to me. Is that clear?'

'Yes, sir, clear.'

'What's your name, son?'

'Stuart Naylor, sir.'

'Okay, Stuart, if I'm not here you'll find me with the governor. Off you go then.'

Newport checks his watch. It's nearing 8 am. They rarely see the governor before nine thirty. He uses that window each day to catch up and collect information on prison matters. Taking out his phone, he returns the call he elected not to take while Stuart was in his office.

'Yes, what is it?' he asks once they answer.

'I have more information for you after speaking with the agency temp again. He claims he placed the extinguisher exactly where he was told. He also remembers someone in a prison uniform moving it when he passed it again, after deploying the others.'

'Did he get a good look at them?'

'No, only that they were wearing a prison uniform.'

'Well, I suppose that's useful information of sorts. If he remembers anything else, I would appreciate a further call.'

He hangs up and settles down to make a start on clearing paperwork. He keeps one eye on the time to ensure that he's ready when the governor arrives for their daily briefing. At around nine fifteen he selects the file needed and leaves his office.

~

Governor Riley arrives at the prison by 9 am. He was still at home when he was notified of another death in his prison.

At nine twenty, Officer Newport arrives in the governor's secretary's office.

'Morning, Cynthia.'

'He's already here,' she whispers, pointing to the governor's office.

'Thanks,' Newport says, knocking on the door.

'Come in,' the governor's voice calls from within.

'Good morning, Governor. Wasn't expecting you this early.' Newport closes the door behind him.

'Yes, I only remembered last night I have a scheduled meeting at the ministry for three this afternoon.'

'About what?'

'They don't tell me beforehand any more. Let's hope it's not about more cuts. Staff levels are already well below that recommended two years ago. It would only affect morale even further.'

'You heard what happened last night, then?'

'Yes, yet another death to deal with. I'm close to accepting that there may well be a virus in this prison. That's three now in the last two months. What do you make of it?'

'I'm like you, entirely in the dark, Governor. Unless medical come up with something, we can only look on this death like the others, as unexplained.'

'Damn it,' the governor curses, and pounds the table.

'His death is a tad inconvenient. Since he was the only one that could speak.'

'That's right, so where are we now with this issue?'

'Setbacks aside, we've still got a thin strand which I'm hoping I can weave into a full carpet.'

'I wish you'd talk straight, Mr Newport. Metaphors are too much for me first thing in the morning.'

The governor's phone buzzes.

'Yes, Cynthia,' he answers.

'I have a warden out here, Governor, who wants to talk with Mr Newport.'

'Tell him he'll be out in a minute.'

'It's that young warden I alluded to, the one I mentioned who is smart and thinks outside the box,' says Newport.

'The same one I advised you to be vigilant of?'

'Yes, that's him, hopefully with information I'm waiting for.' Newport heads for the door, opening it sharply.

Taken by surprise, Stuart Naylor stands up rather hurriedly from resting on Cynthia's desk, an action that doesn't go unnoticed by Newport.

'I have that sequence you requested, sir,' he says, presenting a single sheet of A4.

'Thank you, you've done well. I may call on you again soon to do something special for me. Think you'll be up for it?'

'I'll be up for anything, sir.'

'Good, off you go then.'

Newport can't help but notice the chemistry between Cynthia and Naylor. Something that couldn't have developed in the short time he spent waiting outside. There had to be more to it. Cynthia is single, older and attractively interesting in her own way. But I'm married and don't know how others might be reacting to loneliness. Newport re-enters the governor's office.

'What have you got?' the governor asks.

'I haven't looked yet, but I know what it should be.' Newport places the sheet on the desk. 'Let me explain. None of the prisoners with the tattoos have any way of telling us what they mean. Neither could we work it out, the permutations being far too many to calculate. What we noticed, though, was how they naturally arranged themselves. This represents that observation,' he says, pointing to the sheet of paper.

'And it's telling us what exactly?'

'I'll admit it's nothing more than a sequence. For what? It's still no clearer, I mean it could be map coordinates, anything.'

The governor's telephone rings again with Cynthia informing him this time that the doctor from the medical centre wishes to speak with Officer Newport.

'I'll take it outside, sir,' Newport says, standing up.

'Put it through here please, Cynthia,' the governor orders.

'Are you sure, Governor?'

'Yes, yes, go ahead,' he confirms.

Newport picks up the phone and selects the flashing line.

'Newport speaking… What! Are you sure? Thanks for letting me know so quickly.'

'Have you got something?' the governor asks.

'Yeah, but not good news, Governor, he's telling me that the post-mortem shows that the person who died last night was not our Mr Madas.'

'Impossible!'

'It seems that he may have swapped clothes and traded places with his legal visitor who turned up yesterday and simply walked out of this prison.'

'Shit! That's the bloody last thing I needed to hear right now. I need you, Mr Newport, to look into whether anyone in this prison has been complicit in any way that aided his escape. I've got to get onto the intelligence service immediately and let them know what's happened. It also means he's got a good eighteen hours' head start and could be anywhere in the country by now.'

With news of another unexplained death reaching all corners of Downing, Fat Fingers is none too pleased when he hears the supposed identity of the victim, especially with the agreed money yet to be transferred and the chip secured.

However, he recognises the death as being the clumsy work of

Dozer. Far from being an asset, Dozer is now losing him clients and money. A trend he will not allow to continue indefinitely. This latest incident is just one in a long line that shows his growing lack of respect. Dozer needs pegging back before his actions are seen by others as a direct challenge to Fat Fingers' authority. One thing that Fat Fingers prides himself on is his ability to offer the right amount of money and at a level that even your mother would betray you.

He knows exactly what he needs to do to shrink Dozer down to size. It only requires one phone call and the loyalty of those he really trusts to make it happen.

# CHAPTER 22

The rooms at the ministry reflect its archaic nature, the government's low-spend policy unashamedly retaining the décor of yesteryear. Any reference to its drabness gets one of two rehearsed answers: the need to protect our historical buildings or the lack of any budget for change.

As the clock on the wall nears 3 pm, all attendees gather around a large oval table in the Nelson room. Finding their designated places, everyone quickly settles. Each place has its allotted bottle of unbranded spring water and an A4 notepad in a leather-bound folder. Once they're seated, Sir Edward brings the meeting to order.

'Good afternoon and welcome everyone. I can see we are all here so, let's make a start. First...,'

Sir Edward is forced to halt immediately, taking a side glance in the direction of a mobile that's gradually getting louder.

'Oh, I'm sorry everyone,' the governor apologises. 'I really have to take this call, it's a matter of national security.'

The governor stands and exits the room with his mobile pressed firmly against his ear.

'Martin, thanks for getting back to me.'

'Rick, listen, what choice did I have, if only to tell you that you fucked up allowing a high-risk prisoner like that to just walk out of Downing.'

'I can assure you, Martin, that this embarrassing incident was not an intentional act on our part.'

'Intentional or not Rick, the outcome is still the same, we have a dangerous man loose. The ironic thing is, we had advanced plans to come and fetch him from you, once we were in possession of new intelligence.'

'What new intelligence? We got little to nothing from him.'

'The prisoner calling himself Izsa Madas is in fact Sadam Benwadi, a twenty-seven-year-old Yemeni national who studied Optical Engineering here eight years ago. He was arrested for activities unassociated with his studies as a student and deported. Although his file shows he never finished his degree, it also contains a warning that he's extremely clever and capable of designing advanced weapons systems.'

'Surely you would have picked that up from his fingerprints on arrest?'

'Rick, come on, we do this every day. If there were prints it wouldn't have taken us this long to allow you to lose him.'

'Okay, I take the point, Martin, and again I'm sorry to have let the side down. I've got to get back to my meeting, bye.'

Putting his mobile on silent, the governor re-enters the room, where whatever was being discussed in his absence ends suddenly, with all eyes focusing on him as he takes his seat again. Sir Edward attempts to restart the meeting.

'Joining us today, eventually, is Governor Patrick Riley from Downing Prison, who I believe has served his country and profession with the same tenacity for roughly thirty years. I'd like to extend a warm welcome also to Doctor Minn, who is the main representative for Lotto-Guard, the company in charge of delivering the new court system. Mr Ian Gilby, who's the consultant advisor heading up our prison release task force, and last but not least, Ms Gina Wayne. Ms Wayne is the recently appointed deployment specialist for the Pinpoint system.'

Clearing his throat, he takes a sip of water before going on.

'Now, in this election year, there is no guarantee the public will return us to power. The government hopes, however, that whichever party gets elected, and subject to budget, they will allow this new process to continue. I for one will recommend that they do.

'The purpose of this meeting is to identify the various agencies involved in the release of prisoners. It's been a long-held desire of the government and mine to balance early release with fully protecting the public. There are many factors to consider before any prisoner is eligible, and we've been looking at offenders, their crimes, and the steps taken by prisons to rehabilitate them. And there is of course their level of education; have they been active in trying to improve it themselves? When we arrive at a point where a prisoner is suitable for release, we then weigh up their job prospects, ongoing counselling, family support, housing and mental issues. The pitfalls mentioned are already well documented. What I'm introducing today is a new and radical approach to the parole problem. We've been trialling the use of hypnosis. I believe it can be a cost-effective way to curb

reoffending once prisoners are back in the community.'

'That sounds a ridiculously flawed concept,' interjects Governor Riley, standing up. 'That will never work,' he adds

'Come now, Governor. It's unlike you to reject an idea out of hand.'

'No, and I'm telling you now, there's no way I will have my good name associated with this hocus-pocus approach to dealing with dangerous criminals. We're talking about killers and rapists here. I've dealt with them for near-on thirty years, and that's my professional opinion, backed up by experience.' Riley sits down and scans the table, trying to gauge who would hitch their wagon to his when called to vote.

'I would rather you'd said, "convince me",' says Sir Edward. 'Then I would know that you were not totally closed to new ideas, Governor.'

'Okay, let's try this your way, Sir Edward. Convince me.'

'Well, I'm going a little ahead of the agenda here, but if you could all please turn to the last page of the briefing.'

'What's this?' Ms Wayne asks, briefly skimming through it.

'It's an accord,' says Sir Edward, 'stating that we will work jointly to achieve the potential release of prisoners under this scheme. Code-named "PHP", or Prisoner Hypnotic Programme.'

'And you were expecting us to sign it without question? Was that your plan?'

'Not at all, Governor. But one question for you. Do you take vitamins?'

'Do I take vitamins! What sort of question is that? Do I take vitamins? Vitamins...' Governor Riley's head flops down towards the table.

'Oh, my God!' shrieks Ms Wayne. 'What's happening to him? Is he having a heart attack? Where are his vitamins?'

'Don't worry, everyone, he's fine. It's just a practical demonstration of the programme. Mr Gilby,' Sir Edward nods to Ian to take over.

'Governor, you will concentrate on my voice and my voice only. When I count to three and say wake up, you will awake feeling fresh, with no doubts about this agreement and eager to sign it. One, two, three. Wake up.'

Governor Riley opens his eyes and lifts his head. He takes his fountain pen from his pocket and scribbles his signature at the bottom of the agreement before returning the pen to his pocket.

'And sleep,' Ian instructs him.

'You could be a very dangerous man, Mr Gilby, if you didn't use your skills for good,' Ms Wayne remarks.

'That's not where I'm dangerous.' Ian flirts.

'Ahem, Mr Gilby.' Sir Edward interrupts, forcing him to refocus.

'Governor Riley, when I tell you to, you will wake up and be fully conscious of your actions. One, two, three, wake up.'

The governor lifts his head. He looks around the table at each person.

'How are you feeling, Governor?' Sir Edward asks.

'I'm a little embarrassed, to tell the truth.'

'But why?'

'Because I'm aware of what I've done, but even while doing it I… I was powerless to stop myself.'

'And that's all I've sought to prove in this exercise. Obviously, the first batch of prisoners for release will be under even stricter measures. They'll be electronically tagged and subject to the Pinpoint curfew rules. Also, in line with my earlier statement, I've arranged basic employment, with the kind help of Doctor Minn. This arrangement allows for further monitoring and assessments well ahead of any tag-free release.'

'How many are we talking about?' Ms Wayne asks.

'For the first trial, a maximum of twelve.'

'Do you have the names yet for the first batch?' asks the governor. 'Or should I be redirecting that question to Mr Gilby, as it's now clear to me what he's been doing in my prison.'

Sir Edward passes a sheet to Dr Minn, who passes it to Governor Riley. The governor scans the list, scrutinising each of the names.

'First off, Mr Yip and Mr Earlington are both convicted murderers. I strongly disapprove of their inclusion before they've served at least half their sentences. I don't want that on my conscience when things go wrong.'

'Well, I'm happy to say you will not need to make that decision, Governor. That burden will be mine and mine alone. But let me try to explain a little about my thinking. First, those two were brought to my attention by Mr Gilby. I, like you, had the same opinion about their convictions. But after reviewing their files, I could see why it would be a far better option to tackle them early and before they became institutionalised.'

'I can agree with some of what you've said, Sir Edward, but not all.'

'If I can count on that signature of yours, even with your misgivings, then we can make it work.'

'If everyone feels the same when we vote, then I'll take it on the chin. But, for my signature, it's only right you document my concerns fully,' the governor advises.

'Can we have a show of hands then, please,' says Sir Edward, 'if you will support the trials.'

Everyone raises their hand, except Governor Riley.

'Carried, subject to all noted amendments,' confirms Sir Edward.

Back at Downing Prison, two wardens have turned up at Dozer's cell. The key in the door brings him to his feet.

'What's happening?' he says, as the door swings open.

'Kevin, we're here to escort you to the medical centre for your operation,' one warden tells him.

'I was told it's going be next Friday.'

'Lucky for you, then; there's been a cancellation. Get your toothbrush and let's go.'

'What about eating?' Dozer asks.

'What about it?'

'They also said not to eat anything before the operation.'

'That's old thinking, Kevin. These days they have drugs for everything, don't worry. Let's not waste the slot they've given us to fix you. Besides, the last meal you had was over three hours ago, right?'

Dozer goes to the sink and grabs his toothbrush and toothpaste, putting them in his top pocket. The two wardens escort him to the medical centre.

In the sterile environment of the operating theatre, Kevin is prepared and made to lie on his back. All the medical staff wear caps and masks which hide all but their eyes. It would be a hard task for him to identify any of them. A masked person stands over him.

'Now, Kevin, you will experience a cold sensation in your right hand. We'll be applying an oxygen mask while sending you off to sleep. Are you ready to count for me? From ten backwards, please.'

'Ten… nine… eight…' He falls silent after only three numbers.

'Okay, we have little time. Is the Spatz gastric balloon ready?'

'Yes, Chef.'

'Don't take the piss, or I'll make sure you're next on this table. Listen, we muck this up and Fat Fingers will stop paying for our kids' private education. So, no more fucking around, you got that?'

'Yeah, I'm sorry.'

'Right, is his breathing okay? I'm inserting the endoscope now.'

'Yes, he's where we need him to be.'

'Good. The guide tube is going in now.'

The surgeon inserts the deflated Spatz through the guide tube. He then manoeuvres it into place, guided by the endoscope camera. Attaching a saline pump, the Spatz inflates slowly with the solution while the surgeon monitors its progress on the screen. After only five minutes the whole procedure is complete.

'Okay, coming out now.' He continues to narrate while removing all the tubes. 'I want an adhesive bandage for his shoulder and a sling before he's brought around. We don't want him finding out yet what's taken place.'

They take an awake but groggy Dozer back to his cell, making him comfortable and instructing him to rest. He complains that his arm feels no better but takes comfort from being told it will still be sore for a few days and needs time to heal. The whole experience has left him hungry, so he's looking forward to his evening meal.

Later, in the canteen, Dozer sits and boasts about the damage he wants Ox to suffer now that his arm is fixed.

'Give us the order, we'll grab him and you can give him your special treatment,' one of his colleagues suggests through a snigger.

'No, he's too smart, and they're always together everywhere,' Dozer answers.

'Do you think they're gay, like that foreign one yesterday?'

'Well, you may have a point. They were quick to defend that child molester in Vincent's cell. Anyway, enough of that for the time being. What's on the dinner menu today?'

It's all about food for now, and Dozer is happy to use medical grounds to have his drones fetch his food.

'It's Chinese. What would you like?'

'Surprise me with a little of everything.'

Going to fetch Dozer's food, he whispers out of earshot,

'No surprise there, that's what you always have.'

# CHAPTER 23

Canary Wharf, once the thriving financial hub of the United Kingdom's business empire, is now a semi-desolate shell, still overshadowed by memories of its pre-Brexit prominence. Unlike the majority that voted for change on a wave of populist misinformation, many established companies sought to cut their losses after the bitter divorce from Europe. Shareholders sanctioned directors to move operations to Europe, allowing them to continue their long-running affair with the European Union.

Lotto-Guard's UK headquarters is located within the City and this makes perfect financial sense, since the government is falling over itself to offer tax breaks to halt the increasing decline in British jobs. Dr Minn has used this tried and tested method repeatedly in other regions of the world. His factory, as listed by Companies House, manufactures electronic items from imported components. It's perceived to be a lucrative business after a gigantic deal signed by the European Union and Asia's largest producers reduced imports.

The complex spans several floors. Housing a factory of guarded secrets, it's a wonder the company can keep its real activity from over one hundred employees working there.

Level one contains the heart of Lotto-Guard's operations, with its row upon row of stacked crates as its only identifying feature. There's strictly controlled access to this level from all upper levels. Offices and accommodation occupy the first and second floors, with limited connectivity between all floors.

Hidden below are two further floors: sub-level two, used for car parking and deliveries, and sub-level one for the real and secret purpose of the plant.

It's Monday 17 May 2027 and approximately seventeen days after their prisoner assessment process began. Later than expected, they finally arrive at the factory just after 5 pm. The move began early that morning but a broken-down van saw the process use up the whole day. Each prisoner exiting the bus looks tired from their journey. With their belongings secured in bright red canvas holdalls, they line up in much the same order as they had entered. Dr Minn, flanked by his bodyguard Chi, stands ready to welcome them.

'Good evening, gentlemen. I must apologise for the time it's taken to transfer you from Downing Prison. You must all feel tired. You are the chosen few they will judge the success or failure of this early release project on. We aim here to show you trust and freedom and prepare you for your ultimate release. Make no mistake, though, there's no second chance for failure here. We will ship you right back to resume your sentence. I should add, gentlemen, it could include extra time being added to your sentences. Now, we have many rules here, but only a handful I'll expect you to obey unconditionally. Why are they so significant? Because they provide a framework for your safety, the safety of others and the success of this complex.

'Rule number one: you're not allowed outside these premises. The bracelets on your hands, gentlemen, are Pinpoint-issued.

Designed to guarantee that any attempt at escape before your sanctioned release date will end in failure, possibly death.'

Dr Minn walks along the line, looking into each person's face. His expressionless delivery gives weight to his words. At the end of the line, he turns and walks back.

'Rule number two: I have no interest in the crimes that have brought you here. That is between you, your god and your conscience. I will afford you respect and demand the same from each of you. Now, to welcome you and to make up for your bad travel experience, I've arranged for you to have the rest of the day off. Tomorrow evening at seven and every Tuesday at the same fixed time, you will be allowed one phone call, lasting no more than ten minutes. I'm sure I will impress you with the facilities here. but I also caution, you are here to work. Work which will form part of your release and rehabilitation package, which, unlike prison, will earn you at least a market wage. Mr Chi here will show you to your quarters, and we will reconnect tomorrow morning at eight am sharp. Oh, one last thing. Please ensure that you are within the confines of your own rooms no later than five minutes past the hour of ten o'clock each night. I hope you can all police yourselves without our intervention.'

'This way, please,' Chi announces as he walks towards an industrial-size service lift. Chi's body movement appears comical as his long body and short legs are noticeable and pronounced. One by one the prisoners pick up their belongings and file in behind him.

Scott, an acne-faced skinhead, added later to the scheme, makes a whispered comment to Paul, who follows behind him.

'He's a funny shape.'

'Maybe you can tell him?' says Paul.

'No way I'll mess this up, trust me.'

Once the lift is full, Chi produces an electronic key. He activates the lift, taking them to the accommodation floor.

Each room offers soft carpets and a comfortable bed, together with a few items you wouldn't find at Downing, like razors.

The unexpected bonus and big surprise is the discovery that all room security, including door keys, is under their direct control. For the first time since the start of their ordeal, they are being trusted and treated like real human beings. Settling in will be strange; so much room with so few personal items to fill it. In prison, their challenge was always to try to have the bare minimum, as each item needed two functions, either for bargaining or as a weapon. After unpacking, Chan walks to the room next door to his. He knocks and waits.

'Who is it?' says Ox.

'Me.'

'Come in, Me.'

Chan pushes the door half-open, poking his head around the door before entering.

'Not bad, hey?'

'What's yours like?' Ox asks.

'Same as this one.'

'If I'm honest, it's even better than where I lived before prison. It's almost too good to be true. Do you think there's hidden cameras and listening devices in our rooms?'

'They only need these,' Chan says, gesturing to his bracelet.

'Perhaps. I suppose it's freedom of some sort, that's the main thing. But we must never let go of the fact we're in here for something we didn't do.'

'Forget? No way, never. But we need to think how we go about finding the truth when we get out and what we'll do once we've found it. Until then we trust no one, agreed?'

'Agreed,' Ox says as they high-five their deal.

'Ready to look around?' Chan asks.

'Yeah, let me put my shoes on first.'

Ox sits on his bed, extracts a pair of blue trainers from his holdall and puts them on.

'Should I take my key?' he asks Chan, who nods, producing his from his pocket.

'Okay, let's go.'

Walking out into the corridor activates the lighting system. Every few steps, ceiling sensors trigger the lights ahead to come on and auto-extinguish those behind. They notice light emitting from an open door to a room, the games room, where most of the others have already settled.

'Come in, guys,' says Paul, excited. 'You will not believe this place. The fridge is full of beer and juices. And have you noticed, there's even real coffee, not that instant shit.'

'Have you looked around the whole place?' says Chan.

'Not yet, but I hear there's a gym, a library, and even a fucking cinema. Man, it's like paradise in here. I may never want to leave.'

'Well, we're off for a little wander round ourselves,' says Chan. 'See you in a minute.'

'I don't think so,' says Scott, taking up a position in the doorway, to block their exit. 'You'll wait here until I give you permission to leave.'

'Now, who died and forgot to take you with them?' says Ox, in reference to Scott's pale complexion.

'Let me remind you of the prisoners' code. Technically, we're still in prison,' he mumbles, biting his nails and avoiding eye contact.

'Ah, okay, seeing how you've put that so nicely, I'll offer you only one fuck off. Now move.'

Scott steps towards Ox, but Paul's hand across his chest stops him from getting closer.

'Don't you know who he is?' Paul whispers in Scott's ear. 'He's the guy who retired Dozer.'

Scott's expression and body language visibly alter.

'Look, I'm sorry,' says Scott. 'It's nothing personal, one of the side effects of being in the system too long. I'm Scott.' He steps back, extending his hand. Ox doesn't reciprocate the gesture and pushes past, while Scott stands, unsure what his next move should be.

'Are you coming?' Ox asks, looking back. Chan also pushes past Scott.

'Wait for me,' Paul says, following them out of the room.

Chan rests a hand on Ox's shoulder.

'What was all that about? It's unlike you not to accept a friendly gesture, even though he did get off on the wrong foot.'

Ox exhales, turns and leans for a second against the wall.

'You know that point when you've had enough, but no one gets it, and… and… and you explain the same shit repeatedly?'

Chan knows more than anyone about Ox's temperament. He offers nothing more than silence. Paul, though, can't help commenting on everything as he opens doors for a quick peek before moving on.

The time is closing in on 10 pm, prompting them to return to their rooms. Chan sets his alarm for 6:30 am to ensure enough time to wake up and get ready for the eight o'clock meeting arranged by Dr Minn.

Chan wakes up to a loud pounding on his door and shouts of 'Seven thirty, everybody up!'

Had he slept so deeply he'd failed to hear the alarm? He checks his clock and sees it's only coming up to six thirty. Just then, the alarm sounds and he stops it. Confused, Chan opens his room door and asks the first person passing.

'What's the time, mate?'

'Just gone seven thirty,' the man answers.

'Are you sure?'

'Yeah, none of the alarms worked, that's why they're knocking on doors.'

'Thanks,'

Quick to get ready, Chan leaves his room and goes to the restaurant. Most of the others are already having their breakfast. Sitting next to Ox, there was only one question he needed the answer to. Why had everyone suffered the same alarm malfunction?

'They've given us an extra half hour,' Ox tells him. 'You better get some food down you, and quick.'

It's a little after eight thirty when they're taken down for their first scheduled meeting with Dr Minn.

'Good morning again, gentlemen. I trust you all slept well?' Dr Minn observes a few nods and continues. 'Sorry for the slight delay this morning. Are there any questions from your downtime yesterday?'

'Yeah,' Scott says. 'We felt restricted with more doors locked than open. That's dangerous. If a fire breaks out, we're all doomed.' The others seem to agree with that observation.

'It's very nice that you all took time to explore,' says Dr Minn. 'It's something we expected. However, had you been a little more observant, I'm sure you would have noticed the huge number of sprinklers.'

He points at the ceiling but only a few bother to look.

'If a fire were to break out, you're more likely to drown than burn here. Now, I'm sure you are all eager to find out what field of work you will be doing. The answer, gentlemen, is "money". But before you get any ideas, we are talking Chinese money. We will be printing Chinese money, which is of no use to any of you.'

A group of Chinese men enter the room and line up, mirroring the prisoners. They're dressed in dark pocketless boiler suits and white wellingtons, with white cloth caps covering their hair.

'These are your workmates. Their English is impeccable and they will train you in all aspects of your assigned positions. After one week, you'll all be assessed. Anyone not up to speed will be shipped back to Downing. Good luck, and I hope this relationship will be beneficial to us all.' Dr Minn waves Chi away to escort the men to the lower working area.

A very nervous accountant, accompanied by the operations manager, approaches Dr Minn.

'Good morning, Doctor Minn. You asked to see me, sir?'

'It's Max, isn't it?'

'Yes, sir, that is correct.'

'I must tell you a story, Max. But I don't want you to stop me unless you've heard it before, or fully understand its meaning,'

'I understand, but…'

'But, Mr Max, I haven't started the story and you've forgotten the rule already. Please listen. Imagine this factory is a bakery. Let's say I produce ten lots of dough. I put all ten in the oven. How many loaves of bread should I be expecting?'

'Ten,' answers the accountant.

'So, as my accountant you should be able to help me understand how we would end up with nine loaves in our little bakery?'

'Doctor Minn, I do not know what to tell you. Naturally, I'll look back over my figures again, but I can only work with what I'm given.'

'What's your input to this little mystery, Mr Junjie?' Dr Minn asks the operations manager.

'Could be any number of reasons, Dr Minn. We have been having power problems for months, with machines suddenly stopping. That alone could account for some of the losses. If you could give me a few days, sir, I can report back anything else that I find apart from that.'

'Make it happen sooner, Mr Junjie. I'm sure you don't wish to see your excellent employment record blemished by failure.'

At the end of their first full working day, Chan and Ox are exhausted. The tasks are a little repetitive but, with the clear instructions they've received from their Chinese mentors, they're not complicated. The smell of ammonia in the dye and the long bouts of boredom will be their main issues. Meeting in the rest room after dinner, Paul is keen to find out how their day has been.

'So how easy or what?' he starts, looking for them to acknowledge the same.

'Easy, but boring,' answers Ox.

'I'm not use to being on my feet all day, it's probably going to take me a couple of days to build up stamina, and for that reason I'll be having an early night,' suggests Chan.

'Yeah, it sounds the sensible thing to do,' adds Ox.

'You guys are truly lightweights. The first day we're not locked up early and you're off to bed?' Paul scoffs at their plans for the evening.

Later, Chan double checks his alarm, making sure it's set and ready to wake him early, before going to sleep.


The following morning starts much like the first, with the doors being pounded. As with the previous night, the clocks seem to have lost about an hour. Their employers made a point of saying that timekeeping is important, yet no one in charge seems bothered by what's going on with the clocks.

'So, did you get your full eight hours?' Paul questions.

'I got more than if I'd stayed up any longer. So what did you do when we left, apart from just sitting around?'

'Well, actually I made a phone call.'

'What? Ah, you're right, yesterday was Tuesday, the only day for phone calls,' Chan recalls.

'Why didn't you remind us, and who did you call anyway?' asks Ox.

'You guys never gave me a chance, you were in such a hurry to go and sleep. And as for who I called, that will always remain private, like it should be.'

'He's right, Ox, you have no business asking him who he's been calling.' Chan sides with Paul on this one, to the annoyance of Ox, who is supposedly his best friend.

. . .

On the third night, Chan is finding it even harder to fall asleep, his mind preoccupied with waking up. Frequently checking his clock, he notices that, since 11:45 pm, it hasn't moved for two minutes. The temperature in his room is becoming a little uncomfortable, and Chan soon realises that the air-conditioning system is not functioning either.

Getting out of bed, he puts on a white T-shirt over jeans and ventures out of his room. When he's not greeted by the automatic light system, his first thoughts are that it must be a power cut. It's dark but, being a modern building, emergency floor lighting points the way to the nearest exit. He remembers the first day's exploration and wonders if he'll find all the exits locked.

With only one way to find out, he tries the nearest exit and is surprised when he finds it unlocked. Moving onto a stair landing, well lit by warm fluorescent lights, he's not sure how long he can be away from his room. But based on the previous two nights, he's calculated that he has a minimum of half an hour to explore.

Wasting no time, he goes down a level and finds that floor in darkness too. Not knowing if such an opportunity will present itself again, he's prepared to push his luck and try the next level. The well-lit stairs are helping his navigation.

Down at the next level, all the lights appear to be functioning. It's also immediately clear that work is being done during the night. Chan opens a door and enters, but at the first sound of voices he ducks behind a stack of pallets. The voices seem to get louder, heading in his direction. He checks around but sees no other nearby accessible hiding place.

'This bloody power problem is making us work twice as hard,' a voice moans.

The whistling sound of an electric motor seems to follow the voice, and it gets louder before falling silent. Without warning, two forks punch through the base of the pallets, missing Chan's foot by inches. If they move the pallets, then his chances of remaining undetected drop immediately to zero.

Thinking quickly, Chan steps onto the forks as they lift the stacked crates. The forklift reverses into a ninety-degree turn. Feeling a slight movement from an unsteady top crate, Chan stretches stealthily towards it and uses his strong grip to anchor them together.

The forklift navigates to an even more brightly lit area, slows then stops, causing a further strain on Chan's grip.

'Left hand down, hold it, that's straight now,' claims a different voice. 'Stack it up quickly so we can take our break.'

The forklift ratchets its load towards the ceiling. Chan knows he has two choices: move lower, towards the base of the stack, or keep a firm grip on the top as the ceiling gets nearer. He climbs down but snags his T-shirt on a nail. The driver, sensing some restriction, lowers the load to the ground.

'Why have you stopped?' asks the man on the ground.

'Because this paper is very expensive. I can't afford to damage it. We might as well take our break, then you can help me split the pallets,' answers the driver.

'Help you? Listen, mate, I don't earn those big forklift wages.'

'And that there is the difference between you and me. I get paid the big bucks, as you call it, not to take unnecessary risks, damage stock or listen to anything I'm not supposed to – like you, chattering on about West Ham all day.'

The men remove their hats and overalls, leaving them by the forklift. Their conversation fades as they wander off for the break, leaving Chan to free his T-shirt and quickly descend unchallenged. He borrows a hat and overalls to disguise his clothes.

A chime signals a general announcement.

'Ten minutes before the power is back on the mains, ten minutes.'

Chan follows the two men, keeping within earshot. His new attire blends in with all the other workers, and so does his face, with its Chinese features.

'When are they going to permanently fix that damn power thing?' the men say as they walk.

'They're still waiting for a spare part. End of the week at the earliest, I've heard.'

'It must be cheaper to get it here than bring it all the way from China.'

'Everything they do keeps the money in their community.'

'I bet it's crossed your mind.'

'What has?'

'What just one sheet of this money could do for your bank balance?'

'Yeah, I admit it has, but keeping my balls attached to my body would cost a lot less than having them sewn back on.'

'And what about those new recruits?'

'What about them?'

'Well, they're in the dark about how long they'll be here.'

'Why should it matter to you? Forever doesn't seem too long if you don't know when that is.'

It's an odd conversation to hear after being warned that all printed money has no value unless you're in China. There has to be more to this operation than shown so far.

The answer isn't long in coming. Chan, dressed in working gear, wanders even further into the heart of the operation. He avoids making any eye contact as he witnesses an extra process taking place; the already printed 'Chinese' notes are having a further image added, converting them into crisp fifty-pound notes.

Remembering he has less than ten minutes before they restore the power, Chan extracts himself from any further danger and makes his way back up two levels, to the relative sanctuary of his room.

# CHAPTER 24

The restless night gets no better for Chan as he processes the new information he's gleaned over and over in his head. He needs to recall every detail, if only to convince himself it wasn't a dream.

By the time the daily pounding on the doors occurs, Chan has already been awake and dressed for over an hour. He's more than keen to escape his bedroom so he can see his friend and share the burden of his knowledge.

He knocks once on Ox's door, then forces it open and enters without waiting.

'Come in, why don't you,' Ox barks. He flips back the bedsheet and plants his feet on the floor.

'You'll feel different when you hear what I've got to tell you.'

'Come on, Chan, you know me; any news, good or bad, is better received after that first cup of coffee.'

'I think this news will leave a bitter taste whatever the drink.'

'Go on then,' Ox says, pulling his T-shirt over his shoulders.

'Last night I went downstairs.'

'If you had waited until this morning I could have gone with you.'

'When I say downstairs, I mean two levels. There's more to this place than meets the eye, Ox, trust me.'

Ox puts on his trousers. 'And how did you get down there with all the doors locked?'

'That's the thing. I'm sure you've noticed how each morning the clocks have lost time?'

'Yeah, and?'

'Well, it's because they're diverting all the power from this floor.'

'And you couldn't have told me that after a cup of coffee?'

'What's the matter with you this morning, Ox? You're suddenly not a morning person?'

'Well, with last night being so hot and sticky and having no air con, what do you expect?'

'I expect as my best friend you will at least listen while I'm trying to do my best to explain something serious.' Chan's voice turns staccato in his frustration.

'Shoot, I'm all ears,' Ox concedes, sitting back down on his bed.

'Nothing works up here because they require all the electricity downstairs to power their other activities.'

'What other activities?'

'You know the plates used to produce the Chinese money?'

'You mean that useless Monopoly crap?'

'Yeah, but it's only useless until they transform it into new fifty-pound notes. And there's more.'

'About the money?'

'No, not about the money, it's about the lies they are feeding us all about how long we'll stay here before being released.'

'That Minn guy made it clear. About six months, if that,' Ox recalls.

'From what I overheard, we're not scheduled to leave at all. If you think about it, Ox, if we'd gone into this hypnotised, without Paul's help, we wouldn't have had a clue.'

'Are you trying to say we should trust him, after agreeing when we arrived Monday to trust no one?'

'Look, I know we're not free yet, but we're also not stewing in Downing Prison either, and that's down to him. But more urgent at the moment is that we need to get out of here tonight.'

'Tonight! You're joking.'

'No, I'm not. We need to take advantage of their power problems. It might be our only chance to leave this place.'

'Yeah, but why tonight?'

'Because by the end of this week they'll fix the electricity problem, and after that we can wave goodbye to any chance of leaving here soon, or ever for all we know.'

'Okay, now you really are testing me without a cup of coffee inside me.'

'Can't you stop going on about damn coffee?'

'Yeah, but we need to go for breakfast before they get suspicious.'

'Okay, fine. Let's go.'

In the canteen, everyone else has already made inroads into their breakfast. Chan and Ox put a few items on their trays and move to find two empty seats.

'You.'

Chan pivots on his heels. 'Me?'

'Yes you.' One of the 'workmates' is staring at Chan.

The workmate walks towards him. Chan wonders if he knows something about last night's nocturnal movements. For a second his thoughts race towards being shipped back to Downing.

'What's wrong?' Chan asks. His eyes blur out everything but the approaching man.

'Sorry, I don't know your name. You dropped your napkin.'

Chan regains his focus and looks down. Relieved at being able to mask his feelings of guilt, he bends and retrieves the napkin.

'Thank you,' he says, moving away swiftly to grab a seat.

Ox has already found them two seats. Unfortunately, they're not scheduled to work together, meaning the conversation will have to wait until the evening. Chan and Paul's work routine overlaps. Chan hints that they need to talk urgently but keeps quiet under a barrage of subtle pressure to reveal everything there and then.

'Just come to my room after dinner,' is all he's prepared to trust Paul with for the time being.

The evening can't come soon enough for Paul, who has worked himself into thinking all sorts. Something he's feeling for the first time is being included, and he values it more than anything tangible. Going to Chan's room after dinner, he knocks and waits. He's surprised to hear Ox's voice calling for him to enter.

'I didn't expect to find you here,' Paul says, entering Chan's room.

'Why?'

'No reason, other than Chan didn't mention it, that's all.'

'Play nice, you two. Take a seat,' Chan says.

Paul finds space on Chan's bed, on the opposite side to Ox.

'Right, what I wanted to tell you both is about doing the right thing at the right time. Like you helping us out of Downing, Paul. It's my turn to ask you to trust me. Well?'

'Well, give me a clue at least,' says Paul.

'Not until I know that you're on board.'

'There's always the option to walk away now and forget everything that's said,' Ox tells Paul, glancing out of the corner of his eye to catch his reaction.

Paul is certain they were discussing something important before he arrived. He feels the bond he has built, at least with Chan, is worth the trust. 'Okay.'

'Are you sure?' Chan presses him. Ox rolls his eyes.

'Yeah, absolutely, I'm in.'

'Good. And Ox, you really need to get your head around it too. All three of us are in this together now and we'll need each other going forward.'

'But what does he bring to this?' says Ox.

'He's proved himself already. He's as honest as they come – what more do you need? We're in a situation here and we can't afford to be bickering. If you can't get on board with that, we might as well stay here and rot.'

'It's only for a short time, six months,' says Paul. 'I'm sure I can rough it out if you can.'

Ox sighs and nods.

'This place isn't what it seems, Paul,' says Chan. 'I don't think they intend for us to leave here, at least not for a long time. And the only reason we're ahead of the game is because you kept us from being hypnotised. To stand any chance of clearing our name, we need to leave here, tonight.'

'Tonight? You can't just leave a place like this,' says Paul. 'There's got to be as much, if not more security than there was in prison here.'

'Probably true, but with the power down we can literally walk out of here.'

'Where would we go?' asks Paul.

'If we can make it outside this place, I'll have no problem finding somewhere for us to hide,' Ox says.

'Okay, here's what I propose we do,' Chan explains. 'When the air conditioning goes off, check that your clock has also stopped. If it has, then the power is definitely off. That should give us between fifteen and thirty minutes to get to the lower levels.'

'And then what?' Paul asks.

'And then we leave,' Chan says, rather unconvincingly.

'You're not sure, are you, how we're going to do this?' Paul asks.

A knock at the door forces them to stop the discussion. Ox and Paul shrug; it's not their room, so not their decision to answer.

Chan moves to the door and half opens it, to find Scott shifting about as if he needs the toilet.

'Yes?'

'Is Paul in there with you?' Scott asks. The question throws Chan. He's not sure whether he should answer.

'Yes. What's up, man?' Paul answers, coming to the door.

'I thought you were coming to play cards like we arranged.'

Paul slaps his forehead. 'Oh yeah, I forgot. Give me two minutes, yeah?'

'You're welcome to join us too, you know,' Scott tells Chan.

'It's okay, he doesn't play,' says Paul. 'Besides, it would be like taking candy from a baby,' he jokes.

Scott seems encouraged at the prospect of making extra money.

'That's no problem, we can teach you,' Scott says with a smile.

'When I say, he doesn't play, it's because of his religion.'

'Well, we can always change that for him too. When in Rome and all that, yeah?'

'Two minutes,' Paul says again before closing the door. 'I'm sorry about that, couldn't think of anything else to say.'

'Don't worry. Just make sure you're ready once the power goes off. Meet us on the stairs to the right. All the doors should be unlocked. You'd better go.'

Paul leaves and Chan closes the door behind him.

'I hope to God we're not wrong in trusting him,' Ox says.

'What's happened to us, Ox, shouldn't mean we trust no one again.'

'Maybe,' Ox says, 'Maybe.'

At 10 pm everyone is in their rooms where they should be.

Ox has increased the air conditioner's fan settings so it makes an audible sound, thinking once it goes off, it will be easier to notice. Fully dressed, he lays on top of his bed with all kinds of things running through his mind. His main thought is that if they fail, their problems could turn into a real nightmare.

Paul is also awake, excited yet scared at the same time. He packs his holdall with some personal effects and leaves it by the door so as not to forget it.

Chan too is a little unsure, but his conscience tells him it's the only option. He has time to brush his teeth and agrees with his reflection that there's no turning back.

The digital clock displays 23:50 and marks every second while the air conditioning continues to hum. Ox leaves his bed for the toilet, relieving his body of nervous excess. As he looks into the mirror, negative thoughts about getting caught haunt him. With time drifting, random recollections back to the time of arrest pops into his head. He peers into the mirror and notices a spot near his chin and moves in closer to inspect it. He lifts his chin to peer down his nose.

Then the lights cut out. Still anxious, he feels his way back into his room. The silence confirms the air conditioner has stopped and the digital clock no longer emits any light. Just as he goes to put his hand on the door handle, his door swings open.

'Ox! Are you there?' Chan whispers.

'Yeah, just coming,' he answers in the same whisper.

Through the doorway and guided by the floor lighting, Ox follows Chan towards the emergency exit. Chan opens the door out onto the landing. No alarm, just like last night.

'Okay, let's give Paul a few minutes,' Chan whispers between deep breaths. The prospect of escape is raising his heart rate.

'He should have been here already. His room is closer to this exit than ours. How much time did you say we'll have?'

Ox moves behind the door to look over the rail, down towards the other floors.

'Relax, we'll give him five minutes. Then we're gone.'

The door opens sharply as Paul rushes through onto the landing.

'Where's Ox?' says Paul. 'I knew he'd be the last one here, holding us up.' The door closes, revealing Ox.

'Why have you got a bag? A bright coloured one at that?' Ox is incensed by Paul's stupidity.

'Why have you brought it?' Chan asks.

'I had to bring a few things. Medication and other stuff I need.'

'And how come this is the first we've heard about this?' Ox moves within spitting distance of Paul.

'Look, there are certain conditions you don't mention, even to your closest friends, okay?'

'We're losing time standing here, let's crack on,' Chan says as he starts down the stairs.

Knowing they need not stop at the first level, Chan walks down towards the next, followed keenly by Ox and Paul.

When they reach the landing, Chan tests the door with a gentle nudge. The door swings free.

'Okay, this is where they've been converting the money. The next floor down must be where we came in when we first arrived.'

'We need to go in there before we go downstairs,' Ox says.

'Why?'

'Because we'll need money when we get out of here.'

'No, too risky,' says Chan.

'He's right,' says Paul. 'We can't go out there with no money.'

'Well, I don't think it's a good idea,' Chan argues.

'Okay, you stay here. Paul and I will go.'

Chan shakes his head and disagrees with the whole idea. 'If you're not back in five minutes, I'm out of here, friends or not. You hear me?'

'Yeah, that's fair, we can work with that,' Paul says.

'Well, what are you waiting for? Time is money,' Chan scoffs, before moving aside to allow them access to the door. They open it and disappear inside.

Chan sits on the stairs and confirms the time they left on his watch. It's a process he repeats several times while waiting.

Suddenly, the landing light goes out, bringing Chan to his feet. He looks through the crack in the door and sees that the whole floor, the whole building, sits in total darkness.

With a thud, the door hits Chan in the face, forcing him back against the handrail.

'Chan, where are you?' Ox whispers, only it's far louder than a whisper as his voice echoes down the empty stairwell.

'I'm here,' Chan moans, gripping his face. 'Why don't you tell the world and its dog where we are?' he adds.

'We need to go now,' says Ox.

'What happened in there?'

'Let's go, we'll swap notes later,' Paul says.

They manoeuvre down the final stairs, still in darkness, to reach the lowest level. The parking area lights come back on as suddenly as the other floors went off. Blessed with a fully lit floor and no one in sight, the trio move past two parked cars towards a metal shutter marked 'Emergency Exit'.

'Let's hope our luck holds with this last obstacle,' Chan says. He presses the button that lifts the shutter and then looks around, only to realise it's just him and Ox. 'Where is he?'

'He was right behind me.' Ox throws up his hands in despair as he scans the area.

The lights on a blue Bentley Flying Spur flash in time with the sound of the doors unlocking.

'What the hell does he think he's doing?' Ox runs towards the car, trailed by Chan. They find Paul in the driver's seat, with his holdall dumped on the passenger side.

'Get in,' he says.

'Are you mad?' says Chan.

'Get in. We can't go outside wearing these bracelets. In here there's a chance the glass will protect us from the sensors. Get in!' He repeats.

Opening the rear door, Ox and Chan slide onto the plush leather back seat.

'How do you know so much about the Pinpoint system?' Chan asks.

'I read somewhere that it operates like a passive infrared detector,' Paul says, fiddling under the dash.

'Do you have any idea how to drive this thing?'

'Not the time to be distracting me, guys.'

The car's dash lights up and the doors automatically lock.

'You've got it working?'

'I started it, but whatever's happening now is not down to me.'

The car reverses, swinging left to point towards the exit. The car moves, picking up speed, as all three try opening their nearest doors. They're all locked.

'Paul! Tell me you're in control and driving it?'

'I don't think I can make that claim. This car must have driverless technology fitted, and somehow it's activated, maybe when I hot-wired it.'

'So where is it taking us?' Ox asks.

'No idea, mate, no idea.'

The car climbs the ramp out onto the street, steering as if driven by a ghost, then disappears silently into the night.

# CHAPTER 25

'Can't you do something?' Ox asks as the car moves silently through the streets.

'Probably not. It's auto-programmed, so no.'

'Anyway, where did you learn to break into cars?'

'I'm a thief. Breaking into cars, I'm sure that was like lesson number five. Anyway, might as well relax; we can't do anything about it right now.'

'And the cash?' says Chan.

'What about it?'

'Well, how much did you take?'

Paul unzips his holdall. 'See for yourself.'

The bag is full of bundles of crisp new fifty-pound notes. Chan looks slack-jawed at the bag. He sees something else, thin and shiny amongst the notes.

'What are those?' Chan asks, reaching in and pulling one from the bag.

'The plates needed to transform the money to sterling, and our guarantee they won't rush to announce us missing.'

'And how do you figure that one?'

'Do you think that factory is legit? Of course not. Trust me, they'll do anything to protect what's going on in there from becoming public knowledge.'

'Call me pessimistic, Paul, but I can't help thinking our little escapade is in danger of going pear-shaped. As soon as one problem gets solved, we seem to attract another.'

Chan sits back in silence.

As it's late and after midnight, the car drives through the streets at a comfortable cruising speed. It manoeuvres wide of a cyclist who shouldn't be on the road at night without lights. Up front, Paul marvels at the technology allowing the car to navigate, read traffic signals and avoid hazards, all without a driver's input. He had memorised every turn since leaving the factory, until Chan and Ox's distraction; now he's lost. He pulls out the photo of his daughter and allows himself a smile before replacing it.

The car heads towards a roundabout and slows, allowing it to merge onto it without stopping. After the exit, it goes up through the gears onto a single carriageway and is soon joined by a dark Audi A6, seemingly from nowhere. The Audi's full beams light up the interior of the Bentley. It swerves either side of an adverse camber, trailing the Bentley too close.

'What's this guy think he's doing?' says Ox, peering out the rear window. The trailing car gathers speed, closing the gap before slipping back, then doing the same again. 'If we knew how to stop this car, I'd be up for giving him a little talking to.'

'Maybe they're just in a hurry to get home,' says Chan.

The Audi moves down the offside, clipping their rear wheel arch as it does so.

'In a hurry or not, what did he do? Pass his test on a bicycle,' notes Ox.

It pulls alongside, parallel with Paul. The driver gestures for Paul to slow down and pull over but Paul raises both hands, showing he's not driving. The Audi driver lowers his window as the road goes through a series of bends and mouths in Paul's direction.

'What's he saying? I can't make it out,' Paul says, turning around.

'I think it looks like, "What sort of fucking fool sees a gun pointed at him and keeps on driving".'

'Bloody hell!' Paul shouts, and ducks away from the window as a single shot ricochets off the bulletproof glass back into the Audi. The Audi swerves and drops back. Chan and Ox turn to stare out the rear window and witness the Audi braking hard and losing control before flipping over.

'Now! Don't tell me that was sheer coincidence! Either you or this car is a trouble magnet!' Ox vents.

'He's right, Paul. How do you explain what just took place?' says Chan.

'I can't. I didn't see!'

'Yeah, that's because you hid like a baby,' Ox says.

'Sorry! But I make no apology for hiding; I'm not especially keen on getting myself shot. You want coincidence? The clue is I was shit scared. It must be the car. There's some serious electronics in here that somebody wants. At least I have first-hand experience that you can't carjack a driverless car.'

The Bentley sails on through their argument, and soon all three men fall silent, gazing out the windows instead.

After leaving the single carriageway, the Bentley slows then swings sharply through gates into a private estate. The beams from the Bentley's headlamps are the sole source lighting the road ahead. The car slows, passing several large houses set back on manicured lawns, before turning through the open gates to a large mansion. Loose pebbles on the driveway emit a crunching sound under the weight of the car's twenty-inch tyres, and lights either side of a garage come on as the door opens. The car drives silently into the garage and parks itself beside a gold Mercedes. The doors unlock as the engine powers off.

'Okay, it's open, let's go,' says Paul.

'You don't have to tell me twice,' Ox replies.

Chan looks out of the back window and sees the garage door lowering.

'Guys, we need to be proactive, the door is closing,' Chan whispers, scrambling to exit the car. Paul gets out, taking the holdall with him as the garage door shuts.

'Don't worry,' says a confident Paul, 'garage doors always contain a switch to open them from the inside but having said that, wherever this one is it's not obvious.'

'Have you seen the damage caused by that car hitting us?' Chan says, running his hand over the slightly dented area.

'Don't worry about it; none of us was driving,' Paul answers.

'I don't even have a licence,' says Ox.

'Let's stop worrying about the damn car and concentrate on getting out of here,' Paul snaps.

The garage lighting is on a delayed timer and dims quickly, leaving just a strip of light coming from under the house access door. They follow and Paul leads, trusting his experience as a burglar; he seems happy to assume that role. He opens the door enough to establish that the adjacent room is the kitchen.

Suddenly the motor for the garage door sparks into life and the door begins rising again. The lights flicker as a strong beam from outside climbs the walls as the garage door gets higher.

'Well, no chance now of getting out that way,' whispers Chan.

'Follow me... quick,' Paul says, opening the access door leading to the kitchen.

Outside the garage, Dr Minn and his daughter have arrived home after an evening meal out. As the garage door opens, Chi, driving, checks for the empty space for the incoming car.

'Sir, something here is not right,' he says.

'What is it, Chi?' Dr Minn asks.

'It's the other car, sir. The one stored at the factory. It's here.'

'Impossible!'

'See for yourself, sir.'

The open garage door reveals all the parking spaces as being occupied.

'Wait, sir, let me check first,' Chi says, exiting the car. He walks in front of the car's headlamps, casting a long shadow that stretches ahead as he follows it into the garage. He checks the garage, then the car, and notices the damage to the Bentley.

Dr Minn's mobile rings, prompting Chi to look back towards the car, shielding his eyes from the glare of the headlamps.

'Yes?' Dr Minn answers. 'And you're certain? No, I'll come to see for myself. Half an hour, no more.'

'Is there a problem, Father?' Mai Li asks.

'Nothing for you to worry about, dear. Please tell Chi to come.'

'Are you sure?'

'Sure, it's just an issue at the factory, but it needs my personal input.'

'But it's late, Father. Can't it wait until the morning?'

'No, my dear, and the sooner you go in, the sooner I'll return. Please tell Chi to come now.'

Mai Li opens her door, stepping out onto the drive. Closing the car door, the driveway crunches underfoot as she starts towards the garage, alerting Chi, who looks momentarily in her direction. She can see him at the open door of the Bentley, looking for evidence of who might have used it. He moves to the front, placing a hand on the bonnet to gauge from the heat, perhaps, how long it's been there.

'Father wants you now,' Mai Li informs Chi as she approaches, taking a route around the opposite side of the car to avoid contact, as he rushes out to her father waiting in the car.

'Did you spot anything unusual?'

'No, sir, it hasn't been there long though, the bonnet is still warm. Looks like it's also been in a collision with a dark object, possibly another car.'

'It should have been picked up last week for a software upgrade. I do hope it's not malfunctioned as a result.'

'I'll contact Bentley first thing in the morning to collect it for repair.'

'Okay, Chi, as quick as you can to the factory please.'

In a short moment, the car has manoeuvred out the drive and gone.

Mai Li enters the house through the garage access into the kitchen. Turning on the lights, she finds a clean glass and goes to the chilled water dispenser by the fridge. After drinking the water, she moves to the sink and hand washes the empty glass, placing it on the drainer alongside some clean pans. She catches a shape reflected in a pan, moving towards her from behind.

Grabbing the handle, she swings hard, with all the strength of her small frame, and connects squarely with the side of the head of the person behind her, sending him crashing to the floor. Scared, she raises the pan to strike a second time, only to find her arm held. She looks round and gets her second shock of the evening.

'You! What are you doing here?' she shrieks, recognising Chan.

'I could ask you the same question.'

'I live here!'

The man on the floor, Paul, moves to get up.

'Let go of my arm,' she demands.

'No, he's no threat, trust me. I can't let you hit him again.'

Chan is slow to release Mai Li's arm, which she lowers as Ox also appears from a hiding place.

'What! Is the whole of Downing Prison here?' Mai Li steps back and places a hand over a panic switch.

'I push this and the police will be here in under five minutes, and then you can add housebreaking to your sentence. So, you'd better start talking and making sense.'

'Yes, we're in your house uninvited... but until now, we've committed no crimes. Well, I mean him and me, anyway.' Chan points at Ox.

'And what about him?' Mai Li nods in Paul's direction.

'He'll be able to speak for himself when he recovers from your... attentions,' says Ox.

'Trust me, you're not in any danger,' repeats Chan. 'We want to leave as soon as we can, in search of answers as to who framed us and why.'

'Framed you for what?' she asks.

'For murder,' Paul says, still groaning.

'Shut up, Paul! Or I'll hit you again myself,' Ox warns.

'And you still claim I'm not in any danger?' she questions again.

'You're not. First, because we didn't do it. Second, they arrested us on a fake charge and then when we got to court, sentenced us on a completely different one.'

'Okay, then what were you originally arrested for?'

'Neither of us know,' says Ox. 'Every time we're anywhere near a car like that Bentley, things just kick off.'

'So how did you escape prison to end up here?'

'Technically we haven't come from prison,' says Paul. 'We were in the factory where the car came from.'

'Something doesn't add up here,' Mai Li says. 'What's my father's factory got to do with all this? And why break into our home?'

'We didn't break in, the car brought us here,' says Paul, adding, 'Do you mind if I get up now?'

'No, you stay right where I can see you,' Mai Li says.

'Well, at least can I have something for my head to stop this lump getting any bigger?'

She looks at Ox and gestures towards the freezer. Paul is less than thrilled with Ox's offer of a bag of prawns.

'What! No steak? Or even a bag of peas?'

'Beggars can't be choosers,' Ox tells him.

'I didn't know people were being taken to the factory from the prison,' Mai Li says, steering the conversation back on topic.

'I bet there's a lot you don't know about your father's operation,' claims Chan.

'There's a lot I don't know about my father,' she reveals, pulling her hand back from the switch.

'Look, we're happy to leave and for you never to see us again,' says Chan.

'I must be crazy to even half believe your story. But if it's the truth, I can probably help.'

'Why would you do that?' Paul asks.

'First, I'm not doing it for free. No, in return for my silence, you must tell me everything, everything you know about my father.'

'That sounds fair, but we don't know much,' Ox confesses.

No longer scared, Mai Li moves completely away from the switch towards the door. 'Follow me,' she says, as Ox helps Paul to his feet. Leaving the pack of now thawing prawns on the kitchen counter, Paul picks up his holdall and follows Chan, with Ox trailing behind him. From the kitchen, they cross the Italian tiled marbled floor of the hallway. Paul pauses, looking at the many paintings and objects adorning the walls.

'Don't even think about it,' Ox whispers, nudging him forward.

They take the stairs to the first floor and turn right, which brings them more or less above Dr Minn's office. Mai Li unlocks the door to her bedroom and palms it open.

'Come in, and touch nothing,' she says, holding the door open until all three are in, before locking it.

Her bedroom is spacious, large enough to hold another set of every item and still have space for more. Standing against the wall adjacent to the en suite door is a large glass tank draped with a jade green sheet. Across the room near the window, is a curved glass desk with three large computer screens. The bed appears messy and not made in days. She clears it, dumping everything on a chair that sits alongside her bed.

'I do not allow the cleaners in here. Make yourselves comfortable,' she says, waving a dismissive hand at the mess.

'What's under here?' Chan asks, as he lifts the edge of the

cover of the tank. 'Oh, my God!' he shrieks, as a huge snake presses its head against the glass. He drops the cover. 'You keep snakes?' Chan says, panting, breathing heavily and backing away from the tank.

'I warned you not to touch anything.'

Mai Li turns on her computer and sits waiting for it to warm up. Paul and Chan relax on the bed, but Ox takes a closer interest and stands behind her.

'What are you doing?' he asks as she types.

'I'm logging into the court computer system.'

'I thought no one could do that?'

'Well, that's true in theory, but I'm not just anyone. I worked on some of its development during my Uni studies. So, can you remember the crime number?'

'Somehow you would have thought they would be burned into our heads. But the truth is, we've been trying to forget the whole sorry saga.'

'I think it was something like one, seven, ninety-something,' says Chan.

'Never mind, I'll use something else.' She continues her search. After a few minutes, she says, 'One, seven, nine, two.'

'What? You've found it?' Ox says, as Chan joins him beside her.

'Not quite that number...' She pauses, as a realisation hits her.

'What about that number?' Chan asks.

'Strangely, that number has links also to a Mr James Long. Give me a minute while I dig a little deeper and cross-check it with the court computer.'

'You have access to that too? A woman of beauty and brains,' Ox says, looking across at Chan, who stares back with a look that says 'You didn't need to say it, did you?' reinforced with a shake of his head.

'I'm Sorry, I didn't mean to embarrass you. I mean, not that you're not beautiful... I'll just shut up and let you do whatever it is your doing.'

'You do that,' says Chan, nudging Ox to one side.

'I don't mind. It's flattering really,' she says, as Ox nudges Chan back, regaining his spot.

Mai Li's fingers glide over the keys. She works on all three screens at once, while Ox and Chan look on in silent amazement. Paul's head is still hurting, and he reclines on the bed, closing his eyes.

It's been over an hour and a half when the unexpected knock on the door brings Paul upright, with Chan and Ox both looking towards Mai Li.

'Just a second, please,' she calls out, getting to her feet. She points to the bathroom waving all three towards it. The men move silently into the en suite. Ox and Chan climb into the bath, pulling the shower curtain across to conceal themselves.

'Turn on the shower,' Mai Li whispers to Paul as she pulls the door shut. Quickly finding her dressing gown from a pile of clothes on a chair, she puts it on over the clothes she's wearing before unlocking the door.

'Ah! Father, you're back already. Everything okay at the factory?'

'Yes, just a slight generator problem, but I came straight back. You were right, it will keep until the morning. May I come in, if you are still awake?'

'I'd rather you didn't, Father. I was just about to take a shower.'

'Can I assume then you're not planning to cook the prawns you left out in the kitchen?'

'Oh, I forgot about that. Maybe not, considering I can't cook.'

'You know you only have to ask. We have a fine chef here who could teach you. Anyway, you're right and it's late. Goodnight, Mai Li.'

'Father.'

'Yes?'

'Can I ask you something?'

'Of course, anything. What is it?'

'Do you remember when you asked me to change the codes in the court system? What was that for?'

'That was a while ago. What's made you bring that up now? Let me try to remember. Er... yes, it was the government's additional security checks; they insisted we carry them out before the system went live, and later reversed that request. Why?'

'No real reason, I thought maybe I could get a job working with the court system, since I know so much about it. Or maybe even at the factory. There must be something I could do there?'

'No, I want my daughter to set her sights much higher than that. Besides, we need to get you your passport first, remember? If you have a business idea you want to explore, we can talk about it in the morning.'

'Thank you, Father.'

'Goodnight again, Mai Li.'

Mai Li locks the door and goes to the bathroom.

'You can come out now, he's gone,' she says, pushing the door open.

Paul squeezes past her and resumes his position on her bed.

'I said you can come out,' she repeats as the noise from the shower finally stops. She pulls back the shower curtain, revealing the two soaked friends.

'This is enough of a reason for me to kill Paul,' says Ox.

'He only did it because I told him to, and it saved you from being discovered.' She throws them a towel each.

'We have no other clothes. What are we supposed to do?' asks Chan.

'Take them off. It's easy enough to get them dried.' Mai Li leaves the bathroom as they strip off. She returns to collect the soaked clothes, pausing for a moment to admire Ox's sculpted torso. Noticing that he's aware of her looking, she averts her eyes, only to catch a reflection of Chan's back in the bathroom mirror.

'What's that mark on your shoulder?' she asks, ignoring Ox's tightened stomach.

'I don't know. It's been there ever since I can remember.'

'Would you mind me taking a closer look?'

'Why?'

'Because it looks familiar.'

She moves closer to Chan, appearing more excited at the imprint on his shoulder.

'Could you leave us and go in the bedroom? Please! I need to talk to Chan alone and show him something,' she tells Ox.

'What?' says Ox.

'What?' says Chan.

Ox's face tells its own story as he leaves them and exits the bathroom.

'What's going on in there?' Paul asks, sitting up.

'Don't ask.'

'You know what they say, three's a crowd,' Paul teases as Ox sits on the bed, feeling duped.

It's confusing Ox; he thought Mai Li liked him more than Chan. If her actions of the past few minutes are anything to go by, then this is a race where he'll end up second.

After a further minute, Mai Li and Chan emerge from the bathroom, holding onto each other. There are tears in her eyes, and Chan looks emotional too.

'What have you done in under three minutes that's brought her to tears?' asks Paul.

'Guys, you will not believe this,' says Chan, 'but we're related.'

'That would make it even more gross,' says Paul.

'You know, I thought you shared a lot of similar features, but I wasn't sure if I was just doing the old "they all look the same to me" thing.' Ox is smiling now: in his mind the race is back on.

'That's because we're twins,' Mai Li answers.

'No way! You two are winding us up, right? And anyway, where's the proof?' Ox asks, hoping that it's true and that it clears his path to Mai Li.

'My father has it hanging around his neck,' says Mai Li.

'I bet he'd hang us by the neck if he knew we were here,' says Ox.

'Well, the longer we stay here, the greater the chance of that actually happening,' says Paul.

# CHAPTER 26

Mai Li spent the night in one of the many extra rooms in the house, allowing for the three stowaways to sort out their own sleeping arrangements. As a precaution though, she locked the bedroom from the outside, ensuring that she's the only one with access. Aware of her father's daily routines, she knew it would be easy for her to return in the morning while he meditates. Unlocking the door she still enters her bedroom cautiously.

'It's only me,' she whispers, poking her head around the door.

Going inside, there's no visual evidence to suggest that three men had spent the night in her room. Chan and Ox emerge from the walk-in wardrobe while Paul appears as if by magic from beneath the pile of clothes on the chair next to the bed.

'We need to go before you get into real trouble,' Chan suggests.

'You might as well relax; no one can go anywhere until my father has left the house.'

'In that case, you couldn't find us something to eat?' asks Paul. 'I'm starving.'

Mai Li picks up the house telephone, pressing two digits.

'Candy, can I have an English breakfast brought to my room,

please? Oh, and Candy, could you ask the chef to make three of everything, please? Yes, that's correct, three.'

She hangs up and asks the men about their plans; they've had all night to come up with something.

'Well, we need to find more on this James Long bloke; he may be the key to all this,' Paul says.

'Paul, there is no "we", as in you and us,' says Ox. 'This is not your problem. You're free to step away at any point.'

'What sort of human would I be if I didn't see this through?'

'Just a thief with a conscience, that's all,' says Ox.

'I could take that as you warming to me?'

'Well, don't,' replies Ox.

'Maybe just as a compliment, then?'

'Girls, stop bitching,' Mai Li says. 'We have more urgent things to think about. We need to keep ahead of the curve. Find me something long we can tie around my mobile.'

'How about this lamp cord?' offers Paul, lifting and tracing the flex back to the wall plug.

'How long would you say that is?' she asks.

'I would guess around eight feet.'

'More than enough; find something to cut it.' She grabs one of her two mobiles and dials the number of the other. It rings and she swiftly puts it on silent. She takes the severed cord and promptly secures it around the first mobile in a crude knot. She lowers the phone out the window, down to a position just above the window of her father's office. She increases the volume on the receiving mobile, creating a listening device. Using the redundant lamp moved closer to the window, she anchors the cord.

A knock at the door sends them all into hiding again. She answers, stunned at who is blocking her doorway.

'Chi? What are you doing here?'

'I've brought your breakfast. You ordered so much they weren't sure if you were alone up here.' He turns around and picks up a tray from the trolley parked behind him.

'I'll take that, thank you.' She takes the tray from Chi before moving back into her room. She's barely placed it on her desk when she turns to find Chi right behind her with the second tray and notices how he scans her room.

'What do you think you are doing in my room?' she shouts.

'Just helping with the breakfast trays, that's all.'

'Get out,' she snaps, snatching the tray from Chi's hand. 'You need to wait until you're invited before you invade a woman's private space.'

'I'm sorry, Ms Minn,' he says, backing into the doorframe before navigating his way out of her room.

'And you should be. Wait till my father hears about this, how you forced your way into my bedroom, hoping to find me in my underwear.'

'But that would be a completely untrue version of what's happened.'

'Let's see if he decides this is acceptable behaviour from his employee.' She slams the door before realising she doesn't yet have the third tray.

She picks up the mobile before opening the door again to retrieve the last tray. Chi remains outside, still pleading.

'Please, I'm begging you, Ms Minn. I'm sorry, it won't happen again. I need to keep my job, Ms Minn.'

'You need to move away from this door now, right now before I call him,' she says, holding up her mobile to convince him. As luck would have it, her father's voice suddenly emits from her mobile and Chi backs away from the door with haste. Picking up the last tray, she slams the door shut with her foot, returning inside. She lifts the phone to her ear as Ox, Chan and Paul emerge from their hiding places, then she activates the loudspeaker function so they can listen simultaneously.

'Quiet,' she says.

"Sir Edward, thanks for returning my call and sorry to burden you so early with unwanted news. Last night my facility suffered an unexplained breakout. It's odd, though, Sir Edward, how only three of the special Downing intake are unaccounted for. It's also regrettable that they stole personal items, which I'm hoping we can recover without publicity or involving the police. As they are still within the Link system, we should be able to use the bracelets to find them. I'm proposing to reprogram the system to detect them without endangering their lives... No, no, this is a far easier option than what we did with the court system... I assure you nothing I do will jeopardise our arrangement.'

A few seconds later, the mobile hanging out the window beeps loudly twice.

'Get it up, quick!' Mai Li orders. Paul is nearest and takes charge of the cord, retrieving the mobile. Mai Li instantly removes the flex, looks at the holding caller ID, then answers it.

'Father, I'm in my room, you didn't need to call me.'

'Good morning, my daughter. I know, I was just being lazy, following what young people do these days. Anyway, I have another little correction I need you to implement for me. The type of work you said last night that you enjoyed doing.'

'What? Now, Father?'

'Oh no, sometime this evening will be fine. It's not that urgent.' He tries to mask his true wish that he would like it done sooner rather than later. 'I've got factory business with my solicitor and the accountants which will take up most of my day. Anyway, did you have something planned for yourself today?'

'Well, I planned on meeting up with some Uni friends,' she says, quickly conjuring up a believable excuse, which she thinks could help delay him.

'It's not a big issue. You enjoy yourself. It can even be done tomorrow, although I would prefer having it completed before Monday at the latest.'

'Thanks, Father.' She ends the call, turning off the mobile. 'In around half an hour my father will have left and we can leave too,' she tells the trio.

'What are we going to do for transport?' asks Ox.

'Do you have a car?' Chan asks.

'No, I'm still learning. But if my instructor is free, I can arrange

for my lesson to be brought forward, and that's how we get out.'
She claims confidently.

∾

It's not long before the sound of Dr Minn's car leaving prompts
Mai Li into action. She contacts her driving instructor, who is
more than willing to bring her booked lesson forward.

'You've done too much already and no need to take further
risks,' Ox points out. Mai Li ignores him, choosing to concentrate
on getting the last number her father dialled from the house
telephone. How best to use it is her next thought.

'Okay, give it here,' Paul says, taking the piece of paper on
which Mai Li has written the number.

'What are you going to do?' asks Chan.

'Can I use the phone?' Paul asks Mai Li, ignoring the question.
She hands the cordless house phone to Paul, who dials the
number and listens.

'Good morning, Sir Edward Long's ministerial office, how
may I direct your call?'

Paul disconnects the call and returns the handset to Mai Li.

'Sir Edward Long – he's that MP,' says Ox. 'You know, the one
that's been banging on about law and order. I'm sure that's him.'

'I know Mr Minn is your father, but I can't see how he's not
connected somehow to all the troubles we've been having,'
Chan's quick to point out.

'He's your father too,' Mai Li reminds him.

'Let's forget about all this family history stuff until we've
cleared our names and the dust has settled,' says Ox.

'Well, we only have two clues so far,' says Chan. 'Sir Edward
Long and a James Long. I wonder if they're the same person?'

'Somehow, I can't see it,' interrupts Paul. 'MPs have to be
squeaky clean. A more likely scenario, just probably related.'

'Well, I've got enough to make a start,' Mai Li says, sitting at
her computer again, gently pounding the keys.

The three men don't understand what she's doing. For the moment, Mai Li offers no commentary, seeming to direct all her focus on her computer screen.

'Ah, found something. Good old Facebook, never lets you down.'

'What is it?' asks Chan.

'Sir Edward is the current prisons minister. His brother, James, though, lives a playboy lifestyle with debts to match, it seems.'

'You're good at this,' Paul says, in reference to her skills.

'Wait, there's more,' she adds. 'For instance, James Long is selling a car and there's his mobile number, which means we can use it to get his address.'

'Okay, I vote we let Paul do it,' Ox suggests. 'Make the call, that is. He said he wants to help, and we don't seem to have any luck when it's to do with cars.'

Paul tuts. 'Give me the phone and stop being so superstitious.' Paul takes the phone again from Mai Li and dials the number on the screen. 'It's ringing. Everyone quiet. Oh, good morning, my name is Simon, and I was wondering if the car you advertised is still available?'

'Available till sold,' says a male voice. 'I'll be honest, though, I'm expecting someone this afternoon who sounded keen.'

'And if I were to pay, say, a thousand pounds over the advertised price, that's cash, where would I be in the bidding order?'

'The car would be yours, Simon. A bird in the hand... and all that.'

'Then do you mind giving me your location, please? The postcode and house number are all I need to find the address.'

'You can meet me in North Wharf Road, Paddington W2. It's one-way, so make sure you enter from the Harrow Road, Bishops Bridge Road end. After two hundred metres, you'll find me parked up just before the junction with Hermitage Street.'

'Hermitage Street, okay, I've got that. Should we say about three o'clock, James, or not long after?'

'It might be sold by then. I did say someone was coming and they said two o'clock.'

'Okay, I'm keen too, so should we make that one o'clock then?'

'Perfect, and you already have my number. So, I'd appreciate a call if for any reason you can't make it.'

'I'm ninety-nine per cent sure you'll be seeing us today.'

'Us?'

'Yeah, it's me and my mechanic. I just drive them, it's his job to check them and make sure they run.'

'Oh, okay, I see. Then I'll see you both later, goodbye.'

The call ends.

'All we have to do now is get there without getting arrested,' Ox says.

'A simple task if you're free,' says Chan.

'What about Pinpoint?' asks Paul.

'From what I remember of our arrest, it's only being used in the evenings during curfew,' Ox says.

'Well, my driving instructor will be here soon,' says Mai Li. 'That's our transport out of here.'

'Please don't come,' Chan pleads. 'You've already done too much.'

'No chance. Without me, my instructor won't help you.'

'Have you got a bag similar to this one I could use?' Paul asks. 'This one will attract too much attention.'

She goes to the wardrobe and removes a dark sports holdall from a shelf.

'Will this do?'

'Yes, perfect, thanks.'

After about ten minutes, a knock at Mai Li's door sends them all scrambling to hide while she answers it. A maid informs her of the driving instructor's arrival.

'Where are all the staff?' she asks.

'Having breakfast, miss.'

'Then take this tray with you, have your breakfast, and then come for the other trays once I've left for my lesson; I'll leave them outside my door, okay?' Mai Li says, slipping back into the room to retrieve one tray, which is handed to the maid.

'Thank you, miss,' the maid says, taking the tray and leaving. Mai Li closes the door.

'Okay, time to go,' she informs them, opening the door again to check that the maid has left.

Paul grabs the sports bag before dropping in behind Chan and Ox, who follow Mai Li out the door. She leads them down the stairs, across the hallway and out the front door.

Mai Li gets into the driving seat of her instructor's car. The other three pile onto the rear seats, slamming the doors shut. The instructor looks over his right shoulder in total shock.

'What do you think you're doing? This is a one-to-one lesson! Ms Minn, please explain what's going on here?'

'They're just Uni friends who stopped over last night,' she says. Then adds, 'They need dropping off somewhere.'

'I want you all out of my car, now. I'm a professional driving instructor, not a taxi service.'

'We know. But could you make an exception for, say, four hundred pounds?' Paul produces eight new fifty-pound notes from his pocket.

'If this is something unlawful, I don't know you and don't think you're getting a receipt either.' He stuffs the wad into the breast pocket of his jacket. 'Better still, I'll drive, to guarantee we get there.'

The crestfallen instructor and Mai Li swap seats before the car leaves the driveway and heads back towards the main road.

# CHAPTER 27

Since returning an earlier call to Dr Minn about the factory incident, Sir Edward has been sitting at his office desk in deep contemplation. The missing prisoners mean his long-term plans for prisoner release reforms are in danger of being scuppered without being properly assessed. Less than pleased with the attention he'll now have to give the matter, existing problems like the women in his life, the potential of two babies and next month's general election can't be sidelined for any given length of time either. Frustrated and angry, he knows who needs to provide those answers.

Unsettled, Sir Edward lifts his telephone, intending to contact Ian, hoping for a full explanation that would help salvage his scheme, should there be any possible chance that it could be salvaged. The telephone rings and Ian is quick to answer.

'Edward, I'm almost sure it's tomorrow, not today that you're due to be calling with an update.'

'So, I take it you haven't heard anything then?'

'Anything about what?'

'I was hoping you could tell me, Ian?'

'Look, you're answering questions with questions – what's going on?'

'My prison release project has suffered a major setback and I'm not entirely sure you're blameless.'

'If I've messed up any small details then I apologise, unconditionally of course.'

'You have indeed messed up, Mr Gilby, and I think a face-to-face meeting is the most appropriate way forward at this stage. What say you meet me at the same place as last time, twelve thirty. Does that sound good to you?'

'Yeah, I can do that, I'll see you there, bye.'

'Bye,' Sir Edward concludes his call then summons his secretary, Amy, to his office.

'Yes, Sir Edward?' she answers on entering.

'Amy, please cancel all appointments for the rest of the day, reschedule anything important and find excuses for the others.'

'Yes, sir.'

'If anyone enquiries as to my whereabouts, I'm in meetings all day.'

'Have you called Lady Elizabeth yet, sir? You asked to be reminded after ten am.'

'Thanks, I haven't but I will, but if I don't and she calls, please inform her that I'll be dining out this evening with my brother.'

Sir Edward knows his wife will avoid contacting him if she believes he's with James, affording him the perfect cover to keep his appointment later with Kim.

He leaves his office, taking a taxi rather than his official car.

At home, Elizabeth is taking a day off, hoping to manage her morning sickness better. Since her husband left for work, she's only left her bed twice. She's finding it strange how ordinary things like toothpaste or soap are having such an effect. Her plan to ride out the nausea by sleeping is so far not working well. As she tries to settle again, the bedside phone rings.

'Hello,' she answers, exhaustion in her voice.

'Elizabeth, we need to talk.'

'Who is this, please?' she moans.

'I'm surprised you don't recognise my voice. It's me, Kim.'

'Kim? Have you been drinking?'

'No, but I wish I had. It would make this a lot easier.'

'Make what easier? Kim, look, you know you shouldn't be calling here. And I'm sorry but I can't do this right now either.' She hangs up and takes herself off to the bathroom. The phone rings again almost immediately and Elizabeth drags herself from the bathroom to answer again, feeling angry that her movements are being dictated by Kim, of all people.

'I thought you would have got the message?' she answers angrily.

'Darling, it's only me. What message? I'm just calling to see how you're feeling.'

'Oh, I'm sorry, Edward, that wasn't aimed at you. I'm not handling this morning sickness well.'

'What's this message thing about?'

'Oh, nothing, just a silly call from Kim.'

'Kim? When?'

'Just before your call.'

'What did she say to upset you?'

'I didn't give her that chance, though she sounded desperate to talk.'

'Desperate? Look, you take things easy and don't worry about Kim. Take the phone off the hook if you need to. I'll take care of her. She won't bother you again, I promise.'

'What do you mean, take care of her? We were friends once, you know.'

'Stop worrying, that's just my anger talking.'

'Edward, promise me…'

'I'm sorry, darling, but I have to go.'

The call ends abruptly, and just in time, as Elizabeth needs to return to the bathroom again.

Feeling bad about cutting her off, Elizabeth decides after exiting the bathroom to call Kim back.

'I thought you didn't want to speak with me?' Kim answers, recognising the number.

'You know how Edward feels about it.'

'Wouldn't it be nice, though, if we could patch things up and all be friends again?'

'I know I would like that.'

'Then why don't you come over later? Anytime, we'll have the place to ourselves, we can have a catch-up over some drinks and I'll even order your favourite pizza from a new place opened locally this week. I'm dying to try it – what do you say?'

'Pizza maybe but no alcohol.'

'Anything, just come, please, it will feel like the old days.'

'Maybe, I'll see, I can't promise you.'

'Just try, that's all I'm asking.'

Sir Edward feels incensed by his ex-wife's behaviour. He feels the need to intervene somehow and avert a disaster, should Kim carry out her threats to tell his wife, the press or his party. On the move by taxi, the traffic is slowing and Sir Edward uses the delay to call Kim.

'It didn't take you long,' she answers.

'Actually, I'd planned to call you today. Your silly stunt has only brought that forward, that's all.'

'All I know is that since I told you I'm pregnant, you've avoided me.'

'Kim, you're confusing being busy with avoiding you. We were married once, remember. You've forgotten what my hours were like. And it's an election year, for Christ's sake.'

'At the moment, I've seen no commitment or intent. What are you going to do once your baby is born?'

'To be honest, I haven't had time to think about that problem.'

'But you've had enough time to label it as a problem?'

'Okay, maybe I used the wrong word, Kim, but that's certainly not what I meant.'

'Well, you'd better find your focus, Edward, before I'm showing and have to tell people. Because, believe me, the first person that I think needs to know is Elizabeth.'

'Kim, please listen. Before you do something silly, something I'm sure you'll regret later, we need to meet and discuss things like adults and without the threats.'

'Edward, they're not threats. At the moment, my only desire is for you to acknowledge that we're having a baby together and to promise you will be an active father in his or her life.'

'Does Christine know yet?'

'No, but she brought home a membership form for the health club the other day. Maybe she can already see changes in my body shape, like all mothers.'

'Kim, when are we going to talk? I was thinking maybe later today?'

'Why don't you come over this evening, after eight o'clock? My mother won't be here, she's spending a few days with her sister down in Brighton.'

'Okay, I'll see what I can do.'


With the traffic still ambling, Sir Edward puts his mind to work. For the first time, he recognises that doing nothing is not an option. He looks out the window, watching people milling about, wondering if they have similar problems.

His ideal outcome would be for Kim to lose the baby by natural means, but he hates himself for even harbouring such thoughts.

The taxi's meter continues ticking even though the traffic

hasn't moved for over two minutes. Close enough to the pub, Sir Edward decides to walk the last three hundred metres to clear his head of negative thoughts. His mind is playing the what-if game, but so far, he's lost every round.

He nears the theatre, the final marker before the pub. Sir Edward notices a billboard advertising the current show. It's a comedy, ironically called *Love Triangle*. He walks past and enters the pub. Ian had arrived first this time and found a seat just feet away from where they sat last time.

'Table for one, sir?' asks an attractive waitress.

'No, I'm meeting that gentleman over there, thank you.' He points in Ian's direction.

'Then please follow me,' she says, picking up a single-sheet handwritten menu. 'Here you are, sir. Can I get you something to drink?' She places the handwritten menu on the table.

'Just a cup of Earl Grey tea, thank you.' He removes his mobile from his pocket and places it on the table. Then removes his coat; folding it twice, he places it over the back of a chair before sitting down.

'And how many of those have you had?' Ian's customary glass of whisky with ice sat in front of him.

'What, don't you drink anything other than tea?'

'I have been known to enjoy the odd glass of champagne, or more often a well-chilled bottle of Sauvignon Blanc.' Sir Edward leans in towards Ian, keeping the pitch of his voice low. 'I feel you may have let me down, Ian.'

Ian tries to respond, but Sir Edward cuts him off.

'And I'm not entirely sure what went wrong.'

Ian tries again.

'Please let me finish,' Sir Edward insists. 'Obviously, they passed your test that got them out of prison, but ultimately you've fucked up by not controlling them as agreed. Now, I know one of them is your brother. I half expected it and I would have overlooked it. And in the wider scheme of things the other two…

well, what I mean is, I could have found good reasons, in this election year, to overlook them too.'

'Then what is this great problem?'

'The great problem, Mr Gilby, is that they've stolen something. As I understand it, they took a risk for freedom but in doing so they put their lives and those of the public at risk.

'I don't understand how the public could be at risk?'

'You didn't seriously think that we would release them without additional safeguards. The tags they're wearing are monitored by the Pinpoint system. That targets them and by default anyone within a radius of fifty centimetres.'

'So how do we get past this?'

'That ship has sailed, Mr Gilby. And, if you'll excuse the pun, the spotlight falls on you.'

'Meaning?'

'Meaning, the results of your actions have forced me to suspend the programme. I've already mentioned the lives you've put at risk, and frankly, I can't justify the papers being handed back just yet.'

'Are you saying you're not giving me a chance to fix this?'

'Not unless you know where they are?'

'I don't, that's the truth.' Ian opens his hands in a 'nothing to hide' gesture.

'Then…' Sir Edward shakes his head and has to pause as the waitress returns with his tea.

'Shall I stir for you, sir?' she asks.

'Please,' he says, knowing full well that he's stalling while Ian waits to continue.

After stirring the pot vigorously, she prepares the cup.

'I can do the rest, thank you.' He smiles up at the waitress, covering the cup with his hand.

'Enjoy,' she says with a smile before moving away from the table.

'You were saying?' Ian continues pressing.

'Look, since I've had to suspend the scheme, you need to think about maybe completing another task, to earn your papers.'

'How did I know it would be something along those lines?' Ian says, forcing a half-smile.

'Don't you want to hear what the task is?' Sir Edward cocks his head as he looks at Ian.

'You'll be telling me that there's someone you want killed next,' Ian whispers calmly.

'I thought you couldn't impress me anymore. But if you have deduced that just by looking into my eyes, then I'm impressed.' Sir Edward looks around to check that no one has heard his off-the-cuff remark.

'Don't be. It's a lucky guess. Mind-reading – that's not part of my act.'

'Why didn't you let me keep on believing in the magic of your profession?'

'Because I'm not trying to impress you. I'm trying to get back control of my life.' Ian's voice rises.

'And you will, Ian.' Sir Edward pauses.

'So, who is the unfortunate soul you'd rather wasn't living?'

'My ex-wife. She's got a jealous, disruptive streak that's becoming a problem for my pregnant wife.'

'And how do you think I can help? Because I'm telling you now, I'm no killer.'

'I was thinking that maybe by using hypnosis she could be kept out of our lives forever, for which I would be more than happy to return your papers.'

'Hypnotising someone long term is a big deal that could mess them up mentally. The prison thing, well that's short term until they develop good habits.'

'Well, I wasn't sure how far you'd go, but if you wanted to say hypnotise someone else, who would, so to speak, take care of her, I'd be comfortable with that option too.'

'Don't take it as me agreeing to anything, but something like that would cost far more than my papers. It would mean me having to live with it forever while keeping your involvement a secret.'

'Okay, so this is where you get to name your price.' Sir Edward leans back in his seat in anticipation.

Sir Edward's mobile, on silent, vibrates, turning slightly on the table, with 'James' displayed on the small screen.

'A second, please,' Sir Edward says to Ian, picking up the phone and moving away from the table and the noise.

'Edward, they know. I don't know how, but they do.'

'James, what the hell are you talking about? Who knows what?'

'There was only meant to be two. But four turned up, asking all kinds of awkward questions about that… incident.'

'Reporters?'

'No, they weren't reporters. Three guys and a girl. Originally he said to expect him with his mechanic to view the car.'

'The car I told you to get rid of weeks ago?'

'Yeah, only I thought maybe I could make a few quid on it rather than just having it crushed.'

'Decision-making is your worst quality, James. You're the only person I know that puts his hand back in a fire having being burned once. When will you learn?' Sir Edward turns away from Ian's gaze and shields the mouthpiece.

'The car is in my name, James, and that's the only thing that can be traced back.'

'Yeah, but I know you weren't there.'

'You're not getting it. The car is the original crime scene.' Sir Edward thinks a second. 'Okay, where are you and the car right now?'

'I'm near the taxi pickup point at Paddington Station. I saw those Pinpoint bracelets on their wrists and noticed the way they were trying to avoid cameras. So, I took my chance and just ran over the footbridge and down into the station.'

'Maybe it's best if you spend the night in a hotel, just in case they know where you live. Stay there and wait for me, I'll pick you up in around fifteen minutes. We'll retrieve the car and decide what to do then.'

Sir Edward returns to the table.

'I'm afraid the meeting is over. There's something more important that I must attend to. Go home, Ian, and sober up.'

Producing a twenty-pound note from his pocket, Sir Edward leaves it under the teapot and hurries out of the pub.

He hires a minicab from his mobile as soon has he exits and plots a route to Paddington Station.

The entrance to the station is busy, but there's an area for quick drop-offs and pickups. Sir Edward is about to call his brother when he spots him.

'Just over there by that second sign, please,' he instructs the driver.

The car stops a few metres short of the double yellow lines. James stoops to peer into the car before opening the door and climbing into the back alongside Edward.

'Driver, are you okay to drive us to a few locations?' Sir Edward asks.

'Really, for this to be legal, you should book through the office.'

'There's no way you can help even in an emergency?'

'If you pay extra, I'll take my break and make it happen.'

'Okay, we'll pay extra. Whatever it takes. Go right when you leave the station, then take the third turning off the roundabout.'

They sit back as the car moves out of the station, sweeping right and joining the roundabout. It makes an almost full circle, turning left into North Wharf Road.

'Can you slow down, please?' says James.

'Where did you park it?' asks Edward.

'It should be just down there on the left.' He strains to see out the front window.

'Where? I can't see it,' Sir Edward responds.

'It's gone! I swear that's where I left it.'

'Well, it's either stolen or you didn't read that sign.'

'Which sign?'

'The one that says "tow-away zone".'

'I'm sorry,' James says, embarrassed.

'This day can't get any worse. I may have to report it stolen now.'

'Where next, please?' asks the driver.

'Do you know Shepherd's Hill?' Sir Edward asks.

'If Waze can find it, then I can too,' he answers with confidence.

'How about Highgate Station?'

'Yes, I know that place, on the A1, right.'

'Yes, then head towards Highgate Station and I'll direct you when we close.'

'Okay, boss.' Looking over his right shoulder, the driver moves off.

'Have you had something to eat today?' Edward asks his brother.

'Yeah, I had a sandwich while I was waiting.'

'Something healthy, I hope?'

'When you're scared, all sense of healthy eating goes out the window.'

'James, you're a diabetic. Be more aware, your life could depend on it.'

After twenty minutes, the cab is cruising north along the A1 and nearing Highgate. The brothers haven't risked saying anything in presence of the driver that he could possibly remember. Sir Edward leans forward to get a better view out of the front window.

'Could you take the right turn at the traffic lights, please, and then the first left or it's the second, if you count the small access road,' Edward instructs the driver.

'Where are we going?' James asks.

'Relax. I have to make a quick stop, but the less you know the better.'

James returns to looking out the window.

After five hundred metres the car turns left into Priory Gardens and Edward gives the driver further instructions.

'Can you stop by the first house on the left please, the one with the steps.'

'Who lives here?' James asks. Edward doesn't answer.

'I'll be a few minutes. Ten maximum, I promise. Wait here.'

Sir Edward leaves the car and starts up the steps.

Unseen, on the opposite side of the road, a car pulls in a few metres further along. The occupant stays in the car but adjusts their mirror and seems to be taking a very keen interest.

Kim is quick to answer the door, as if she is expecting her caller.

'Edward! You're a little early, but thanks for keeping your word this time. Come in, come in,' she says, smiling.

'Kim, before you get upset, something very important has come up and I can't stop, but as you see, I've made the effort to come and tell you in person.'

'Something always comes up. Isn't this also important to you, Edward?' She turns away and starts crying.

'I'm sorry, Kim.'

'Why do I feel that this so-called very important thing is another woman?' She dries her eyes and turns with a half-smile that seems to only affect one side of her face. Looking past him, she sees movement in the rear seat of the cab.

'Is your bit of important in that cab with you? Is that why you can't stay focused for five minutes?' She pushes past Edward and down the steps. Knowing her temper, Edward responds and follows after her.

'Kim, wait. Please don't make a scene.'

The tinted window obscures the passenger's identity. Kim jerks open the door.

'Are you aware that we're having a baby?' she screams, loud enough for half the street to hear.

'I wasn't, but I am now.'

'James!'

'Hello, Kim.'

'What if that had been Elizabeth in there?' Edward says with some anger.

'I'm sorry, it's hormones,' she says, resting her head in her hands to conceal her embarrassment.

'Why don't you ever listen? If you want to be the headline in tomorrow's papers, then you're going about it the right way.'

'I'll talk to James, he won't say anything,' she says in a lower, more controlled tone.

'Trying to back me into a corner – that's what you call love?'

'I'm sorry, Edward.'

'Sorry solves nothing. We need to leave.'

'No, no, please, I don't want you leaving here angry.' She bends down to talk with her former brother-in-law. 'James, can you please come inside for a moment? We can order another cab.'

'It's Edward's call,' he answers. Kim looks back up at Edward.

'I suppose it's better than doing this in public,' he sighs. 'Go in with her please, James, while I pay the fare.'

James exits the car and follows Kim up the steps to the house. He stops to answer a call on his mobile.

'Hello… I'm surprised you've found the courage to call my number… No, he's not with me right now.' James is being careful and elusive.

Sir Edward goes to the driver's window. 'I'm sorry about all that. She's my former wife.'

'My friend, I have three wives and same model at home,' the driver boasts.

'Thanks for understanding.' Sir Edward hands the driver a large tip and allows the cab to leave.

Straightening up, he's aware of his mobile buzzing in his pocket. There are three missed calls from Elizabeth.

'Oh, hi, dear,' he answers the current call.

'Where are you, Edward? Why haven't you been answering your phone?'

'I'm with James, at a restaurant.'

'It doesn't sound much like a restaurant.'

'No, I'm outside, about to leave for home.'

'Can I speak with James, please?' She's trying to wrong-foot him.

'Sorry, dear, he's in the loo. I came out to look for the cab. In fact, that could be them trying to call me back now. Is everything okay?'

'I'm still feeling rough and I can't seem to keep any food down unless it's toast, only we've run out of bread. You know, that special one I like?'

'That's no problem, apart from the all-night shop being in South London. Anyway, I need to go, dear. See you later.'

Sir Edward moves quickly up the stairs and into the house. He calls Kim's name as he enters.

'We're in the kitchen,' she calls back.

Entering the kitchen, Edward sees that a cup of tea is ready and waiting for him.

'I'm sorry, but I have to go. James, you can check into a hotel tonight and I'll speak with you sometime tomorrow to sort that other thing.'

'Give me a second to finish my tea and I'll leave with you.'

'Don't be silly,' says Kim. 'If it's only one night there's no need for a hotel. We have a good guest room upstairs. Please stay.' She's trying to impress on Edward that she still cares for his family. James looks at his brother for approval.

'It's your choice,' says Edward. 'I have to leave now, though.' He turns and heads towards the front door.

'Let me see you out,' Kim says, following him. 'Again, I'm sorry,' she says at the front door. 'Call me tomorrow so we can start again, like a family.'

'I told you, Kim, the best solution for everyone would be for you to abort the baby.'

He walks out the door and Kim closes it behind him, applying the security chain. Turning, she sees James standing in the kitchen doorway and realises he must have heard their full conversation. She hides her distress with a wan smile.

'Come, let me show you where you'll spend the night and later I'll order a pizza and we can relax.'

Elizabeth is still outside, parked over the road, when Edward leaves Kim's house. She lowers herself into the car seat as he walks past on the other side of the road. She takes out her mobile, unlocks it, then dials the only contact that has no photo ID beside the number.

'Hello, who's this?'

'It's Lizzy.'

'Lizzy, what's wrong? Remember this number is for emergencies only.'

'It's Edward, Dad. Lately he's been acting odd.'

'How do you mean? What's going on?'

'I've just found out he's been seeing that bitch, his ex-wife.'

'Seeing someone doesn't mean anything is going on.'

'Then why would he have to lie about it?'

'Where are you now?'

'In a friend's car, outside Kim's house.'

'I take it she's at home and he's with her?'

'Yeah, at least he was. God! I feel like going in there and ripping out every strand of her fake hair, one root at a time. And to think I felt sorry enough to come all the way over here to see her on the promise of a pizza and chat. How can he do this, Dad? After all, I'm the one giving him a child, something she didn't even want.'

'Listen, Lizzy, go home. I'll think of something.'

'How are you going to fix this one, Dad? Just when I need him, I can feel her breaking us apart. And that's without even thinking about the impact and damage it could do to Edward's career.'

He can feel her emotion from the breaking up of her voice.

'Lizzy, stop crying. Listen to your father and go home now.'

It's almost 5:30 in the afternoon and Fat Fingers' mobile vibrates. Removing it from its secure hiding place, he answers it.

'Yes?'

'Mr Fingers, I wager you were wondering if you'd ever hear from me again?'

'Yes, I'll agree I did, but I suspected that someone else might get in touch.

'So, you're not surprised?'

'Only that for a dead man, you sound very well. Then again, I guess a man that can get himself into prison must have good plans, likewise, to get himself out.'

'A sad and unfortunate side effect of our plight that another person had to die to save thousands of others. That's why the pace of progress to meet our deadline is so important.'

'Sorry, some people in my service are not up to my current standards.'

'If the task is too much, don't be embarrassed to say, Mr Fingers. But it will mean the return of the cash already being wired to you. If you need more time, that's the one commodity we don't have, nor can we control it.'

'I guarantee the chip is being secured as I speak. But I'd be exposing myself to the vulnerability of the information I already know, and seeing how easy it was for you to get access to me, I need assurances, other assurances separate from the money.'

'If you are saying this will put us back on track, then I'm listening, Mr Fingers.'

'I want you to do something for me that will balance the scales. That way I'll have something on you and vice versa.'

'The term is a Mexican stand-off, but then I get the chip, right?'

'Do this tonight, then call, otherwise I'll return your money and sell the chip to the highest bidder.'

The line goes silent, with only static for a moment.

'Okay, but only tell me the net result you want and I will take care of all the details.'

It's five minutes before ten in the evening when Fat Fingers receives a call. A voice simply says "all done" before ringing off. He knows the clock has properly started, and so, armed with a number for Paul's brother, who he needs to contact for the first time in years, he dials the number, not sure how the call or the fact that it's him calling will be received. After two rings a slurred voice answers.

'Hello, who's this?'

'Is this Ian I'm speaking to?'

'I'm not sure I should even talk to someone that knows my name but answers my question with a question.'

'Knowing my name might not be helpful at this point.'

'You can always test your theory, although there's something hauntingly familiar about your voice.'

'What if instead I mention Paul, your brother?'

'If you're the police, I don't know where he is, and even if I did, he can stay and rot there. If you... I mean... when you find him, you can even quote me on it.'

'I can find him but I'm not the police.'

'Then if you know where he is, why the hell are you calling me?'

'You don't sound sober at all, Ian.'

'I'll tell you what, if you need to kill him, go ahead. You would be doing us both a favour. At least then he can't ruin any other chances, and I get to put my past behind me.'

'I'm sure no matter how much you claim to hate him, you don't really want him dead.'

'How would you know what I want?'

'Because you once looked up to me as your father.'

'And there's your first mistake; that tells me who you are. I know influential people who could see you remain there for the rest of your life.'

'That's already been taken care of, but there's two sides to every story and most of what you'd heard or read was just sensationalised press, trying to sell newspapers.'

'And so, you put Paul straight, yeah? With the truth or your version of it.'

'With the truth, yes, I had nothing to lose or gain.'

'So, what is the truth? According to your sick mind.'

'The truth will always be the truth, but can seem more distorted when you're drunk.'

'Whisky and me go back a long way, so you can speak to us as a pair or not at all.'

'Okay, the first time I met your mum was on the streets. She asked if I could spare some change to get a bus home, because she had lost her purse. I liked her and followed her just to see which bus she would take so that maybe I could run into her again. When she stopped at a doorway, I knew if she opened the door then she had conned me as it was nowhere near any bus stops. It looked like someone had dumped a big box of rubbish in front of the door. I expected her to brush it aside, put a key in the door and enter. Instead, she opened the box and carefully lifted out what looked like a folded blanket. Then she climbed into the box, and I heard a baby crying. She was trying to settle the baby; it would have been too cold to even consider breastfeeding. The easiest thing was to just leave and come back in the morning, or not at all, but knowing even a healthy person would struggle in such low temperatures, I couldn't leave them there. I only had a small one bedroom myself, but it was warm, and a step up from the doorway where I found her. I didn't ask about her past and in time we grew closer. Your mother kept secrets, though. Even after your brother was born I did not understand how she was still being controlled by your father. The day you came home from school and found me trying to make drugs was one of the lowest points in my life. When she was carrying Paul, and I now suspect it was during both pregnancies, she would transport drugs for your father. She was always high because she would pinch a little of it for herself. What she didn't know was he set her up to be robbed, so she would forever be indebted for the value of the lost drugs plus interest that doubled every two days. I couldn't earn enough to pay that debt in full and that's why I attempted making some, just tried to win somehow and keep the family together. The night she died, though, I remember so clearly. I had bought you a present for your eighth birthday but it just happened to be the day it coincided with her finding out I'd been unfaithful. When she went into the kitchen to fetch a knife, I saw you and Paul go into the bedroom where you always hid when we argued. I thought the knife was to cut the cake, but then she started searching for you and Paul, saying that she would "take you both to the grave with her" and that I couldn't have loved her or you kid's if someone else was having my child. I realised straight away what she was planning and I struggled with her, trying to get the knife. She bit me in the stomach and I just lashed out, and she fell. It happened so fast I didn't realise in the confusion I had already taken the knife and literally severed the side of her face.'

'You're telling me you saved our lives? Yet I can't understand why it's taken this long to find us and explain what really happened.'

'The answer is two angry boys that grew up into two angry men.'

'And that's all?'

'No, and also a big favour to ask.'

'You said that you could find Paul. Get him to do your favour.'

'Look he forgave me some years ago and if his circumstances were different, I know he would do it.'

'Well, he's not me and I did Paul a big favour getting him out of prison, just because he was my brother. I suppose if I felt that I owed him, I must owe you too, at least a favour for saving my life, but I'm not getting involved with getting anyone else out of prison.'

'No, and I wouldn't ask you to. This is a simple job of delivering something important for me.'

'I don't mess with drugs either, and if it's simple why can't anybody do it?'

'It's not drugs, I've just run out of people that I can trust and it was Paul who suggested you. He may not show it but he looks up to you as his big brother.'

'And that's it?'

'That's it.'

'Well, I'm almost out of whisky,'

'And what does that mean?

'It means I'm sleepy, my glass is empty, the bottle is empty, my mobile battery is almost... empty and I need to sleep then piss, no that should be piss then sleep. Anyway, you arrange for me to meet Paul, then after I've spoken to him, I'll decide if I'm going to help you or not.'

'Okay.'

The line goes silent, a sign that Ian's battery may have finally died.

# CHAPTER 28

The sound of Elizabeth heaving in the bathroom acts as the alarm that wakes Edward.

Come the weekend he prefers a lie-in, getting up around ten. He turns over and half sits up in bed, adjusting the pillows to support his head. The television is on but muted, a sign that Elizabeth has been awake for a while. She soon returns and sits on his corner of the bed.

'Ohhh, I'm sorry if the noise woke you,' she says, caressing his face.

'Don't be silly. Hopefully, you won't feel like that for the entire pregnancy.'

The television's newsflash banner below his ex-wife's picture catches Edward's eye.

'Where's the remote?' he asks. Elizabeth retrieves it from her bedside table. She increases the volume and leaves it on the bed.

*'Police this morning confirmed the death of Kim Long, the former wife of the current prisons minister, Sir Edward Long MP. The discovery of her body this morning by her mother has left the family in deep shock. It's understood the property showed no signs of a forced entry, but police say*

*they are still treating the death as suspicious. It's expected that a full post-mortem will reveal the exact cause of her death. In other news, a Bentley showroom was broken into last night. The manager reported that thieves appeared to have only targeted one vehicle, stealing its radio system —'*

Edward sits up higher in the bed after turning off the television. They're both shaken by the announcement of Kim's death.

'I feel sick,' Elizabeth murmurs. 'It was only yesterday she called. It's hard to imagine she's dead.'

'Come on, darling, take a deep breath. We don't know yet what's really happened.' He tries to console her, putting an arm around her shoulders as she sighs.

'I can't help thinking… if only I had listened to her, Edward. It's obvious now she wanted to tell me something.'

'Don't work yourself up. Remember, stress isn't good for the baby.'

'Yesterday, what did you mean when you said you'd take care of it and she wouldn't bother me again?'

'Is that what's upsetting you?'

'Swear on your baby's life this had nothing to do with you.'

'Elizabeth, how can you even hint that? You know I was home about two hours after we spoke. It would have been even quicker if I hadn't needed to go to South London for your special bread.'

'I was asleep. I'm not quite clear what time you arrived home.'

Edward climbs from the bed, going to the chair where the suit he wore yesterday hangs on the back.

'Well, at least the receipt from the store should show the date and time printed on it.' He looks around at Elizabeth. 'Where is my shirt? The receipt was in the pocket.'

'Sorry, I put a wash on early this morning while you were sleeping.'

'So, you question my word while at the same time you've destroy my alibi. Let's hope that the shop's surveillance system can back me up. I'll be in the shower should you wish to accuse me of anything else.' He goes into the bathroom.

'I didn't mean to sound like I was questioning you. I'm just thinking how hard it is to create life and how it can so easily end in a moment, that's all,' she says, rubbing both hands over her tummy with a maternal instinct to protect what's growing inside.

The noise from the running shower filters Elizabeth's voice into the background. Edward is grateful for the bathroom's sanctuary, allowing him to gather his thoughts and get his head straight. He's in no doubt his brother James has questions to answer. Yes, Kim's death is a tragedy, he can accept that, but he can't fathom why James would be so stupid for a second time.

'Bloody déjà vu,' Edward mutters to himself as he stares into the mirror.

After his shower, with a towel covering his lower body, Edward returns to the bedroom to find Elizabeth still sitting in the same position. He sits on his side of the bed in silence and then the phone rings. Elizabeth moves to answer it.

'Yes, he's here,' she says, offering Edward the phone.

'Who is it?' he asks.

'Your brother.'

'James, good morning,' he says after taking the phone.

'You've seen the news?'

'Yes, I have.' He looks away from his wife's gaze.

'Edward, please believe me, Kim's death had nothing to do with me.'

'Look, I'm just out of the shower; let me call you back once I've put some clothes on.' He hands the phone back to Elizabeth to replace.

'What did James want?'

'To ask if I'd seen the news.'

'And you had, I heard you tell him. So why promise to call him back?'

'Like him or not, Elizabeth, he's still my brother. There are family matters that need discussing with James, so you'll just need to trust me.'

'I'm worried about his lifestyle having a negative impact on your campaign.'

'Did I say he was in trouble? No, I said family matters.'

'And that's your code for trouble, isn't it? He never contacts you otherwise.'

'I wasn't aware that the little incident between you two was still having such an effect.'

'That little incident, others would call attempted rape, Edward. And on our wedding day, no less.'

'He was drunk and apologised as soon as he sobered up.'

'Sobered up? I should have had him locked up or at a minimum put on the register.'

'Look, I don't want to argue about James yet again. He's my brother, and my problem. I've worked hard and continue to work hard trying to keep you two apart.'

'And you're satisfied that I'm emotionally not happy with that arrangement?'

'Emotionally, I can admit to having my head in the sand. But I'm not clueless about the promises and vows I've made to my wife. A wife I love and who's having my baby.'

Hearing Edward say the word 'love', something he hasn't done in a while, makes Elizabeth feel wanted.

'Do you want to know something ironic? I hate James so much, yet I still called him yesterday when you didn't answer your phone.'

'You should understand that, sometimes, doing what you wish is not always just your decision. I'm thinking maybe after the election, whether I lose or I'm re-elected, we'll take that well-earned break to Italy. You know, that full honeymoon we never had. What do you think?'

'I say we've both said things we need to think about,' Elizabeth answers. She stands up to add a few more when the doorbell rings.

'You're not expecting anyone?' she asks, walking over to the window. 'It's the police.'

'You'd better let them in and tell them I'll be down in a minute, once I'm dressed.'

Elizabeth leaves the bedroom as the doorbell rings a second time, with the caller using the door knocker too.

'I'm coming, please wait,' she calls out, navigating the stairs cautiously. She unhooks the security chain, opening the front door just a little.

'Yes, can I help you?' she says to the two officers standing on her doorstep.

'Good morning, Lady Long. I'm Detective Inspector Ryan Chase, and this is Detective Sergeant Fairbank. Is your husband at home?'

'Where else would you expect my husband to be?' Elizabeth answers.

'May we come in? There are a few questions we need to put to him.'

'What is this all about?' she asks.

'I'm sorry, but I can only discuss that with your husband, Lady Long.'

'Okay, then,' she says, fully opening the door. 'If you would like to go straight through, he's getting dressed and will be down with you in a minute.' She guides them towards the spacious living room.

Edward soon appears, giving them no time to settle.

'Officers, to what do we owe this pleasure?'

'Good morning, Sir Edward,' says Chase. He introduces himself and Fairbank again.

'Good morning, gentlemen. Are you here about my stolen car?'

'Sorry, no, we're here on a separate issue. As you may by now be aware, your ex-wife was found dead early this morning.'

'Yes, I woke up to the news. Surely they could have suppressed it for a little longer?'

'These days it's a big problem trying to stay ahead of social media and the release of information.'

'Do we know the circumstances of her death?'

'Our investigation is at an early stage, but we're following all leads as and when received.'

'So, there are leads then?' Elizabeth says.

'Not exactly. Mrs Barton has made serious allegations about you being implicated in her daughter's death.'

'Me? That's an outrageous slur. We've never seen eye to eye, but I never expected she would sink this low.'

'I need, however, to ask about your whereabouts during the last twelve hours.'

Edward looks at Elizabeth before responding.

'Well, I got home just after ten thirty last night. Before that, I was in South London picking up bread.'

'It's a long way to go for bread, if I may say, sir,' says Fairbank.

'Well, it's not just any bread. My wife being pregnant means going that extra mile for whatever she craves.' He glances at Elizabeth again.

'Oh, congratulations, Lady Long,' says Fairbank.

'Thank you. My husband's receipt for the bread would have confirmed what he's just told you. But sadly, I didn't go through his pockets before doing the laundry this morning and may have destroyed that piece of evidence. However, the tag on the packet carries the store's name. I'm sure they'll have CCTV records. I'll get the information for you, Inspector.'

Elizabeth leaves the room.

'So, no other clues?' Sir Edward asks.

'Well, we've learnt there was a pizza delivery. However, witnesses have given conflicting statements about the delivery rider. One claims he was only five feet tall while the other puts him nearer six and a different build. We're checking with the company which rider made the actual delivery.'

'Here you are, Detective,' Elizabeth announces, as she re-enters the room with the details scribbled on a Post-it note.

'Thank you, Lady Long,' says Inspector Chase. 'I believe we've taken up enough of your time.'

He closes his notebook and they all follow Lady Elizabeth. As she opens the front door, the inspector's mobile rings, and he halts to deal with it. Ending the call, the inspector's face shows a deeper sadness.

'What's wrong, Detective? Is there something else?'

'More, yes, but it's quite sad I'm afraid. It appears Kim's stomach contained traces of pizza, even though the pizza we found was untouched. Added to that, they've also confirmed that Kim was pregnant when she died. That's such sad, sad news,' he concludes.

'Oh, my God!' Elizabeth says, covering her mouth and pushing past everyone to get to the downstairs cloakroom.

'Are you sure?' asks Sir Edward, seizing the unexpected chance to have his reaction officially recorded.

'Sadly yes, and the evidence so far points to it looking more and more like foul play.'

'And if that's the case, what happens next?'

'First, we will need to wait for the full post-mortem to confirm the foetus's age. Anything over twenty-four weeks, and we'd have no choice but to treat it as a double murder.'

'I don't think Kim would have been twenty-four weeks without me knowing.'

'Interesting,' the inspector makes his own off-the-cuff remark. 'and why do you believe that, Sir Edward?' He asks, looking seriously at him in anticipation of his answer.

'Well we were married for some time, Inspector, and I'm certain she would have told me.'

'So, when was the last time that you actually saw your ex-wife sir?' The inspector asks as Elizabeth exits the cloakroom.

'Ah, I think that was about three and a half weeks ago, Tuesday the twenty-seventh of April to be precise.' Lady Elizabeth knows that her husband has lied and shields her face from the detective.

'Congratulation on having such a remarkable memory, Sir Edward. Anyway, thank you again for your time.'

'I don't think I've been much of a help, Inspector, sorry. Look, despite the relationship breakdown with my former mother-in-law, I would appreciate being kept in the loop.' He lowers his voice to ensure his request is only heard by the inspector. 'And I would respectfully request you consider the condition of my wife and allow me to inform her of any new developments coming to light.'

'We understand, sir. Goodbye.'

'Oh, Inspector, one final thing, if I may. Someone stole my car yesterday.'

'Yes, you mentioned something about it when we arrived.'

'If I gave you the details would you be able to chase it up and report back?'

'Sorry, it isn't really my department, but leave it with me anyway, although I can't promise anything.'

'Thank you, Inspector, I'll write down the registration for you.'

Sir Edward hands over the note before closing the door.

Elizabeth comes out of the bathroom, dabbing her eyes with a tissue.

'Why don't you have a lie down, dear?'

'I might just do that. I've been up since early this morning.'

Edward watches his wife climb the stairs. He waits until she's out of sight before using his mobile to call his brother.

'James, it's me. The police just left my house and I need to hear the truth from you.'

'What do you mean "the truth", Edward? I've told you that earlier. I'm just as much in the dark even though I was there.'

'What is it you're not telling me, James? There must be something you've missed?'

'What I'm not telling you, Edward, is lies. I had nothing to do with Kim's death. That's what you need to believe, Edward, because it's the truth. Look, after you left she ordered a pizza. But my levels were already too high, and I knew it would have put

259

me over the top. So, I watched Kim eat at least two slices, then I wasn't feeling too clever, so I went up to bed. I remember hearing the doorbell again around ten minutes later. Anyway, in the night I got up to get some water and maybe help myself to a slice of pizza if there was any left. I found the pizza box on the kitchen table. All the slices were there, untouched, which puzzled me. I wasn't sure if I'd imagined it or if it was an effect of the diabetes. Because I was sure I'd seen her eat at least two slices. That's when I saw her on the kitchen floor, by the sink. The tap was still running and she was lying in a pool of water. Now I think about it, the water could have been from the broken glass beside her. It looked like she might have been getting water when it happened.'

'Maybe you could have saved her if you'd called an ambulance then?'

'Edward, you forget, I've been there before. She was dead, stone-cold dead. All I could think of was not being found with another dead body. I was feeling dizzy and panicked. I just wanted to get out of there. I went upstairs and got my jacket. When I came back down, I remembered that my fingerprints must be all over the cup from the tea I drank earlier. I found the cups in the dishwasher but it wasn't obvious which one I'd used. So, I put the dishwasher on and cleaned anything I'd touched before leaving.'

'And that's everything?'

'Honest to God, that's everything.'

'Okay, James, I'll be in touch, bye.'

Edward sees no reason to disbelieve his brother's version of events, but there are little elements of uncertainty creeping into his thoughts.

It's Sunday morning at Downing Prison, and the quietest day of the week. The prison chapel sees an unlikely array of inmates taking advantage to spend two extra hours away from their cells in the name of religion. Mr Salerno, having denounced all forms of deities, has this option removed from his file and so sits in his cell, relaxing to some classical music on an old cassette player. Noticing his illegal mobile vibrating, he stops the tape to answer.

'Mr Fingers,' the voice opens. 'If you've had access to news in the last twenty-four hours, you would have heard conclusive evidence that I've kept my end of the bargain.'

'No, I've heard nothing since a brief call on Friday. I don't want to press you for uncomfortable details but I would like to know, how?'

'Well, seeing that you only allowed us the small window on Friday to complete your task, we had to pool a few resources to keep things on schedule to make it happen. I sent people to the address immediately to scout for any clear opportunities to complete the job quickly.  It was just our luck that a pizza delivery turns up not long after they arrived, and they made use of it.  She had ordered a special two-for-one pizza. So, they put an order in for another, ate one pizza, and delivered the other, after adding a toxin to the topping, courtesy of some Russian friends. Naturally, she was very vocal in her complaint about the order being short. She calmed a bit when they explained that she was entitled to a discount and didn't have to pay until the order was completed and the rider would be back in under ten minutes. She started eating immediately, insisting she wouldn't wait as the pizza that had been delivered would get cold. When the second pizza arrived, she left our rider at the door and went back into her kitchen supposedly to fetch her purse, and that's when the poison finally took hold and she collapsed. Instructed to retrieve the treated pizza, our rider carefully entered and walked through the hall to the kitchen where she found her, on the floor by the sink. She had begun foaming a little around the mouth, gasping while clenching her stomach. That's when she begged for water and help, because she was pregnant.'

'Okay.' Fat Fingers sighs. 'I think I've got enough details.'

'Then I can expect the chip to be delivered sometime today then, Mr Fingers?'

'No, not until this coming Wednesday.'

'Why the extra three days? I thought you said you already had it in your possession?'

'And I also mentioned some trust issues that I'm having, So, your courier will be someone I can trust, like family. Just a few more days and you'll have it, that's a promise. I'll be in touch.'


Fat Fingers ends the call and restarts the cassette player.

# CHAPTER 29

After their failed expedition to Paddington on Friday, Chan, Ox and Paul have found a room for refuge in a secure but dilapidated boarding house close to Ladbroke Grove. They hope that the local activity surrounding the start of a week-long protest by Extension Rebellion will help screen them from easy detection. Ox and Chan are also pinning their hopes on Mai Li finding crucial evidence that's useful enough to prove their innocence of murder, and soon.

'Surely, we could have afforded somewhere better than this dump,' says Paul. 'A nice hotel or something, with a little more room, a mini bar perhaps or even a spa?'

'Get real, Paul,' says Ox. 'Fugitives living the high life, that's the quickest way of getting noticed. To be on the same page as us, you need to read from the same book.'

'You know he's right,' adds Chan. 'Flashing that much cash will draw unwanted attention. So, let's wait for Mai Li as agreed. We've survived so far, haven't we?'

'To be fair, it's been more luck than skill,' Paul points out.

'I could say the same about throttling you,' Ox responds.

'If that's how you guys feel, would you also begrudge me

taking a few steps outside in the fresh air? I'll keep the bracelets covered.'

Ox and Chan shrug as they watch Paul get up and exit the room.

'When it comes down to it, we owe him for getting us out of prison,' Chan says.

Ox sighs. 'I'll go find him and apologise. He won't have gone far without the money, and he sure as hell won't be expecting the apology to come from me either.'

Ox gets to his feet and leaves the room. After taking two flights of stairs and the hallway in relative darkness, he exits the building into bright sunshine. He looks for Paul up and down the road but he's nowhere in sight. He moves down the steps in front of the building and twenty metres along to the corner, two buildings away, in time to catch sight of Paul exiting a silver 7 Series BMW with private plates. Ducking back to avoid being seen, Ox observes him leaning back through the open car window before stepping back and checking around.

Paul looks about to return as the car speeds away, prompting Ox to do the same, avoiding any chance of being noticed. As soon as he's back in the room, he tells Chan what he's seen.

'Something's not right. I've just seen Paul chatting to someone in a BMW.'

'Who though? Nobody knows we're here,' says Chan.

'Except Mai Li, and she doesn't drive. I'm telling you, something doesn't add up, Chan.'

The door handle turning is their cue to stop discussing the subject. Paul walks back in.

'I needed that,' he says. 'A change is as good as a rest, as they say.'

'You're back quickly,' says Ox.

'Yeah, I got downstairs and realised I wasn't being fair, or a team player. So, after a few minutes, I came straight back.'

'Hey, we know.'

'Know what?' Paul looks a little surprised.

'We know, being cooped up in here is making us all tense,' says Chan, 'but don't worry, we appreciate everything you've done for us.'

'Back at you. I'll never forget that you guys were there when I needed you.'

Chan's words are at odds with what he's thinking and feeling; and Ox has never trusted Paul. The glance they share says as much.

~

News of the missing prisoners has reached Downing. Governor Riley is feeling quietly smug about the whole thing. He was right to be against the proposal, even warning them it would end badly.

'They only needed to ask me, Mr Newport,' he starts. 'With my years of experience in containment, I told them that madcap scheme would never work. Now we've got two murderers and a thief loose in the community. How can we protect the public when they disregard such experience?'

'I blame the ministers, sir. I think they should try a spell in here.'

'Perhaps a spell in here wouldn't be a bad idea. Please ask Cynthia to come in on your way out.'

'Governor,' Officer Newport tips his cap in response as he leaves the office. Opening the door, he's surprised to find Stuart Naylor draped over Cynthia's desk. Stuart is just as surprised; standing up sharply, he steps away from the desk.

'Cynthia, the governor is ready for you now,' Newport says. He watches until she enters the governor's office, closing the door.

'Mr Naylor, so what brings you, yet again, to the governor's secretary's office?'

'I had a fifteen-minute break,' says Naylor. 'I came for a chat.'

'And can you explain why, out of the hundred and twenty prison wardens, it's you I keep finding here?'

'Cynthia and I get on, sir.'

'You get on. I presume you like this job?'

'Yes, it's a great place to work, sir.'

'Then allow me to do you a favour and make this explicit. If I so much as smell you've been in here unauthorised again, then you, my friend, and possibly Cynthia, will need to find another employer. Clear?'

'Clear, sir.'

'Good, now go.' Newport follows Stuart to the door, closing it. He turns to find Cynthia returning to her desk.

'I hope you're not encouraging that young warden to visit you during work hours? It's unprofessional.'

'I've told him, Mr Newport, but he continues coming. Sometimes he brings little gifts.'

'Gifts! Like what?'

'Well, today he's given me these Post-it notes. They contain uplifting messages on each corner, look.' She points them out on her desk. However, Newport spots something of more interest.

'Did he give you this phone charger, by any chance?'

'I don't remember. It's been on my desk for a while now. I've meant to ask a few times, but when he's here he has a charm that makes me forget almost everything,' she recalls, smitten by the attention.

'Have you tried using it with your mobile though?'

'Yes, once. But it didn't work, hence why it's permanently plugged into the mains.'

'Would you mind if I look? I'm not familiar with that make.'

Cynthia nods. Newport picks up the charger and twirls it in his grip. If not for his curiosity and scrutiny, it would have remained undiscovered. He places the charger back on her desk.

'From the little I know about these devices, this one could drain your battery in just a few minutes, especially if they're not manufactured for that phone.'

'Oh, I didn't realise. I've barely mastered my mobile. I'm glad you spotted the problem.'

'It's no trouble at all. That's how our little prison family works. I'll pick it up later and have it fixed and returned to you in no time.'

'Thank you, Mr Newport.'

For the time being, Newport leaves the charger where it is with Cynthia, entering the governor's office with a finger over his lips. The governor looks up, curious, as he didn't bother to knock before entering.

'You know the little problems of leaks from this office?' Newport whispers.

'Tell me you've found its source?' The governor perks up, hoping they can seal the hole in the information dam.

'I've not just found it; we can use it to our advantage. The good news is, Cynthia knows nothing about it.'

'What has Cynthia got to do with it?'

'Only a small part, Governor. She's being exploited. I'm satisfied we've found the source and I'm aiming to set up our own device to sit alongside theirs. It should function rather like a two-way mirror, only with sound.'

'Then you'd better carry on, since you're the only one that understands whatever it is you're trying to achieve.'

Leaving the governor's office, Newport stops to collect the charger from Cynthia's desk.

'Cynthia, Mr Naylor should not be in this office. I've had to have a word with the governor to safeguard your job.'

'I didn't think it could affect my job,' she says, alarmed.

'That's what our little work family is about, helping each other. I also had a word with Mr Naylor, because I like him too. He's a nice kid. So, don't go embarrassing him about not getting this charger thing right, okay?'

'Trust me, Mr Newport, I won't embarrass myself, let alone him, by bringing it up.'

# CHAPTER 30

At home, Dr Minn emerges from his sanctuary. He follows the same routine each morning before breakfast. For only the second time he can remember, his daughter sits waiting for him. Dr Minn ignores her presence and chooses the spiritual route of silence as his method of finding out what brings her there, and so early. He was very lucky if he saw her before 10 am each day.

Walking near to where she sits, he simply smiles and continues on his way to breakfast, prompting Mai Li to get up to follow.

'I'm not in need of an escort. I can find my own way to breakfast,' he tells her coming alongside him.

'You're still mad at me, aren't you?'

'Mad at you, why would I be mad at you?'

'For stalling on making changes to the Pinpoint computer, to find your missing property, but I have my reasons.'

'Let's hope then that your reasons match my patience on the matter.'

'That's what I want to talk to you about.' She still makes no eye contact.

He stops and turns to face his daughter, waiting for her to open up and explain.

'Did you really love my mother?' she asks, catching him off-guard again.

'Where is this coming from, Mai Li? And where is it leading to?'

'I want to see it again, that pendant you showed me once. Please, I need to be sure.'

'Of what, Mai Li?'

'Well… I have to be sure that the person I've found is your son and my twin brother.'

A hopeful expression Mai Li has never seen before passes over her father's face.

'How long had you been searching?'

'I didn't have any information to search but sometimes when you look for something you can never find it and other times when you don't it's there right in front of your eyes.'

'That mature thinking makes you sound so grown up,' he says, taking a deep breath before opening his shirt to reveal the pendant. The sight of it brings instant tears to Mai Li's eyes.

'Well?' he says, looking down at her.

'We've found him, Father.' She suddenly looks emotional. 'We've really found him,' she repeats.

Her words bring more tears and to Dr Minn's eyes too.

'You must tell me where he is so I can send Chi to fetch him.'

'The only reason I delayed amending the Pinpoint system, Father, was that if I did, then your own son, Chan, risked being killed, because he's part of the system.'

'Chan? You even know his name?'

'Yes, I do, and I also know he will not meet with you without proof.'

'I must ask you a question, my daughter. Your answer needs to be the absolute truth and you won't be in any trouble for telling me. Is Chan one of those released from prison? Is he one of the runaways?'

'Yes. But you can't involve the police. They are innocent, Father.'

'And how would you know this?'

'Because we made that happen; the codes you had me change in the court system convicted your own son of a murder he didn't commit.'

Dr Minn seeks the aid of a nearby chair and sits, shaking his head. 'I'd no idea. That must have been bad karma for agreeing to do so in the first place. What do you need to persuade him to come home and maybe even forgive me one day?'

'Just the pendant. That's the only evidence he needs.'

Dr Minn reaches behind his neck and uncouples the gold chain, placing it in Mai Li's open palm.

'Take good care with this. It's all I have to remember your mother by.'

'I will. I'll bring them both back, I promise.'

Mai Li leaves her father deep in contemplation. Once she is out of sight, he summons Chi.

'I have an important task for you. Mai Li will leave shortly. I want her followed.'

'Is Ms Minn in danger, sir?' asks Chi.

'She doesn't feel she is, but I'm more than sure you will find my stolen property at any address she visits.

'Do you mean the missing bank-note templates, sir?'

'Yes, Chi, you are to retrieve them and bring everyone back here safely. Do you understand? I want no one hurt unless you're prevented from carrying out those orders.'

'I understand, sir.'

'Good.'

Amy, Sir Edward's secretary, enters his office with his preferred morning drink of Earl Grey. As she places the cup in front of him, his desk telephone rings and she answers it.

'Sir Edward Long's office, who's calling, please?'

With her hand covering the mouthpiece, she conveys that a Mr Gilby wishes to speak with him. Sir Edward takes the telephone and waits for Amy to leave before speaking.

'Ian, sorry for not getting back sooner. Since our last meeting, I've had several issues to deal with.'

'No doubt one of those important issues being the death of your ex-wife?'

'Yes, when we heard the news Saturday morning, it was a shock and a tragic loss of life.'

'But more or less what you wanted.'

'What is it you're suggesting, Ian?'

'I'm talking about our conversation where you expressed a desire for her to be out of your life, that's all.'

'Then let me clarify for you that at no point in our conversation did I ask you to kill her.'

'Well, I have a tape that says otherwise.'

'I've warned you in the past about recording our conversations.'

'Yeah, I know, but this one is about you wanting your ex-wife harmed and now she's dead. '

'Well, the police have already interviewed me, so it sounds very much like it would be a case of my word against yours.'

'With the tape, Edward, it will be your word against the tape, which is also your word. At the moment, the police are rushing around with no leads. Just think how bad your life would become if they had this recording, and with the election coming soon. So, if those papers aren't with me within the hour, then the police and anyone who will listen will hear what you were asking me to do.'

'Checkmate, Mr Gilby. You've proved to be a darker horse, maybe, than I gave you credit for, but the fact remains, I didn't kill her, so who did?'

'Not my problem. For you the clock is ticking, don't waste the time.'

'I'll get it arranged. So, I guess this is the official goodbye.'

'Let me assure you, it hasn't been a pleasure, Edward. One last thing.'

'Go ahead.'

'I just want to make you aware that before meeting you, I'd planned to vote for your party, but not anymore.'

'Harsh but understandable under the circumstances, Mr Gilby.'

The phone line falls silent and Sir Edward summons Amy back to his office. As he removes a brown envelope from his bottom drawer, his phone rings for the second time and Amy answers it again.

'It's a Detective Ryan Chase, regarding your vehicle, sir.'

'Thank you, Amy.' He hands over the envelope. 'Can you see that this gets sent by courier ASAP?'

'Right away, Sir Edward. I'll do it now.'

Edward waits again for her to leave the room before turning to his caller.

'Hello, Detective Chase, sorry for keeping you waiting.'

'No problem, Sir Edward. They've located your car, sir.'

'Oh, they've found it, that is fantastic news, Detective.'

'Fantastic in one sense, given it wasn't stolen. However, it turns out that it was removed for a parking violation.'

'So, I can expect its immediate return then, on payment of any fines and, of course, any storage costs?'

'Ordinarily, yes, Sir Edward, but since you reported it stolen, the detectives were keen to gather more clues, to help solve the theft. I understand they're also checking for any links to other crimes.'

'Well, in this case, it's probably a waste of their time and taxpayers' money. My brother admits to having parked the car and whilst he was away from it seeking directions, he found it gone on his return.'

'As helpful as that is, Sir Edward, I did say that it wasn't my department, so once I'd made them aware who the car belonged to, they were keen to resolve the case quickly and efficiently. They stepped up their enquiries with forensic tests and I believe they are working to bring us the results as we speak.'

There's an uneasy pause.

'Hello? Still there, Sir Edward?'

'Ah, yes, sorry, Detective. I got distracted, some election material just landed on my desk. Speaking of which, I hope my party can count on your vote in the upcoming elections?' Sir Edward tries a subtle change of subject.

'Afraid I'm undecided at the moment,' the detective reveals.

'Well, I hope over the coming fortnight, as the face of law enforcement, we can convince you that our party wholeheartedly supports giving the police more powers to do their job.'

'I'm sorry, Sir Edward, but I need to go.'

'Detective, before you go, any further news on the Barton case?'

'Nothing to report at the moment, sir. Your story about the bread checked out, and I will, as promised, keep you informed.'

'Thank you, Detective.'

Sir Edward stands up and goes to the door to speak to his secretary.

'Amy.'

'Yes, Sir Edward?'

'Over the next two weeks, the election campaign will keep me away from this office, so I wanted to take this opportunity to thank you for your selfless service, and the late hours you've put in over the years.'

'Thank you, Sir Edward.'

'I'll be off shortly for my press conference with the Prime Minister. I probably won't be back until after the election,' he jokes.

At that moment, a smartly dressed young man enters Amy's office.

'Good morning, Sir Edward, I'm Matthew Robinson from the CBB.'

The 'Commercial British Broadcasting' company is the public company that took over after they finally abolished the TV license fee.

'I'm here to introduce myself and let you know I'll be shadowing you throughout the election, sir.'

'Matthew, you're most welcome. I only have one request of you, and that is, that you run everything by me before broadcasting.'

'What about freedom of the press, Sir Edward?' Robinson challenges him, raising his eyebrows.

'If you want freedom, then I suggest that you use the same door you came through. If you want exclusive access, then it's my way or that doorway. Make your choice, Mr Robinson. There's a re-election looming with my name on it.'

Mai Li takes a minicab straight to the three-storey building in Ladbroke Grove, unaware she's being followed. Leaving the car, she appears relaxed and oblivious to Chi, parking up close by.

Chi waits a few minutes in the car before he follows Mai Li inside. With no clue where in the building she may be, Chi starts his search from the bottom, aiming to check every apartment right to the top if needed. He stops at each door to listen for any signs of activity before moving on to the next. With this approach and some luck, he's banking on the element of surprise being in his favour.

As he reaches the last door on the second floor, it's opened by a scruffily dressed man. Chi's huge frame causes the man to look twice as he closes and locks his door.

After clearing the second floor, Chi starts up the next flight. He hears voices even before reaching the landing. The easily identifiable voice of Mai Li confirms the exact door. Chi stands at the door, his bulk almost filling the frame. He knocks loudly, knowing his presence will be a complete surprise.

Paul answers the door. He looks at Chi and takes in his full height, leaving him speechless. Ox calls out from within the other room.

'Who is it?'

Chi walks in, forcing Paul backwards. The scene from Chi's point of view is of Chan lying shirtless on the bed, Mai Li sitting next to him with her hands on his back and Ox's hand on Mai Li's shoulder.

'Chi! What are you doing here?' Mai Li's eyes are wide with surprise.

'Your father sent me to protect you. Have you no shame, being in this garbage hole with three men?'

'It's not what it looks like,' she says. Chan rolls over and sits up.

Ox stands up to face Chi.

'Don't even think about it.' Chi wags a finger at Ox.

Mai Li grabs Ox by the hand, holding him back. 'Don't. He's my father's guard dog. He's trained and very dangerous.'

'What is it you want?' says Paul, stepping further back into the room. 'Is it the money?' Paul feels for the holdall by the side of the bed, keeping his eyes fixed on Chi. 'It's all there, most of it anyway.' He opens the bag to reveal the money and the plates.

Chi holds out his hand and Paul zips the bag before handing it to him.

'You, get dressed,' he says, looking at Chan. 'My boss is expecting all of you.'

'You have the money, the plates. So, what's the problem?' says Ox.

'Can't you forget that you've seen us?' says Paul.

'My problem is that I have seen you. Now you have two choices; either you return without pain with me or you return with pain, but still with me. I know which I would prefer.'

Back at Dr Minn's home, Chi leads all three men into the drawing room to await their host. Mai Li seems to be holding onto Ox too tightly, adding to Chi's annoyance. Dr Minn enters the room and gestures for them to sit, taking a seat himself.

'I'm glad to see that none of you were foolish enough to turn down my invitation. Before I get to why you were brought here, I'd like to share something with you, especially you, Mr Yip. I've been fortunate to have had the chance to know and raise my daughter. But I discovered not long after her birth she was a twin, and it left me in pieces. After searching unsuccessfully in various state-run orphanages, someone took me to an unsanctioned one run by two priests. The conditions they worked under reflected their struggle to keep the children safe and to remain undetected. Moving around an already overcrowded room, it was heart-breaking to see so many of the children without even a single piece of clothing.

'Then I spotted Chi here. They told me that all the children were roughly the same age, but he seemed to be smaller than the rest. There was no information on any child other than what the priests could recall from memory. Sometimes, the abandoned child was just left on their doorstep. It may have been guilt at not finding my child that led me to offer Chi a home. As was the case back then, he came with many medical dependencies, of which his growth was the most challenging. I could not get treatment for him – his parents never registered his birth. In the eyes of the state, he didn't exist. So, using the same network of unfunded and unprivileged people, I got hold of growth hormones they said would help. What you see today in Chi is a product of my attempt to help give him a normal life. Although I've never told him this, I've always considered him as a son.'

Chi rocks and adjusts his stance, moved by the revelation.

'So, Mr Yip. If you are my son, then you'll be sharing that status with Chi.'

Dr Minn gets up and walks to within a few feet of where Chan sits. Chan looks up but says nothing. Chan looks over at Chi, who looks back.

'He is your son, Father. Check for yourself.' Mai Li hands back the pendant to her father.

Chan stands up and unbuttons his shirt. He lowers it off his shoulders, turning to expose his back.

Dr Minn raises the pendant, his hand shaking as he hovers over the scar. It appears to mirror the dragon's side of the pendant perfectly.

'That's all the proof I need,' he announces tearfully. 'The journey to find you is finally over.' Chan pulls his shirt back over his shoulders.

'What happens next?' asks Ox.

'He will enjoy, for the rest of his life, every luxury I can give him.'

'I meant about us?'

'I'm a fair man, Mr Ox,' Dr Minn says, returning to his seat. 'Any grudges I've ever held were never without good reason. Do you consider what you've done as giving me a good reason?'

'Look, it's him that stole your stuff,' Ox says, pointing at Paul. 'We've just been trying to clear our name, that's it, nothing else.'

'They're telling you the truth, Father,' says Mai Li. 'And I told you those changes you had me make to the system ended up putting them in prison.'

'And what about the thief, what do I owe you?' Dr Minn asks. Paul stands before being forced back into his seat by Chi.

'Well, if it wasn't for me, you might still have been searching for your son,' Paul answers.

'So, nobody owes anyone anything, and everything has worked out perfectly, except for one enormous problem. I'm talking about the hundreds of workers and their families who now have no work because of your actions.'

'He's sorry. Aren't you, Paul?' Chan attempts to use his new-found status.

'I am… truly sorry, sir,' says Paul.

A few seconds pass while Dr Minn appears to be deep in thought. Finally, he raises his head and speaks.

'Chi will show you to your rooms. We all need some time to understand everything that's happened, and to see if or how we're to move on.'

# CHAPTER 31

Officer Newport sits in the governor's office to update him on the progress since his discovery of the listening device attached to Cynthia's phone charger.

'How did they manage this under our noses?' the governor asks.

'It was simple, yet clever, Governor. Whoever set this up must have had access to prison plans and electrical design. With the prison built as a single-storey structure, it was easy for them to use the ring main to both access and transmit signals over our network.'

'And this device?'

'So, this device will convert their signals to radio waves, then it transmits them without altering the original. The only drawback is the delay when they're converted back. Other than that, we're good to go, and with everything digital these days, they won't suspect good old-fashioned RF.' Newport grins.

'RF, Mr Newport?'

'Yes, Governor, radio frequency.'

'Well then, no time like the present, Mr Newport, switch it on.'

Activated with a small switch, the unit makes a weird noise as it self-tunes before settling to a steady hum. They listen for anything from the receiver, anything that would show the exercise is worth it. Silence, apart from a few burps of static noise. The governor, unimpressed, sits back in his chair after two minutes. Then, a sudden crackle brings the unit to life.

*'I'm glad he persuaded you and some thanks from me too, for agreeing to do this favour for me.......................... Let's not waste your time. The only thing that's important is to make sure you're at the side gate of Lotto-Guard HQ, Canary Wharf, at four thirty pm today. It's all arranged, they will meet you there..................... No, ask no questions, and once they're satisfied, just walk away, forget everything, and I mean everything.'*

'Why can't we hear the other side of the conversation?' the governor whispers.

'It only monitors a device that would have been monitoring you, Governor.'

'Did you pick up on the essence of what they said?'

'I did and wrote it all down, sir.'

*'Do this right and it will be your part of someone's fifteen minutes of fame.'*

The voice concludes with the receiving unit falling silent again. Newport asks what he should do with the information.

'Inform the police, Mr Newport, as any decent citizen should.'

Inspector Chase parks up close to the side entrance of Lotto-Guard in his private car. Never switching off, he was on route to drop Fairbank home when he received a personal call. He reaches for the radio's volume switch but halts on hearing the end of the news.

*'Investigators in the Kim Long murder case have disclosed today that the ex-wife of the current prisons minister was pregnant at the time of her death.'*

'Why do they always say the ex-wife of the minister?' Fairbank asks as the inspector lowers the volume after the news until it's hardly noticeable.

'Just a lot easier for people to place exactly who they're talking about, that's all.'

'And how come we've stopped here?' Fairbank continues with another question.

'A reliable tip-off.'

'What are we looking for, anyway?' Fairbank says, reclining his seat.

'What every policeman should look out for, Mr Fairbank, suspicious activity. Maybe less of the questions and a line in that empty notebook of yours might help you remember that.'

'Noted here,' Fairbank says, pointing to his temple. Chase checks his watch, tapping the face.

'Never got around to having this looked at. What time is yours showing?'

'Four twenty-eight, sir.'

'Okay, it's time to be the suspicious bastards that criminals hate us for.' Chase makes a 180-degree visual sweep of the location.

'What about him?'

'Where?' Chase looks out Fairbank's window.

'Over there, by the gate,' Fairbank says, raising his reclined seat back to its original position.

The figure stops and looks behind him. He checks his watch then looks around again, spotting their unmarked vehicle. With an aluminium briefcase held tight in his grip, he starts towards the car.

'Shit! He's coming over.' Fairbank panics, looking at Chase.

'Relax, be calm, and eyes on me. Let me do the talking.'

Ian Gilby casts a shadow over the passenger window as he approaches, tapping on the glass to get their attention. Chase lowers the window and joins Fairbank in staring out at Ian, who leans down to the open window.

'Any chance you're here waiting for me?' he asks.

'Why, who are you?' Chase casually enquires.

'Sorry, mate, my mistake,' Ian says, turning and taking himself back across the road as the side gate opens, and a large number of men dressed in dark clothing file out of the building.

'Looks like crude oil, spilling onto the pavement,' Chase remarks, smiling at his own joke. 'What day is it today, Fairbank?'

'I don't know, sir. Your birthday?'

'I'm talking about the day of the week.'

'Oh. Wednesday, sir.'

'That's right, Friday is mosque day, so what's going on in that building?'

Ian stands out amongst the crowd of people because of his height and the paleness of his skin. The crowd disperses, leaving three men standing by Ian. Two have their backs to the car. Chase half recognises the third man, confident he'd seen his clothing recently. All four step back through the gate and out of sight.

'We need to get inside that building. Any ideas, lad?' says Chase.

'How about... we suspect the factory of running a modern-day slavery operation?'

'I'll say one thing for you, Fairbank, going to university hasn't made all the tools in your box dull.' He picks up the radio.

'Thank you, sir.'

Chase calls in for a warrant and backup from the elite

intervention team. Expecting it will be at least half an hour until the elite team arrives, Chase leaves Fairbank in the car while he goes to scout the building.

Fairbank adjusts his position, twisting to see out of the rear window. His knee accidentally opens the glove compartment, and he moves to close it when the sight of several old police notebooks piques his curiosity. He removes the elastic band securing them and flicks through a few. They represent a few months of the inspector's old arrest notes. Laid out in neat handwriting, each entry has the familiar marks used by police to identify ethnic groups. It jumps out at Fairbank that the inspector, during his entire career, had a bias when it came to arrests.

Chase is on his way back and Fairbank is quick to replace everything. He closes the glovebox seconds before the inspector reaches his window.

'Anything, sir?'

'No, there's only a single security guard at the main entrance.'

'Check behind you, sir. That guy who spoke to us earlier just came out the gate.' Chase turns for a second and watches as Ian leaves the factory, heading back in the direction he came from.

'Shouldn't we stop and question him?'

'Call it instinct, Fairbank, but those left inside are of more interest,' says Chase.

That is clear evidence, if Fairbank needed it. He wonders if, in the past, Chase has ignored other evidence to feed his preference for targeting ethnic groups.

The elite team's two marked vans roll down the road, parking up opposite. Chase walks over and greets the commander as he steps down from the vehicle. 'What's the deal, Chase?' he says, shaking hands.

'There are people of interest inside this building. My sources believe they could impact on national security. And after seeing a familiar individual, it makes me even more suspicious.'

'And we know how suspicious you can be. So how do you want to do this?'

Fairbank comes over to join them.

'Who is this, Chase? Your new puppy?' says the commander.

'Detective Sergeant Fairbank,' says Fairbank, introducing himself and ignoring the comment.

'Leave two here watching this gate and the rest can come with us,' Chase instructs the commander.

'What about the warrant, sir?' Fairbank interjects.

'You wait here for it while we go and solve crimes – that's an order, Fairbank.'

They're behaving like schoolboys back together again after the long summer break. Fairbank has no problem working on his own, but he isn't happy being forced to do so without information.

The team make their way round to the main entrance, finding all the doors locked. They pound on the door to get the security guard's attention.

'Okay, okay, hold your horses,' the single security guard says, moving from behind his desk towards the front door. It seems to take him forever. With his large, noisy bunch of keys, he unlocks first the bottom, then the top lock.

'Can I help you, gentlemen?' he says, cracking the door.

'Is there anyone still working in this building?' Chase asks.

'And who would you like me to direct your enquiry to?'

'That will be you. Is there anybody still working in the building?'

'Who are you, and why do you wish to know?'

'My name is Detective Inspector Ryan Chase,' he says, showing his badge. 'Can we come in?'

'Not without a warrant. Do you have one?'

'It's on its way.'

'Then I will decline your request until it's here.'

The guard tries closing the door, only to find a size eleven obstruction wedged between it and the frame.

'Look…' Chase says.

'No, you look. Either you remove your foot or I'm calling the police.'

'That would be a waste of time since we're already here.'

Chase responds to a tap on his shoulder. He leans slightly back to receive whispered information.

'I'm sorry. As soon as the warrant arrives, we'll be back.' Chase withdraws his foot, allowing the guard to close and secure the door again.

~

'You're sure we've got access?' Chase asks as they walk back towards the side gate.

'Yeah, two blokes came out and we stopped the gate from closing.'

'Where are the two men now?'

'You weren't specific, Chase, your instructions said nothing about detaining them. Besides, until your warrant arrives, we're not legally authorised to arrest anyone,' says the commander.

Angered, Chase looks around for Fairbank; he needs to let off steam at someone and spots him getting out of the car and crossing the road, holding his mobile.

'Do you also need a nap after making private phone calls in the middle of my operation?' the inspector says, challenging Fairbank.

'It was a call to get the warrant emailed to my mobile. See,' he says, holding up the phone and pointing to the screen. Annoyed, he adds, 'Don't forget, I was off duty on my way home.'

'Let me remind you, as police, you're never off duty. These guys out of university do things so differently,' Chase jokes, looking around for support from his old team. 'Okay, you take it to that nosy security guard. We're going in here. Let's go!' Chase orders. The team file through the gate behind him.

Beyond the gate, the ground slopes down into a basement car park. Automatic lights illuminate the area.

Back in reception, cameras have picked up the illegal entry. The security guard idles between answering Fairbank's knock at the main door and raising awareness of the basement intrusion.

'Just a second,' he calls out to Fairbank, holding his hand up to acknowledge seeing him.

The guard adjusts the microphone and makes a broadcast.

'Mr Junjie, you're needed in reception. I repeat, Mr Junjie to reception immediately please.'

The announcement registers throughout the building. Mr Junjie takes less than a minute to appear in reception.

'Sam, what's going on?'

'We have armed police in our basement, sir, and someone is causing a nuisance at the front door.'

Junjie picks up the telephone, calling the factory owner.

'Hello!'

'Hello, who is this?'

'I'm calling from the factory, the maintenance manager Junjie, sir. This is the only number I've been given for contacting the new owner.'

'And what's the problem?'

'There's armed police inside your factory. How soon can we expect you down here?'

'Well, not immediately, I'm detained elsewhere. So, what is your plan for dealing with this, Junjie?'

'Well, at the moment they're in the basement. I'm sure their intentions are not to stay there. It's only a matter of time, though, before they gain access to the rest of the building.'

'If they're contained, that should give you plenty of time to destroy any sensitive papers from the office.'

He turns away from Sam and whispers. 'And what about… the cash, sir?'

'Burn it, destroy everything.'

'Understood,' says Junjie.

With his new orders, Junjie ends the call and turns to Sam.

'Okay, take your time dealing with the idiot at the door and try to keep the police in the basement,' he says, leaving through a heavy security door.

Sam starts towards the front door.

'What is this emergency that you need to break my door?' he asks Fairbank, who flashes his badge.

'Detective Sergeant Fairbank, I believe you're waiting to see the warrant for this operation?'

'Where is it, then?' asks Sam, expecting the warrant in paper form.

'It's here on my mobile, sir.' Fairbank hands Sam his phone.

'I'll need my glasses to read this. Please wait there.' Sam goes back to his console. The security monitors still show the team scratching around in the basement.

'I think the police could face a charge of breaking and entering. Because they already entered the basement ahead of you presenting this warrant,' Sam informs Fairbank, returning to the main door.

'For a security guard, you sound like you know something about the law.'

Sam smiles. 'Yes, two years ago I was only six months short of completing my law degree when my father got sick, then he died. So with the fees not being paid I lost my place. But qualified or not, being of colour here even in 2027 doesn't guarantee you a good job, and maybe it never will… the black lives matter back in 2020 has changed very little.' He adds while continuing to check the warrant line by line, which further adds to the delay.

Suddenly, several men rush past Fairbank, grabbing Sam who

drops the mobile as they force him down onto the buildings hard marble floor. Fairbank's mobile smashes in half cracking the screen with the battery ending up several feet from the case. The unsuccessful attempt to gain access from the basement has brought the elite squad back to the main entrance.

'Find the control room,' orders Chase. 'Secure it and get all these bloody internal doors open, and quick.'

The team spread out from reception into the interior of the building.

All but maintenance workers have dispersed for the day. The team work to round up anybody found in the factory. They all speak little to no English, except for two who speak little to no Chinese. English or not, they know how to comply when faced with the sight of guns.

Midway through the search of the factory, the team stumble upon a locked door. Their attempts to gain access are halted for several minutes as they search the immediate area for a key or some device to open it. Thwarted long enough, one officer picks up the nearby fire appliance.

'Step back, quick, stand aside,' he instructs.

With one heavy blow, he shatters the timber frame surround, and the lock, screws and part of the door splinter into small bits of debris and drop onto the floor. Navigating the broken door, the officer enters carefully. The team have found a hidden control room, containing up to fifteen surveillance monitors, all showing rooms elsewhere in the building.

'Sir, you'll want to see this,' the officer says.

'What have you got for me?' Chase asks, following the officer into the concealed room, with Fairbank trailing. After viewing several of the monitors, Chase turns to Fairbank.

'Slavery. Was a good call, Sergeant. But we now need to locate those rooms on the monitors and collect supporting evidence.'

'Look, sir, those lifts must work,' the officer says, pointing to one monitor showing a figure exiting a lift and carrying a large bag.

The team continue to search, finding their way to the first-floor offices, where they encounter Junjie sitting at a desk near a window at the far end of the open-plan office.

'Met Police! Stay where you are, keep your hands where we can see them!' shouts the lead officer.

Junjie stops what he's doing and raises his hands. The shredder continues running for fifteen seconds while Junjie sits, statue-like, unable to complete his task of destroying all key documents.

'Who else is on this floor?' says Fairbank.

'Just me,' Junjie replies, as they circle his desk, the red dots from their guns dancing within a two-inch radius of his heart.

'Name?' Fairbank asks.

'Junjie.'

'And where are the accommodation rooms located?'

'That would be top floor, I think,' Junjie answers.

Fairbank recognises Junjie as the person seen on the monitors leaving the lift.

'Your lift badge please?' Fairbank asks.

'Don't know where I left it.' Junjie searches the top of his desk, shuffling items to make them less visible.

'Try the drawers,' says Fairbank.

'No, it won't be in there.' Junjie keeps rummaging.

'How do you know it's not there unless you look?'

'Because this isn't my desk,' he pleads falsely, looking up with no hint that he's lying.

'So why hide this?' An officer turns over a framed photograph showing Junjie, a woman and a young child. The officer raises his gun and steps back, giving clear instructions to open the drawers slowly. As the top drawer opens, the officer's eyes widen. Crammed into every inch of drawer space are bundles of fifty-pound notes.

'Either your employer pays exceptionally well or you have a little operation of your own running here. At a wild guess, I would say people trafficking, maybe?' Fairbank suggests.

'No, no no no no, I only took the money because I was desperate.'

'Desperate, to get rich?'

'No, to see my family again. I pay twenty-thousand pounds to bring my family to England, and they say I must pay again.'

'Mr Junjie, I'm arresting you under the Modern Slavery Act 2015 and suspicion of trafficking. You don't have to say anything, but anything you say will be recorded and could be used as evidence in a court of law. Do you understand?'

Junjie offers no further comment; a simple check of his pockets reveals his security pass. Armed with access to the lifts and all floors, Fairbank leads a team of three up to the accommodation floor.

Going room by room, anyone found is first searched then taken to the canteen. Most are Asian, and when questioned they offer similar stories: no English, no address and no identifying documents. There's nothing either to suggest their ages or place of birth. It will be easy for immigration to offer the theory that they are illegal migrants in the UK, either through being trafficked or, as is so often the case, just over-staying their visa.

Several of the men detained speak good English but insist that they are legally there, under a government-backed prison release scheme.

After uncovering Junjie's stash, the team are convinced there must be more hidden in the building, launching a more extensive search. A forensic team arrive within the hour, to add weight in numbers for collecting the mass of evidence. They're taken to the factory's secret processing area found on sub-level two. The printing machine used to convert Chinese notes into pounds is old.

'It's in good nick for its age,' one officer observes on seeing the machine when he enters the room.

'I would have left it in the museum,' another says, offering his opinion.

'It's dusty,' the first remarks, after running his fingers over it. 'And the plates are missing too,' he adds.

The light layer of dust is a clear sign the printer had not been operated for a while. The plates, however, are nowhere to be seen, prompting an intensive search to find them. Another team finds the large quantity of cash awaiting the conversion process.

As the search process continues on all floors of the factory, Detective Inspector Chase takes a break and reflects on not listening to Fairbank. Feeling, as was suggested, that he should have at least questioned the tall man seen outside the building, he's not about to change his ways and praise him for his contribution. Wanting to say something, he turns to Fairbank.

'Aren't you glad, Mr Fairbank, that I didn't drop you home, otherwise you wouldn't have been here for the kill?'

'I'm not sure how you would like me to respond to that, sir?'

'A simple thank you is enough, Fairbank.'

'I suppose when I think about it, I should thank you for my phone being smashed into pieces and spraining my wrist trying to avoid it.'

'You need to toughen up, Fairbank, if you want to remain in this game. Imagine meeting a criminal face to face and your first reaction is to be worried about breaking his nails.'

Fairbank has had enough of his superior for one day. He decides to take a taxi home, rather than wait for the detective. On finishing up their investigations, they seal the factory and all prisoners under the government scheme are transported back to Downing. Forensic tests carried out have confirmed that the paper used is of the highest quality with the operation at the factory earning the title, 'the largest currency forgery in British history'.

# CHAPTER 32

I t's 5:30 am on Thursday 27 May. And even though it's thirty-six minutes after sunrise, the sky above the capital is still dark. While most of the population sleeps, the heart of the transport system is already hard at work. On a Northern Line train heading south sits the lone figure of Sadam Benwadi, who has so far stayed off-grid since his bold escape from Downing Prison. Clean shaven and in a suit, he's dressed like any other office worker, and with a black woollen hat pulled over his ears and a scarf doubled around his neck, he can avoid the main features of his face being identified. With both hands resting on the aluminium briefcase sitting on his lap, he's nervous and holds it with a firm grip.

Sadam removes a small folded piece of paper from his coat pocket and studies it before putting it back in the same pocket. His intended destination is Fitzrovia's Goodge Street station, and because he's not familiar with the line, he checks the tube map above the seats opposite frequently. He notes there are only three stops left as the train leaves Mornington Crescent station and mentally prepares himself for the brisk walk when he gets there.

Mr Benwadi has also gathered statistics about his destination, from its height of 191 metres to the fact that there are 36 floors.

He needs to arrive in Cleveland Mews at precisely 6 am to meet the cleaner recruited to help him gain access to the secure building. The train pulls in to the station and he stands, ready to exit. As the doors open, he brushes against a middle-aged lady in a rush to enter the train. She looks on him with some anger as he tries to avoid eye contact or confrontation. Following the crowd, he takes the stairs towards the lifts, but slows as two of the three lifts are out of order and a crowd waiting is several layers deep. Checking his watch, he decides, like a few others, that the stairs would be quicker and wastes no time starting up the 136 steps.

The ascent to ground level takes him longer than expected and, out of breath, he finally exits the station onto Tottenham Court Road. Checking his watch once again, he turns left towards Euston then takes the first left into Tottenham Street, followed with a right at Charlotte Street. Then after three blocks, another left into Howland Street. Checking his watch again, he's got a little over two minutes left to make the rendezvous point before the whole exercise would need rescheduling. With Cleveland Mews metres, away on his right, he can see just one security camera, located above the street sign, covering the one-way street's exit.

On time, too, is his contact Ishmael, as pre-arranged standing by the blue railings at the rear exit gate by the smoking point. The contact looks up and turns back into the gate as he approaches, using his head to signal the direction he should take to enter the gate.

'You just about made it, another minute and the security

cameras would begin recording again,' Ishmael informs him, checking his watch.

'Have you got something for me?'

'You first,' Ishmael answers.

Sadam extracts an envelope from the breast pocket of his coat and hands it to Ishmael, who puts it straight into his back pocket without checking the contents.

'Here,' he says, passing a building security pass to Sadam.

'This looks nothing like me,' he says, removing his hat and stuffing it into the coat pocket.

'It's okay, you won't need to show it, it's been stolen specifically just for access to the lifts and certain doors,' Ishmael explains, locking the back gate. 'Follow me. This route will by-pass the main cameras by the entrance that record twenty-four seven.'

Sadam is led up some stairs and along a corridor towards the front of the building. Needing to get to the fifteenth floor, he will need to pass through security. Ishmael puts a key into a service door, opens it then exits into a passageway leading back to the security desk at the main entrance. Confirming the coast is clear, he opens the door fully.

'Okay, it's clear,' he says, closing the door after Sadam has exited. 'This is as far as I can take you, down there is reception and the security barriers,' he whispers. 'Use the pass to tap in, you'll find the lifts to all floors just behind the barriers.'

'Thanks,' he says, before turning and moving off towards security, with Ishmael moving in the other direction.

As he approaches reception, Sadam can see the lifts in the background. Producing the pass, he taps the pad with confidence, which parts the barriers. Lifting the aluminium briefcase over the top, he moves through to the other side.

'Excuse me, sir.' A rather portly security guard halts his progress before he can take another step towards the lifts.

'Yes, is there a problem?' he nervously answers, keeping any verbal to a minimum.

'No, it's just the first time that I've seen you. You must be new?'

'Yes, only started last week.'

'Well, we have a random bag checking policy here, and I would like to try and get one out of the way before the big staff rush at eight o'clock. So, would you mind opening your case for me, sir?'

Caught out by the request, it's the one thing they hadn't planned for. He moves tentatively towards the security console, placing the case on top. Bending to see the combination, Sadam opens the case, spinning it to face the guard.

'Isn't that one of those Mega-Light torches?' The guard notices the first item on top.

'Yes, I live in the countryside and sometimes have to walk home from the station in pitch darkness.'

Seeing a torch up close he wants to get himself seems to have left him satisfied.

'Thank you for that, sir.'

'Not at all, thank you, you're only doing your job,' Sadam says, closing the case.

'Have a good day, sir.

'And you,' he replies, lifting the case and moving away.


Heading straight for the lifts, he's aware of another looming check-point to deal with upstairs. When the lift arrives, he presses for floor 15 on entry and watch as the sliding doors close. On reaching the thirty-fifth floor, he exits the lift and sees the door to the control centre. He needs, however, to take the stairs to the Aerial gallery, which is located on the next floor up, then gain access to the outside ledge. Taking two flights of stairs to the next floor, he reaches the external door. Setting the case down, he opens the main section to reveal a few tools. Taking the wire strippers, he carefully exposes the wires leading from the door contacts. He also removes from his case a metre-long piece of red electrical wire, fitted with crocodile clips at each end, attaching one end to the door's stripped connector wire and the other to the wire that sits above the door frame. Satisfied, he tests the connection by pushing the door bar, breaking the contact. With the indicator light above the door still off, he knows it's safe to continue. Extracting the torch, he uses the case to wedge the door and stop it from closing, before going outside.

It's windy and cold, and looking down, Sadam feels the effect of his vertigo. He puts his hat back on, then turns the torch on, pointing it towards a green patch of land two blocks to the north. The light acts as a beacon, and after forty seconds the buzzing sound of a drone gets closer to the light. It hovers steady a foot from the ledge, allowing Sadam to retrieve a package suspended from its undercarriage. The drone's operator can view its delivery through the on-board camera and recalls the drone immediately. Moving back inside, Sadam removes his hat and places the package in the case along with the torch. Closing the door, he unfixes the wire, also storing it in the case.

Back again on the thirty-fifth floor, he uses the same security pass to get access the control centre. Inside, the room contains over fifteen aisles of data cabinets. Checking the piece of paper in his pocket again, Sadam moves straight to the location where the cabinet labelled Lotto-Guard stands. Placing the aluminium case on the floor, he opens it and removes the package. Lifting the inner dividing flap, he also removes an anti-static grounding wrist strap, which he puts on his wrist, then anchors the other end to the cabinet, before he opens it. Counting from the top, he half pulls out the ninth module, exposing its electronic components towards the back. Unwrapping the package delivered by Fat Fingers, he removes the chip and connects it to the module's spare power supply. Taking out his mobile, he attaches a USB lead between the module and the phone to install the software needed to support the chip's function.

After five minutes a beep confirms the installation and is also his cue to think about his exit strategy. Removing the cable, he slides the module back, closes the cabinet and detaches the anti-static strap, placing it, along with the USB cable, into his briefcase. The control centre door opens suddenly, forcing Sadam into a nearby aisle to avoid being detected. The engineer that enters doesn't stay long after rebooting a module. As soon as he's able, Sadam leaves the control room and moves straight to the lifts. On the way down, it stops three times, taking on half a dozen more people before arriving at the ground floor. The journey down seemed a lot longer than going up.

Following others exiting, Sadam has no trouble leaving the BT Tower through its main entrance. Going down the steps to the pavement, he turns right into Maple Street and is soon lost in crowds of people heading to work in all directions.

# CHAPTER 33

It's early morning, and all is quiet at Dr Minn's home. The new guests have the run of his house with plenty of space to adjust and settle. His natural son is eager for a one-to-one chat, hoping to learn something about his mother and perhaps anything on his father and their missing years.

Knowing he must address this at some point kept Dr Minn awake for most of last night and is the main reason he's late getting to his sanctuary this morning. As always though, he uses it to meditate and seek spiritual guidance whenever there are tough choices. He's surprised but heartened to find his son sitting silently by the water feature on entering the main chamber.

'Mr Yip, a refreshing and welcome surprise to discover you here. I've not been able to coax your sister into joining me as yet.'

'I'm surprised, she's never been in here?'

'No, never.'

'And yet it was her that suggested it as a place where we can be candid about our feelings.'

'And which of them do you need to be candid about?'

'Well, some of them I don't even think I could explain. I learnt very early that my parents had adopted me. I don't remember exactly when, but I was about seven, I think. The subject only came up when they couldn't explain why other children were tormenting me about my eyes. In my school, you see, the only people being picked on more than me were the black kids. I suppose that's why as outsiders, Ox and I have remained good friends since then. He didn't accept it for long and taught me how to fight back; they soon moved on, picking on easier targets, like the bullies they were. I was carefree up to that point; something about not being aware buffers you from life's cruel realities. Then, over the years, the need for real answers about my past started chipping away at me. Those feelings only stopped after being imprisoned and replaced by "who framed us and why"?'

'Added to all your troubles should be my failure to learn of your existence before it was too late.'

'No, not a failure at all, I heard what you said about Chi. In the same way that you offered him a home, someone gave me one too.'

'We will sort this out soon, I promise, and you will get your life back.'

With the father and son relationship rekindled, Dr Minn asks Chan to join him for breakfast so they can continue to foster it.

As they leave his sanctuary, it turns out that everyone is up early. Chi sits outside, restless for a word with Dr Minn. He stands as they near.

'Good morning,' says Chi, greeting them.

'Good morning,' they both reply.

'Sir, I was wondering if you would allow me the chance to talk with you privately, please?' Chi asks.

'Can it wait until after breakfast?'

'I would appreciate that opportunity now if you could spare the time, sir.'

'Okay, please go ahead and I'll join you as soon as I can,' he tells Chan.

After Chan has moved away and out of sight, Dr Minn sits and invites Chi to do the same.

'Now, what is so urgent that I've had to delay my breakfast?'

'It's about your daughter, sir.'

'Mai Li?'

'Yes.' Chi lowers his head.

'Chi, I've known you most of your life, and I hope I've always encouraged you to be assertive. Whatever you want to say, I can only hear when you actually talk.'

'I'm in love with your daughter,' Chi finally blurts out.

'And I take it from your nervousness that Mai Li knows little or nothing of this infatuation?'

'Sir, it's more than infatuation, but she seems to spend more and more time with your son's friend, Mr Ox. A word from you is all it would take.'

'All it would take for what?'

'For her to notice me, sir.'

'Chi, you've already heard me describe you as being like a son to me. I have no better influence or experience in matters of the heart than the next man. With my daughter, I have none at all. She is, and always will be, a free spirit, a bit like her mother I suppose. Gone are the times when you could rely on a father's opinions being obeyed. I couldn't guarantee that any intervention would deliver your desired outcome. Her future partner needs to be her choice, and hers alone.'

Chi looks deflated as Dr Minn leaves him sitting to ponder the reality of the situation.

Elsewhere, it's the second day of the general election campaign and Sir Edward is visiting a police cadet college in North London, invited by the police commissioner to boost both their profiles. They hope to bring awareness to the young minds of the harsh reality of prison.

They've assembled everyone in the main hall. The chief instructor takes to the stage to announce his guest speaker.

'Good morning, ladies and gentlemen, and welcome to our last assembly together, with you as cadets. In under a week, most of you will complete your final exams, and before long you'll be on the road to your chosen career paths. As I've got to know most of you over these last three months, I'm reminded that society is not without its share of social and economic pressures that will impact all our lives. To apply what you've learnt in training will allow you to discharge your duties in an efficient and professional way. Today, with crime at the forefront of all our minds, my guest speaker is the Right Honourable Sir Edward Long MP, the current minister for prisons.' The instructor initiates the clapping as Sir Edward moves centre stage, placing his notes on the lectern.

'Good morning, everyone,' he begins. 'It's a sad fact that our prison population has a far higher proportion of young people than many of our European counterparts. The measures this government has introduced over its tenure have seen these figures stabilised, but there's still a long way to go. The coming weeks will see my party publish more measures to further reduce this number. Over the last five years, I've been immensely proud of my contribution to the reduction in knife crime. Now, every one of you will have sworn the oath to protect and serve the public. You should keep in mind that everyone is someone's son, daughter, aunt, uncle, sister, brother, cousin... you get my meaning. What I'm saying is that all life matters, and not just those we hold dear. So here is my oath to you all. Because of the continued dangers faced by our police force, I've agreed with the Chancellor to introduce an above-inflation pay increase. In a few weeks, to coincide with the start of your careers, every basic salary will see a significant uplift of around two thousand pounds.'

The cadets applaud like he's a rock star. Closing on a high, he asks the audience for questions.

'What made you go into politics sir?' a female cadet asks.

'As soon as I was eligible to vote, I couldn't decide on which party or which candidate to give my precious vote to. Why? Because they all advocated similar policies. I decided that if I wanted the changes not being offered, then the only way forward was to become an MP myself. This would ensure that the public could judge my ideas for putting the country right in the same way I had done.'

Another hand goes up.

'Yes, you, miss.' He nods to a girl further towards the back, who lowers her hand and stands up.

'Would you say you have achieved what you set out to do in politics?' She sits again quickly.

'The thing about politics is that sometimes you get things right and at other times it can go spectacularly wrong. That's why a government needs more than a five-year term to see the benefits of its policies. Next question, please... yes, you, sir.'

A tall, fresh-faced young man stands up.

'What is it like working in a prison?' he asks.

'I think you may have misheard the introduction.' Sir Edward smiles. 'I'm the minister for prisons; I don't actually work in one. But if you are thinking about a career in the prison service, then it's both challenging and rewarding. You get satisfaction from knowing you are helping to protect the public while rehabilitating those that want to change their lives.'

The chief instructor returns to the stand to close proceedings.

'I'd just like to thank the minister for taking time out of his busy campaign schedule to be with us this morning. I'm sure you will all join me in wishing him good luck in his election campaign. Thank you, Sir Edward Long MP, thank you.'

The students stand, on the command of the instructor, to join in applauding the minister off the stage.

The reporter Matthew Robinson waits with his cameraman and live-links to the morning news to interview Sir Edward as he exits the college with the commissioner.

'Sir Edward, CBB live news reporting, can you give us an

update, sir?' The reporter manoeuvres the microphone closer to Sir Edward's face. Judging interviews as free publicity, Sir Edward stops his exit and is more than willing to be interviewed on camera.

'Sir Edward, can we have your comment on the latest reports this morning that Lotto-Guard, a company hailed by you as being the answer to our courts and prison system, has been exposed as a fraudulent cover for people trafficking, amongst other things?'

For a second, Sir Edward appears paralysed by the question. He reacts, though, as any seasoned politician would when confronted with unexpected questions.

'Sorry, I'm unable to comment without having at least seen the facts. I'm sure the police, who do a fine job, would not wish me to speculate on any investigations that are ongoing. Thank you.'

Sir Edward moves off camera quickly, leaving Robinson hovering with his second question, which he's forced to direct at the police commissioner instead.

Later that evening, Sir Edward sits in his living room, in a comfortable chair by the fire, working to complete a speech for the following morning. The house telephone rings and breaks his concentration.

'Good evening, who's calling?' he answers, hoping it's a sales call he can cut off quickly.

'Evening again, Sir Edward. Detective Inspector Chase here. I have the results from the tests carried out on your car.'

'Good, I trust everything is in order?'

'Not quite, sir, some stains found in the boot of your car turned out to be human blood.'

'Blood? I don't understand, Inspector.'

'They extracted the DNA and found a match on the national database.'

'Are you telling me that a crime has been committed involving my car?'

'Yes, sir. In fact, they've linked it to a specific murder case.'

'I can't see how that's possible.' Sir Edward tries to mask his knowledge.

'The case in question is technically closed, after the two individuals who pleaded guilty were imprisoned.'

'So, what is the answer, Inspector? The car was reported stolen.'

'Look, it's no use asking me, but if I was a betting man, I wouldn't put it beyond them trying to establish how the victim's blood got into your car and whether it was pre- or post-murder.'

'Are you saying they might re-open the case?'

'I can't confirm anything, but if they do, it won't be for a few weeks at least. Anyway, the real reason for my call was to share some more information about your ex-wife's case.' Chase sounds more confident when dealing with his own case.

'Go ahead, Inspector'

'From CCTV footage, we've tracked down the owner of a second delivery scooter. He claims that he accepted an offer of three hundred pounds' cash from a stranger to hire his scooter for an hour. For a biker who only earns thirteen pounds or less an hour, I can see the attraction and why he never came forward. Anyway, the most interesting fact is that the other rider was a woman.'

'Can she be identified?'

'Sadly not, she reportedly wore a scarf that covered most of her face. She left the delivery worker keys to a Range Rover as security.'

'Then what about the car's number plates?'

'They turned out to be false too. Cloned from a car registered in Scotland. We will eventually turn up something, for sure, that will lead us to the killer.'

'Thanks, Inspector, much appreciated.'

The call ends as Lady Elizabeth comes into the room. She

caught the tail end of Edward's conversation and is keen to know the details.

'I know some of that was about Kim, wasn't it?' she asks.

'Yes. They have a lead involving a woman, and he's sure they will soon have information that will lead them to her.'

'Information such as what?'

'I'm sorry, darling, but I have an important call to make. I promise to tell you everything the inspector said afterwards.'

'You seem to spend an awful lot of time on the phone. How about maybe asking how my day has been?'

Elizabeth's complaint falls on deaf ears as she watches him leave the room, mobile in hand and already dialling.

'Good evening, Doctor Minn.'

'Ah, Sir Edward. So nice to have you return my call. I called Wednesday, you know, only to hear a recorded message informing me to call back after the election.'

'It's been hectic, you know what it's like. Anyway, I was wondering if you still have the wherewithal to access official records?'

Dr Minn is a little hurt that Sir Edward has made no attempt to enquire why he had called him in the first place.

'Wherewithal?' He finally answers. 'I'm a little embarrassed to admit, Sir Edward, but I'm not familiar with that English word.'

'Let's call it resources then.'

'Ah, I might have to disappoint you again. The resources needed to fulfil any requests are… unavailable.'

'When you say unavailable, you mean temporary?'

'No, I'm no longer the owner of Lotto-Guard UK.'

'Aargh!' A cry from the living room prompts Sir Edward to end his call rather abruptly, 'I have to go,' he says, ringing off.

'Elizabeth, darling, what is it, dear?' he calls ahead as he rushes back into the living room.

'Something's not right, Edward. My stomach feels all knotted with pain.' She groans again as tears begin streaming from her eyes.

'Sit back, try to relax, dear.'

'Aaaaaargh!' Elizabeth cries out and doubles over on the sofa, cradling her stomach tightly.

'Hang on, dear. I'm calling for help.' Still holding his mobile, he pushes nine three time rapidly.

'Nine nine nine emergencies, which service please?'

'Ambulance, please. Hurry.'

# CHAPTER 34

'The Friday morning headlines: the prisons minister, Sir Edward Long, resigned his government post last night citing personal reasons. In his statement, the minister said that he will also not be seeking re-election. Speculation surrounding his decision broke late last night after an ambulance rushed his wife to hospital. In the last hour, the hospital confirmed Lady Long had suffered a miscarriage. It's understood the couple, who were expecting their first child, are in deep shock. A spokeswoman for the family said they hoped the press will respect their wish to grieve their loss in private.*

Other breaking news reaching us this morning. Police say they've received the same coded terror warning sent to all major news agencies about an imminent attack. It is understood that no specific targets were mentioned; however, a group calling themselves 'YLA' have warned that they will unleash an unstoppable devastation on the people of London if the terms of their demands are not met. We understand from our notification that they are demanding that the British government halts all arms sales to the Middle East immediately. Security forces are checking for links to all known terror groups. In response, the government has issued a public statement saying that Britain will not *bow to any terrorist threats or ask its citizens to hide in their own country. They've also added that apart from the increased security measures for all key public services, the UK threat levels will remain the same.'*

≈

The day begins at Downing Prison with Governor Riley in deep contemplation just sitting. Looking childlike in one of his own guest chairs, he stares down at his feet to avoid having to look up. His pose is not unsimilar to a naughty schoolboy waiting outside the headmasters' office, given time to reflect while waiting to learn his fate. Officer Newport has been summoned to the governor's office but seems to be taking a while, affording the governor even more time to think on what troubles him before his pending arrival.

Notified by Cynthia when he arrives that the governor is expecting him and to go straight in, Officer Newport stops anyway to say good morning and check if she knew whether the governor would have seen the early morning news?

'I don't know,' Cynthia answers, leaving him no better informed to continue into the office and meet the unacceptable sight of Stuart Naylor occupying the governor's chair.

'What's going on in here? And who's given you permission to sit in that chair, lad? Give me a second, Governor, and I'll have him out of your recliner and this prison.' Newport moves towards Naylor, who does little more than glance up as he nears the side of the desk.

'Mr Newport! Please – restrain yourself.' The governor is firm in his order. 'Mr Naylor is not who you assumed he was.'

'You're right, Governor. Whatever I thought of him, he's clearly punching above his weight and overstepped the mark this time.' Newport feels the need to flex his authority muscles.

'Mr Naylor is with HM Inspectorate of Prisons,' the governor blurts out, as if he'd unearthed the information personally. 'I do distinctively recall warning you about this, and your out-of-the-box thinker.' Governor Riley adds.

The news appears to place an invisible barrier stopping Newport, who retreats to the front of the desk, taking a seat in the other vacant chair.

'Now that the formal introductions are out of the way, I can finally turn my attention to the real reasons for me being here,' Stuart begins. 'Questions regarding the running of this prison. Contracting-out to the private sector still remains a controversial topic. Many argue that the private sector's involvement should have created a more diverse market by now, driving up standards and promoting efficiencies. Others, though, see imprisonment as a function which the government should not delegate or profit from. So, my question to you, gentlemen is, which category would you file this prison under?'

Governor Riley and Officer Newport glance at each other, with neither offering to say anything that might incriminate or confuse the situation further until Stuart has at least revealed how many aces he's holding.

'Okay, then let me help with some possible answers,' Stuart offers. 'In the short time I've been here, I've witnessed some fine work. For example, it impressed me how Mr Newport went about trying to crack the code needed to find a terrorist target. Whilst it turned out to be nothing more than a distracting exercise, the core drive and ideas put forward to resolve it were his. That fact alone may well offset sections of my report.'

Newport's expressionless face stares back at Stuart in silence. He shifts his position in the chair as Stuart stands and moves to the front of the desk, leaning back on it, before he continues.

'Initially, my remit was to investigate the unexplained deaths in this prison. But it soon became clear there were other things happening.

'For instance, if a fire broke out – could we rely on the safety equipment in this prison? And I mean all of them?   Yes, I stumbled across your little network almost by accident. And before you assert that it does not exist, perhaps you won't mind me reminding you, Mr Newport, about my time in narcotics? So, after finding the empty fire extinguisher, I knew there was something more going on, and in my experience, most prison deaths have some correlation with the supply or use of drugs.'

'Then with your experience, Mr Naylor, you more than anyone should appreciate and understand, how all prisons have some small element of drug use.' Governor Riley breaks his silence, with his head still low, hiding his guilt.

'Indeed, Governor, but my discovery exposed the fact that we were not talking about small amounts – and why I needed to unravel the network to find the person at its helm. Starting, obviously, with how the drugs were being distributed around the prison undetected. I was aware of Mr Salerno's influence in this prison, and sure enough he'd know something, even if not involved himself. The cell search on the night of the lockdown gave me my first clue.'

'Mr Newport can confirm no drugs were found in Mr Salerno's cell,' the governor interjects again.

'That's correct, I can and you were there.' Mr Newport breaks his silence too, concurring with the governor's statement.

'The clue was, whoever searched Mr Salerno's cell the first time, never found what they were looking for. I also calculated, since there were no drug dogs involved in our search, that they were clearly looking for something else. The answer – well that came later in the medical unit. When I arrived there, Mr Salerno had already been given medication to help him relax. He was mumbling all sorts, names and dates, which linked me back to Cynthia. I found out it was her responsibility to schedule the staff patrol that kept officers away from key locations whenever the drugs were being moved. Then again, I'm not telling you anything new, am I, Governor? – And why? Because she did directly as you ordered.'

'Are you suggesting that she was being blackmailed because such accusations require actual evidence to back them up? Do you have such evidence, Mr Naylor? The governor feels more confident that, without it, he'd have nothing to answer.

'No.'

'Then your action is no better than a witch hunt.'

'But I said nothing in regards to Cynthia being blackmailed. No, she was a willing participant in your deception, considering you were in a relationship with her and planning to run off together.'

'Where do you get this nonsense from? I've known Cynthia for over twelve years and the Governor and his wife even longer.' Newport joins the governor in trying to undermine Mr Naylor and relieve the pressure.

'On the contrary, she was very supportive, if misguided, but it was your name, Governor, that came up several times whilst I was observing Mr Salerno. To confirm my theory, I had the doctor check his medical history, which showed he suffers from a condition called 'somniloquism.'

'A what?' Officer Newport grunts.

'Just means he talks in his sleep, Mr Newport,' the governor explains.

'And why, being aware of his own condition, Mr Salerno did everything to ensure he never shared a cell with anyone throughout his prison life,' Stuart confirms.

'I don't think you know him as we do. He's pure evil – not just here, it's his record in every prison he's been in,' Newport recalls.

'And so, we come to you, Mr Newport, someone who the governor has known for a long time but doesn't seem to have afforded you that same trust with any key information?' Stuart asks.

'I've given him no reasons not to. We go back a long way, as I've said, and I trust him fully.'

'And I trust you fully too,' the governor professes.

'Then let's examine that trust, shall we? Tell him, Governor, what you were really searching for in Mr Salerno's cell?'

Governor Riley remains silent, prompting Newport to offer his answer.

'If you must know, the governor suspected him of having some device, possibly a mobile phone.'

'No, he was searching for evidence. Evidence of records he was sure Mr Salerno kept on their operation.'

'Records! What links has Mr Salerno got with the governor?' Newport asks.

'Mr Salerno keeps everything in his head, a fact I was referring to in a roundabout way earlier. So, the governor sent you in merely to clear up his failed attempt to find a physical ledger, detailing their many transactions. So, I don't think the governor has been open with you on anything,' Stuart explains further. 'His exit plan had two parts: first to transfer all the illicit proceeds into his wife's name, which he achieved, including your percentage, which he named the retirement fund, Mr Newport. His final plans were to transfer the money offshore, but he got a little ahead of himself in carelessly leaving a cheap do-it-yourself divorce petition, which his wife discovered, along with his plans to marry Cynthia.'

'Is what he's saying true, Governor?' Newport asks.

'If Mr Naylor was an artist, then he would paint the most wonderful pictures.'

'I asked you if it were true, Governor.' Newport presses for a real answer.

'I would take the governor's silence, Mr Newport, as the admission of a guilty man,' Naylor suggests.

'What's going to happen now?' Governor Riley asks, knowing his career is at its end.

'My report will contain only the facts. I have no interest in the trivia surrounding the relationship between you two. If you ask me, though, I don't see how you'll avoid prison. For how long, that will depend on the amount of cooperation you're willing to give to the enquiry.'

At Dr Minn's home, the breakfast table, like those in prison, provides a meeting place for all the guests staying. Paul's silence prompts Chan to instigate a dialogue.

'What's up with you this morning?'

'What do you mean?' Paul says, avoiding eye contact.

'You seem detached, that's all,' Chan says, as Mai Li enters the kitchen.

'Good morning.' She greets everyone with a smile then tones it down when she notices Chi staring from the staff table. Her smile alone said it all – no stress and no worries. A collective 'good morning' greets a cheerful Mai Li. Even the servants acknowledge her.

'What's got you smiling this morning?' asks Ox, who was pleased to see her.

'Well, it's another day, and we are all alive. Oh, and I changed the system last night, so you guys are no longer linked to that murder.'

'Seems like things are working out for you guys, I'm happy for you really. Sounds like my cue to leave and sort out my own life,' says Paul.

'Where do you plan on going?' says Ox. 'There's still your sentence to consider.'

'Yes, and I'm sure you guys not being linked with me will help get your lives back even quicker.'

'Where are you heading, back to Ladbroke Grove? And whoever it was you met outside, in that car?'

'You weren't meant to see.'

'But I did. And from what I did see, you didn't appear to be in any danger.'

'That's because it was Ian, my brother, you know the one you met in prison. Yeah, my father sent him.'

'Your father! How did he know where to find you?'

'I suppose it makes little difference telling you now. In my daughter's picture is this small tracking device.' Paul produces the picture, pointing out the slight bulge at one corner.

'I knew there was something you were keeping from us and why the photo was so important to you,' Ox says.

'Everyone has a father, right? I guess mine is a little more protective about his kids than most.'

'Why so?' asks Mai Li. 'You're a grown man.'

'When I was small, my father used to take me with him "on the rob",' says Paul.

'"On the rob." What does that mean?' Mai Li asks.

'It means stealing. It wasn't until my first arrest that I realised the game he'd taught us, hiding sweets around the house so we'd have to go through some small gaps to get them, was a backdrop to my life of crime.'

'And your mother?' Mai Li asks.

'From what I remember, she spent a lot of time in her room, off her head, drugged up.'

'And where is he now, your father?' Mai Li continues.

'Quit asking, he may not want to tell us.' Chan offers Paul an escape route from her questioning.

'No, he's where all failed criminals like me end up – prison.'

'If you don't know where he is, I'm able to help you, you know,' Mai Li offers.

'No need, he's in Downing.'

'Paul, you're a real dark horse,' says Chan. 'You never mentioned him once while we were there. We could have even met him and not realised.'

'Well, that was one reason for dropping my double-barrelled name at eighteen. It avoided people making that same link.'

'You should be proud of your family no matter what,' Mai Li says.

'That's true, as you'll never know when you might need them,' adds Chan.

'Except when you realise how your father's actions may have contributed to the death of your mother, you might take a different perspective. Besides, she was planning to leave him the wrong way, by committing suicide and taking Ian and me with her, after she found out about his affair and a daughter he fathered.'

'I'm sorry. At least it's nice to know you have a sister out there,' says Ox.

'Sorry for what? Look, I've never met her and have no information about her at all. Anyway, time I was on the road,' Paul says, standing up.

'You can't leave yet,' Mai Li insists. 'We need to get those bracelets removed first. We'll have to use some sort of an electronic bridge to keep them linked while being removed. I'll get Chi to take them off before you go.'

'Thanks.'

'In fact, let's do them all now. Come, follow me, all of you.' Mai Li leads the trio out of the kitchen into the garage.

After an hour-long effort, the bracelets are all removed, allowing Paul time to say a final goodbye.

'You guys keep out of trouble,' he tells Ox and Chan.

'And you, more than us, need to do the same,' Ox answers.

With the borrowed bag, he leaves the house, getting into a waiting cab as Chan, Ox and Mai Li look on.

'I'm still curious, about his father being at Downing,' Chan says, waving as the car moves further down the drive out the gate and away.

'I can find out for you... brother.' Mai Li feels strange yet happy calling Chan her brother.

'I know, you're brilliant, and I've a lot to learn and thank you for. I've already learnt how life is too short, and I'll be honest, if it were me, I'm not sure I wouldn't have given up looking for my family a lot earlier.'

'Want to know what I think?' says Ox. 'I'm glad your sister

didn't give up her belief that one day she might find you. I'd take that outcome any day.'

'It's no trouble checking who Paul's father is. I've got a backdoor to the prison's computer system anyway.'

'I need to reclassify what I said about you earlier, from brilliant to dangerous,' Chan says, smiling.

Mai Li, using her computer skills, soon finds Paul's real surname: Gilby-Salerno, but has to wait when a live news pop-up appears on her screen.

*'We're receiving graphic and disturbing news this lunchtime, of fatal incidences, in and around central London. It's reported so far that hundreds of people may have lost their lives with many more severely wounded. Police are now trying to disperse a large crowd which had gathered in Trafalgar Square in defiance of this morning's terrorist order. They're concerned that the mass gathering may have contributed to the high death count. We are going live to our reporter Karen Brown, who is with an eye-witness just off the square. Karen.'*

*"Good afternoon, I'm here just off Trafalgar Square with an eye-witness who was visiting the National Portrait Gallery. Can you describe to me, sir, what you saw?"*

*"I couldn't believe it at first. The crowd didn't stand a chance, especially those who had brought small children with them. No one could work out which direction it was being fired from. It seemed to target anybody with those things on their wrists."*

*"You mean the Pinpoint bracelets?"*

*"Yeah, and anybody standing close enough to them were just in the line of fire."*

*"Thank you. As you can see from the live pictures, London is facing a major disaster. A policeman I spoke to some ten minutes ago spoke of the scale of the operation they'll need, just for the recovery of bodies. This is Karen Brown for CBB News, handing you back to the studio."*

*'Thank you, Karen. The Prime Minister, we're told, has cut short his visit to France and will visit several sites this afternoon ahead of a*

*televised response to what can only be described as a day when we've all witnessed the mass slaughter of innocent people.'*

'We need to watch that later,' Chan suggests, while Mai Li is quiet after she minimises the pop-up screen to continue.

'Are you alright?' Ox asks, seeing that Mai Li has become a little emotional.

'Yeah, it's just hard to think that if you guys were still out there and wearing the bracelets, anything could have happened to you,' she answers, looking up at Ox, who places his arms around her shoulders in a quick embrace, before she focuses again on her screen. Checking the name against prison records, there is only one match, Avion Salerno, also known as Fat Fingers.

'Aren't you glad we didn't keep pushing him to tell us?' Chan jokes with Ox.

'That's my lesson learnt. Never again am I going to judge people solely on what I think I'm seeing,' states Ox.

'You shouldn't be so quick to change your opinion on someone,' Mai Li suggests.

'Why?'

'Because two of father's paintings from the hall are missing, plus I think he also stole some special money my father kept here,' Mai Li says.

'Why didn't you tell me before he left? I would have been able to stop him,' Ox claims.

'I didn't say anything, because I hate those paintings, I'm glad they're gone,' she answers.

'Then what about the money? Ox presses the point.

'Don't worry, I think they were the early samples, He won't be stupid once he realises.'

'Maybe he just can't help himself: once a thief, you'll take any opportunity,' Chan adds.

≈

At home, Sir Edward takes a break from packing a light case with toiletries and fresh clothes to take when he visits his wife Elizabeth later, who remains in hospital for observation. Sitting for a moment on his bed, he contemplates his actions and the decisions he's taken over the last couple of months. The decision to resign still rests heavily on his conscience since he had so many ideas needing a platform. But between the two babies and now none, a murder case and the collapse of his scheme, he feels he's made the right decision. Following the news events unfolding all day, he's shocked at the scheme he championed causing so much death. He increases the television volume to hear what his Prime Minister has to say.

*'There now follows a public broadcast from the Prime Minister:'*

*"Good evening. It's with a heavy heart and deep sadness that I address you directly tonight. The Pinpoint system was deployed to bring more control over known criminals who were out at night committing more crimes whilst awaiting justice. Today we saw this same system used as a weapon, targeting randomly innocent members of the public. The warning we received this morning from an unknown terror group gave insufficient information to prevent this attack. Details not made public earlier I can share with you now. This group said that any attempt to shut down the system would also result in shutting down our entire financial system, costing our economy billions for every second it was down. Faced for the first time with an attack of this sophistication, they, whoever they are, have rendered our normal protocol useless. I'm asking the public to stay calm, vigilant and, for now, to remain in indoors, only venturing out when absolutely necessary. One thing that has not changed is our need for the public's support so that it won't be necessary to reintroduce measures similar to the Covid-19 crisis of 2020.*
*Please continue to report any suspicious or unusual activity to the police. Everything is being done to identify this group or individuals and*

bring them to justice swiftly. Out of respect for this unfolding tragedy, the government has cancelled the upcoming general election set for Thursday the 10th of June until further notice. Our intention as a government was never to stay in power without backing from the ballot box; however, today we all witnessed these extraordinary circumstances.

We estimate that there are between nine and eleven thousand Pinpoint bracelets in circulation. The terrorist who we have not yet identified could even be sitting next to you right now, listening to this broadcast. If you are, take note that Britain will never give in to terrorism. God bless you all, and good night."

'In other news, police arrested this man today trying to pass a large quantity of fifty-pound notes while placing a bet. An astute cashier noticed the similarity between serial numbers on some notes presented and notified the police. He's been identified as Paul Gilby.'

'A debate is growing for the government to reclaim full control, after Lotto-Guard's collapse and the announcement that the election has been suspended. Calls to abandon the high-tech court system also gather pace and this looks more likely following an online poll in favour of the move, topping two million. Legal experts have highlighted that thousands of cases will have to be reviewed. It's understood that the number of new appeals for unsafe convictions is rising. Human Rights groups say if necessary every case should be reinvestigated to ensure that the correct people responsible for the crimes, are arrested and brought before the courts to face due punishment. A leading advocate for the old court system concluded an interview today with the following comment: "A drastic audit is the only way to correct and preserve the integrity of our once world renowned legal system."'

## THE END

Now you've finished the book, what can you do? Visit Amazon and Goodreads to leave a review! Send out a tweet, maybe even a like on Facebook. This will both inspire the author and help others to appreciate this literary treat.

If you have enjoyed this book, please also consider leaving a review or rating on Amazon, Goodreads and/or the site where you purchased it. Readers reviews aids new Authors work to be discovered.

You can also connect with Delton Pink online to discuss the book and to be the first to hear about other titles and projects in the pipeline, he's looking forward to hearing from

## CONNECT WITH THE AUTHOR

www.deltonpink.com

Facebook.com / deltonpink

Twitter.com / @deltonpink #HypnoticState

Goodreads.com / deltonpink

# ACKNOWLEDGEMENTS

To my daughter, Marisha Pink (*Finding Arun* and *Last Piece of Me*), my heartfelt thanks for helping me to learn a lot about the many processes needed to bring my imagination to life.

To my son, Kishan Pink, who has reversed the role of support coming from a father to his son. I know he'll be a good father himself and is clever beyond his years.

To my wife, Nina Pink, who allowed me to get through the process of many hours of writing and rewriting in solitude.

To my Proof-reader and Editor's, who deserve more than thanks especially Richard Sheehan, editor to the stars and me, a true professional who helped me through a process that forced me to dig deeper, guaranteeing that I achieved a level above the one that I had set myself.

To all of the beta readers, but mainly Stuart Henry for sticking with it even though there were changes before he had even read the title, I'll be forever humble for your support.